Uns

Heather Critchlow grew up in rural Aberdeenshire and trained as a business journalist after studying history and social science at the University of Cambridge. Her short stories have appeared in crime fiction anthologies *Afraid of the Light*, *Afraid of the Christmas Lights* and *Afraid of the Shadows*. She lives in St Albans.

Also by Heather Critchlow

The Cal Lovett Files

Unsolved
Unburied
Unsound

UNSOUND

HEATHER CRITCHLOW

First published in the United Kingdom in 2024 by

Canelo
Unit 9, 5th Floor
Cargo Works, 1–2 Hatfields
London SE1 9PG
United Kingdom

Print ISBN 978 1 80436 262 4
Ebook ISBN 978 1 80436 261 7

This book is a work of fiction. Names, characters, businesses, organizations, places and events are either the product of the author's imagination or are used fictitiously. Any resemblance to actual persons, living or dead, events or locales is entirely coincidental.

Cover design by Andrew Smith

Cover images © Shutterstock

Look for more great books at www.canelo.co

Printed and bound in Great Britain by Clays Ltd, Elcograf S.p.A.

1

For Will, Rachel and Adam

PROLOGUE

EDINBURGH

ARRAN, 2010

He's not sure how long he's been unconscious, but when he wakes, it is still dark. The metal is like ice against his skin – it admits no forgiveness, offers no warmth. The pain in his leg is excruciating and his body is stuck in the strangest position, as if he's fallen down a rabbit hole and is looking at the darkness like Alice, standing on her head in that story his wee sister Kirsty loves. He doesn't know where he is. He throws his arms out, feeling only the cold, hard metal, and sets off a clanging, booming echo that deafens him. There is no white rabbit.

Tears refuse to come. Just a low keening, like the cattle in the fields at home. He can almost smell the byres and imagines himself on his early-morning rounds atop a frozen blanket of snow, lulled by the crunching squeak of his feet on the icescape.

There he is, seen from above: filling the troughs, calling to the dogs, doing his father's bidding. Strange, though, he can hear Kirsty playing her violin in the background. A sweet clean sound in his ears. Maybe she's left her window open and the music is dancing out to him. He never did watch her play at Hogmanay – the failure to keep his promise is a sudden piercing regret.

What he wouldn't give to be back there now, on the farm with them all, where he belongs. There is so much to tell them he's sorry for. But he's in Edinburgh and they are miles away, perched on the edge of the Highlands. It might as well be the moon.

Arran drops into unconsciousness for a time. It can't be long, because it's still dark when he wakes. Above him, he can see the bright distant pinpricks of stars. He's stopped feeling cold now. A crystal-clear moment of soberness and pain.

He needs to live. He needs to be able to tell them he's sorry.

He shouts and thrashes, calls for help, but the sounds crash around him and he has no idea if they travel anywhere other than into his own head. He bites down on his lip and forces himself upwards, screaming with the mind-dissolving pain of it, using his fingernails to brace and pull. He's so weak after these past weeks but he throws everything he's got into it, like a spider trying to climb out of a bottle.

It isn't enough. His fingernails break and tear; the only warmth he feels is the blood where he rips them, adding a dull aching agony to the rest of his shattered, stinking body.

At what point do you give up? When the faces of the people you love no longer flash through your mind? When your body becomes so cold that it's impossible to move your limbs? When a flush of heat and delirium make you believe the sun is shining and the waves are tossing their foaming bodies to shore? When you start to see the funny side?

Before dawn, he fancies he hears his name called. Just once. He almost recognises the voice, and then it is gone. He opens his mouth to reply. But... what's the point? Maybe he'll just sleep now. Maybe a dark sort of peace will come.

CHAPTER ONE

CAL

The lights are dazzling and hot. Beads of sweat dampen Cal's collar and push up through the thick stickiness of the make-up clarted on his face. He resists the urge to smear it away with the back of his hand, reminding himself that orange is a good look on camera. It's the same with shirts – his producer insisted on sending this one next-day delivery. She knows leaving it to him would be pointless. He'd just have worn a decade-old T-shirt. As much as he pretends he doesn't like Sarah's strict fussiness, he wishes she were here now. There's not one friendly face in sight.

As crowds of people fuss around the chairs and a microphone is attached to his shirt, his heart is drumming a beat and he's acutely aware of how ridiculous these nerves are – it's only a television interview. Yes, millions of people will be watching, but he's a *media professional*. Not that anyone would put his work in the same bracket as a live national breakfast show on TV.

His throat is dry but it feels too late to ask for a glass of water, so he swallows repeatedly and hopes his words don't dry up too. The make-up lady finishes powdering Jacinta's face and the army of acolytes retreat from the breakfast show host, back to their enviable positions in the dark behind the cameras.

This, he thinks, pinned like a butterfly beneath the glare, is why he loves being a podcaster. He can record episodes in his pants if he wants. No one gets to see his lack of dress sense. Or the fear and uncertainty in his eyes.

3

The countdown switches from verbal to hand signals and Jacinta, who hasn't so far shown the slightest interest in Cal, swivels to face him as if someone has pressed a button on her back and turned the electricity on. The transition is unsettling. He buries the sudden nervous urge to laugh.

The screen behind them changes and he is aware of his sister's face reflected in all the monitors around the studio. He doesn't need to look closely to picture her red curls and wry smile, arms crossed over her chest. It's not his favourite image of Margot, but it's the one the media have been using more these days. Taken just after her nineteenth birthday, only weeks before she went missing. She isn't smiling; she looks challenging. He loves that. Not everyone feels the same. How long, he wonders for the millionth time, before victims don't have to be 'perfect' to deserve sympathy.

'This morning, we're talking to Cal Lovett, host of the successful true crime podcast *Finding Justice*. Cal, welcome to the show.'

'Thank you, pleasure to—' he murmurs, but she carries on over him.

'Normally, Cal spends his time interviewing families of missing and murdered people, including the high-profile case of missing Aberdeen woman Layla Mackie, which led to the discovery of her bones and, ultimately, a conviction. Now, the tables are turned and he's the one being interviewed. Cal's hoping for a conviction closer to home. As listeners to the podcast will be aware, Cal's older sister went missing when he was a child. Her remains were found in a Tamworth scrapyard almost two years ago and, this week, a man goes on trial for her murder.'

Jacinta pauses, flicking to sympathy mode.

'This must be very difficult for you.'

'Well,' he says, still not sure if this is the moment for him to speak or if she is going to carry on. 'Actually, it's a relief.' Jacinta's eyebrows jump together, though her forehead remains

4

smooth. 'It's been almost forty years since Margot went missing and we've waited a long time for answers. My father died before she was found, so he never knew what happened to her. Nothing can change that, but it would bring my mother comfort to have this resolved and to see Margot's killer held accountable.'

Jacinta tilts her head. Her eyes are beady and focused. He's reminded of a bird. When she speaks, he feels chastised.

'Obviously, we can't talk about the specifics that might come up in the trial itself.' She turns, in an aside to the camera. 'Don't want to prejudice anything.' Then back to Cal: 'How much do you think your sister's disappearance has damaged your life?' He wonders if she's going to use Margot's name at all.

'I don't know about damaged—'

'Yes, but...' She sounds impatient and Cal flounders, trying to work out what she wants from him so he can give it to her. 'How much does it have to do with your career choices, for example?'

'Everything,' he says, trying to sound lighter than he feels, more conversational. 'I do feel driven to seek the truth in cases that have been forgotten about. I think what Margot's case shows is that it's never too late – it's never over.'

'But what effect has it had on you, personally? Her disappearance.'

Jacinta leans forward. Her body language may be warm and she's smiling, but Cal feels a ruthless chill emanating from her. He doesn't want to answer the question. Doesn't want to be here at all.

'I can understand, better than some, how the families feel – how difficult it is to live not just with loss, but uncertainty as well,' he says. 'Many of them can't grieve until they have answers.'

'And will you be able to grieve now?' she pushes, picking up his words and tossing them back to him. 'Once the trial is over?'

'I hope so.'

She segues so fast into the question he can tell she's really been waiting to ask that he barely has time to recalibrate. 'And what would you say to the people who think Jason Barr is a convenient scapegoat?'

He forces his hands to remain flat on the arms of the purple velvet chair, fighting their desire to curl into fists at the mention of Barr. Not this again, he wants to shout when he finds his bearings. The ex-bouncer with a history of violence against women has developed quite an online following. He's become the poster boy for a backlash against previous advances in the courts and justice system.

Cal thought all that had died down, but even now, the judge has ruled that Barr's previous attacks cannot be brought as evidence or discussed in the media, in case they prejudice the trial. Just one example of several rulings that have gone against the prosecution.

He becomes aware that Jacinta is waiting. 'I'd urge them to wait for the trial,' he says. 'The police have a strong case and I'm confident we'll get the right verdict.'

'Or at least the one you want,' she barks, throwing out a laugh. 'Thanks for coming on the show, Cal.' She swivels to look at a different camera. 'We'll be back in a moment with our top tips for autumn footwear.'

Blindsided, Cal doesn't react: he just sits still as a technician takes the microphone from his shirt and Jacinta swigs from a coffee handed to her, reading a sheaf of notes and ignoring him completely. A runner gestures for him to rise and follow. He opens his mouth to say goodbye but the host doesn't look up.

Out in the corridor, the runner thanks him and asks if he wants to use the gents before he goes. Cal, realising his mouth is still hanging open, closes it and feels the dryness turn to nausea.

'That was...'

The runner nods and turns a Jacinta-style fake beam on him, holding her thumbs up. 'You were great.'

The insincerity floors him. He is too slow to correct her, to make it clear that he wasn't asking for feedback on his performance. She's already backing away, her eyes glazed as she contemplates the next task. He sags against the wall, watching her speed down the corridor. That wasn't what he meant at all.

CHAPTER TWO

Welcome to Scotland.

The sign flashes past as they sail across the border. Usually, he feels nothing but joy when crossing this line, but today Cal's heart sinks as they draw closer to their destination. He flicks his gaze to the rear-view mirror; no matter how many times he checks, Chrissie is still in the back, headphones in, red curls drawn back from her face, piles of belongings around her. Allie is dozing in the passenger seat beside him.

The world tilts. They could be back ten years ago, setting off on holiday together – all they need is the dog in the back with Chrissie, and the years of turmoil and divorce would unravel. If it was safe to close his eyes, he'd be there in a second. *Would he?*

The past lurches away without discussion, leaving only the problematic present.

He sighs.

'It's really only for a few weeks,' Allie says, stirring. 'She's talking about coming back for the verdict, after all.'

'I thought you were asleep.'

She stretches, rolling her neck, as he glances her way while checking the blind spot so he can pull back into the slow lane after overtaking a lorry. Allie doesn't answer. She seems to be taking it all a lot better than he is.

'You're acting like it's forever,' she says a minute later.

'I didn't say anything.'

'You don't have to. I was married to you for eighteen years, remember?'

8

'How could I forget?' he jokes.

'Rude.' She laughs, turning to look out at the wet countryside. 'Weeks pass between you and Chrissie seeing each other, Cal. It's really not that different than when you go away on your podcast investigations.'

There's an edge to her tone. It's been some time since they had this discussion – he's having flashbacks to their marriage and the reasons it failed. Allie couldn't take another case swallowing him whole, he knows that. But it's sad that their relationship crumbled right at the moment when it had all come together professionally.

'It just feels different, that's all.'

'Because you're the one being left behind?'

Now it's Cal's turn to fall silent.

He doesn't want to argue. She's right, though. He doesn't even live with their daughter full-time, so why does taking her to university feel like he's losing her?

Chrissie lifts her headphones away from her ears.

'Are you two fighting?'

'No!' they chorus.

'Good. You're not going to be embarrassing when we say goodbye, are you?'

Cal glances at her in the mirror again – she's looking at him.

'Of course not,' he says, but he feels the look that passes between his ex-wife and his daughter. If he focuses on the road, maybe the urge to cry will pass.

–

They stop at a service station – a nice one, with gift shops and proper food. Cal had envisaged a leisurely meal and a chance to soak up the last moments before the change that's coming, but Chrissie is antsy, keen to get back on the road, to start her new life.

'Will Robbie be there to meet you?' Allie stretches her arm and loops her fingers through Chrissie's. He doesn't often see them together, but the friction between his ex-wife and daughter has completely faded in the last couple of years, Cal realises. They found their way back to each other. It makes him happy.

Chrissie shakes her head at the mention of her boyfriend. 'No. I've asked him to stay away for a few days, let me settle in without him.'

'Sensible,' Allie comments.

Cal conceals his disappointment. He likes Robbie – more than that, he has felt bound to him since, two years ago, he helped to investigate the death of the boy's mother on the west coast of Scotland. They are different ages and backgrounds, and yet so similar in the loss they've experienced. Cal has learned to treasure that cross-generational connection with the once-floundering kid.

Robbie has pulled himself together, while the rest of his family has fallen apart. Cal knows, rationally, that the seeds of that implosion were sown fifteen years before they met, but he still can't help feeling responsible. The boy has been left with family in name only. Almost three years older than Chrissie and in the second year of an engineering degree, Robbie is steady and Cal trusts him; he is delighted by the thought that they're going to be in the same city.

As they walk back to the car, Chrissie takes his arm, rests her head on his shoulder a moment.

'I'm going to be fine, Dad,' she says.

'I know.' He plants a kiss on her curls and forces a laugh.

She stops and looks at him. 'It's you we need to worry about.' Her green eyes exude their usual soft kindness, but her eyebrows have pulled together and her brow has little furrows. Allie has moved ahead of them.

Chrissie has had a front-row seat to the stresses of the past months, as the police and prosecutors have been preparing for the trial of Jason Barr, the ex-convict that Cal is sure killed Margot thirty-eight years ago. They're now two weeks in and, though the evidence is limited, Cal is praying it's enough to have the man put away for life.

The media coverage has been intense, frequently straying over the lines of what's acceptable. Somewhere along the way, Margot transformed into a different person – promiscuous and partying – not the nurturing older sister he remembers. He was nine years old when she went missing, and the twisted narrative spun by Barr's slick legal team has had him second-guessing his memories.

'I'm sorry the last few months have been hard,' he says. 'We're almost there.'

And in so many ways, they are. Soon, they'll have a verdict. Jason Barr will be imprisoned for killing Margot. Finally, she will be avenged. Cal is desperate to cross that border, to move beyond this constant aching search for justice, but he'd be lying if he said he wasn't also afraid. What happens when the thing that's been driving you is gone?

He follows his daughter to the car. Trying, so very hard, to let go.

CHAPTER THREE

They reach the halls of residence after taking several wrong turns. Chrissie's leaning so far forward in her urgency to get there that she's almost in the front.

Eventually, they find somewhere to park. Chrissie goes to collect her key, and Cal and Allie stand by the car, stretching their legs and taking in the dramatic hulk of Arthur's Seat above them. The grandeur of Edinburgh's buildings nestles next to the wild, as if you could step from one to the other in a second. He glances up and wishes he were up on the hill now, looking down on it all. The wind is strong and bitterly cold. Cal zips up his coat, putting his hand against his nose to warm it.

Chrissie is beside herself with excitement when she returns with a key card and an information pack. Cal, handed the documents to carry, looks at the list of things to do upon arrival – open a bank account, register with a GP, make arrangements to pay tuition fees – and it hits him how she is a woman now, not a child. A pang inside his chest, like a falling away. His instinct is to tell her to be careful, and yet it is impossible to feel sad, so infectious is her anticipation.

'There's a ceilidh tonight,' he tells her, instead of all the warnings that flood his mind. 'That sounds fun.'

It takes a few trips to carry Chrissie's things to her room on the second floor. They pass other parents doing the same and there is a sense of nervous camaraderie between them all – jolly voices disguising the advancing heartache of the empty nest. Cal's stomach flutters with apprehension, as if it were his first day, not Chrissie's.

Allie and Chrissie go about finding a place for everything while Cal goes back for the final load. He weaves his way through groups of students who talk loudly and somehow fit here, making him feel irrelevant in this place. He stares at the now empty car, already feeling how lonely it will be as he drives on to Aberdeen. Allie is catching the train back. Their display of unity is for their daughter, and it's enough for both of them.

He waits an age for the lift and when he reaches Chrissie's door, a girl is standing just inside the room.

'This is Yara,' Chrissie says, her voice higher and a bit louder than usual. Cal automatically reaches out and shakes the hand of the tall, skinny girl with a bare midriff, realising too late that the handshake was a mistake. 'Right,' Chrissie says, a quirk to her mouth.

Cal lifts the final box onto the side. He hopes Chrissie has her toy sloth in there. He hasn't seen it yet and it's been on her bed her whole life.

'Are you going to unpack this? I could take the box back?'

She shakes her head. There's a glowing nervous energy coming from her as she looks around the room. 'I can finish it later. Yara and I are going to go and check out the student union after lunch, so…'

They'd agreed they would take her for lunch before they left, but Cal wonders if it's a mistake, if she'd rather plunge into her new life.

'We don't have to go for lunch,' Allie says gently, lightly, though Cal knows she dreads leaving as much as he does.

'Oh, no, I want to,' Chrissie says quickly, a flash of uncertainty behind her eyes. Maybe she isn't quite ready to be let loose yet, either. He catches the way she glances at Yara.

He clears his throat and does the right thing, rather than the selfish one. 'Would you like to come with us?'

The girl looks uncomfortable. 'I don't want to intrude…'

'You wouldn't be,' Chrissie says, looking at her mother for confirmation, and Cal watches her smile and insist.

It's strange walking out onto the road that leads into the city centre, he and Allie following the girls as they ask each other the getting-to-know-you questions, awkwardly eager but tentatively forming a connection. They find a crowded cafe that has a smattering of other parents and new students clearly doing the same as them. The smiles are a little too bright. Cal's eyes pinch and he swallows away the feelings; there will be time for that later. They wait five minutes for a table, and order soup and sandwiches, large slabs of cake and coffees. 'This is our treat,' Allie tells Yara pre-emptively, nudging Chrissie. 'The last chance to feed you both up for a bit.'

In the end, Yara acts as their bridge – like they're passing their daughter into her new life, instead of pushing her off alone. She lightens the atmosphere, forces them not to dwell or become maudlin. Cal listens to her explain that her mum and dad dropped her off early, as they had to get back to their catering business and her two younger brothers. 'I've been unpacked for hours,' she jokes.

Cal hands over the information pack he's been guarding, so Chrissie and Yara can pore over the pages of events and socials, making plans, bolstering each other. He realises, as the other girl relaxes, just how nervous she was in the room before. The apparent prickliness was an illusion.

Chrissie looks at her watch and startles. 'We're meeting Helen in half an hour,' she tells them, reaching for her phone. 'Should I text her and push it back a bit?'

'No, love,' Allie says. She looks at Cal for confirmation. 'Let's get the bill and then we can walk you back up and leave you to get on with it.'

Chrissie nods, takes a deep breath, and Cal can see her relief and fear weighing equally. He squeezes her shoulder as he rises to pay, hiding his anguish. At the till, he asks the server to put another four chocolate brownies in a box. 'Here,' he says, out on the street, handing it to Chrissie. 'Sustenance for all that work you'll be doing tonight.' He raises an eyebrow at Yara to let her know that he's joking and she giggles.

The walk back vanishes. Cal wants to hold it and examine it from every angle. They'll never have this again. One child. One moment like this to savour in all its painful bittersweetness.

'We won't come up,' Allie says decisively when they reach the halls. 'Your dad needs to drop me at the station.' His ex-wife puts a hand on his arm. It feels like a warm anchor in a storm. He knows that Allie cannot take any more, because he can't either. Even though everything inside him is screaming to hold on.

'Bye, then, love,' Cal says, opening his arms wide. She steps into them and he squeezes tight, pressing his nose into her hair and inhaling deeply, trying to make it enough. 'Have fun.' He waits until she pulls back and then he relinquishes her, holding a hand up to Yara. 'Lovely to meet you.' Allie hugs Chrissie and whispers in her ear, and then she wrenches herself back too. There's a lump in his throat so big, it's going to choke him.

They stand, drinking in the sight of their daughter, and watch as the two girls find their key cards and walk to the entrance.

'Your parents are great,' he hears Yara say as they pull back the door. His heart swells. Chrissie's reply is swallowed by the building.

'Come on,' he says to Allie. They turn and walk in the direction of the car.

The campus pulses around them: people laughing, shouting to each other – freshers' week fever is in the air. It's surreal. All Cal can picture is Chrissie as a chubby toddler with red ringlets and a gummy smile. He can feel the weight of her on his shoulders, her little hands gripping his forehead.

When they reach the car, he turns and looks at Allie. Tears start to slip from her eyes and the sight makes him well up too, pride and sadness chasing each other through him.

'Oh, Cal,' she says, as he steps forward and pulls her into a hug. 'Our girl.'

'I know.' He feels like he's standing on a beach with the tide running out and the sands shifting beneath his feet. 'It's gone so fast.'

He fights the panic that comes from that thought – that there's an hourglass somewhere that's running out, the grains of his life slipping through his fingers.

CHAPTER FOUR

Cal is stiff and tired by the time he reaches Shona's new house on the outskirts of Aberdeen. Nestled on the edge of the green belt near Blackburn, the newly built wood-clad building overlooks startlingly bright fields edged with very dirty, miserable sheep. A horizontal rain has driven the poor creatures into the corners and they're stoically chomping grass as water fills their fleeces.

He leaves his bag in the car and darts to the door just as Shona opens it for him, wearing black leggings and a cream jumper, thick woolly socks on her feet and her short blonde hair clipped up on top of her head. She always wears it that way when she's cooking and, sure enough, as he wraps his arms around her, he smells the rich, spiced stew that is one of his favourites.

This isn't his home, yet. But it could be. A sanctuary from the feelings the day has dredged up, and far from the trial and Jason Barr. It's a relief to be here.

'Hey there, stranger. I missed you.' Shona squeezes him tightly and then reaches behind him to slam the thick door shut. It's immediately cosier with the sound of the rain dulled. 'How was it?'

Cal thinks back to the long journey, sniping with Allie, but then remembers the time spent with Chrissie and her new friend, the painful joy of it all. He finds it impossible to describe to Shona the sense of pride and loss he feels. The thought that she wouldn't understand because she hasn't got a child of her own flits disloyally into his mind. He shoves it away, hating himself for thinking it.

'Saying goodbye to Chrissie was worse than I thought it would be,' he tries. 'It just feels so seismic. Where did all the time go? God, I sound old.'

He follows Shona's chuckle into the main room that runs along the back of the house. A bottle of white wine sits on the kitchen island, a corkscrew half in.

'You didn't embarrass her, did you?'

She's joking, and Cal tries to laugh with her but finds he isn't in the mood, suddenly almost tearful. He wants her to know, without being told, how awful he feels. This is desperately unfair, but somehow he and Shona have been struggling to communicate. Do all relationships evolve this way? Does the early ease have to dissipate? There's a headache starting in his temples; his eyes are gritty from driving so far, his back stiff. It's probably a bad idea to drink on these feelings, but he forces a smile and reaches for the bottle of wine, unscrewing the cork. Shona watches him quietly.

'Sorry.' He pinches the bridge of his nose and tries to lighten the heaviness in his expression. 'I'm just tired. Today was... strange.'

'It's fine.' She slides two glasses across the counter towards him. 'I'm glad you're here. I've missed you.'

Cal crosses to her and pulls her close again, kissing her properly this time and banishing the ridiculous thought that he'd like to be with Allie right now, sniping or not, just to be with someone who understands this particular wrench of the empty nest. Although, to be fair, his ex-wife seemed to be coping better than him, and it's not like they have a nest any more.

'That's better,' Shona says, sliding her hands beneath his T-shirt and running her fingers over his skin. As their kisses deepen and his breath thickens, he feels the displacement retreating. He laughs as they crab-walk to the sofa, bashing into furniture in the still-unfamiliar room, unwilling to take their hands off each other. The present flies back into Cal – the out-of-body feeling gone. This is who he is now; he is where he wants to be. He is so lucky to have this incredible woman in his life. It's just been too much today – the ongoing trial and Chrissie starting university.

The rain increases its tempo. Across the room, the stew bubbles and condensation runs down the glasses of wine to pool on the counter. Nothing matters in these moments, only his fingers in Shona's hair, the warm silk of her skin, and the total and utter loss of control. Her voice echoes in the room around them.

Afterwards, they devour the stew and drink the wine in front of the fire, pink-faced and wrapped in blankets, the smell of sex on their skin. His headache has reduced to a dull pulse.

'You know,' Shona says, mopping gravy from her plate with a thick hunk of bread, her feet entwined with his, her hair sticking up in a bleached halo. 'After the trial, you could spend more time here.'

Cal smiles and kisses her shoulder. 'I'd like that.'

She sets down her plate and turns towards him. 'I mean, a lot more time.' Her blue eyes pin him to the spot. 'You could move in.'

He runs a finger along her arm, playing for time. The idea should be alluring, not frightening. 'You'd want that?'

Shona is fiercely independent. After a disastrous relationship in her twenties with a man who turned into a stalker, she's lived alone and he's always had the impression she likes it that way.

'I think so.' The lightness in her voice has sunk to the bottom.

Cal's eyes drift around the room, taking in the neatness and style that are so lacking in his own Midlands flat, grasping at his thoughts. 'I wouldn't drive you mad?'

'No more than you do anyway.' She laughs, but Cal can hear the hollowness in it, the vulnerability. Then her tone rises. 'I want to be with you all the time, Cal, not just in fits and starts.'

'That's fair enough.' And it is. But he has the terrible sinking familiarity of conversations he used to have with Allie. The nature of his work, making true crime podcasts and document-aries, means he is often away for long stretches of time. And he isn't sure Shona does want him here all the time anyway. She values her space and he doesn't want to become a nuisance, an invader. But that's not the heart of it, he knows – he's afraid. He isn't ready to harness himself to someone, to fully depend on them. His split from Allie happened years ago and yet it is still raw and painful.

'You aren't exactly biting my hand off here…'

'Hey…' He shuffles forward. Her chin tilts upwards, eyes filled with uncharacteristic uncertainty. Is that resentment there too? 'Look at me. I love you.' He punctuates the point with a kiss. 'I'd like nothing more than to be here with you all the time. It's just complicated, with my mum and Chrissie.'

He pictures his stooped and brittle mother, how the last time he saw her she was even more unsteady on her feet, visibly declining. It is a heavy burden to bear and, as the only surviving child, it is his alone. Not that he can imagine Margot would have been up for a caring role had she lived. She and their mother didn't see eye to eye. 'Mum's going to need care at some point. And she's not exactly easy to help. I worry that if I'm not close then no one will know what she needs.'

Shona nods, all too aware of the precariousness of that rela-tionship.

'And Chrissie.' He pictures the room in his flat that is hers, covered with her drawings, and the shells and ephemera she collects to paint. It's her home too. It's not the childhood home she still shares with Allie, but if he moves away, will it weaken their connection? 'She'll be coming back in the holidays. There's her room to think of.'

'She could come here,' Shona says. 'There's a spare room and she loves Aberdeen.'

It's true. She does, and she regularly visits Jean and Tam, the parents of a missing woman whose case Cal helped to solve. They have become pseudo-grandparents. But it wouldn't be the same. This is primarily Shona's home, her space.

20

Cal feels a ripping inside him, divided needs and desires. He smiles but the muscles in his face don't co-operate as well as they usually do.

'I can't easily move,' Shona says, quietly. 'My work...'

She's right – as a top forensic anthropologist, she's affiliated to the university, teaches classes, runs a lab. Cal is a nomad: he travels to where the stories take him, pinging back to his roots when needed. And he isn't being honest. It isn't just about the practicalities.

'No, it definitely doesn't make sense for you to move,' he says, kissing her hair. 'Even if you hadn't just bought this place.'

Cal suddenly feels exhausted. The headache is back, front and centre, nudging at him. He stifles a yawn.

'Today wasn't the right time to bring this up,' Shona says, a flatness in her tone that he wishes wasn't there. He needs to change the subject, quickly.

'I guess things are just all over the place right now. Chrissie flying the nest bothers me more than I realised it would, and the verdict could be any time. I just feel like I need to get through that, get the result for Margot, and then I can breathe and think. Plan for the future.' Punt the decision down the line, is what he doesn't say.

Shona leans against him. He can tell she is troubled.

'What is it?' he asks. 'You can say.'

'I'm just worried that you might be heading for a crash,' she says eventually. 'Depending how things go with the trial, what comes out, it could be really hard. You can't rely on other people, an external outcome. You need to rely on yourself, to move forward without condition.'

A shiver runs through Cal. He tries not to think about the details. But in court, he's had to listen to the sparse evidence there is about what happened to his sister almost forty years ago. Her body decomposed and decayed in a tarpaulin underneath a scrapyard for so long that it has taken many secrets with it, but there is forensic evidence and speculation and guesswork.

Then that man, across the courtroom, posing as a pillar of the community with his wealthy wife. The thought of it makes his skin crawl.

'I know,' he says. 'I do.'

Shona nods and snuggles into him.

Pulling her close, Cal decides not to mention his plans yet. He hasn't really told anyone about the podcast he's been working on, the story he's planning to tell – only his producer knows. When Barr is found guilty, he'll finally be free to do justice to his sister. For people to know what she was really like and what that man did to them by taking her away. There's a part of him that knows this is wrong, that he's constructing a safe shell around himself, pushing Shona away, but he can't think about that today.

CHAPTER FIVE

ARRAN, 2009

Lots of the others have parents bringing them. It makes Arran feel lonely and superior at the same time. The woman's voice across the corridor is loud and plummy. He caught sight of her when he peeked down the hallway at the chaos – her hair is swept up in a stiff beehive, her perfume a cloud in the air that he can smell from here. Nothing like his own mother, last seen wearing an apron covered with flour, shooing a hen from the kitchen.

He hurriedly shuts his door to avoid being noticed. 'Are you sure?' he can hear her saying. 'It's very basic. You don't have to…'

But he doesn't catch the rest, only the tone of lazy amusement in her son's reply. They're all tanned – it looks as if they've come straight from the beach. Arran hasn't been abroad. Ever. The idea is mystical. Holidays are at Loch Morlich, in the caravan his maternal grandparents passed on to them – freezing navy water and hot chocolates to warm up. He loves it there.

'Come on, now. Time to leave him to it. Boy has to make his own way. Doesn't need us mollycoddling.' That's the father – navy suit and grey curls on a white collar, and a gold watch that he looked at no less than three times in the brief moment Arran peeked out. The man seems severe. Reminds Arran of his own father, as different as this man's life must be. He thinks of the barns at home, the wild open spaces and the mud on his father's boots. Feels a pang akin to regret, as well as the burn of curiosity, the jitter of anticipation. For these few years, his life will be different to what it has ever been.

Retreating, he lies down on the bed, which accounts for almost half of this pod-like space. He has already unpacked, lined his pens on the desk and plugged in his clock radio, and there is nothing else to do. Not yet. Not until the other parents leave. Then he'll have to make himself go out there and do introductions, though the thought of it makes his pale skin flare with heat, turns his hands clammy. What is he going to have in common with these people? It doesn't matter. He'll meet the other people doing his course on Monday and they'll be more like-minded, that's what his mum said.

Maybe he should have let his mother drive him. But he'd persuaded her to drop him at the station in Inverness instead. They said goodbye outside WHSmith in their characteristically understated way, his younger sisters left at home despite their protests. None of these loud proclamations. He chuckles at the thought of his mum talking to the beehive woman. She's a farmer's daughter and a farmer's wife, tough and practical. He could see no tears in her eyes when she hugged him and tousled his hair – more of a sort of wistful longing and release. He felt it then, that moment of stepping over a divide, leaving them behind.

'You don't need to wait,' he'd said, his voice deeper than usual. 'I'll be fine.'

When the train rolled into Edinburgh, with the drama of the sheer stone walls stained by the weather and the castle high above, he'd been struck by memories of a school trip, of jostling pupils with clipboards and mackintoshes. Toying loosely with the memory, he'd walked up the hill to the halls, his heavy bags burning lines on his shoulders and his stomach hollow. He paid attention to every coffee shop and pub – would those be places where he'll soon be sitting with friends, drinking beers, having coffees, meeting girls? Endless possibilities swarmed like the tourists he had to step around.

And now, the corridor is filled with loud goodbyes and tearful parents, a last rise in volume as they emerge from rooms, and he thinks it's time to get off the bed and head for the little kitchen, where he's decided he'll make himself a cup of tea and open the packet of biscuits he discovered his mother had tucked in the rucksack without him knowing. But, before he can make himself move, there is a knock on the door.

Arran freezes and then it comes again, and his words trip over themselves.

'Aye, come in, like.'

He pushes himself to sitting on the edge of the bed just as the door swings back, and the tanned boy with floppy hair and a lazy kind of smile is there, holding out two bottles and rolling his eyes.

'Fucking hell, glad that's over. Can I interest you in a beer?'

Arran wants to say: 'interest you'? Roll the words over his tongue, imagining his sisters giggling at the language.

'That'd be fine,' he says instead, feeling his face flush beetroot but standing up and letting the boy press a cold, wet bottle into his hand, all thoughts of tea and biscuits vanishing.

'Got the paternal units to spring for a mini-fridge,' the boy drawls. 'Got to have the priorities right, eh?'

In the absence of words, Arran makes an appreciative noise and swigs at the beer, almost choking on the froth and bubbles. He feels like a right eejit.

'Oh, forgive me,' the boy says, extending a hand for Arran to shake, wrist adorned with a chunky watch in the same style his father was wearing, though his eyes have warmth in them instead of steel. His skin is smooth. It feels expensive beneath Arran's farming callouses. 'I'm Jonno.'

And for a moment Arran can't get beyond the sense of wondrous amusement, but then they move to Jonno's room to inspect the mini-fridge, and others join them: a girl with dyed-red hair and owl-like glasses, her fingers heavy with silver rings and her feet encased in Doc Martens boots; another with a pale pink sweater and blonde hair scraped into a bun that makes him think of a ballerina. Jonno holds court in an inflatable chair he has squished into a corner, while the three of them sit on the bed.

The conversation is stilted to begin with, but as the beer flows and the girl with owl glasses – Colleen – returns to her room for a bottle of wine, Arran feels himself start to unwind. He leans against the wall, his face flushed, chattier than he would usually be with his pals at home. They've all known him so long – here he can be anyone.

He listens to Colleen, pink and excited, explaining how she wants to focus on feminist discourse in dystopian literature and he has no idea what she means but she's so passionate about it that he finds himself being caught up in her flow, trying to contribute.

'You've never read *The Handmaid's Tale*?' she exclaims when he loses the thread.

'Er...'

'You're kidding?'

'It's hardly compulsory,' Jonno says languidly from his inflatable throne. No one has anointed him but he is already king of them all, and they stop and listen. Arran smiles in gratitude, as Colleen gapes in outrage.

'Have you got a copy?' he asks Colleen. 'Can I borrow it? Not now...' he calls, but she has already bounced from the bed and pelted away to her room.

For some reason, most likely related to the beer and wine they've consumed, this strikes the remaining trio as unbearably funny. When Colleen returns, they are lost in their laughter, tears pouring down their cheeks. She stands over them with her hands on her hips, the novel in one hand, until she catches the bug and her sternness dissolves. Arran feels warm in a way he has never done before. Hilarity is squashed in his house – it is silliness, an indulgence that wastes time. Here, he does not have to stop their conversation to go and feed the beasts or grease machinery. He is free to laugh as long as he wants. It feels so good. He holds his hand out for the book and places it reverently in his lap.

'What are you studying?' The girl in pale pink – Olivia – asks when they have all calmed down, and he stumbles over his words as he tells her about the rural resource management course. Without being asked, the words spill out of him, and he explains about the farm and the plan for him to take it over from his father – it's been in the family for a hundred years but it needs to change, modernise, diversify. He doesn't mention the arguments between his parents, the fact that he was almost not allowed to go.

'Only two certainties in life,' Jonno butts in. 'Land and taxes.'

Colleen splutters wine and shoves Jonno from where she is sitting on the floor – Arran has noticed her edging closer to him as the afternoon has gone on. 'Death, you moron. It's death and taxes…'

At first, Jonno looks annoyed. 'I can't believe you're all laughing at me…' Arran sees how tight his face is, wonders if he's not used to this kind of banter. But as he looks around at them chuckling and sees they aren't really mocking him, Jonno's face seems to relax. Maybe he isn't the only fish out of water, Arran thinks, tilting back his fourth bottle of beer, surprised to find he's reached the last drops. All of a sudden, he realises the world has gone fuzzy at the edges. So much alcohol on an empty stomach.

'Anyone hungry, like?'

'Yes!' Colleen leaps to her feet. 'Starving.'

She reaches down and offers Jonno a hand, pulling him to his feet. Arran notices the way her face shines, though she turns away and tries to hide it. He thinks maybe Colleen is barking up the wrong tree. He's caught Jonno looking appreciatively at Olivia a couple of times and he can understand why. She's quieter but somehow has more of a presence. Her skin glows. She smiles at him now and he ducks his head, afraid she can see his thoughts.

'Shall we go out for something?' Jonno suggests. 'The canteen looks a bit school dinnerish.' He screws up his nose.

The others chorus agreement and Arran presses down the misgivings that jump into his head – he has to be really careful with money. There's only just enough if he doesn't splurge, and he'll need to get a job to make ends meet as it is. But it's the first day, and he's making friends, so what can it hurt? They jostle along the corridor together, knocking on doors and gathering others for the expedition. Arran notices how loud they are, how unapologetic about themselves, already a pack that belongs. When Olivia turns and smiles at him, he grins from ear to ear.

CHAPTER SIX

CAL

The windswept wildness of Balmedie beach, with its flat golden sands and dunes covered with waving grasses, is the perfect place for Cal to decompress. As he and Shona walk along the shoreline, arms around each other's waist, legs in sync, he can almost feel the wind blowing away the troubles that have surrounded him at home. In the distance, two riders urge their horses into the cold foaming water, and they stop to watch the animals swimming in the surf.

Both of them have kept the conversation light for the last couple of days, though Cal has noticed the quiet watchfulness on Shona's part. He hates feeling that he's disappointing her or taking her for granted but his mind won't settle on future plans. He doesn't want to think about these things now. There is too much on his plate as it is. He's leaving tomorrow, driving back down south like he's drawn by the tide, the regular patterns of their lives pushing and pulling him up and down the country. Their relationship has always been dictated by circumstances and commitments beyond their control, and if he's honest, he's fine with that, doesn't need more.

Shona has never asked him to leave the Midlands before, knowing Chrissie spent nights with him every week. Of course, he realises now, it makes sense that she's been waiting for this moment. While he is caught up in the trial and the long-awaited justice for his sister, she's coming to the end of patiently biding her time, wanting the next phase of her life to start. He feels foolish for not having anticipated the problem and suddenly perceives the absence of a close friend, who would have asked some pointed questions.

'Why do you keep checking your phone? Am I boring you?'

He jerks his head up guiltily, relieved to see that Shona is laughing, though he thinks there's an edge to her tone.

'Caught. Sorry!'

'It's only the billionth time today.'

'I know, I know. It's just that I'm waiting for Chrissie—'

'She'll be fine,' Shona says, linking her arm in his and turning him back down the beach. 'She's just making friends, establishing herself, that's all. In the nicest possible way, you're the last person on her mind.'

Sometimes, Cal finds the disconnect between him and Shona hard to get past. With her logical, scientific mind, she's so often right. He's used to being guided by his gut, by emotion. It's not always rational, but it has served him well in a career where instinct can be the key to unlocking a mystery. Shona would say that's the brain picking up on clues, but to him it feels more than that.

'Maybe I should just send another message. Just in case...'

'No, you don't.' Shona grabs his phone and hares off across the sand with it. Her short blonde hair takes off, whipped skywards by the breeze, and her laugh floats up and is whisked out to sea as she runs.

Cal runs after her, his feet pounding the wet hard-packed sand, and relief at this glimpse of the woman he fell in love with thuds inside him. She's fitter than he is, and he's wheezing and out of breath by the time she flops down in the lee of a huge sand dune, her face pink and her eyes sparkling.

'I can't breathe.' He sinks down next to her.

When they've both stopped laughing, Shona touches his arm.

'You already sent a message. I know it's hard, but you should wait, give her space.'

'But what if she's lying in a gutter, drunk and abandoned?'

'You're only half-joking, aren't you?'

Cal dips his head in embarrassment. That is by far the tamest nightmare scenario he's envisaged in the forty-eight hours since he left Chrissie in her halls of residence. His mind is creating reel after reel of worst-case options. It's not rational, he knows that.

'I guess I'm scared. I didn't expect to feel this way about her going to uni.'

Shona cups his cheek. Her hand is small and soft, chilled by the wind.

'This has come at a bad time for you,' she says. 'You're on edge with the trial. That's all it is. Chrissie is smart and sensible. It's far more likely that she's too busy studying and finding the lecture hall than lying paralytic on a pavement somewhere, isn't it?'

Cal nods.

'Don't crowd her – let her find her own way. She'll call.'

Cal wishes he could soothe the feelings of loss and instability that have appeared so suddenly. Even more, he wishes he could turn back the clock and appreciate every second of Chrissie's childhood.

'You're very wise,' he says instead, leaning forward and finding her lips. Shona pulls him in closer for a deeper kiss. When she releases him, he holds his hand out for his phone.

'Fine. Helicopter parent.' Shona scrambles to her feet and stretches a hand to pull him up. They stare at the sea together and he tries to find the right words to move their conversation along.

'Look…' she says, when they're walking again. 'There's a case I want to talk to you about. It might be something you're interested in. An old friend of mine, whose son went missing in 2010, has recently got back in touch – I hadn't seen her since we were wee. I know now isn't the time, but maybe let me know when you've got the headspace?'

Cal's heart sinks a little at the thought that he's going to have to confess his Margot podcast plan. But Shona wouldn't ask if it wasn't important.

'Sure,' he says, wrapping an arm round her. 'Just as soon as the trial is out of the way.'

CHAPTER SEVEN

That night they drive along the coast and are settling themselves into a red leather booth in a Turkish restaurant overlooking the churning sea, when Detective Foulds calls.

'Is now a good time?'

Cal feels like a stone has nestled in the base of his throat. He can tell by the tone of her voice that something has happened.

'What? What is it?'

'I wanted to be the one to tell you. We've had a bit of bad news about the trial.' Cal's heart swoops. Shona frowns as she watches his face. 'The judge has had a bereavement.'

'Oh. God, that's awful.'

'Yes, his wife died suddenly on Friday and so, clearly, he can't continue for now.'

Cursed. Everything about his quest for justice with Margot is cursed. 'No, of course not. What happens now?'

'Well, if it were a juror, they'd just use a substitute. But this is a little trickier – either we need to rerun the trial with a new judge...' Cal groans. 'Or we wait for him to come back. He's insistent that he's going to come back to work, so right now we're minded to wait, as honestly that might be quicker, but we're looking at that taking at least a month. Earliest.'

All the air in his lungs rushes out.

'A month?'

'I'm sorry. It could be more.'

'We were so close.'

Foulds sighs. 'I know. It's a huge blow.'

'Will the jurors remember everything?'

'They'll do a recap, go over anything that's needed when it restarts.'

'Better than a mistrial, I suppose.'

'Yeah, having to go through it all over again wouldn't be ideal.' Foulds injects a note of forced cheerfulness into her voice. 'But we will, if we have to.'

–

When he hangs up, he swears, trying to push back the tears and the overwhelming sense of unfairness – he knows he needs to be an adult about it when, actually, all he wants to do is run into the surf and scream at the sea.

'What's going on?' Shona's face is creased with worry. Cal brings her up to date and she looks even more tense.

'I'm sorry,' she says, squeezing his hand. 'You will get there. It's just going to take a little longer.'

Cal stares at the road outside the restaurant. The sky seems darker, the world greyer than a moment before. Even the yellow sands seem dull.

Shona nudges the menu in his direction. 'Come on, let's eat. Maybe that will help.'

He stares at the choices. The only thing that will help is seeing Barr in prison.

'You choose,' he says, not caring what they have. 'It all looks delicious.'

After mezze and seafood, they sit picking at baklava.

'What are you going to do in the meantime?' Shona asks eventually, her lips shining with the honey coating from the dessert.

His work has been the elephant in the room for a while. He's been making short documentaries, as well as researching and recording segments for other podcasts, unwilling to commit to a new series until the trial has taken place. This freelance work pays the bills – just – but isn't as exciting, fulfilling or lucrative as his own podcast. His agreement with his production company

34

includes a cut of advertising revenue and that boost would really help while he and Allie are putting Chrissie through university. Cal doesn't want to plunge into another investigation and have to leave it at a crucial time, but the news from Foulds means he can't just sit around and wait.

It takes it out of him, immersing himself in another family's pain, stepping into their lives and trying to imagine himself in the shoes of the victim. It enters his dreams, distorts his waking hours. He's going to have to deal with that. It's on the tip of his tongue to tell Shona about his plans to do a podcast on Margot and Barr, but he isn't sure she's going to see it as healthy, especially as he'll be taking on more financial risk to do so.

Her words interrupt his thoughts. 'It's just that I have a suggestion.'

Cal picks up his tiny coffee cup and sips at the bitter liquid. 'You do?'

Shona takes his hand and squeezes. 'The case I wanted to talk to you about? It's a family we were friends with when I was growing up. Their daughter was a bit older than me but we met on holiday at Loch Morlich one year and stayed in touch.' She stumbles over her words. 'Anyway. She grew up and married a local boy whose family had a farm near Inverness. They took over the farm and had kids of their own. The oldest son, Arran, got a place at Edinburgh University.'

Cal stills at the mention of the institution where he has just dropped off his daughter.

'I know.' Shona winces. 'Maybe this isn't the best time to ask, but he's been missing thirteen years now. Angela said he came back for Christmas and just wasn't right, but he wouldn't say why. She couldn't get anything out of him, so she left it.'

Cal's heart stutters at the horror. It's exactly the kind of panic situation he's been trying to divert himself from all weekend. He doesn't want to hear this, but he has to. He swallows. 'Go on.'

She shrugs. 'That's it. He's never been found. No trace and no real leads. The police have long given up.'

Cal exhales. 'That's awful.'

Shona copes with all manner of difficult cases and grieving families in her work, but to make it to her, there have to be bodies and remains, a certainty of death. Cal can see how troubled she is by the absence of evidence, of something she can tackle with science. The waiter appears to clear the table, and she drops Cal's hand and swivels to look out at Aberdeen beach, clearing her throat.

When he's gone, Shona turns back.

'So, how can I help?' he asks unwillingly, trying to push the sense of foreboding away. He's bombarded with requests for help from all directions – Shona knows that. She knows how hard it is to say no.

'I know this is a big ask,' she says. His chest tightens. 'But the police won't investigate. They say he ran away or died by suicide.'

He tries to make his voice gentle. 'It sounds like that's likely? If he wasn't right when he went home… Maybe the pressures of university were too much. It can be hard being away from home, in a new environment.'

He tries not to think about Chrissie in that same position. His mind keeps returning to Margot's trial… He doesn't have the capacity for this.

Shona shakes her head. 'Angie is adamant that Arran wouldn't do that.'

Cal tries to keep his face neutral. They both know that many families find death by suicide impossible to accept.

'I know what you're thinking,' she says shrewdly.

He holds his hands up in surrender. 'I have an open mind.'

'I can't explain it,' she says, 'but there's just something that isn't right about this one.'

'I'm not sure how you think I can help?'

'Well, I just thought that maybe while you wait for the trial to restart, you could dig into it a little. It would mean you could live with me as a halfway point.' There it is again. The moving-in question. Shona pushes on, 'You can get to Moray and Edinburgh from here. Could visit Chrissie too.'

She watches for his reaction and he sees that Chrissie is her trump card. His mind is spinning – Cal feels hemmed in, his options shut down, and he needs a moment to collect himself.

'How come you haven't mentioned this before?'

'I didn't know about it. We lost touch until a couple of months back. She called me because she's desperate. Everyone seems to have given up and she's got no answers. I decided not to mention it before because I know there's a lot of demands on you. I do know that. I feel shitty asking.' Shona's blue eyes have clouded like the sea on a rough day.

'No,' he says. 'You can ask me anything. Always.'

He hates the thought that she's been dealing with this alone. That he's been so preoccupied with the trial and Margot that he hasn't prised it out of her.

'Cliff said I should just ask, but I wasn't sure.'

She glances out at the surf again. It's started to rain and a pedestrian is running from their car to the restaurant, head down against the battering might of the weather.

'Cliff knows?' Her younger colleague is usually the source of humour and scrapes rather than counselling.

She looks back, surprise written on her face. 'We don't have many secrets. I have to listen to his yapping all day, so it seemed only fair...'

He smiles but underneath feels a lurching instability. It's not that he's jealous of Cliff, who is more like a son to Shona than anything, but he's hurt that he isn't the first person she's told. Cal hasn't been there for her.

'They're devastated, Cal. Arran was studying rural resource management, keen to take over the farm. He had plans but he was also their future. They're facing having to sell up or divide the farm, though I think their daughter is determined to take it on.'

Cal realises he has no choice but to come clean. He now really wishes he'd brought it up before, but it's too late for regrets. He takes a breath and plunges in.

'Look,' he says. 'There's something I should have told you. About my plans.'

Shona sits up straighter. Her grip loosens on his hand and he squeezes to hold on to her, to reassure himself as much as anything.

'Once the trial is done, I'm going to do a podcast on Margot and the other Barr victims, all the way through from the assaults he previously did time for. And there's other unsolved cases I want to cover, ones that could have been him. I've talked to Sarah and we're thinking twelve episodes initially, with scope to extend. She thinks she can get me a better contract with the production company – maybe on more of a partnership basis. Fifty–fifty.' The excitement is threaded through his voice.

'Wow.' Shona leans back. 'You've planned this out? Talked to Sarah?'

'It's not exactly planned…'

'Right.'

Shona catches the waiter's eye and signals for the bill. The relaxed atmosphere of earlier has been punctured.

'I'm sorry,' he says, pulling his wallet out so they can do their usual fight over who pays. 'It's just that I've waited a long time for this opportunity…'

It's impossible to explain how much this means to him. It's what's been driving him forward recently. He owes Margot. To right the misconceptions in the press, to set the record straight.

'But then, it's not going to be over, is it?'

Shona's voice is thick and her face pale. Cal worries that they've done too much. She gets more easily tired since the car accident a couple of years ago.

'What do you mean?'

Shona's shoulders deflate. 'I thought… I thought after the trial that would be it.'

Cal stares at her, horrified that she's waiting for it to be over. How can he possibly explain that it will never be over. Margot looms as large as ever. He dreams of his sister, he sees her image in his daughter, mourns her without the support of his mother. Shona understands this, doesn't she? His mind inexplicably flits to Chrissie's boyfriend Robbie – the only person in Cal's life who absolutely gets this.

He opens his mouth to speak but, with epic timing, the waiter appears and they fall silent as Cal pays. He knows from the fact that Shona doesn't put up any resistance that she's rattled.

When the waiter leaves, she stands and pulls on her coat. He follows suit, a stone in his gut at the way things are between them. They walk from the restaurant without touching – out into the dusk and the assault of the weather. She flips her hood up so he can't see her face. Without a word, she starts to run for the car. All he can do is follow.

CHAPTER EIGHT

'Well, that sounds perfect.' On Monday morning, after Shona has gone to work, Cal calls Sarah with the news about the trial and the new podcast proposal. He's hoping she'll tell him not to do it. 'Take the case.'

'You make it sound so simple.'

He sets down his coffee. As is always the way, he's barely had a chance to take a sip before Sarah launches in, somehow finding the heart of the matter like a heat-seeking missile set to total destruction. From the laptop screen, she's looking at him with her head tilted and one eyebrow reaching for her hairline. He's barely made it out of bed but her black bob is immaculate, and she's wearing a full face of make-up and a statement necklace. He stares at the spiked metal as she speaks.

'It is simple: you're a bit fucked. You need a new series. Quick. This sounds flexible. If you need to pause to go back to court, you can.'

'But this is a case linked to Shona. I'm not sure how ethical…'

Sarah makes a snorting noise into the espresso she has lifted to her lips.

'I object to that,' he says. 'I've always been above board.'

'Oh, come on. You're going to make a podcast about the man who killed your sister.' She blanches at the look on his face. 'Sorry. You are, though. And, for what it's worth, I think it'll be great.' She keeps eye contact with him and his chest warms slightly at her support. Sarah could never be accused of pandering to someone to make them feel good, so if she gives any praise, she means it. 'But it isn't exactly "ethical".' She hooks her fingers in the shape of quote marks to make the point.

'So, what are you saying?'

'Since you don't exactly do conventional, I'm confused as to why you suddenly seem to have doubts about this particular case.' She does the eyebrow raise again.

He scans the room for an escape or a distraction. 'Astute.'

'Why, thank you.' She knocks back her coffee. 'But tell me, what gives?'

He's not going to tell her that he's scared of moving in with his girlfriend. He's desperate for advice, but not that desperate. 'It's complicated... Overwhelming. There's all the trial stuff, Chrissie going to uni, my mother back home getting frailer, Shona... I just want the world to stop and let me breathe for a minute.'

'Don't we all.'

'I know we need a new series. Something.'

She sits back and folds her arms. If Cal has changed in the time they've worked together, then Sarah has too. Her edges aren't quite as sharp. These days she at least waits a second or two before admonishing him.

'Well, why don't you use this waiting time to have a nose around? No pressure. We reconvene in a month and if there's nothing doing then you walk away from this one.'

He pictures his empty flat, his mother's house. Can he just leave everything for a little while? Then he looks around Shona's house – the dripping green of the fields that surround it, the turning leaves and the morning bite in the air. Her warm fires and comforting cooking in the insulated refuge, while the storms rage at the long glass windows. He pictures her face, her head bent over her laptop, hands tucking blonde hair behind her ears. He tries to be rational, to tamp down the urge to flee. Things are good here. He should stay.

'That could work.' The words come reluctantly, in the absence of another option.

'Great, sounds like a plan. You can send me a first episode any time.'

His mouth drops open, fish-like. 'Wait, you said...'

She grins. 'Record as you go, just in case. That's your thing now, anyway. It's more efficient.' She waves her hand at him. 'Got to go...' Classic Sarah – leaving just to win the argument.

'You only just called.'

'Bye, Cal. Keep in touch. I'll have some conversations with advertisers and media, just in case...'

'But...'

He's talking to an empty screen. Cal stares into the dregs of his coffee. Exhales. Battles the rising sense of déjà vu.

CHAPTER NINE

ARRAN, 2009

The first week is like being in a foreign country. Arran, used to waking early to help on the farm before going to college, can't adjust his body clock. He finds himself staying up late but still waking with the first light when the halls are silent, bar the occasional bleary-eyed sportspeople venturing out for training runs or to swim in the Commonwealth Pool.

Everything around him seems a novelty, drawn in colours brighter than he knew existed. He calls home once or twice and they are happy to hear from him but it's hard to connect with the person he used to be there. He could close his eyes and conjure the hills and the fields in a second, but he chooses not to, feeling midway between two selves. He's left the Highland Arran behind for a time, but it's not yet clear who he's going to be here and he's conscious that he will have to go back to his old skin at some point. This is a hiatus.

The tiredness he feels as he drags himself out of bed for lectures lends the city a blurred and ethereal feeling. He marvels at the great buildings, the wide streets and vistas, the grand architecture; he raises his collar and shoulders against the violent winds that whistle down the streets and then drop suddenly, making way for temporary bursts of sunshine and warmth. The sound of the piper on Princes Street makes his heart swell in his chest.

He has to get to grips with finding the faculty, the lecture hall, his first tutorial. There are coursemates to meet, and first drinks that start awkwardly and then become easier as the beers slip down his throat, his face flushed and his shyness retreating. Practical and outdoorsy, his fellow 'agrics' – the rural resource management students – are more like the people he's used to than his corridor mates.

Even so, he notices that he's gesticulating more, speaking more than he would at home. He briefly feels self-conscious about it, almost hearing the piss-taking that his family would engage in if they could see him, and then decides he doesn't care.

Jonno seems to know everyone. He rapidly makes friends with the entire corridor and though Arran occasionally winces at the loud, posh tones that moderate for no one, he can't help but admire the confidence with which Jonno moves through the world. He's never met anyone with such self-assurance, so lacking in self-doubt. Where Arran's from, it would be unattractive, unacceptable even, but he marvels at the way his new friend – for they are becoming friends – takes control of a room, drawing people in with a joke or a back slap, effortlessly flirting with every girl he meets.

He takes to calling Arran 'Farmer Boy' – affectionately, of course. He gets used to his door being barged open and Jonno insisting he has to come to the bar now. Once, when Arran is dressing, he is shocked to notice Jonno just brazening his way in and sitting on the bed, picking up a magazine.

'Um, I'm getting dressed here,' he says, grabbing his towel and covering up as best he can.

'Boarding school,' Jonno says, flicking the page. 'Seen it all.'

Arran doesn't feel he can protest, so he turns his back and pulls up his trousers quickly, his still-wet legs sticking to his jeans. He's annoyed and in awe, and that's annoying in itself.

'So,' Jonno says. 'I need a wingman tonight. You game?'

'A wingman?'

'Met these two lovely English Literature students.' Jonno makes the shape of breasts with his hands. Arran is annoyed with himself for blushing. 'We're going to meet in the union and then go on – I said I'd bring a friend.' He turns his hands into guns and points them at Arran.

'Me?'

Jonno has a steady stream of posh, pink-shirted, cords-wearing friends with floppy hair and equally loud voices, any of whom Arran would have expected to be a more obvious choice. Most of them are living in the en-suite versions of halls, or even in flats paid for by their parents, instead of the uni residences. They like coming to ogle Jonno's 'digs', marvelling at how small the room is and the fact that he has to share a bathroom.

Whether or not Jonno's choice of accommodation was made for this reason, Arran can see he enjoys it. Never mind that he has expensive sheets, while most make do with polycotton, as well as a designer rug and a six-foot-tall pot plant in a brass container – it's still seen as comically slumming it by the boating and polo set.

'You free?' Jonno raises an eyebrow and waits for a response, though Arran can see that he knows perfectly well the answer is yes. There were tentative plans for some of his coursemates to meet in the Illict Still but he's still waiting for a text. And Jonno always gets his way: he turns on the charm and you somehow end up falling at his feet.

'Aye,' he says. 'I'm free.'

'Get in. I said we'll take them for some drinks and then on to Big Cheese.'

'Really?' Arran has heard of the cheesy music night that is an Edinburgh University institution but hadn't really seen it as his scene, or Jonno's. 'I'm more of a pub and cinema guy myself.'

Jonno stares at him. 'But how are you going to get girls with an attitude like that?'

'I do okay.' Arran thinks of Natalie, one of the girls on his course, and the way she's been smiling at him in lectures. She always seems to end up sitting in front of him, smelling of fruity shower gel and flicking her hair. It's early days, but there are

45

plans for a night out soon and then maybe… It's just hard to tear his thoughts away from Olivia and the feeling of diving, his stomach dropping away, that he gets when he sees her. She's out of his league, he knows that, but it's her face he sees when he closes his eyes at night.

'Of course you do.' Jonno looks like he doesn't believe a word.

'I do!'

Jonno springs from the bed and to the door. 'Pick you up at seven.'

CHAPTER TEN

CAL

The farm is bigger than he'd imagined. The barns are huge, industrial-looking buildings, with space for hundreds of cattle which are currently dotted around the fields. He parks his car in front of a white-painted farmhouse that looks like it had been there long before the modern additions sprung up around it. As he steps out, a clutch of hens run towards him to investigate – their beady eyes and dinosaur-like gait make them seem like little prehistoric busybodies.

Most of Cal's cases come about because he feels a strong connection with the victim that pulls him into their orbit. The podcast he was hoping to start will be the ultimate connection – all of the people whose lives Jason Barr damaged or destroyed, giving them voices at last. Instead, he faces this new challenge. Can he forge a connection with missing Arran?

Part of the problem for the boy's family is just this: he isn't an alluring news story. Not a vulnerable child, nor an attractive woman, he's last on the list for news coverage; his plight twangs fewer heartstrings. Cal winces at the trap he's fallen into, relieved to feel the stir of injustice that is so often the emotion to drive him. It flows into his veins like impatience. Arran is someone's son, a brother, a missing soul. *Come on, you can do this. Stop wallowing. Snap out of it.*

A dog starts barking – a collie that comes close but won't get within petting distance. Cal looks around for someone, but there is no one. He'd pictured a set-up akin to the crofting existence that Jean and Tam have in Aberdeenshire, but this is an entirely different, grander, operation. He's tired and his legs are stiff after a couple of hours in the car, driving towards the Highlands, stopping just short.

And then she is there. A woman who must be the same age as Shona, but seems two decades older. Angela's hair is grey and pulled back from her face, though frizzy wisps stand out around her like a halo. She's wearing an apron, on which she is wiping her hands. She doesn't shush the dog, just watches Cal for a moment, almost like she's weighing him up. He approaches, trusting that the collie is more bark than bite.

'Cal?' Her accent is thick, her tone wary.

'Yes. You must be Angela?'

'Aye. Jet! Wheesht!'

The dog slinks away from them and the absence of sound is a relief. Cal can hear the sound of machinery now – a tractor perhaps.

'I've to get the scones in the oven,' she says. 'They'll be in shortly for their break. Away and come in.'

She waits by the gate, her eyes round, and Cal feels like she both wants to pull him in and bar the way. He goes slowly and softly along the path. The house is surrounded by a wall and a gate, perhaps to protect it from the livestock. Certainly, it makes no difference to the chickens – one leaps onto the wall next to him, making him jump. Angela smiles at the movement and her face transforms. He recognises her, then, from the pictures Shona has shared with him.

He sits at a huge, scrubbed kitchen table while she busies herself with the scones, cutting them out and putting them on a tray, then into the Aga. He gets his equipment ready, setting the microphone carefully in the middle of the table so it will pick up their conversation, as well as the hum and everyday nature of the activities.

She lifts the cover over the range and fills the kettle, which spits at the base before settling. She adds teabags to a chipped teapot. He looks around while she works: the kitchen is big, the floor covered with dark red flagstones, and horse brasses hanging round the large fireplace. There's a box of newspapers in the corner, shoes piled by the side of it. Every surface seems to have something on it: a job half-done or a project frozen.

A cat is curled contentedly on an easy chair in another corner.

'Here.' Angela sets a mug of tea down in front of Cal. 'The scones will be oot in a minute.'

'Will you sit down with me?'

Angela looks around, her eyes raking the surfaces, refusing to rest on Cal. 'I've so much to be getting on with...'

Cal thinks of the need to get some thoughts recorded, of the limited time he has to be here. He needs her to calm down, loosen up. 'Angela...' He keeps his voice soft. 'Shona said you wanted to tell me about Arran, to see if I can help?'

She looks at him then, lets him see her pain. Cal feels it hit him inside, like jumping into cold water on a winter's day. He doesn't look away; if you fight it, it hurts more. You have to accept the cold. It doesn't make things any warmer – you just get used to the chill.

'He was a good boy.' She sinks onto a chair opposite Cal, but only half on it, perched like she isn't really taking a break. 'He was such a good boy. My easy one.' Her hand goes to her mouth. 'God forgive me for saying it, but he was. Do you have children?'

'One. A daughter.'

'Well, maybe it's different with one, but the girls have always bickered, fought like cat and dog. Maybe because they're close in age, I don't know. They're my daughters and I love them, but they drive me mad. Arran was always a quiet lad. Not nervous or shy, just steady. Easy-going.'

'And he planned to take over the farm?'

'Yes. It's difficult, as a farming family. There's a pressure that comes with it. Someone needs to step up. We knew that, Bill and I, but we didn't push him. He wanted to do it. He was excited about it...' Her voice drifts. 'He was.'

'How did the girls feel about him taking it on?'

'Kirsty wasn't bothered. She's always been one for the music, wanted to get away. She's in Glasgow now, plays the fiddle. We've been once to see her and I couldn't believe it was her away on the stage. But Gillian always found it hard, I think. She's got the blood. The farming blood.' Angela knits her fingers together. 'She's taken his place, in the end.'

Cal tilts forward, as if in an effort to soften his words.

'The police seem to think Arran took his own life.'

Angela shakes her head, the colour rising in her already-flushed cheeks. 'He would never. Never. It just wasn't him. I'm his mother, I would know.'

He can see that her belief in this is unshakeable. This was the issue that worried him about taking on Arran's case. What if everything points that way in the end?

'What do you think happened to Arran?'

The tears come then, though she wipes them back before they have time to hit her cheeks. 'I don't know,' she says. 'But something happened that first term. When he came back at Christmas, he was different. He just wasn't my son. Something happened to change him.'

—

Cal takes notes for a while: any names Angela has of school friends, new university friends, and places or things Arran mentioned.

'He had a girlfriend,' she says, her eyes watery, voice shaking a little. 'Natalie. But she said they broke up after Christmas. She was a nice lassie. She helped me look for him a bit.'

'Angela,' he says, leaning forward. 'I'm sorry to ask you this, and please know I have no reason to believe it to be true, but could he still be alive somewhere?' Her face blanches and she starts shaking her head from side to side, but he carries on, determined to say it, knowing his listeners will ask the same thing. 'Maybe taking on the farm was suddenly too much for him, or could he have had some kind of breakdown?'

'No. It's not possible. It just isn't. We've followed every lead, every report of a young man who's turned up in hospital or been found. I've seen five dead bodies...' Her voice thins, before she continues, 'And none of them were him.' She pauses, clearing her throat and pressing her fingertips on the table, like she's on the edge of a cliff, hanging on. 'I've walked the streets in Edinburgh, Glasgow, Aberdeen – even London. I've talked to homeless people, showed his picture, left word that he should just tell us he's safe, even if he doesn't want to come back. Everything. I've done everything.'

'I'm sorry,' he says. The word is ineffective, but it's all he has.

'His bank cards have never been used either and we've kept the account running, just in case. But the real reason I know, is that I *know* my son. He just... wouldn't.' Her expression hardens, takes on a fierceness. 'Your daughter – are you and she close?' Cal nods. 'Would she just vanish? Walk away without telling you?'

Cal pictures Chrissie. He can conjure her laughing face, the dimples in her cheeks and the bouncing red curls so easily. 'No,' he says. 'If she was in her right mind, there is no way...' Because the truth that Cal knows, after years of documentary making and now podcasting, is that we never really know what someone else will do.

'That's what everyone said.' Angela sounds disappointed with him for leaving the caveat in. 'That either Arran was depressed or had an episode of some kind. That he walked into a river, or the sea. But he has never washed up anywhere. How does someone just vanish on their own like that?'

'And you don't believe that's true, anyway?'

'No. I never have and I never will.'

The kitchen timer rings and Angela leaps to her feet as if scalded, grabbing the oven glove and taking a tray of twelve perfect scones out of the oven, sliding them onto the side. 'They'll be here in a moment,' she murmurs. 'Like clockwork.'

The back door bursts open, as if it had been waiting for her signal. Feet and loud voices, a bustle of people that turn out to be only three figures. An older man in a blue boiler suit, a woman younger than Cal – maybe thirty – wearing a faded waxed jacket, and another older man in a pair of ripped jeans and a jumper with holes in the sleeves. 'It's the axle,' the woman is saying. 'I swear to God, Dad.'

'Will you nay listen…'

'Boots aff,' Angela bellows. Cal stands, waiting to be introduced.

'Bill,' Angela says, queen of her own domain, all standing before her. 'This is Cal, the man from the podcast.'

Bill, Arran's father, is tall and well built, his hair receding and greying, with the look of a man who's worked outdoors his whole life. His face hardens, but he nods and extends a hand for Cal to shake. 'Afternoon.'

'And this is Gillian, our daughter. One of them.'

The woman looks at him, her face neutral – neither welcoming, nor hostile. Cal smiles. The middle child.

'And Bobby.'

'All right, Angela?' Bobby looks from one to the other of them, clearly reading the room, shifting from foot to foot uncomfortably. The man must only be in his fifties or sixties if he's working the farm, but he looks older. His stubble is grey and he's missing a few teeth. Cal can see there's a hole in his sock as well. 'Actually, I've a call to make,' Bobby says. 'I'll maybe take a cup out with me, if that's okay?'

Gillian smirks.

'Bring it back,' Angela says, pouring him a tea and dumping three sugars into it, as well as passing him a hot scone. He pulls his sleeve over his hand to hold it.

'Will do, Angela, will do.' Bobby shoves his feet into his boots and is out of the door even quicker than he came through it.

Cal turns and smiles at the others. There's an atmosphere in the room and he doesn't know how this is going to go. Gillian breaks the stillness by pulling out a chair and pouring tea. 'Here, Dad, get that down you.'

But Bill is looking at Cal. When he sits, it is slowly, in a considered way, indicating he is working round aches and stiffness. There's something shuttered in his slow movements, his body language closed, protective. It's understandable, but behind his eyes, Cal can see the same brokenness that exists in Angela, and in his own mother.

'Can you find out what happened, then? After all this time?'

The room is quiet now, as they all wait for his answer. 'I won't promise you anything,' he says. 'That wouldn't be fair. But someone must know something. They always do. Maybe doing a podcast about Arran will shake some people loose, maybe someone can help shed some light on things. It's been thirteen years. The people Arran was friends with may even have children of their own. That changes people, it makes them think.'

'Aye,' Bill says, sipping his tea but keeping his eyes on Cal. 'It would do.'

—

They talk for a little while, but the atmosphere is different with all three in the room, and Cal soon takes his leave. This is just an introduction: he'll come back when he has more information, more questions to ask. It's too early in the process now.

He says his goodbyes and Gillian gets up to walk him out. He has a feeling she wants to speak to him without her parents there.

'They're impressive, keeping all this going in the face of such grief.'

She looks out at the fields, hands in pockets. Her hair is scraped up into a knot on the top of her head, wisps escaping like the straw that blows across the yard. From this angle, he can see the resemblance to her brother. He gets the feeling Gillian isn't a person who shows vulnerability.

'Is there something you wanted to mention?'

When she speaks, there is no hint of a waver in her voice, no suggestion of tears. Her jaw is set.

'I remember that Christmas. The one he came back different.'

'You'd have been, what, fourteen?'

She nods. 'Just. We argued, Arran and I. The whole time. He was thin and quiet, and just absent. It freaked me out. I think it made me provoke him more, you know? I'd been in his room and damaged some of his things. I was a real bitch to him. It was never about that, really. He was going to get the farm – he was the son and the older one, and it wasn't fair.'

'You resented him.'

'No. I resented them.' She inclines her head towards the house where her parents are. 'I took it out on him, though. I was so angry. Arran and I were similar. Not like Kirsty, with her music. She never wanted this.'

Cal isn't sure where this is going. He looks at her, waits.

'Now I have it: everything I longed for. Dad is grooming me to take over.' She tilts her chin and he sees the anger that she mentioned surfacing, making her face contort.

'You have it, but you can't enjoy it.'

'The guilt,' she says. 'It eats you inside. I know it's stupid. I was a kid, wishing for things. But it's always felt like my decision: that I gave him up to have this and I can never take it back.'

'It's not your fault,' he says. 'I know that's hard to accept, but it's not.'

She nods and looks at her boots; Cal doesn't have the impression that his words have given her any comfort.

'And what happened before he left?'

Her gaze shifts. There's something here, Cal's sure of it. He felt it in the kitchen, when he talked to Angela and Bill. A gap in the narrative, like a missing stepping stone.

'This didn't come from me.'

'Fine.'

'They argued too. I was in bed, but I heard the shouting one night. Dad... He never really shouted – he's never needed to. Losing Arran changed him, but back then he was pretty much the law here. You did what he said. Mum worked on him a long time for Arran to be able to go away. He always thought the university course was a waste of time, but he let him go. I don't know what happened with Arran before that Christmas, but he was so different. Then there was a horrible row at Hogmanay. It was all my fault. I was jealous and I wanted him to go.'

She holds his gaze for a beat. The pain is hard to stare into. Then the back door opens and Bill appears, pulling on his boots. 'Gilly,' he calls. 'Quit jabbering.'

–

The darkness he found in the farmhouse stays with Cal on the two-hour drive back to Shona's. It mingles with his own memories, the sense that a clock stops and the whole room freezes. You can never go back and make it right. When he ponders Arran's case and feels the usual determination rising, despite the hopelessness of it all, it is not his parents he thinks of first. It's Gillian: a woman who, as a child, wished her brother gone, and her wish came true.

CHAPTER ELEVEN

EPISODE ONE: AN EMPTY SHELL

Arran McDonald was a good boy. Farming stock. The first in his family to apply to university. Thirteen years ago, he left his Moray home for Edinburgh, swapping vast fields and an endless sky for the grandeur of Scotland's capital city. But only for a time. It was meant to be a brief hiatus before returning to the farm to take over the running of the family business. Arran loved the land, the cattle, the sheep, the outdoors. He understood the graft that would be needed, what it meant to have farming in his blood.

'It wasn't ever about persuading him to do something he didn't want to do.' That's Angela, Arran's mum. 'Arran wanted this life. He chose it.'

The family were excited to have him home for Christmas, the first holiday since he took up his university place. Angela picked him up from the station in Inverness and drove him back to the farm. She wasn't prepared for the changes she saw. 'He was thin, his hair looked greasy and his skin was pale.' Maybe that's standard for an undergraduate who hasn't yet learned to look after themselves while partying, studying and working a part-time job, as Arran was. But that wasn't the worst of it.

'He was gone. When he left, he was Arran. *The person who came home looked like him, talked like him, but he wisnae. He didn't speak to his sisters, to any of us, really. Even the dogs didn't want to go near him. He stayed in his room. Didn't smile, not really. When you were watching him, he'd move the muscles but if he didn't think you were looking, his face went blank. Empty. Something had happened. I know it had.'*

Angela expected Arran to improve with home, rest and routine, but things only got worse as the break progressed. He refused to open up to his family, insisting everything was fine and that he was just tired. Despite her encouragement, he didn't pick up with his school and farming friends. On Hogmanay, when he was supposed to take part in the usual celebrations at home to drink in the New Year, the nineteen-year-old left the farm abruptly and headed back to Edinburgh.

From then on, he didn't pick up the phone when his parents or siblings called. 'I didn't know what to do. I should have acted sooner. To my dying day, I'll wish I'd listened to that instinct.'

But she did act. After a few weeks, she tried to raise the alarm. Only, Angela's calls to the university took time to reach the right person. She was passed from one office to another – no one was taking her seriously.

'I knew. I just knew something was very wrong.'

She's being too hard on herself, in the way that all parents of missing children are. If only: the familiar litany among those who have no answers, beset by questions and regrets. Angela did travel to Edinburgh, when she couldn't reach Arran. She talked her way onto Arran's corridor in the halls of residence. She found his room unlocked and sat in there for two days, patiently waiting for him to come back. She questioned other students in the corridor, but no one seemed to know much about the boy in room twelve. Or if they did, they wouldn't talk. His reports of a corridor full of friends were false. No one seemed to have noticed he was missing.

Angela checked the hospitals and reported his disappearance to the police, but was initially treated as an overprotective mother with a son who was most likely on a bender, being a typical student, enjoying his freedom and sleeping at a friend's or girlfriend's flat. Desperate, Angela kept pushing. Calving season was just around the corner, but she was determined not to go back to the farm. Not without answers.

She still doesn't have the answers today.

Arran hasn't been seen since.

His tutor confirmed the student hadn't been to lectures or tutorials since November. He was on a final warning. The university IT department checked his email account: it hadn't been used since early

January. By then, it was February. The police started an investigation. Desperate, Angela printed posters, handed out flyers in clubs, bars and on street corners. Have you seen my son? But days turned into weeks, and all leads ran cold.

After a while, the other students began to resent her constant presence in their corridor. They were uncomfortable with the questioning, her quiet distress. Complaints were made. The university sent someone to suggest, politely, that it was time for her to leave. They agreed to keep his room as it was for the rest of the term, just in case he returned.

Angela is a farmer's wife, capable and practical.

'I washed all his clothes, before I left, you know? Put them in his drawers all neat, like. So they were ready for him. I cleared all the rubbish and the things he'd left out — it wasn't like him to live like that. Did the bed and dusting...' She has to take a moment before she finishes.

'If I'd known he wisnae coming back, I never would have done it. It washed away the smell of him. Forever.'

This is Finding Justice and I'm your host, Cal Lovett.

CHAPTER TWELVE

ARRAN, 2009

It quickly becomes apparent that he has little in common with the pair of English Lit students that Jonno has persuaded to double-date them. Both are tall, willowy, blonde and very posh. Arran is wearing a soft blue shirt with his smart jeans, and yet he feels cheap and underdressed. He can smell the aftershave he doused himself with – insistent, next to Jonno's subtly expensive look and scent – but he tries to banish the insecurity, to give it a chance. He's out meeting new people and having new experiences. This is fine.

Edinburgh looks beautiful at night, laced with the lights that cast shadows on the historic buildings, catching their edges. The place looks eerie and watchful. They're down on George Street, in a glossy cocktail bar whose prices make Arran quail. He swallows hard and reaches for his wallet when the two of them go up to order, but Jonno waves him away, wafting a gold Amex at the barman lining up their happy-hour drinks. The gentle look that the other student gives him lets him know Jonno is aware of the difference in their economic circumstances. It brooks no opposition. Arran feels relieved, grateful and oddly resentful. He gathers the drinks into his hands.

Back at the table, Arran passes the elaborate concoctions to the girls, noting their long and perfect manicures and comparing them with his sisters' short and grimy equivalents. Kirsty would love nails like these, and the glossy hair like horses' manes, but Gilly would scoff, he knows. She couldn't care less.

These nails wouldn't last two minutes on the farm, and that's all Gilly would bother herself with.

The sight of the nails exacerbates the gulf he feels between himself and these confident creatures. He feels even further adrift as he listens to the others chat about ski trips and boating holidays. Their voices are like polished glass. Why is it that he feels the outsider, the curiosity, in his own capital city?

'So good to blow off steam before the hard work starts,' one of the girls, Amber, is saying.

'Totally,' Jonno agrees, though Arran's instinct is to laugh – university isn't work. He's here for a break. Real work is his day-to-day, out in the fields all hours, fixing tractors in temperatures so cold that his hands go numb and bleed.

'Where did you go this summer?' Sienna, his date, cocks her head, her glass raised. Arran startles from his reverie.

'Oh. Loch Morlich,' he says. 'We go every summer.'

'Do you have your own place? A cosy lochside cabin sounds divine!'

Arran pictures the comfy caravan on the park he's known his whole life: the games room with its pool table and the laundry where you feed pound coins into the slots to dry your washing. He tilts his beer to his lips – he's pretty sure this isn't what she means.

'Something like that,' he says, a moment later.

'How long were you away?'

'Two weeks,' he says. Sienna's face creases in concern – the horror of such a short break. 'We can't leave the farm for long,' he goes on, feeling the need to justify. 'My father never comes for all of it. I went back early with him this year to help.' He doesn't mention how much of this was to keep the peace and be allowed to take up his university place, something his father sees as an unnecessary indulgence, a criticism of his own lack of further education.

'You work on the farm?' Amber's nose wrinkles. 'Isn't that really smelly?'

'Yes.' He grins. 'And long hours. When the lambing's on, we can be up all night.' Just for a second, he feels a piercing desire for a mug of his mother's hot chocolate in the kitchen in the early hours of the morning, an orphaned lamb or two in a box by the Aga, the smell of their fuzzy long-legged bodies. So far from this buzzing, elegant bar in Edinburgh.

'Lambs?!' Sienna squeaks. 'How cute. I love lambs.'

'Aye.' He smiles at her. 'They are nice, like.' He doesn't think she'll want to hear about the birthing – the smell of the barns and the slick slide of the afterbirth, the sadness of the stillborn ones and the way their mothers nudge them to move – so he lets her keep her white fluffy image.

The conversation slips on and he is glad to sit in the background – though, as Jonno slides his hand around Amber's waist or touches her hair, leaning in towards her, he starts to feel how much of a mismatch and disappointment he is to Sienna. This is not a partnership that's going to work. He tries subtly to look at his watch, wondering if he could make his excuses and go back to halls, instead of on to the club night. Colleen and Olivia were going to the bar. He'd far rather be there with them.

But, when it's time to go, Amber protests at having to walk back up the hill to the student neighbourhood, insisting on them all bundling into a black cab, which deposits them at Potterrow, behind the Festival Theatre, no time to deviate. Arran sits with his back to the driver, while Jonno, Amber and Sienna laugh on the seat together. He's going to have to see this through. The others, staggering and laughing, all seem to be more drunk than he is.

He follows them into the dimly lit room, where the happy, cheesy tracks vibrate the air around them. Journey's 'Don't Stop Believin'' pumps out of the speakers and the girls twist into the heaving mass on the dance floor – a crush of bodies and grinning faces – joined by Jonno, arms raised, their voices lost in the wall of sound. Noise and excitement whip around Arran. He's an alien life form on an alluring planet. Telling himself it's just the same as the one nightclub he and his school pals used to go to, he follows them.

But, as the night ploughs on, it becomes clear that Sienna is desperate to lose him. As Amber and Jonno stick to each other, sweaty-slick bodies touching in the swarm of drunk students, Sienna sidles further, eventually finding other people she seems to know and joining their group without a backward glance. Arran's shoulders drop from their tight position as he lets her go.

With no need to dance, he heads for the edge, thirsty and deciding he will have one beer and then signal to Jonno that he's leaving. He looks over to his friend to see if he can get him something, but his lips are locked with Amber's, his hand on her mini-skirted behind, so he pushes through the crowd alone.

At the bar, it takes an age to get served. Happy not to be dancing, Arran lets a couple of girls go ahead of him. He stares around at the mass of faces, seeing others who look less than confident. From a distance, everyone looks so happy, but zoom in and you see those feeling out of place. It calms him. He's so busy scanning the writhing mass of humanity that he doesn't feel the hand tugging his sleeve at first.

When he turns, he sees a girl with dark shoulder-length hair and flicks of black eyeliner, wearing a strappy top of black lace over cream. She's much shorter than him and he thinks she's going to ask him to move so she can get to the bar, but then realises she's saying his name. His brow furrows in confusion, until he sees the line of silver rings in her ear and realises he knows her.

She clocks his uncertainty and laughs, putting her hand on her collarbone. 'Na-ta-lie,' she says slowly.

Arran slaps his forehead playfully. 'I didn't recognise you. You look...'

'Bit different without the scruffy trainers and jeans.'

'...gorgeous.' She blushes and he casts around for something to say. 'Are you trying to get to the bar?'

'Oh, no.' Her breath is hot against his ear. 'I saw you standing here. Are you with friends?'

'Aye.' He gestures at the dance floor. 'Somewhere, like.' Natalie laughs again and he feels tension unwinding inside him. 'Do you want a drink?'

She nods and asks for a vodka and Red Bull, and Arran feels a wave of relief that he doesn't have to stand here on his own. When they have their drinks, he leans close to hear what she's saying, drawn like a magnet to her. Natalie touches his arm to make a point; her eyes seem big in the gloom, fixed on his face. Her skin is flushed.

Once they've had their drinks, they move into the crowd and he doesn't feel self-conscious as he dances with her to the cheesy pop tunes. Once, he catches sight of Jonno, now with a bigger crowd of polished-looking people, and he is relieved to be where he is. Natalie grabs his arm and he looks back to see her getting swept away in the crowd, so he lifts her clear and closer, the two of them laughing, faces inches apart for a moment.

At one point, a man jostles into him, so hard that if Arran hadn't held him up, he'd have hit the floor. He's about to shove him away, annoyed, when he realises it's someone he knows.

'Arran! How ye dein, pal? Arran!'

Donny. He was in the year above him in school, but Arran doesn't know him that well, although he remembers now that he's also at uni in Edinburgh. Donny's black hair is plastered to his head with sweat and he's much thinner than he used to be. Arran claps him on the back in greeting, conscious of Natalie standing back and waiting, the thrash of the other dancers around them and the flashing lights making their faces strange and sickly.

It's impossible to talk here and he's having a good time, wants to suggest that he and Donny catch up later, but the other boy leans in.

'Aren't you going to introduce me to your girlfriend?' Donny slurs into his ear. His breath is meaty and sour, like something inside him has curdled.

'This is Natalie,' he shouts back, waving across at her, wincing as he watches her try to smile. 'She's not my...'

But Donny slides towards Natalie before he can finish, pulling her into a clumsy embrace. Arran sees Natalie's look of discomfort. Taken aback, he steps forward. Maybe it's just the crush of people and the fact that Donny isn't steady on his feet that's making him seem this predatory. Arran feels embarrassed for the other boy. Responsible for his weird behaviour.

Donny holds his hands up. 'Sorry, pal, no harm meant, eh?' He doesn't look at Arran, keeping instead an assessing gaze fixed on Natalie. 'Later.' He peels away from them, shoving his way through the crowd. Other students turn and then fall back when they see his face. Arran sees Natalie's disquiet and feels tarnished by the association.

She leans in close to him. 'How do you know him?'

'We went to the same school. He was the year above. We weren't friends.' He feels the need to distance himself. 'Are you okay? Sorry about him. I think he's really pissed.' But he's not totally sure how true that is. There was a meanness in Donny's gaze, a glittering hardness.

Natalie puts a hand on his chest and he feels his heart beating faster at her touch. The track changes and the room roars at the song that has been the soundtrack to the summer. Her face lights up and they jump in time with the beat, at one with the heaving crowd that has closed around Donny like water.

He is hot, sweaty and euphoric, and hardly notices the time passing until it's three in the morning, and the music is switched off and the lights go up. When he bends close to listen to what Natalie is saying, because his ears are ringing, she presses her lips to his and he goes with it, liking the feel of her arms snaking around him, their mingled taste of Red Bull and beer, the comfortable way they have between them and the flattery of being sought out by her. Then her flatmates are calling her, laughing and making kissing noises, pulling her away, and she grins – and for a moment he thinks she's going to ask him to go with them but he waves at her and she's borne away, her face turning in the crowd to look at him.

Arran looks around for Jonno, but he can't find him. Out in the drizzle, he tries again, turning on the spot to search for his friend's distinctive floppy hair in the streetlights. He waits, his own hair and shirt misted with rain as well as sweat, ears thick with the relative quiet of the street and his mind exhausted but awake. The street empties fast and he is resigned to walking back to halls alone, when a cab pulls up next to him and a tousled fair head leans out of the window.

'Farmer Boooooy!'

'Shhhh.' An amused voice from within. 'People are sleeping.'

Jonno's eyes are wide with drink as he looks at Arran and stage-whispers, 'Yeah… shhhh.' He presses his finger to his lips but misses the middle.

Arran starts to laugh.

He opens the door to the cab and is startled to see Olivia and Colleen, not Sienna and Amber as he expected. His heart kicks. 'Oh my God, what are you doing here?!'

The girls pull him into hugs and he feels emotional as he smells the familiar shampoo and perfume, so recognisable from halls and so different to the hostile polish of the women from their date – he must have drunk more than he realised.

'I kidnapped them,' Jonno shouts as the cab lurches off in the opposite direction to the way they should have been going.

'You called us and asked if we wanted to go to a *speakeasy*,' Colleen says, leaning forward. 'I wouldn't call that kidnapping.'

'A what?' Arran says.

'Peasants…' is Jonno's lofty response and Colleen whacks him in the arm.

'I was asleep.' Olivia laughs. 'This better be good.'

Jonno pouts. 'It's going to be brilliant.'

Arran feels, once again, like he's a visitor to another planet. His duties on the farm seem a million miles away. He's filled with laughter, like liquid brimming over and spilling out of him.

'This is crazy,' he says. 'I have no idea what we're doing, but I'm in.'

The cab stops at the end of a dead-looking alley and Jonno presses a twenty-pound note into the driver's hand, telling him to keep the change and apologising for the noise. Arran only vaguely knows where they are as he steps out onto the wet pavement. He helps Jonno out of the cab, which then pulls away fast, leaving them alone on the deserted street. A cat darts across the opening at the far end in a black and white blur.

Olivia keeps her hand on his arm, warming him and making him forget Natalie. The earlier part of the night vanishes like smoke. There is only now. 'Jonno, are you sure about this?'

Jonno seems to have sobered up and is now the picture of a gentleman. 'Perfectly. Oh ye of little faith.' And he strides forward into the dark, rapping on a door in a part of the alley that smells of piss and takeaways. Nothing happens. Colleen groans and Olivia lets out another giggle.

'Oh, man,' Arran says. 'You've finally lost it.' Jonno swipes playfully at him and then turns back to the door. Arran's about to suggest they run back and see if they can wave down the cab, when the vast door opens a crack, revealing a sliver of a person – a suspicious eye peering at them.

'Not tonight,' the voice says.

Arran feels himself rocking backwards, deflated. But the words have the opposite effect on Jonno, who rises a step and holds out a card he has pulled from his blazer. He says something that sounds like 'salt' or 'saltire' to Arran's addled ears and the door swings back. Before he knows what's happening, Olivia grabs his hand, her skin warm and smooth as silk. Arran is up the steps with the rest of them and they are swallowed by the house.

The man who opened the door is dressed in black tie. He takes their coats and gives Jonno a gleaming brass disc with a number on. Jonno hands over a credit card and Arran says, 'Can I...' but Jonno shakes his head.

'You have to be a member,' he says.

'How do you even know about this?' Colleen looks both awed and disapproving. Arran can see she feels as much a fish out of water as he does, but her dislike of privilege and pomp are holding her back. Jonno doesn't answer, is already following the man through a series of poorly lit rooms sheathed in dark wallpaper, where dripping plants and sumptuous velvet furniture make it glamorous and cosy at the same time.

He takes Colleen's arm and leans in to whisper to her.

'I never do anything like this. Let's enjoy it?'

She looks up at him, face clouded, but then it clears of guilt and a grin spreads over her lips. Arran straightens his back, tries to pretend he's born to this and follows the others.

They are led to a booth so circular that it's like a teacup ride at the fair. The walls are lined with ancient-looking books, and voices sparkle around them, refracting from the crystal chandeliers and the glasses and bottles on the bar. Men with slicked-back hair and embroidered waistcoats shake cocktails and bring dishes of nuts and crackers to place before them.

Arran looks at Jonno, perfectly at home, with his arm slung over the back of the booth, and a burst of love and envy explodes inside him. As they nestle in and talk, dissecting their lives, the people around them in halls, the things they feel so deeply, he experiences a level of connection and happiness so strong that he thinks it cannot be contained.

Jonno sees his face, reaches out and ruffles his hair. They all lean in together in one amorphous heap of warmth and Colleen, several cocktails down, mumbles what Arran is feeling deep inside. 'I think I love you guys.' No one laughs at her.

When Colleen and Jonno are engaged in an intense debate on the fairness or unfairness of inheritance tax, Arran turns to Olivia. She is incandescent, her blonde hair down for once and tumbling around her face. He's reminded that she was asleep until Jonno roused her for this adventure. To him, she looks like an angel.

'I'm glad you got out of bed for this,' he says.

'Me too.' Her fingers entwine with his and it's hard to explain, but there's no expectation or agenda between them. It's more than that. He drinks in the proximity of her, happy to sit here forever just to be close to these people. He's never had friends like this before.

It's a grey dawn when they finally leave the house and stumble out into the main street. They were almost the last ones left inside.

'When does it close?' Arran asks in wonder, looking back at the alley, which seems to his exhausted eyes to have melted away. Maybe all of this is a dream or an illusion.

'It doesn't,' Jonno says. 'As long as people want to drink, it stays open.'

'Imagine not knowing what time you're going to finish work,' he mutters, without thinking. Jonno roars with laughter and slings his arm around Arran's neck.

The street is still wet, but the rain has stopped and the early-morning quiet is punctuated by the clip of the first commuters on their way to work. What do they think of these drunken students in their midst? What would his father think if he could see him now? He pushes the thought away. It wouldn't be good. He's here to work, to learn and then implement. Not for frivolity.

'Bacon rolls, anyone?'

Arran is saved from introspection. They all chorus their agreement and link arms, following Jonno as he leads the way once more, a Pied Piper taking them into another world.

CHAPTER THIRTEEN

CAL

Shona drops him off at the station. They talked last night, about Arran. Cal gently suggested that suicide looks a distinct possibility – the personality change, the absence of a body or a lead. Shona was adamant that Angie knew her son, that this wasn't an option. It's so unlike her to be irrational. It's almost as if he and she are taking different sides on this because it's the easier fight to have. She hasn't brought up the topic of him moving in again, but it's there, hovering between them like mist.

'I'll call you later,' he says, leaning in for a kiss.

'Aye,' she tells him, accepting rather than returning it.

The train from Aberdeen to Edinburgh takes two and a half hours. Cal watches the sea, grey and rolling, as the carriages make their way south. He has called Chrissie to let her know that he'll be there for a few days, making enquiries, but he hasn't heard back from her yet, though he keeps checking his phone.

To distract himself, he goes through the notes he made when talking to Arran's mother. Arran had told her he was friends with people in his corridor – a boy and two girls – but she wasn't sure of their names. None of them materialised when she was there, looking. She thinks maybe the girlfriend, Natalie, might know more.

The lack of detail strikes him hard in the gut. He makes a mental note to ask Chrissie the full names of her friends, in case he ever needs them. Maybe she should give him their numbers too. Just in case. At least Natalie has been easy enough to track down. She now works in policy in the Scottish Executive and has agreed to meet him for coffee.

At Waverley station, he leaves his bag in left luggage and walks up in the direction of the Scottish Parliament. Arthur's Seat looms over the city; the sky above is laden with heavy clouds, not so much threatening as promising rain.

Cal waits for Natalie in a small coffee shop painted purple – even the tables and chairs are shades of indigo. A glass-fronted display houses an indecent number of cakes, cut into doorstop-shaped wedges, and he imagines bringing Chrissie here at some point, feels the need to see her. He checks his phone, but she still hasn't replied. Lectures, perhaps. He hates the swelling feeling in his chest that accompanies this lack of contact. It's the habit of anxiety, that's all.

After a few moments, a woman in a pair of smart black trousers, turquoise shirt and beige mackintosh enters the cafe and hovers just inside the doorway, scanning the patrons. Her brown hair is neatly clipped back. Cal stands and waves uncertainly, and she crosses to him, relief on her face.

'Natalie? Thanks for meeting me.'

'Not at all. I don't know if I can help, but I'll try. Arran disappeared in our first year – it seems such a long time ago.' Her brown eyes are big and soulful, her most distinguishing feature. Cal wonders what she was like as a student in the city. Will his daughter seem this grown-up soon?

'Let me get you a coffee.' He stands in the queue for drinks for a few minutes, shifting from foot to foot, wishing the barista would stop chatting, as Natalie is giving up her lunch break for this and will have to get back soon. But when he looks over at her, she's gazing out of the window, not checking her phone. Her posture is so still, it's unnatural, like she isn't actually here at all.

'I still think about Arran quite often,' she admits when he sets the latte down in front of her. 'It's the not knowing that kills you. I can't believe it's been thirteen years. I used to think about him constantly, even when we left uni. Used to see him in the street. The number of times I ran after some poor man and scared the life out of him.' She looks down, her cheeks reddening.

'Forgive me, the only information I have is from Arran's family so far. His mum seems to think you and he were—'

'Yes,' she cuts in, instead of dancing around the topic. 'We were together. I fancied him rotten from the first time I met him.' Natalie cups her hands around her coffee and looks down into the foam. 'We started going out a few weeks into term. He was my first proper boyfriend, really. There had been one or two at school, but this was different, you know? Being away from home. Being an adult.'

'What was he like?'

'You'll have seen the pictures. He was good-looking, tall and strong from all the time outdoors on the farm. It wasn't that he was quiet in a shy way – he just didn't always seem to need to talk, to be the centre of attention. But people looked up to him. He was confident and good at what he did. Everyone on the course liked him.'

'You must have spent a lot of time together, then? Doing the same course?'

'Yeah, he hung out with us sometimes, but he had this intense thing going on with some people in his halls, so he spent a lot of time with them too.'

'His mum seems to think he was friends with someone called Jonno. Is that who you mean?'

'That's him: Jonathan Keble. Very posh, moved in different circles to the rest of us. His father was a lord, I think, had some big estate somewhere. And two girls, Olivia and Colleen.'

'They were close?' Natalie nods. 'If you were seeing him, you must have spent some time with them too.'

'Not that much. The four of them were such a tight unit. There wasn't really room for anyone else. It was a bit of a bone of contention between us, to be honest.' She looks uncomfortable. 'We used to invite him out all the time, for drinks and things. He came sometimes, but it always felt to me that he was waiting to get back to them, if you know what I mean?'

Cal nods. 'Have you heard what they're up to now?'

'I don't know about Jonathan, but Olivia did law and works in-house for a big Edinburgh landlord now. I have a friend who works there – I can dig out the details if it helps?'

He pauses, scribbles down some notes. 'That would be really helpful. And the other girl?'

'I'm not sure about Colleen – she was hard work, to be honest. Always had a cause she was invested in and prickly about, but I don't know what she went on to do. I don't think she liked me very much.'

'Do you remember what Arran was like before the Christmas holidays?'

'He was quieter than usual, a bit withdrawn. I didn't worry too much about it at the time. It was the end of the first term, we were all knackered. There were loads of Christmas parties and plenty of hangovers. Everyone needed to go home for a break. I got the flu for the last few days so ended up shut in my room until my dad came to pick me up.'

Natalie shifts in her seat, glancing at the crowds in the street outside. It has started to rain and people are pulling up hoods, some unwisely wielding umbrellas against the stiff wind. She has barely touched her coffee. He feels like he's losing her.

'And were you together when Arran went missing?'

Then Natalie hunches in on herself, and he realises she's actually trying to hide tears.

'I'm sorry, asking these questions after all this time.'

'No...' She sniffs. 'It's fine. If any of this helps... then it's worth it.' She clears her throat and takes the tissue that Cal has fished from his bag.

'We had a huge argument a couple of weeks after the Christmas break. He was different when he came back, really

72

moody and preoccupied, didn't come to lectures. He said he'd had a row at home, a really bad one, but he wouldn't talk about it.' Natalie drops her head into her hands. 'I should have been more understanding.'

'None of this is your fault.' Cal leans forward, trying to help her see that he means it. The legacy of blame and guilt left behind when someone goes missing is breathtaking. His mind is spinning, though, remembering Gilly's words.

'There was something else weird going on…' The words spill out of her. 'I think maybe, I thought… he'd had something with Olivia behind my back. He swore that wasn't it, but she wasn't speaking to him and he was so cut up about it. It's all he seemed to care about. I'd be talking and then I'd see he wasn't even listening to me.'

'That must have been hard.'

'I flipped out at him.' Natalie takes a shaky breath. 'He just wouldn't tell me what was wrong. I screamed at him in the street and we broke up. I thought he'd come after me, I didn't really think that was it. That I'd never see him again. I sent him so many messages on Facebook but he didn't reply.'

'When was this?'

She looks up at Cal, no longer trying to hold back the tears. 'It was the day he went missing. That afternoon.'

'That must have been awful.' Something strikes him about what she's just said.

'I didn't think Arran used social media.' He remembers what Angela said. All they had was his university email account and there was nothing useful in there.

Natalie looks up through her tears. 'He didn't, really. But we had a group for our course, so he set one up. It was a joke between us all how little he looked at it.'

It takes a few moments for Natalie to collect herself.

'I feel so responsible.'

'Natalie, people break up. You couldn't have known. Did you tell the police all this at the time?'

'Yes. I said we'd had a fight.'

The lack of police interest is starting to make sense now. Teenage boy has bust-up with his girlfriend and vanishes – doesn't sound like foul play. In fact, Cal has a strong suspicion that the explanation is actually this simple. Poor Natalie.

But, he hears Shona's words in his head, he is jumping to conclusions. If that's the case, what happened to his body? Why has he never been found?

'Natalie, do you think Arran would have done something to himself?'

'That's just it,' she says. 'Before that day I never would have thought that. But he was so lost and angry… I don't know.'

She stares back at the rain-soaked street, dotted with churning puddles. The cafe window is misted with condensation, the door swinging wildly when someone leaves. Her eyes are distant, lost in past thoughts and memories.

'I just wish we knew,' she says finally. 'Dead or alive, how does someone just vanish into thin air?'

CHAPTER FOURTEEN

ARRAN, 2009

They sleep for most of Sunday and then bundle into Olivia's room for pizza, mugs of tea and biscuits to feed their hangovers, slouched in pyjamas or joggers and T-shirts. Olivia's skin is pale and her hair scraped away from her face – Colleen's still dripping from the shower. When someone knocks to return a textbook, Olivia squeaks, 'Oh God, I'm such a state, don't let them see me!' So Arran opens the door and takes the book from the surprised coursemate.

It doesn't matter that they can see the state of each other – it's different. They're a unit, bonded in a way the outside world could not understand.

'Thank you.' She smiles at him when he hands it to her and he feels his skin going hot under her scrutiny.

They collapse in a line on the bed, leaning on each other, watching films on Olivia's laptop, barely talking, only playing rock, paper, scissors to decide who's going to make the next round of tea. At midnight they separate, heading to their rooms. Jonno clasps his shoulder.

'Just so you know,' he says, 'Olivia has a date with a guy from her course this week.'

'Oh… right. Why would that matter to me?'

Jonno just gives him a sympathetic smile and shuts the door.

When he gets to his first lecture on Monday, Natalie is waiting outside the room, a folder held tight against her chest, biting her lip and shifting from foot to foot. Even Arran, usually oblivious to these things, can tell she's waiting for him. Her face flushes when she sees him and her smile makes him feel better again. In a flash, the club on Saturday comes back to him – normal life bursting the false bubble he has been enveloped in.

It's easy to fall into step with her and take the seat next to her in the lecture. As they listen to their tutor and he takes notes, he's aware of her beside him, can feel the glances she throws his way.

After the lecture, a group of them go for coffee together. It's cold, but the sun is shining so they sit at an outside table with their cappuccinos, talking about the course and their backgrounds. He can't help but compare the earnestness and lack of laughter with the hilarity at the speakeasy.

Several of them are the children of farmers, like Arran, learning the latest thinking at a time when the industry is squeezed and struggling, trying to keep family businesses going for the next generation, bound by tradition in some ways but desperate to innovate in others.

'How about you?' he asks Natalie, who's seated by his elbow, one of two women in the group of eight. He's noticed how a couple of the other lads keep looking at her for approval when they speak. He doesn't know how he feels about that. Only one kiss, he can hardly lay claim, yet something about being chosen sets a flutter inside him.

She shrugs. 'My dad's trying to persuade me to choose something else.'

'Sounds like the polar opposite to mine, then.'

'He always wanted to travel and never got to. He keeps saying he doesn't want me to miss out.'

'He sounds great.'

'Yeah, he is.'

'What does your mum say?'

Her face clouds and she glances across the table to where most of the others are laughing at Tommy, already the clown of the group. She lowers her voice so he has to bend towards her to hear. 'She left when I was little. Farming wasn't for her. My auntie moved in to look after me and my brother.'

'I'm sorry. Do you get to see her?'

Natalie shakes her head. 'Once or twice, but not really. When I was fifteen, she showed up and said I could come and live with her.'

'Wow. What did you say?'

She looks up at him, brown eyes close and mesmerising. 'I told her where to go.'

'That must have been tough, though.' He's conscious that one of the others has started to listen to their chat, so he squeezes her hand beneath the table, just for a second. Then drops it, along with the conversation.

He barely notices the time passing until the clouds come in front of the sun and he realises how cold he's getting. He doesn't usually sit still outdoors. When he gets up and announces that he needs to go, he catches the twinge of disappointment on her face, but she soon starts to get ready to leave too.

'Which way are you going?'

He gestures in the direction of halls. 'Back to my room. I said I'd meet some friends. How about you?'

'Same way,' she says. 'Mind if I...'

'No, go ahead.' He falls into step beside her, feeling a gangling giant next to her diminutive frame and having to slow his pace to match her smaller stride.

There's a moment's silence and then they both speak at once. Arran laughs. 'After you.'

Natalie's face is a deepening shade of pink. 'Oh, it's nothing, really, I was just wondering if you wanted to go for coffee sometime.' She looks back in the direction of the cafe they've just left. 'I mean. Again... with just us.'

Arran stops and she hugs the folder even tighter, her face painted an excruciating shade of embarrassment, but the deep brown eyes meet his.

He feels a flicker of regret about Olivia. But she's seeing someone and she's out of his league. That's what Jonno was trying to tell him last night. He's not stupid. Natalie is fun and pretty and she likes him. He likes her too. 'I'd love to. Give me your number?'

They move to the side to let others past and fumble with phones, each of them smiling. She has dancing eyes, he decides as he types in his number and passes her mobile back to her; he then makes sure that he saves hers when she presses dial.

'Great,' she says.

'I'll text, shall I?'

Natalie nods, her brown ponytail bobbing behind her.

She gestures back the way they came. 'I wasn't actually going this way...'

They both laugh and he feels a warm twist in his centre, something easy and recognisable. 'Right, see you then.'

When he's walked a little way, he turns back to look for her: she's almost out of sight, mixed in the swirl of student and tourist traffic. Her brown bobbing hair and a bouncing step. But over to the other side of the road, another figure catches his eye. What is Donny doing? Is that even him? The boy seems to be meeting a stocky man, seemingly as wide as he is high. The man shoves Donny and then the pair melt down a side alley, lost from view.

CHAPTER FIFTEEN

'Ooh, looking fancy.'

Colleen is sitting on Arran's bed, highlighting almost every line in a heavy textbook. Her hair is now a lurid purple. The dye stained the sink and shower in the bathroom until it looked like a violet crime scene. The cleaners were furious and it was pretty obvious who the culprit was, so she's been given a warning.

At her words, he looks up to see Jonno at the door in gleaming black tie, his hair gelled back and his face freshly shaven, an expensive-looking wool coat over his arm. A cloud of aftershave accompanies him, catching in the back of Arran's throat and making his nose itch. He tilts his chair back and whistles at the sight.

'What are you two doing?' Jonno points at Arran's laptop, the pens strewn around Colleen. 'It's Friday night. Are you *working*?'

Colleen sags back against the wall, and picks up her textbook and highlighter.

'First essay due Monday,' she says. 'We're working till ten and then hitting the bar as a reward. Olivia's coming after her dance class.'

'Where are you out to in that get-up?' Arran asks. 'Come meet us after?'

They've slotted into such a natural foursome that, though he sees other people too, Arran is starting to feel that Jonno, Olivia and Colleen are his university family – the priority, with their mad exuberance and sarcasm, their drunken wit and lack of restraint. He laughs less without them. When they get back late, they congregate in someone's room and lie around, listening to music, drinking endless cups of tea and eating toast. They don't have to talk every second and he likes that, just as he marvels at the whirl of fun and laughter that surrounds them at other times. When they're out, he sees other people looking at them, feels their envy.

Jonno groans. 'I can't. This thing's going to go on late.'

'What thing?' Colleen's watching him closely. She drops her highlighter on the bed.

Arran's noticed she can be possessive of Jonno – good-looking and confident, he attracts attention wherever they go. He's pretty sure Colleen has feelings for the other boy; she's always finding excuses to touch his hair or lean into him. He's wondered about warning her off, in case she makes a fool of herself, but Jonno's words about Olivia still sting and he can't bring himself to do the same to someone else.

'Just the sons of some friends of my father's. Bit of a drag, really.' He shrugs again, an uncertain movement that's out of place on him. Arran is intrigued to see the discomfort. But then, he hates even putting on a shirt and tie, so he doesn't blame him.

'Is that one of those networking clubs?' Colleen's face has twisted.

Jonno shrugs. 'I guess. I wouldn't go, but…'

'You don't always have to do what your dad says.' Colleen's textbook follows the highlighter onto the bed and closes with a heavy thump. Her voice is pinched, combative. Arran recognises an argument in the offing.

'You haven't met him.'

'But that's ridiculous. You're at university now, not some kid.'

Arran, seeing Jonno's discomfort, thinks of his own father. Going against him is easier said than done.

'Sounds like it might be a good opportunity anyway,' he offers, tentatively. This isn't his world, but he can see it matters to Jonno.

'Only if you'd rather spend the evening with a load of posh boys,' Colleen bites back before Jonno has a chance to reply.

'Jonno *is* a posh boy,' Arran jokes, hoping to lighten the sudden uncomfortable atmosphere in the room.

But Jonno's lips are pressed tightly together, and he isn't laughing. 'I better go,' he says.

Colleen sniffs and returns to her textbook. 'I thought you had more balls than that.'

There's a moment of silence and discomfort.

He rolls his eyes at Jonno, hoping to defuse it, but receives only a tight smile in return. Arran hasn't ever seen him annoyed before. It changes the shape of his face, shutting down his features, turning them cold.

'These things can go on quite late, but I'll see you in the bar if I can.'

'Cool.' He smiles at Jonno. 'Maybe see you later, then.'

They listen to the click of his smart shoes in the hallway as he walks away.

'That was a bit...'

She looks up. 'What?'

'Why do you care if he does what his dad tells him?'

'Do you know what these "networking" groups get up to?'

'Networking?'

'You're so naïve.' Arran blanches. She's not wrong. 'It's all horrible initiation ceremonies and objectifying women and holding on to privilege so no one else gets a look in, ever.'

He thinks of their amiable friend: always so sure of his place in the world, yes, but also kind and generous. 'That doesn't sound like Jonno.'

'But we haven't really seen what he's like when he's with his posh boys, have we? When any of them call, it's like we don't exist. We're the second-rate friends.'

Arran frowns, unsettled by her skewering of Jonno's character in a way that isn't entirely untrue – Jonno hasn't introduced them to his friends properly. But then, Arran's also shied away from introducing them to Natalie or any of his other course mates. And that's not because his friends from halls are second rate, by any means. Quite the opposite. He shakes his head.

'Colleen, I need to write this essay.'

She huffs at him. 'Fine.'

He pauses and makes his tone light. 'You should highlight the rest of that book… I think you've missed a few lines, there.'

He knows she's forgiven him when she throws the highlighter pen at his head.

–

Jonno doesn't meet them in the bar. Arran thinks he sees him at one point and cranes his neck to look, but it's another guy in a dinner jacket, coming in out of the rain and shaking the drips like a wet dog.

Colleen watches him, slugging beer from a bottle, her eyes glittering in the low light. He never feels as comfortable when it's just the two of them. She sees him in a way the others don't, he thinks. He and Colleen come from more normal backgrounds, where money can be tight and life harder.

'He's not coming.'

Arran shrugs. 'Having fun, I guess.'

Colleen arches an eyebrow and shakes her head in a way that says she is so much wiser than he is – it's a movement his sisters have also perfected and maybe that's the reason it makes his skin crawl.

Arran swigs at his beer and wonders why Colleen cares so much – it's almost like she has this idealised view of Jonno and can't cope with him not living up to it. Arran doesn't share this need to homogenise, though maybe that's because he can't. Almost everyone here is different to him, with different futures and possibilities. He knows exactly where he's going. At home, he fits perfectly. At least, he did, before.

Saving him from delving further into Colleen's disapproval, Olivia slides into a seat opposite them, hanging her coat on the back of the chair so the drips immediately pool on the floor beneath. 'Oh my God, it's a storm out there!' Strands of her hair are wet where they've escaped from her hood, and her face is pink with the rush from the cold outside to the heaving bar. It always takes him aback when he sees her, how luminous she is. He feels an unwinding at the sight, his fingers relaxing from their tight hold on the bottle of beer. He suppresses the urge to reach out and push the fronds of hair from her face.

He stands. 'What are you having?'

'You sure?' Her face is make-up-free, and she's wearing leggings and a soft pink jumper from her dance class. Why does he always have to actively try not to blush in her presence? 'Glass of white wine would be great,' she says. 'Any type is fine.'

'And I'll have another…' Colleen turns the bottle so he can see the label of her beer, and gives him an impish smile, knowing full well he bought her the last one but that he won't make a fuss in front of Olivia. Arran doesn't care that much anyway. He has managed to get a job making pizzas three nights a week, so that has taken the pressure off.

When he has fought his way to the front, been served and carried the drinks back, he finds Olivia listening to Colleen, who is red in the face, the effect of the beers she's drunk kicking in. He and Olivia share a look as he passes over her glass. Their fingers touch and it sends a little dart of electricity into his arm. Is he imagining things? He knows she's been out with this boy from her course a few times. Is it serious?

'How was dance?'

'Tough – quite a workout.'

Arran frowns. 'I never really realised…'

'You thought it was all delicate spinning and prancing around?'

'No… Yes…' He pulls a face to emphasise his ignorance as she laughs. 'One of my wee sisters did ballet on a Saturday morning for a while, but she started making a strop so Mum stopped her going.'

'Ballet was my main discipline.' She laughs. 'Sometimes going on pointe made my feet bleed.'

'Fuck, no. Gilly's better off with the cows, then. She can wear her wellies.'

For a moment he can see Gilly filling the troughs with food for the stirks, but then Olivia tilts her head back and laughs. The image vanishes in the distraction of her pale throat. She raises the glass of wine to her lips and he has to force himself to look away.

'Olivia could have been professional,' Colleen puts in, sitting forward and dropping the scraps of label she's been peeling from her beer bottle onto the table. They scatter and melt into the puddles of condensation from the drinks.

'Well, no,' Olivia says. Her eyes slide to the distance for a second and her smile drops just a little. 'I did think about dance school, but you have to be really... dedicated. Law just seemed more future-proof.'

'You'll be a great lawyer,' Arran says, though in truth, he can't reconcile her calm kindness with his vision of a suited and severe professional – admittedly, a vision that largely comes from the television programmes his mother watches.

'What about you?' Olivia asks. 'Any change to your grand life plans?'

'Pretty set in stone,' he says, his hands going to his beer bottle, hugging it. 'I'll be taking over the farm from my father. There's no one else.' For the first time he feels a gape inside. When they leave university, will the others be able to live together, stay in the same city? He'll be alone on the farm, without the sunshine of their company. Something like anguish grips him but he shoves it away. They have four years together.

'But...' Colleen butts in again. 'What if you change your mind, decide to do something else? You're only nineteen. Isn't it a bit soon to decide? Might be better to keep your options open.'

Why does Colleen always have to punch to the heart of the matter?

'Well, there aren't really other options. I'm needed.'

'That's awful, then. You're trapped.'

'No...' He tries to find the words to explain how he feels about the farm, how farming runs in his blood – it's when out in the fields or fixing a tractor in one of the barns and lambing in the early hours that he feels truly free and himself. Being here is more like being trapped, hard to breathe even in Edinburgh's wide streets.

Two of Colleen's friends join her end of the table and she is distracted away. Arran waves at the newcomers and squashes up on the bench as another couple follow. He feels Olivia's eyes on him.

'So, you know exactly what you'll be doing with your life?'

He nods. 'I guess so.'

'I envy the simplicity of that,' she says. 'Knowing what's ahead of you must be nice. You can't really take a wrong turn.'

Her blue eyes seem darker for a moment; maybe it's just the murky light in the bar, but her gaze holds his and he feels connected to her, understood.

'I can imagine you running things,' she says gently, stretching out her hand and putting it over his. Arran's body stills. 'Can we come and stay sometimes? Help with bottle-feeding the lambs?'

His face, already warm from the heat and the alcohol, splits into a grin. 'Aye,' he says. 'That would be grand.'

Olivia squeezes his hand and his mind flicks uncomfortably to Natalie. They're not official, but they've been meeting up, kissing, getting closer on the narrow single bed in her room that is piled with cushions. It's not the same as the connection he feels with Olivia, Jonno and Colleen. Sometimes he resents the time it is taking away from them.

Olivia seems to read his mind. 'Natalie not coming tonight, then?' Her words are light, but is there something else behind them?

He blushes. 'No. Don't know what she's doing. What about...'

'David?' She wrinkles her nose a little. 'No, he's busy, I think.'

They stare at each other. The rest of the bar melts away.

Olivia twists her fingers in his. 'Do you ever think...' She tails off.

'Think what?'

She takes a breath then shakes her head, pulls back her hand. 'I'm being silly,' she tells him. 'Way to ruin everything.'

Before he can say anything more, she reaches for his empty beer bottle and nudges Colleen to get her attention. 'My round.'

Breathless, Arran watches her twist past a group of students he recognises, sees the admiring glances some of them give her. Olivia always seems to glide – maybe it's her dance training. Whatever it is, it's like being caught in a spell. He should tell her. He needs to say something or he's going to burst. But when she gets to the bar, a tall dark-haired student hails her and crosses the floor towards her, slipping his hand around her waist and leaning down for a kiss. David. Here after all. Everything inside him contracts. Telling her would be foolishness. She's right: it would ruin them all.

CHAPTER SIXTEEN

Arran hears Jonno in the early hours. He's fallen into the habit of listening to the radio when he can't sleep. Tonight, thoughts of Olivia circle his head, no matter how much he tries to put them aside. It's hopeless. He's bound to the farm and she would never give everything up to be a farmer's wife. It would be like freezing a butterfly, he knows that. He should be content with her friendship, with her promises to visit.

There's a crash and a wet thud in the hallway. He opens his bedroom door to find the other boy in a puddle at his feet, soaked and half-unconscious. Whisky fumes rise up to meet him, along with the strong, acrid smell of cigar smoke, which seems to be lingering in a toxic cloud.

'Oh, pal,' he whispers, hoping not to wake the rest of the corridor. 'Come on, you can't stay there.'

Jonno gurgles some words in response, but he can't tell what they are.

'Where's your key?'

More unintelligible words.

It's no good — he has to slide his hand into Jonno's jacket and feel in his pocket, past a collection of coins, a lighter and his phone, to find the room key. Jonno slurs and gesticulates while he does.

'At least you didn't lose it. Shhh… It's late, keep it down a bit, eh?' He looks nervously at Colleen's door down the corridor. The last thing they need now is a lecture from her about the ills of the posh boys' network.

Arran opens up the door and holds out a hand to Jonno, but the other boy can't get to his feet. He looks again and sees that his legs are tied together with bungee cord. That explains the crash. An initiation? He unhooks the cord and it pings off. Jonno groans in relief. 'Can you stand? Jonno?'

Arran gives up and gets round behind him, putting his hands under Jonno's armpits and pulling, in an undignified drag-and-shove method that seems to work. He's had to help his dad do this for his pal Sandy after Hogmanay enough times.

Manhandling his friend onto the bed, he flicks on the small lamp. It's strange seeing Jonno in this state of dishevelment. He's always so styled, so well put together. He considers him, lying on the covers like a beached fish, and fights the urge to laugh.

'Come on.' He nudges Jonno, trying to rouse him. Nothing doing.

Arran sighs and unlaces the polished and heavy shoes that Jonno is wearing, sliding them from his feet and putting them neatly at the foot of the bed. He leaves what appear to be silk socks. Cashmere – the word comes to him from nowhere.

With little help from the pissed Jonno, Arran wrestles him out of his dinner jacket, which is wet and reeking of smoke. It goes on the chair by the desk.

'We could light your breath,' he murmurs, rolling Jonno onto his side, into the recovery position. He turns and scans the room, finding the bin and bringing it over to the floor next to the bed. Not that it would do much good right now – he can barely lift his head.

It's cold and he desperately wants to go back to bed but doesn't want to leave Jonno alone, so Arran leaves the door unlocked and crosses to his room for his duvet and a spare blanket. Jonno is lying on top of his own bed covers and there's no chance of shifting him, so he puts the duvet over the other boy and settles himself in the chair in the corner.

From here he can doze and watch over him. It's curious, being in the same room. Strangely peaceful. As he drifts into sleep, Colleen's words float into his mind and he ponders her derision at the network Jonno is part of. Does he feel a twitch of envy at the opportunities available to his friend?

He opens his eyes and checks again. Jonno's handsome face is a greenish shade, his lips twitching in stupor. He doesn't think it's envy he feels. It's just that Jonno is living in another world – another option locked to him. The thing that stings is the freedom, not the privilege or the being part of a society. If Jonno falls in love, he can follow his heart to the ends of the earth.

–

Jonno is sick twice in the night, incoherent and stinking of whisky and vomit. Arran manages to make it to him with the bin each time, supports his shaking frame, feeds him sips of water and tucks him back on his side. He cleans up and returns to the chair, not really sleeping until the first streaks of light paint the sky outside and Jonno's breathing evens out, making it clear the danger has passed.

Arran is jolted awake by a groan, automatically unfurling his legs and raising his cricked neck to grab the bucket, but he finds Jonno sitting up by himself, ashen-faced, hair flopped in his eyes. The other boy gives out another groan that hits the notes between hangover and mortification.

'Oh God. Tell me this isn't what it looks like.'

'Morning. Or not quite.' Arran laughs, checking his watch and seeing it says it's five o'clock. He's more uncomfortable now that Jonno is conscious and looking at him than he was in the small hours, holding his head over the bucket. 'You look a bit wabbit, pal.'

'I look like a rabbit?'

'Wabbit. Tired. Not full of beans.'

'Oh.' Jonno flops back onto his side. 'I don't remember what happened. How did I get back here?'

'No idea. You had a bungee cord around your legs.'

'They must have carried me.'

'And dropped you. I heard a massive crash. It's lucky it was me that woke up and not Colleen, given her thoughts on drunken initiations.'

Jonno winces at the alternative scenario. 'Could you, maybe, speak a bit more quietly?'

'I can do you one better and head off.'

'But we were having so much fun.'

'Yeah. Loads. Can I have my duvet back?'

'Huh?' Jonno looks down and sees he's tangled in Arran's bedding. 'Oh, sorry. Where did you sleep?'

'On your chair. I wouldn't recommend it.'

Jonno shuffles off the bed and hands over the duvet. Then, as Arran heads to the door, he pulls back his own cover and slots back into bed. 'Sorry.' He buries his head under the pillow. 'I owe you.'

'Nay bother. Your key's on the side there.'

He doesn't wait for the response. If he crawls into bed now, he can have a couple of hours before lectures. He knows already that they won't discuss this with Colleen and Olivia.

CHAPTER SEVENTEEN

CAL

Sitting in the snug bar of his small hotel, Cal sips a pint and tries to warm up in front of the fire as he goes through his notes. After leaving Natalie, he walked back through the rain to the station for his luggage, giving up against the onslaught and taking a taxi up the hill to the no-frills accommodation.

He stares into the flames, thinking about Arran and his turbulent first term at university. He's going to have to ask Angela about the family row at Christmas. Does this add to the likelihood that Arran took his own life, after arguing with his girlfriend and falling out with a supposedly close group of friends as well? Was the boy's life imploding? Did he feel he had nowhere to turn? Cal has a creeping feeling that this case will turn out to be both simple and unsolvable. He also needs to ask her about a Facebook account – maybe that will provide some insight into his state of mind, though he doesn't hold out much hope.

He needs more information on Arran's friendship group, so Cal orders another drink and starts with Jonathan Keble, typing the man's name into a search engine. His efforts quickly lead him to a London-based boutique investment firm with an expensive-looking website that houses very little real information, aside from oblique references to real-estate portfolios and alternative assets.

Further searches reveal countless images of Keble at parties. He's a good-looking man: brown hair streaked with gold that either comes from an expensive hairdresser or reflects a large number of foreign holidays. Cal would bet on the holidays – he finds pictures of Keble skiing with groups of friends, faces glowing with the après-ski in Val d'Isère, Courchevel and Aspen. Other images show him drinking cocktails in a villa overlooking a startlingly blue ocean, his head tipped back and arms around a pretty blonde woman who looks younger than him.

Can this man really be the person Arran was so close to in his first term at university? He couldn't be more different than the quiet Highland teen who apparently dreamed of taking over the family farm. But the dates on his biography check out, so Cal calls the number on the website and asks to speak to the man. The default response is clearly about to be no, but when he says he's calling because he's making a podcast, he feels the receptionist's attitude change from gatekeeper to welcoming committee.

He doesn't mention the type of podcast he's making.

Just like that, he is through.

'Jonathan Keble.' The voice oozes charm and confidence. Cal can imagine how easily he carves a path through life. He feels like he should dislike Jonathan, but there's a warmth there that stops him writing him off immediately. He introduces himself and rushes on, trying to strike the balance between putting him at ease and quickly getting the information out. Cal is used to people hanging up on him.

'I'm making a podcast about the disappearance of a man I think you were friends with at university.'

A long pause – does Cal imagine the intake of breath? How is Keble going to play this?

'Arran. You mean Arran?'

'That's right.'

'I see.' The earlier confidence has evaporated, as though it were mist. 'Wow. Why now? Is there any news?' Cal tries to read into the tone. It's frustrating being unable to see the other man's face, but clearly Arran still means something to Keble.

'No, I've been asked by the family to take a look, that's all, so I'm trying to speak to all of Arran's friends at the time, to build a picture of the kind of person he was, and see if we can learn anything.'

He waits to be told to go away, but instead Keble releases a long exhale of breath. 'I thought you were going to say you'd found him. After all this time, you keep hoping...'

'So, how did you meet?'

'We had rooms opposite each other in halls for that first term.'

'And you hit it off?'

'We were completely different background-wise, but yes, there was something about him... He was just so easy to get on with.' Jonathan's voice tails off into wistfulness. 'He was a good friend for a short time.'

'And who did you hang around with? I've been told there were two girls in the corridor—'

'Yes. Olivia and Colleen. We were inseparable for a bit. I wonder what happened to them.'

'I'm going to try and speak to them – you aren't still in touch, then?'

'No. Olivia moved out after that first term, into a flat. I did too. We all went our separate ways.'

'Really? Isn't it unusual to change accommodation midway through the year?'

'Yes, I suppose so, but my father had been nagging me to move into an investment flat – he was going to buy it for me, you see, but I was determined to be independent.' He chuckles, though Cal senses more sadness than mirth behind it. 'My father is used to having his own way. In the end, it was easier to give in. Do what I was told.'

'So you'd moved out before Arran went missing – did you still see him?'

'Yes. He came over, once.'

'And what about Olivia? Did she also keep seeing him?'

'You'd have to ask her.'

'Was there some sort of row between you all? A reason you stopped being friends?'

Is it Cal's imagination, or does Keble hesitate for the smallest fraction of a second?

'Of course not. It was our first term at uni and we were finding our feet. Just because you end up in the same corridor, it doesn't mean you'll be friends for life. No big drama.'

Cal thinks of Chrissie, currently navigating these same waters, trying to find like-minded people. It takes time, missteps, wrong choices. Is that what this was? But Natalie said the corridor friends were inseparable. So much so that she felt excluded.

Keble fills the silence, his voice softer than before. 'We really didn't have much in common, other than being allocated rooms next to each other. I guess you could say Arran was the glue that held us together.'

'But you didn't realise he'd gone missing?'

A long beat, in which Cal listens to the breath on the line and holds his counsel.

'No. I guess I was preoccupied. Time moves quickly. I thought maybe he was busy, that he'd turn up on the doorstep when he was ready. But he never did.'

Cal leaves Jonathan Keble with a promise he'll be in touch. When he ends the call, he sits very still for long moments, staring at the reflection of the flames in the dark glass window across from him. He can't pinpoint exactly what, but something isn't right.

CHAPTER EIGHTEEN

Natalie comes through with contact details for Olivia, and he takes the opportunity to ask her about the Facebook account again, hopeful she'll have remembered more.

'I don't suppose you remember the name Arran used for his Facebook account? Or the email address he used to log in?'

'It was just his first name and initial, I think. He let me log into it once – he… Hang on… It's on the tip of my tongue.' She hums and strains to remember, and Cal's chest briefly swells, but to no avail.

'I'm sorry, it was so long ago.' Natalie sounds crestfallen.

'Don't worry,' he says, hiding the disappointment. 'Maybe it will come back to you.'

Tired of being in his room, Cal ventures out into the city, taking advantage of a momentary lull in the rain to suck in the cold, clean air; he walks up the Royal Mile to the castle and drinks in the views around him: the streets are thronged with tourists and street performers, even in this weather.

He tries to call Shona but her phone rings out and he doesn't leave a message. She's probably still at the lab. The crowds around him emphasise his spiralling solitude. Even in a city this busy, you can be lonely. All around him, people are laughing, talking, connecting with each other. Is this what it was like for Arran? Being lost in a crowd? How did everything spin out of control so quickly for him? A young man with a plan, with promise and hope. How do you lose that in only a few weeks?

He's saved from further introspection by his phone ringing. He's disappointed to see it isn't Shona. The way they left things has him on edge. If he could just speak to her, he'd feel better.

'Cal Lovett? It's Olivia Carmichael. I believe you called to speak to me?'

–

Cal meets Olivia in a smart bar just off George Street, a far cry from the dingy pubs he's been in so far in the city. She's exactly on time; her blonde hair is pulled off her face in a simple bun, and small pearls shine in her earlobes. She orders a sparkling water and slides her smart tan-coloured jacket off, hanging it on a hook beneath the bar. Everything about her is professional and calm, but nothing is relaxed – her face is held so carefully, every muscle poised. She seems so tightly strung beneath it all, and that makes him nervous.

'Do you want to eat something? I appreciate you meeting me on your lunch break.'

'I don't really take a lunch break,' she says. 'I can grab something on the way back to the office.'

'Do you mind if I record this?'

Olivia shrugs and smooths her skirt down, then grips one of her hands with the other on her lap. 'That's fine, but I don't think I can help you very much, I'm afraid.'

'I'm just keen to get a sense of Arran and what he was like back then. Honestly, any memories you have of him are helpful to building a picture of who he was.'

She lifts her glass and sips clumsily from it; a couple of drops of water fall onto her skirt and sit as beads. He passes her a napkin. She thanks him, dabs at the fabric. He pictures Natalie – her openness and ease – and finds it hard to imagine that Arran could get on well with both women. They're so different.

'I gather you were close for a time – you, Jonathan and Colleen?'

Her head jerks up again, her focus once more on him. 'I suppose so. For a short time.' There it is: the ghost of emotion that vanishes so quickly, it's like breath.

'What was Arran like?'

She frowns. 'It's such a long time ago. I remember he was quite quiet and chilled – compared with Jonno and Colleen, especially. I liked chatting to him. He was a good foil for their effervescence, I suppose. They could be so loud, the pair of them.'

Olivia is hard to read. Her smooth, polished face barely seems to move as she talks. 'We went out for drinks and chatted in halls, but it was the first term of university and we were just finding our feet, I guess.'

'And then you moved out of halls?'

'That's right. It wasn't a good fit for me, in the end. Too noisy. I moved in with a friend from school who had a spare room.'

'Did something happen to cause you to make that decision?'

There's a glacial silence. Cal watches Olivia's perfect composure slip, though she rapidly reasserts the blank elegance. For a moment, he saw fear.

'No. Of course not.'

He doesn't believe her. 'So, there wasn't any issue – an argument, say, between you all?'

'Not at all.' Frustration stirs inside him. Usually, he can get people to open up.

'And you didn't really stay friends with the others?'

Her face compresses into a frown. 'Actually, I did. Colleen and I are still in touch. She lives in Edinburgh. She's always looked out for me and I count her as one of my closest friends.'

This short speech is the most she's given him. 'I'd really like to talk to her too.'

'I can ask her to give you a call.'

'What was Jonathan like?'

97

Olivia is back to being a blank page. 'He was easy to get on with… charming, I guess.'

The whole conversation is bizarre. She seems to have few memories, little insight; nothing she says brings Arran, or those months he spent in Edinburgh, to life for him. He can't use this in a podcast episode, and yet he has a feeling there's more behind the facade.

'How did you find out he was missing?'

She shrugs. 'It was all over the university. His mother handed out leaflets everywhere.'

'And yet you never spoke to her?'

Another shrug and what Cal thinks could be the briefest flash of irritation.

'Do you have any thoughts about what happened to Arran?'

'I guess maybe he killed himself.' She says it baldly, without apology.

'You think so? Did he seem unhappy, when you knew him? Like he was hiding some sort of distress?'

Olivia thinks for a moment, shakes her head. 'No,' she says. 'But I guess you never really know what's going on in someone's mind, do you?'

She's right. He has no idea what she is thinking right now. But some moments, Cal feels like he has a tiny glimpse of insight into Arran, like he's waiting to be found. Then it flashes away from him.

When they part, she walks away from him at a clip, phone cradled in her manicured hand like a safety blanket. Maybe she's late for work, maybe she always moves at that pace, but Cal has the uncanny sensation that she's running away.

–

In the evening, he calls Shona from his hotel room, lying on the bed, staring at a crack in the corner where the ceiling meets the wall. The paint is yellowed. It looks nicotine-stained, though it's been over a decade since the smoking ban. He thinks Shona sounds hesitant when she picks up the phone, but maybe that's because he's looking for problems, aware that they haven't been connecting recently. Determined to improve things, he asks her about her day, listening carefully to the stresses and strains caused by some lost samples for an important case. Worry reverberates in her voice as she tells him about it.

'I know Cliff can be a bit of a clown,' she says. 'But that's just for show. He's methodical and dedicated. I just don't think he'd lose something this important.'

'Could it be foul play?'

'What, deliberate?'

'Maybe that's unlikely...'

There's a long silence, as Shona thinks. 'It's worth considering,' she says. Then a rush of breath. 'Thanks. I didn't think of that.'

'No worries.' He smiles. 'You just needed someone more paranoid.'

They laugh and for a moment he is lighter again.

'I'm sorry,' she says. 'I haven't asked about how you're getting on. Have you seen Chrissie?'

'No, I think she's pretty busy.' Cal glosses over his hurt that she hasn't had time to see him yet. Instead, he talks Shona through his chats with Natalie and Olivia, knowing how important this is to her, how much she wants to help her friend.

'Have you spoken to Angela?' she says when he tells her about Natalie's belief that there was a big family argument before Arran came back to uni. 'Maybe she can clear things up. That doesn't sound like them.'

Cal tries to ignore the sense that Shona is partial in this case. Doesn't bring up the truth that she doesn't know the family that well at all, only her childhood friend. He always knew how hard it would be for her to maintain a professional distance from this case – that was one of the reasons for his hesitation before taking it on.

'Not yet. I will,' he says. 'Though Gillian told me something similar when I went to the farm, so—'

'Really? You never said.'

Cal almost groans at his mistake. He isn't used to having to hide things from Shona. She's his sounding board, his voice of reason. 'Please keep that to yourself,' he says quickly. 'I don't want to upset her.' Or tip her off – is what he doesn't say.

'Of course I won't. You don't need to ask that.' Shona sounds annoyed and he sighs, sad that the conversation has been derailed from its earlier levity.

'I'm sorry,' he says. 'I miss you.'

'I miss you too,' Shona tells him. 'I'm sorry if you felt pressured to take this case because of me.'

'I didn't,' he lies. 'I'm just in a bit of a holding pattern because of the trial – Foulds says it should restart in a few weeks.'

Shona is silent for a moment and he has no idea what she is thinking.

'I better go,' she says eventually. 'Early start tomorrow.'

When she's hung up, Cal stares at the crack in the corner. He could swear that it's bigger now than it was this morning.

CHAPTER NINETEEN

Persistence bears fruit. He finally gets a message from Colleen, grudgingly agreeing to meet him in her office the next afternoon for a quick chat. She's a social worker, and he can see from her online presence that Colleen is an activist – causes are plastered over her posts, saturated with an anger that, in his experience, comes from more than just a sense of injustice about the world.

He sits in a dingy reception area for twenty minutes before she appears, looking harassed, her eyes almost challenging him to expect an apology. Cal wouldn't dare.

'Thanks for seeing me,' he says when they're sitting down.

She has a full mug on her desk but hasn't offered Cal a drink. He gets the impression he won't be staying long. The knowledge sharpens his mind, years of interviewing giving him the skills to recognise when to fast-forward to the important questions in case you're tossed out on your ear.

Colleen slugs her tea and grimaces.

'Cold. Look, it was thirteen years ago and we didn't know each other for very long. I'm not sure how much I can help you, but I'll try.'

She looks at her watch.

'How long have you been a social worker?' Stocky, and dressed in black biker boots, black jeans and a leather jacket, Colleen gives the impression of being a bulldog for the families she fights for. She's tightly wound, perched on the edge of her seat, her brown hair embellished with a lilac streak and her hackles almost visible. So different to Olivia's remote sophistication – he's having trouble imagining chalk and cheese together.

'Since I left uni.'

The line of photos tacked to the wall is the only indication of her softer side. Children grin toothily at the camera. In one, a small boy with a blue rucksack on his back hugs Colleen, his thin arms not meeting round her waist. She catches Cal looking at the snapshots.

'My success stories,' she says, her cheeks flushing pink. 'The failures would need more walls.'

'It's a hard job,' he says, hoping to build rapport.

Her eyes narrow and the prickliness returns. 'Aye, cleaning up after the fuck-ups men make.' As she stares at him, Cal is acutely aware of his male culpability.

He thinks of thickset Jason Barr, of his scarred knuckles and his sister's bones in a tarpaulin underneath a scrapyard, her swallow necklace tangled in the remains. He grimaces. 'I hear you,' he says. 'I really do. But Arran is a victim here, too. He was only nineteen when he went missing.'

'I know how old he was,' Colleen snaps. Her lip curls. 'And I wouldn't be so sure he was a victim.'

'What do you mean by that?'

Her mouth closes and she shakes her head from side to side in economical movements. 'Nothing. I used to think some men were different, better than others.'

'And you don't any more?'

'Time has proved the contrary, over and over.' Her eyes flick to the photographs. 'It does something to you.'

She cares too much. He sees it clearly. It will be her self-destruction, this constant fuelling of hurt and anger. Her choice of career will burn her to ashes. It makes him sad. It's a profession that benefits from being peopled with those who care. She gives the impression of cynicism but it's a thin crust, so easily pierced. He's seen it in journalists too. You have to be able to detach. He used to be able to do that, once upon a time.

From his side of the desk, which is towering with files, Cal can feel the searing heat of Colleen's anger and he's going to use it. Her upset is so close to the surface that it's almost bursting. More information will spill out if he pushes in the right places. He's just not sure if it relates to Arran, specifically, or the cases she sees day in, day out.

'I appreciate you talking to me when you're so busy,' he says. 'To be honest, it would just help to have some background on what the beginning of university was like, as well as your initial impressions of Arran. I'm not asking you to sugar-coat things, just tell it as it was. Anything you remember.'

This, he is sure, is how Colleen operates anyway. Bluntness is her currency. Holding his phone up in question, he waits for her nod and then presses the button to record, sliding the handset across the desk, closer to her. He lets the silence hang between them.

Eventually, she breaks it. 'We got on well at first. It was him, me, Olivia and Jonno – Jonathan.' A certain wistfulness crosses her face as she mentions the other boy. He takes a mental note. Curious. 'We had rooms in Pollock.' Cal knows the set of buildings. It's where Chrissie is now living.

'And were you all doing the same course?' He knows the answer to this, but he wants to put her at her ease, to see how she acts when she is telling the truth. Maybe, then, any lies will be more obvious. He also wants her to feel in control, to quiet some of the anger that ripples just beneath the surface.

'No. I was doing English, Olivia law and Jonno economics. He used to tease Arran about being a farmer.' *Jonno* again, that same softness – a weak spot? A vulnerability?

As she talks, Colleen seems to tune out of the cramped and overheated room they're in now, the reality of her heavy caseload replaced with more carefree memories. 'We were in and out of each other's rooms all the time. Arran was probably the most conscientious, apart from Livvy. But law was a tough course.'

'So, you socialised together?'

'Actually, not as much as you'd think. We were more like a family. We'd come back after nights out and gather together.' Her face darkens. 'Look after each other.'

'Do you remember what things were like in the lead-up to Christmas? Before Arran went missing?'

Colleen grips the table. She's wearing rings on most fingers, and they glint in the light from the small window.

'Why are you doing this?'

'The podcast?'

'Aye.'

'Trying to find the truth, to give Arran's parents and sisters some answers. They're stuck – not knowing what happened to him and why.'

Her face softens slightly. The door behind him opens and a colleague barges in.

'Oh, sorry, hen. I didn't know you were busy. I'll come back.'

Colleen's hardness returns. 'Five minutes,' she calls. Cal's frustration builds. There's something here, he knows there is.

'I'd be careful,' she says to him. 'Arran wasn't always as nice as people claim. He had some dodgy friends. Has anyone mentioned Donny?'

Cal shakes his head.

'Well,' she says, standing. 'You need to do some research. He was always hanging around and he was bad news.'

CHAPTER TWENTY

ARRAN, 2009

Arran is walking across The Meadows when he registers a threat, skulking in the shadow of a tree, moving round the trunk as if not wanting to be seen, but watching all the same. He braces himself, sliding the second strap of his rucksack onto his shoulder, muscles tensing, aware of his wallet resting in his back pocket. It's quiet – darkness falling, the light low, so he almost thinks he's imagined the shadow but, no, there's someone there.

He squares his shoulders. He's on the way to meet Natalie and in danger of running late because his mind is on Olivia and whether it's fair to see Nat when he's so confused about it all. Keeping his eyes swivelled to the side while appearing to look ahead, he recalculates the decision to take the shortcut across the green space instead of going round the edge, wondering if he should just run now – he doesn't want a fight if he can avoid it.

Almost past now. Breath of relief that he isn't going to be held up, while also feeling stupid that he's seeing a threat in ordinary city movements, isn't yet comfortable living among so many people.

But then a voice calls out and his step falters.

'Arran, pal, is that you?'

He swivels, just as the shadow steps into the light, spectre-pale, eyes dark holes in the gloom. His heart thumps a dancing beat and his hands curl into fists for a moment.

'Donny?!' He tries to map the features of the boy he knows from home against this roughened specimen, looking even more hardened than he was that night in the club a few weeks ago. Donny sniffs and slides the back of his hand beneath his nose, and then he's moved forward, clapping Arran on the back, his touch spiky and painful. He must know how hard he's hitting him.

It's a shock to see him looking so different. 'All right, min,' he says. 'Give me a bit o' a scare.'

Donny squints at him – Arran sees the calculation in his eyes, a smirk. He wants to get away but Donny is from home and that means he owes him the courtesy.

'How you getting on, like? With the studying?' Donny smells stale, of old cigarettes and damp.

'Not so bad. Getting ma heid round it. You?' It does feel good to drop into their broader tones. For weeks now he's been speaking differently so that the people around him understand. This is like putting on an old coat, finding you've left something in the pocket.

Donny shrugs. 'Not really my scene.'

'What you studying again? Sorry, I canny mind.'

'Taking some time.' He laughs. 'Bastards kicked me oot.'

Arran is distracted. His skin crawls at the state of Donny's appearance. The boy's teeth look furred and yellow as he bites at a nail.

'I better get on,' he says, thinking of Natalie waiting for him.

But Donny advances, getting close into his personal space. 'Listen, pal, you needing onything?' He draws a small plastic bag from his pocket, containing something that looks like weed.

He shouldn't be shocked, but all the same, there's a beat where Arran feels a kind of stunned dismay.

'Nah, I'm good, thanks.' He starts backing away, but Donny is still coming after him, not letting him go. 'Not your bag? I have other options…'

Before Arran can stop him, Donny's pulling more little baggies, some with white powder, others full of tiny pills. They look battered and smeared, well-fingered. Several spin out of his grip and fall to the floor. Arran bends instinctively to help, not wanting anything to do with it.

'I don't need anything,' he says looking around, alarmed to see a pair of joggers approaching. 'Put them away.'

'Too good for it, are you?' Donny sneers, suddenly veering from hapless and friendly to harsh and frightening. His face is too close, his breath venomous.

'No, I just… I don't have the funds for that kind of caper.'

He tries to bring the levity back between them but a switch has flicked.

Donny pushes the bags back into the pockets of his baggy coat. When he withdraws his hand, there's the gleam of a blade in the streetlight.

'Woah…' Arran staggers back a step, glancing around him. The joggers have passed and there is no one near.

The other boy sneers. 'No need to panic, chill oot, min.' He slides the blade out of sight, but still it sits between them. Arran doesn't want to turn his back.

'Are we okay?'

'It's just a way to make a wee bit of cash. I dinna ken fit you're fussing aboot.' Donny's voice is harsh, chastising Arran for overreacting.

Arran thinks of Donny's parents. They're not filthy rich but they live in a nice house and run a small chain of local bakeries. They'd be horrified if they could see their son now. He makes his voice as casual as he can, trying to return them to safer ground.

'Where are you getting it, like?'

'Boats that come in near home. I pick it up and drive it down… Easy pickings.'

'Oh, aye, right.' Arran pictures the coastline, the wild and isolated bays you could moor up by night. Lights on the ocean, packages washed ashore.

Donny takes a hold of his shoulder. His fingers are bone, pinching. 'You wanting in? I can introduce you. I thought when I first saw you that night in the club—'

'Oh, no, that's okay. I'm a wee bit busy with the course.'

The other boy casts his head back and sucks his teeth. He lets out a single laugh, a derisive sound that sends chills through Arran. He wants to be off the dark ground, safe in the pub with Natalie.

'I should be getting on,' he says. 'I'm meeting someone.'

'Not going to invite your old pal from hame? Too good for the likes of me now?'

'Dinna be soft.' He shudders, hoping Donny can't see his revulsion.

'I see you around,' Donny whispers. 'With your posh friends. Pretty girls you hang about with. I might have to join you sometime. Get a bit o' that action.'

He doesn't like the hard gleam in the boy's eye. 'Aye. Well. Good seeing you, Donny. Catch you later, then.'

And he doesn't wait for an answer, just jogs into the streetlight-orange glow, running like a child from the monster beneath the bed.

He's out of breath and strangely shaken when he reaches Natalie. She's standing outside the pub, wrapped in a big coat, scanning the street for him. He comes up behind her, puffing and hot.

'I'm sorry.'

'Oh!' Her face breaks into a relieved smile. 'You're here.' She'd thought he wasn't coming. The black smudges of eyeliner give her a dark feline look. He feels the urge to kiss her, to be back in the light, to banish the crawling feeling.

Their hug is awkward. 'Really sorry,' he repeats, though she isn't making him feel bad. He holds the door to the bar open for her, and they're hit by a wave of warm and loud student life, the dark cold of the park a shrinking image in his mind. 'I bumped into an old friend.'

If he were to tell her now, to try to explain how spooked he feels, it would sound like an overreaction. Laughable. So he just looks over his shoulder as he follows her inside. He thinks he sees the shadow of Donny, still watching him.

CHAPTER TWENTY-ONE

EPISODE TWO: CCTV

At the time of his disappearance, Arran's case came under the remit of former regional force Lothian and Borders Police – now part of Police Scotland. A review of Arran's file requested by the family for this podcast has brought to light new information about his disappearance that was not shared with them at the time.

It transpires that there is in fact CCTV footage of a young man matching Arran's description in the Leith Docks area of the city. The video, from a local warehouse, is not good quality but it appears to show a man in a shirt and bow tie, missing his shoes and staggering as if heavily intoxicated. In the twelve seconds of footage, the figure walks in a zigzag line to the end of the street and disappears into the darkness. He does not reappear.

'We checked all other active cameras in the area at the time,' says Detective Austin. 'Right up until the same time the next day. Unfortunately, this is the only sighting.'

'And did this lead you to form a hypothesis about what happened to Arran?'

'Obviously, this investigation is not closed and we would look at any new information that came to light, but yes, given the conversations we had with family and friends about Arran's state of mind at the time and the apparent intoxication of the man appearing on camera, one line of inquiry is that he came to harm, either accidentally or intentionally, most likely from going into the water. Although, another thought was that he went on board a vessel.'

'A vessel? You think Arran may have boarded a boat?'

'It's a possibility, but I'm afraid I can't comment on that aspect of the inquiry.'

'I just don't think Arran would have chosen to end his life.' That's Angela, Arran's mother, who spoke to me in the first episode. 'I'm angry that we weren't given this information about the CCTV footage at the time.'

'Does this change things for you?'

'We still don't have the answers we need. Arran didn't own a bow tie and suit. Granted, it looks like him, but if it is him, we don't know what he was doing there or where he'd been. If there was some sort of accident… We just want to be able to put him to rest. To do that, people who knew him at university need to come forward. All we have right now is a wall of silence. It doesn't make any sense to me. People need to help us. Please, if you're listening and you know what happened to my son, please help us.'

CHAPTER TWENTY-TWO

ARRAN, 2009

They're playing Twister in the corridor. Colleen has a bottle of peach schnapps which she's adding lemonade to, the liquid fizzing and bubbling over, making their fingers and the mat sticky. All of their faces are flushed and Arran blushes as he twists his body around Olivia's. She's holding an impossible position with a dancer's poise and his arms are strong from farm work. Jonno is hopeless and Colleen's arms are shaking with the effort of holding herself still.

Then a burst of uncontrollable laughter, and the whole pile collapses; Arran braces with his arms to stop himself landing on Olivia and squashing her, hurting her. He looks down, his face close to hers.

'Sorry.'

Her eyes are dark and depthless, her breath sweet as liquid sugar from Colleen's vile nectar. A beat when she looks into his eyes and everything stills, then he's pulling back and onto his knees, freeing her, laughing along with the others, coming back to himself.

'What time is it?'

'No idea,' Jonno slurs, happily, braced against the wall of the corridor. Someone stuck their head out of their room earlier to tell them to shut up, but that just made them all laugh harder. He's supposed to be meeting Nat at six and Arran's reluctant to leave.

He looks across at Olivia again. She is drawing back strands of her hair so she can drain the last drops from her glass. It's in that moment that he decides: he needs to break up with Natalie. This isn't fair. The feelings are so different: he loves being with Nat, basking in her kindness and adoration, and they have fun together, but his feelings for Olivia are a vortex – he is powerless to resist. Once the decision is made, he feels everything inside his mind clearing. Of course, this is what he needs to do. It's so obvious.

'Come on.' Olivia catches his arm and yanks him back towards the mat, where Jonno is teetering on one foot. 'Your turn.'

The door opens at that moment and even though Arran has his back to it, he can tell who it is by the look on Olivia's face. Her eyes brighten and then her gaze shifts to him, in... what? Brief regret – or is that his imagination?

'David! You're early.'

He lifts her into a kiss and Arran feels the hairs on his arms rise, wishes he could look away because it's only hurting him to see this. 'No, I'm right on time.'

Arran's mouth tastes sour now. He raises his wrist to check his watch and sees with a jolt that time has slid past them.

'Shit! It's gone six. I'm supposed to be meeting Nat...'

'Run, or you'll be in trouble!' Colleen giggles.

Their happy afternoon atmosphere is well and truly punctured. Arran chances a glance at Olivia. She doesn't say anything, her smile neutral. He's so physically aware of her – can still feel the warmth of her against him. But she's with David. He's been fooling himself. He thinks of Nat's open and trusting face, and feels a dart of shame piercing the fuzz of alcohol and temptation.

'Bye,' he calls as he grabs his coat and wallet. 'See you later.'

He runs along the twisting paths, covered with foliage, to get to the bar. By the time he makes it to the door, he's panting. Slowly, he pushes his hair back, away from his face. He feels another barb at the sight of relief sweeping her pinched features.

'Nat, I'm sorry. I lost track of time.'

She tilts her head and he kisses her, but immediately her nose wrinkles and her eyes narrow slightly, though she laughs.

'Oh my God, what have you been drinking?'

'Some disgusting peach stuff Colleen likes.' He wipes his mouth with the back of his hand, like that could work. 'Sorry. We were playing Twister.'

'What do you want to do?' Nat's tone is tighter than usual. He's created the atmosphere by being late, but for a moment he feels inexplicably annoyed with her, wishes he could rewind and go back to the fun and laughter in the corridor, wishes David weren't a reality, that things were different. He immediately feels cruel.

'I don't mind – do you want a drink?'

Her mouth twists. 'Maybe we should get you a coffee. I thought you were writing an essay this afternoon.' She keeps her voice light, but the edge of accusation is still there.

'I was. It was just a couple of drinks,' he says. 'As a reward.' Though that isn't true. He lost track. His essay is languishing, seventy words in, and Colleen's sticky bottle of schnapps is almost empty. His stomach rumbles. He needs to eat.

'How about we get a pizza?' he suggests. Nat's body language relaxes slightly.

'Maybe we could watch a film in my room,' she suggests, holding his gaze so that he sees that's not exactly what she's asking.

The figures in the corridor return to the front of his mind. His gut twists at the memory of David's fingers in Olivia's hair. He swallows and forces a smile onto his face. Nat is wonderful. He should be thanking his lucky stars that she likes him. 'Sounds perfect.'

She takes his hand, and they queue for pizza and carry the boxes down the road to her shared flat, just off a little square.

'So, who were you playing Twister with?'

'Oh, the others: Jonno, Colleen and...'

'Olivia,' she finishes lightly. 'Sounds fun.'

He feels like there's a tightrope he's walking here. 'A bit silly,' he says, looping his fingers more tightly with hers, feeling the press of her arm next to his body. Another fleeting memory of Olivia, looking up at him earlier, that fresh citrus scent that accompanies her movements. He pushes the thoughts from his mind. Olivia is with David. He's here now, with Nat. And he really likes her – that should be enough.

At her flat, they bypass the kitchen and her flatmates, heading straight for her room. Arran shrugs off his coat and the cold air that still clings to it. He sits next to her and, thinking they'll eat, reaches for the pizza boxes, but Nat's kneeling on the bed next to him, her breath hot on his ear, her lips on his cheek.

Her kisses land slow and enticing, and a wave of desire for her sweeps away all thought. Arran turns and the usual dance of having to wait to see if someone is as keen as you are vanishes. It's not him initiating, it's Nat pulling at his clothes, and they're falling back onto the bed together, her tongue in his mouth, her skin so warm and smooth, and his senses overwhelmed – he's slept with a couple of people in the past but those were stolen moments, in a bedroom at a party, in a car. Now they are adults and away from home, and have their own space. They have to be a bit quiet, because of Nat's flatmates, but he allows himself to be carried away, awed by Nat's desire, her sweetness replaced with a sort of hunger he didn't know she had. He makes the thoughts that intrude lie quiet. Olivia is his friend. Nothing more.

Afterwards, they lie under the covers, eating slices of pizza, crammed into the single bed, her legs entwined with his, one arm across his chest – a pleasant weight that grows heavier as they stay there, like she's holding him down, stopping him from blowing away, claiming him.

CHAPTER TWENTY-THREE

CAL

Another evening in the bar at the hotel, shuffling thoughts in his mind and getting nowhere. This was one of the evenings Chrissie said she might manage. Cal stares into the flames until a text comes through from her, finally.

> Sorry, Dad, haven't had a chance to come back to you. Out tonight but coffee tomorrow morning?

He replies, telling her to have a good time, but her message has punctured his hopes of seeing her this evening and he can't shake the bitter lump that's wedged inside him. All of a sudden, he isn't needed in the way he was even a few months ago.

To distract himself, he searches for information online about the Leith Docks area of the city. Having served as Edinburgh's port for hundreds of years, it's now awash with restaurants and bars, cafes and galleries. There's even a floating hotel. When Arran was a student here, Millennium Project funding had been used to complete the Water of Leith Walkway, a footpath and cycleway running beside the river. If that's him in the CCTV footage, is that the route he took to get there? The river winds through the city on its journey from the Pentland Hills to where it meets the Firth of Forth. He likes the fact that the watercourse is called the Water of Leith. It sounds grand and historical, like the city itself.

He focuses on the Leith Docks, scanning pictures of the Royal Yacht *Britannia* and taking in the size of the ships that can enter the deep-water harbour. As he does, the police theories circle. What if Arran didn't walk into the sea? Maybe he left these shores thirteen years ago. Could he have smuggled himself on board a boat, or taken a job as crew and left Scotland entirely? If he did, he could be anywhere in the world. How plausible is that? Would he really just go, leaving so much heartache behind him?

None of these theories really fit the profile he currently has, reinforcing the sense that there's more to Arran than appears. Distracted, he orders some food at the bar and picks up the phone to call Shona, wishing he was back in her house, tucked in against the weather.

They talk about her day – a quiet one in the lab – before she asks about the case. He's about to launch into his worries, when he stops himself, remembering that she isn't the impartial observer she usually is. He hasn't updated Angela yet – is he putting Shona in an impossible position if he confides in her?

'It's going okay,' he tells her. 'Not much to go on, yet.'

'But what do you think happened? If you had to call it?'

'Oh, you know...'

'No.' She sounds both amused and annoyed. 'You can tell me, you know. I'm not going to run to Angela with everything you say. I'd have thought you'd know me better than that.'

'I'm sorry,' he says. 'I'm just aware that this is personal for you. If I find things about Arran that they'd rather not know—'

'I'm not going to blame you,' Shona says shortly. 'No matter what you find.' The line is so quiet for a moment that he can hear the shifting of logs in the hearth at her house. If he was there, he could look into her eyes and see what she's really thinking, see if things are okay between them, if this slipping he feels is real or not.

'I miss you,' he tells her, closing his eyes for a moment.

'You too.'

The silence between them grows, awkward and unsettling. He needs to say something, bring them back to each other. The door to the bar opens and a group of poncho-clad, dripping Japanese tourists make a rowdy entrance, faces glowing.

'I'd better go,' he says.

When she's hung up, he watches the tourists settle themselves at a table and order glasses of whisky, feeling desolate in the face of their camaraderie. Alone in a thriving, humming city. Too late, he remembers he promised to call and speak to his mother today. Yet another notch of failure. He gathers up his papers and reminds himself that he has a job to do. That a family is missing their son. There's just so little to go on.

Up in his room, he turns the television on low and crashes unexpectedly easily into sleep. He dreams of a shifting Edinburgh, with its tall tenements and dark wynds and closes. He dreams that Arran is alive and that he finds him, tucked away on the staircase to a basement flat. He tries to return him to his family, but the boy won't go, tugging away from Cal. *I like it here*, he says. *This is where I belong.*

CHAPTER TWENTY-FOUR

EPISODE THREE: DONNY

'Donny wasn't a bad lad when he was at school. But after he went off to university, he came off the rails. It's real sad what happened to him, like.'

In an effort to work out what might have happened to Arran all those years ago, we've been looking into his friendship with Donny Mulligan, a boy who attended Arran's school and went to Edinburgh the year before him to study computer science. Customers at a bakery once owned by Donny's parents remember a cheeky but likeable lad, getting into the usual teenage boy scrapes but nothing more.

That was to change. Once in Scotland's capital city, Donny seems to have fallen in with a rough crowd. What started as taking drugs on nights out moved on to him getting involved in low-level dealing to pay for his own habit.

By the time Arran bumped into him the following year, that low-level habit had become a serious problem. Donny was failing his course, was behind on rent, and had a string of cautions and charges from police for possession. In fact, friends believe he was transporting drugs off boats for gangs – using his home connections with local fishermen and his knowledge of the area to receive imports on isolated beaches and drive them to Edinburgh.

'He was a really unpleasant guy,' Arran's girlfriend, Natalie, remembers. 'We bumped into him a couple of times and he was always out of it. Arran would give him money, pop round with food sometimes. I'm not sure what he saw in him. I think he felt responsible. Because they came from the same place.'

This discovery sheds new light on possible reasons for Arran being in the Leith Docks area late at night. At this point, records show that Donny was in police custody, awaiting charges for possession with intent to supply. Could Arran have been helping him, meeting his contacts and passing on money or drugs while Donny was unable to do so? Is it possible he fell foul of Donny's associates that night, or that he was also involved in the drugs trade? Could he have been forced aboard a boat in the docks or attacked in that area? If so, where is Arran now?

Unfortunately, Donny is unable to help us with our inquiries. Three years after Arran went missing, he was found unresponsive in a basement flat in the Wester Hailes area of the city. He was taken to hospital but died of a heroin overdose the following day.

CHAPTER TWENTY-FIVE

The phone wakes Cal from sleep, early, and the possibilities ricochet inside his mind – Chrissie, his mother, Shona? It feels like only disaster can come from a dawn call. But when he fumbles for the handset, completely awake, he's surprised to see it's Natalie.

'I'm sorry to ring so early.'

'No, it's fine. I was just about to get up,' he lies. It's before seven. 'What's up?'

Natalie sounds breathless. 'His Facebook account,' she says. 'I remember the login.'

Cal sits bolt upright. 'Really?' He scrambles to reach a pen from the bedside table.

'I was so jealous of him and Olivia. I thought there was something going on, and he said I was paranoid but let me log in. He watched me do it. I know it was wrong, but I did it a few times without him. I was so stupid.'

'And what did you find?'

'Nothing,' she says. 'Nothing at all. I felt so awful about it. I had a glass of wine last night and I was thinking about him and… it just came back to me again.'

'Did you log in?'

'No.' She sounds firm. 'I can't go back there again. It took me so long to move on…'

'I understand.' It's the age-old issue with investigating a cold case: bringing back the nightmare for those left behind.

'The email is a Hotmail one. He used morayfarmerboy or farmerboymoray, I'm not sure which, but the password was his date of birth. I told him how stupid it was but he didn't care, said there wasn't anything sensitive in there anyway. Unless he changed it, that should work.'

'That's amazing, thank you.' At last. A crumb.

'Maybe he's used the account.' Despite her protestations, Natalie's voice is filled with hope. 'Will you let me know if he's alive?'

'Of course.' His heart cracks for her.

–

Outside, the sky is a brittle blue, in compensation for yesterday's storm. He'll be seeing Chrissie soon and at the thought of her, his spirits lift. But he has time to try the login first. It's probably going to come to nothing, but at least he'll be able to tick it off his list. He sits down with his laptop, trying the combinations Natalie suggested, and soon he's hit gold. The account opens. He's in.

It feels wrong, snooping around in Arran's private affairs. It always does when he's investigating the missing and murdered. But, immediately, he can see that the account is dormant. No posts, barely anything in the feed. Another dead end.

Cal closes the laptop. Then he remembers Messenger. He opens up the account again and clicks on the icon, just to be sure.

So many unread messages from Natalie. He's about to close it down when he notices an anomaly. Another unread message, sent by Anony4321, right at the bottom of the unread messages, dated the day after he vanished. It's probably spam, but Cal clicks on it anyway. His fingers freeze on the keyboard as an image loads.

He leans forward to see better, confused, unsettled.

The image is a close-up, slightly blurred, as if the hand that held the camera was shaking, or moving closer. He thinks it's Arran. The boy is topless. He's outside and it looks like there are other people around him, but Cal can only see little snippets.

Someone out of shot is holding a bottle of vodka to Arran's lips. Maybe there would be nothing remarkable about the image, just some students having fun, but there's something in the stance of the fully dressed onlookers that sends a shudder through him. It's glee, a sort of *Lord of the Flies* feeling. Arran is outnumbered, unclothed. He looks distressed.

All there is in the message, besides the picture, is a laughing emoji. It doesn't appear that Arran ever opened the message or saw the image. Cal doesn't know what to make of it. He paces the room, returning to the picture again and again, knowing that he needs to share the photo with Arran's parents. How can he do that? How can this be the last image they see of their son? What will it do to them?

He calls Shona, hoping to catch her before work.

'I don't know what to do,' he says, when he's explained the issue.

'You have to send it to them.'

'But…'

'There is nothing worse for them than not knowing.'

There is, he wants to shout – there really are things worse than not knowing. But Shona is right, and this isn't his choice. He needs to give Angela and Bill the opportunity to decide.

When he speaks to Arran's mother, he describes the image, trying to prepare her.

'It could be nothing,' he says. 'But you won't be able to unsee it.'

There is a long silence down the line.

'I need to look,' she tells him. 'I need to know.'

Cal sends her an email, telling her to call him back if she wants to speak when she has it. He is in danger of being late to meet his daughter, but Chrissie will understand. He showers quickly, trying to wash away the unease, though the image stays at the front of his mind. He can't fully explain the feeling

122

it inspires in him: hairs prickling on his neck, that sense of someone standing behind you when you're in an empty house. Maybe it's simply the knowledge that this is the last-known picture of Arran. The last sighting. It's been waiting there, all this time, in a forgotten message.

Angela calls him back just as he's about to leave.

'What do we do? What does this mean?'

'I don't know,' he says. 'Maybe nothing. But I'll share it with the police, just in case.'

'And this came from Natalie?'

'Yes. She remembered the details after we spoke.'

'I liked her,' Angela says. 'She was the only one of his friends that helped me, back then. The only one that seemed to care.'

'She still misses him.'

He hears the tears in her throat.

'Can this help, then? Will it help us find out what happened?' A toxic combination of desperation and hope infuses her voice.

'Let me have a think,' he says. 'Maybe someone can help us work out where it was taken and who else is in the picture.'

'Share it,' she says. 'If you need to. I just want to know what happened to him.'

'Do you want to talk to Bill about that first?'

'No,' she says. 'Just do it.'

—

Cal uses an app on his phone to scan the image. As it loads, he remembers the last time he used this technology – to scan pictures of his sister for newspaper articles that he hoped would redress the balance in coverage between her and Jason Barr. It makes his chest hurt, thinking about a time when he believed that the jackals would see sense.

Once the image is scanned, Cal sends an email to the police with a copy, and then loads it onto the website for the podcast. Fans are always keen to see images of the people involved, and he has already added a few basic shots of Arran as a child and teen. He writes a brief caption and headline for the anonymous picture, appealing for information. Then he crosses his fingers and closes the laptop.

CHAPTER TWENTY-SIX

Despite the frantic rush, Cal arrives early at the coffee shop that Chrissie suggested near The Meadows, so it makes sense that she isn't there. While he waits, he checks his messages and loads the Maps app on his phone, thinking of Arran, staring at the meandering curves of the Water of Leith, the river winding its way to the sea.

But Cal can't concentrate for long. There's a fluttering excitement inside him about seeing Chrissie. No one prepares you for this – how much you will miss your child when they leave home. He shakes his head at himself, imagining how she will laugh at him when he tells her. He's not sure what she'll want to drink, so he sits at a table to wait, toying with a sugar sachet and watching the door.

It's strange – the moment she walks in, he almost doesn't recognise her. Only a few weeks into student life and she looks so perfectly at home, a forest-green hat pulled down over her curls and a striped scarf wound around her neck. These must be new purchases; they reflect the Chrissie she is today, the person she is choosing to become.

Cal stands, grinning, and waves at her. She smiles and crosses to him. They hug and he makes himself let go when her arms loosen, though in truth he wants to hang on.

'Nice hat,' he says, as she pulls it from her head and shrugs off her faded navy peacoat, hanging it on the back of her chair with a worn satchel that he recognises – a familiar friend. His smile is so wide that it's hurting his face.

'I needed it. It gets so cold here and umbrellas are useless – I've lost two to being turned inside out. The wind is strong.' Her eyes glitter, lined with kohl, and he takes in her differences, loving that some student clichés are immortal. She looks like Allie, though she wouldn't thank him for pointing that out. He just hopes she isn't doing *everything* he and her mum did. But then, she's Gen Z, he reminds himself – they're far more sensible.

He goes to the counter to order their coffees and the flaky pain au chocolat that she loves. He can't stop turning and checking she's there, she's real. When he sits back down, he wants to know everything.

'Well? How's it all going?'

'It's great. I love the course, and Edinburgh is amazing. It's an artist's dream, with all these twisting streets and hidden graveyards, so many people coming and going. I want to draw all of it.' She chuckles. 'I'm going through an urban phase.'

The tension running across his ribs loosens as she talks – they've always referred to her drawing obsessions as 'phases', like she's Monet or Picasso. The more she speaks, the more relieved he is. She's fine. She's still his girl. They can drink coffee, have lunch, and he has cleared the whole afternoon for her.

'That's brilliant. How's Robbie doing?'

Chrissie's face clouds.

'I meant to tell you, Dad, we're not actually… together.'

She picks up the teaspoon from the saucer and scrapes it round the foam on the edge of the cup, not meeting his eyes.

'Oh.' He flounders, unprepared for this. Fierce protectiveness surges inside him and he tamps it down, confused because he feels so protective of Robbie as well as Chrissie. She's his priority, of course, but ever since he encountered the lost teenager, who featured in one of his podcast series, he's felt drawn to him. A kindred spirit. Ridiculously, he feels like Chrissie is rejecting him as well as Robbie. *Don't react, Cal, don't react.*

'What happened?' he asks. 'Was it… a mutual thing?'

Chrissie winces. 'Not exactly,' she says, letting the teaspoon drop. 'He'll be okay, Dad. I just don't want to be in a serious relationship, I'm too young. I really liked Robbie, but it was getting too... much.'

He swallows and smiles weakly. 'That's understandable. Are you okay, though? Do you want to talk about it?'

Finally, Chrissie raises her gaze to his. 'I was a bit scared to tell you, Dad. I know how close you and Robbie are after everything you went through. But Mum said I should.'

Cal, feeling the hit in his solar plexus, shakes his head emphatically. He's felt that she's been avoiding his calls. Is this why? 'You're my daughter, Chrissie, your happiness is the number one thing. I never want you to feel you can't tell me something. Robbie is a grown-up – he'll be fine. Though I do feel sorry for him, for losing you.' He tries to inject lightness where he feels so heavy. 'You're pretty great, you know.'

Her frown softens. 'Thanks.' Has she worried about disappointing him? He hates the thought. 'I don't need to talk about it. I just wanted you to know.'

'How about another coffee? I thought maybe we could squeeze in lunch and a walk after? Happy to buy a starving student dinner too, of course.'

'Oh, Dad, sorry...' Her face twists. 'I'm meeting up with some of my tutor group this afternoon. I've only got an hour.'

Cal focuses on keeping a neutral mask while his stomach drops. 'No problem. I'm just glad to be able to see you.'

'I wanted to ask you about how you're doing? About the trial delay? And Gran?'

Now it's his turn to look into his empty cup. 'I think we definitely need another coffee, then.'

'I'll go.' She pushes back her chair.

Cal scrabbles for his wallet. 'Here.' He grabs for a Scottish ten-pound note, struck by how beautiful they are, both familiar and foreign.

'Dad.' She grins. 'It's not that bad. I can buy you a latte.'

Reluctantly, he folds the note into his palm. While she forges a path to the counter in the now-busy room, he slips it into her bag for her to find later. Then he leans back and tries to overcome his disappointment that the afternoon he'd hoped for isn't going to happen. His head is spinning, watching her change and grow, discard the things that no longer fit her life. Robbie was such a kind and stable presence, exactly the kind of boy a father hopes his daughter will choose. But that's not his decision to make. He knows that.

When she's back, he swallows down the sadness, and fills her in on the likely trial restart and his mother's health.

'Don't panic! We're here!' A loud voice interrupts their conversation. It takes Cal a moment to register that the two people bearing down on them are someone his daughter knows. A boy with a pale, elfin face and long limbs, wrapped in a similar striped scarf to the one Chrissie was wearing, and a girl with warm brown skin and a sleek bob bring the cold air with them in a cloud, their faces bright and their voices loud.

Chrissie swivels and her face loses its tautness in a second.

'You're early!' But she doesn't sound disappointed.

'Sorry... he couldn't be held back.' The girl grins, sliding her arm into the boy's companionably. She waves at Cal. 'Hi!'

'Dad.' Chrissie turns to him. 'These are my friends Harry and Anoushka. They're on my course.'

He greets them, liking Anoushka in particular. She seems so exuberant and open. Disobediently, his mind slides to Arran, Jonathan, Olivia and Colleen in their first term. Those early dynamics – feeling your way into new friendships and rein-venting yourself. Did Arran reinvent himself too? Is that why he vanished? He pushes the thought away. It's too early to know.

'Do you want a coffee?' he offers, but he can tell by the way Chrissie is already twitching in her seat that the answer will be no. A slight awkwardness has descended that has never been there with Chrissie's school friends or Robbie. This is separate – just for her. And though it has to be, the sting of it lashes him.

'We'd better get on – sorry, Dad.' She stands and pulls her coat from her chair, slides her arms in. He wants to pull her back to him, freeze their time together just for a few more moments, but that's selfish. Harry snatches up Chrissie's green hat and positions it on his own head while Anoushka admonishes him, and he sees that they are still that dangerous and delicious combination of children and new adults. He feels old.

'So good to see you, Dad. I haven't had a chance to ask you about your case.' Chrissie looks worried as she pulls back from hugging him. He can feel how torn she is, so he summons the most genuine smile he can manage, adjusting the muscles on his face into position, making it reach his eyes. This is his job right now: letting her go.

'Another day,' he says.

She nods, and he thinks he sees in her eyes the knowledge that she is pulling away and it's hurting her as well as him. Then he's waving goodbye to the three of them, and they are out of the door and in the street in a noisy cluster of warmth and laughter. The air in the cafe stills around him, suddenly cold.

CHAPTER TWENTY-SEVEN

Cal walks slowly when he leaves the coffee shop, trying to take in the changes in his daughter and his life. They've always been so close. It shocks him that she hid her break-up from him. He thought she could tell him anything, and would. But then, the last few months he has been distracted. Barr's trial has overshadowed everything.

He thinks of Robbie, also feeling bad that he hasn't known to reach out to the lad. The unspoken bond they have is so hard to articulate to others. He's not sure even Chrissie knows how deeply connected to Robbie he's felt since he met him on the west coast. Since then, the broken boy has turned into a young man with promise and prospects, despite his family trauma. Does he assume Cal will no longer want to talk to him, as he's not with Chrissie?

Aghast at the thought, he reaches into his pocket for his phone, retreating to the safety of a grand but blackened doorway to message him. Robbie doesn't have the support Chrissie does. The need to make sure he's okay is urgent. Once he's typed the message, he feels somewhat better.

After ambling around The Meadows under a foreboding sky, Cal spends the afternoon researching. There is no shortage of little coffee shops he can work in, though he switches to decaf as he feels the buzz of anxiety rising, stemming from the mounting feeling that this case is impossible. Apart from Natalie, no one seems willing to speak or has anything illuminating to say. He needs an 'in', some sort of a lead. Right now, he is treading water.

When his phone rings, he answers it without paying much attention to the fact that it's a withheld number. His head is so far into Arran's world that it takes him a long moment to realise that it's Detective Foulds.

'I've got good news for once.'

'You're getting married?'

'That would not be good news. Never again.'

Cal laughs, and his chest fills with a hope-shaped balloon.

'Is it the trial?'

'Judge is back. Determined not to let grief get in the way, apparently. We start two weeks Monday.'

He lets out a strangled noise.

'I know. It's a lot. Where are you?'

'Edinburgh. On a case.'

'Can you get away?'

Cal thinks of Arran, of Angela and Bill desperately waiting for news, and his heart clenches.

'Yes,' he says. 'I wouldn't miss it.'

He forces himself to stay calm. Yes, he has to get back to the Midlands, but he has time – there's a lot he can do to make progress. After ending the call, he checks the photo again on his phone, staring at the image until it blurs, and the people become only shapes and dark motivations. Is Jonathan Keble in this picture? Is he going to have to go to London and doorstep the man to find out?

Cal flicks back to the brief article he added to the website before meeting Chrissie, what feels like a lifetime ago. There are already comments.

> Why is he bothering with a drunk student?

> Totally. Aren't there missing children he could be looking for?

Cal rolls his eyes. There are always trolls finding fault. It used to make his palms sweat to see the vitriol and aggression in some comments, immediately convinced that he'd done something wrong, but he's become immune to the nonsense that certain people spew when they are safe behind their screens. Having to read the things written about his murdered sister inoculated him against these tamer opinions thrown into the ether. The only guarantee is that someone will hate what you're doing. He hopes Sarah isn't reading, though – as a producer, she is acutely aware of audience numbers and the competition out there for sympathy.

He's about to close the browser, to call Shona and tell her about the trial date, when his eye is drawn to a comment further down, not immediately obvious, as it's nested under an innocuous observation about the shape of a building in the background.

> I'm sure I recognise it, though. Isn't that down in
> the Leith area? The view looks right.

A tingle runs through his limbs like caffeine.

Leith. There it is again. That's too much of a coincidence, surely? The CCTV footage of Arran placed him in that area, after all.

Another comment below the first:

> Aye, right enough. That's Leith.

As he watches, another comment pings up, disagreeing with the first two, but it does nothing to neutralise the alertness that is making the hairs on his arms prickle. There is a thread on which to pull, a place to start.

Energised, he opens another browser window and starts pulling up map images of the area, trying to line up the buildings and work out if the backdrop matches. He stares at the screen for ages, clicking forward and back, frustration rising. A few months ago, he helped to make a documentary about teams of volunteers who use open-source information to pinpoint locations and activities. Without leaving their desks, they can identify war crimes, missile movements and mass graves in far-off countries, combatting fake news with time and freely available data.

He types an email, explaining the situation, and sends it over to the group he spent the most time interviewing, in the hope one of them can help, or at least point him in the right direction.

By the time he looks up, it's dark outside and the coffee shop has emptied. Cal's stomach rumbles and he realises that he never did have lunch after seeing Chrissie. The plans didn't feel fun without her. Packing up his laptop, he loads his rucksack and leaves a sizeable tip in the jar by the till to make up for being there so long. Outside, the air bites and the thought of returning to the drab hotel sucks the energy from him.

As he walks, a text comes in from Robbie – thanking him, telling him he's okay. The message is more formal than in the past, and there's something jarring about the words that makes him think Robbie is far from okay. Cal has always felt a responsibility to stay in touch with the families he's helped, to let them know that they're more to him than a story he can easily forget. He takes their memories, experiences and pain on board with his own, adding them to the burden. At night, they come to him in dreams, the details fixed in his brain, the last moments of their loved ones haunting him, alongside Margot's. He texts back:

> I'm in Edinburgh this week. You're probably busy but I have a free evening tomorrow if you fancy a drink.

As he walks back in the direction of the hotel, his feet hurting from today's wandering, Robbie replies.

That would be really good. Thanks so much. I
know you don't have to do this.

The effusive nature of the words tells Cal all he needs to know
about how the boy is really doing.

CHAPTER TWENTY-EIGHT

EPISODE FOUR: THE GRAIN WAREHOUSE

A picture has been found of Arran McDonald, believed to have been taken the night he went missing. It's not for the faint-hearted. In the image, the student is shirtless, head tilted back, drinking what appears to be vodka straight from the bottle. What's the big deal? Typical student behaviour, right?

Wrong. We've posted the image on the Finding Justice *website so you can see for yourselves. The picture is disturbing – the look on Arran's face is one of fear, not merriment. Can we be sure it's him, and taken that night? The answer is yes, fairly sure.*

The moon indicates the photograph was taken at the time of the month when Arran vanished, and it was sent to his social media account right after he was last seen. The timing also corresponds to the CCTV footage we covered in a previous episode – of someone matching Arran's description in the Leith Docks area that night.

In the background of the picture, the edge of a tall building and a part-view of the city are visible. Thanks to some of our listeners narrowing down the area in which the building must be located, our open-source experts have been able to pinpoint the exact spot. The night the photograph was taken, Arran was several miles from the city centre of Edinburgh, on the roof of an abandoned grain warehouse.

'If you look at the lights there, they correspond to these buildings in the background.' That's open-source expert Darren Hawes, taking us through the evidence that he and his team have amassed. 'The corner of the building that appears above him is actually the far end of the grain warehouse, and not a separate structure. We've cross-checked this with mapping software and photographs found online.'

'So, just to be clear, how sure are you that the grain warehouse is the location where the photograph was taken?'

'I'm a hundred per cent sure. It all fits.'

The confirmation of Arran's location that night is a massive step forward in the hunt for the missing student. It seems he was with a group, drinking alcohol. None of these people have ever come forward and spoken to police or to Arran's family. So we don't know what Arran was doing on the roof of the warehouse, and where he went from there.

If anyone who was there that night is listening to this, please, come forward. Maybe you've been holding on to a secret for years, maybe you haven't known where to turn, maybe you've been protecting someone. Now, it's time to speak.

CHAPTER TWENTY-NINE

'You're meeting Robbie?'

'Yes?' Cal pauses, confused at Shona's disapproving tone.

He's just got through updating her on the events of the day –
from the trial news to the open-source investigation techniques
that have helped him decipher the location in the disturbing
picture of Arran. He'd only told her about Robbie as an afterthought.

'Even though Chrissie's broken up with him?'

'Yes. What's wrong with that?'

'Does Chrissie know?'

'No, I haven't had a chance to tell her.' He can hear Shona
sucking her teeth in the background. 'It wasn't acrimonious,
she just isn't ready for that sort of relationship. Maybe they'll
get back together in future, you never know...'

'Cal...' she warns.

'It's not that I expect that.'

'Uh-huh.'

'Really! And anyway, you know what Robbie's had to deal
with, Shona. Chrissie aside, I can't just walk away from him
after everything that happened.'

She sighs but her voice softens. 'I know. Poor loon. I just
don't think it's simple, that's all. You need to tread carefully,
Cal.'

'Have you ever known me do anything else?' He aims for
mock outrage, keen to smooth over the wrinkled feeling he's
getting from this call. Shona's instincts are always good, but
what choice does he have? He isn't going to walk away from

Robbie, so he's got to just make the best of it. He thought she'd understand that.

–

Cal is on time, the next night, but Robbie is already sitting in the dim pub when he arrives. He's seen Robbie at his worst, and that isn't the case now, but as they hug and backslap, he notes that the boy is thinner than when he last saw him, his movements slow. He draws back and takes in the blank expression on his face; his skin seems colourless and his eyes tired. Cal feels a swooping sense of responsibility.

'Shall we order some food? Dinner's on me.'

He's painfully aware that he could have been out with Chrissie tonight. As they take a seat, Cal wishes it was the three of them, him feeling like a spare part with his laughing daughter and this serious young man.

'I'm not really that hungry...'

'You look like you need a good meal.' Cal pushes a menu on him. 'Pick something and I'll go and order.'

Robbie doesn't smile, but he doesn't argue, either. Cal goes to the bar and comes back with a pint for himself and the bottle of beer Robbie has requested. He watches as the boy fiddles with the label, instead of drinking.

'How's the course going?' he asks.

At the same moment, the words burst out of Robbie: 'Have you seen Chrissie?'

Cal nods. 'I'm sorry, Robbie, I can't really get between you.'

'I know. Just... Is she okay?'

His eyes are almost pleading and Cal can't work out what answer he wants – will he be able to cope with the truth that Chrissie seems fine? He sensed no heaviness in her mood. She's starting a new life and wants to be free of the old one for a while, or maybe forever. He takes a swallow of his beer and rubs the foam from his lips.

'She seems fine.'

Robbie nods. He sniffs and Cal thinks he might cry, but then he forces what must be intended to be a smile onto his face. 'I think it's just going to take me a little while to get over her.'

Cal feels a lump in his throat but is saved from answering by the arrival of two steak and ale pies. The portions are hill-walker fare, and he feels warmed and reassured as his belly fills and the second beer makes his cheeks glow. There's a fire in the corner that makes the pub seem so safe and cosy – bodies pressed in at the bar, and music playing behind the roar and fall of the conversation.

As they eat, Cal sees the colour returning to Robbie's cheeks. He still looks sad, but less like he might keel over. They chat about Robbie's engineering course and the placement he did over the summer months, steering carefully around any mention of Chrissie.

'How's your dad?' he asks tentatively, unable to banish the memory of the way Angus looked at him the last time he saw him. In finding answers for Robbie, Cal's podcast dismantled his father's life like a house of cards.

Robbie shrugs. 'We're not really in touch. I send messages now and then. I wrote to Sean for a while, but he doesn't want anything to do with me right now. Blames me...' He gives a hollow laugh. 'Would you believe?'

'Sometimes it's easier to find a scapegoat than admit the truth.'

'Aye.' They finish their food in silence, but Cal isn't worried. He and Robbie understand each other, feel the same sort of grief. Sometimes just being quiet together is enough.

'Are you here for work, then?' Robbie asks when the plates are taken away, and Cal has ignored his protests and ordered two chocolate brownies. He pushes the tight waistband of his jeans to the back of his mind. He'll be healthy another day.

'Yes. I'm investigating the disappearance of a first-year university student thirteen years ago. He came back from the Christmas holidays and vanished. Has never been heard of or seen since. We're about to start airing the episodes.'

Robbie stares at Cal, his eyes wide. 'Where's he fae?'

'Moray,' Cal tells him. 'The edge of the Highlands. His family have a farm there. He came here to study and was then supposed to take on the farm.'

'And what do you think happened?'

Cal fills Robbie in on the little progress he has made. He takes out the photograph and shows him the comments online. The police have failed to respond to his email, beyond a brief acknowledgement, and Cal is impatient for progress. Robbie studies the image, his face grave. He's so absorbed that the pinched sadness in his features drops a little.

'And this is where you think it was taken?' He looks at the image sent by Cal's contacts, tracing the labelled skyline with his fingertip. 'These details are so small, how can they possibly be sure?'

'They're convinced,' Cal says. 'But I need to go and take a look. To confirm and to work out what the hell he was doing there. I've been trying to contact the owners but there's a series of shell companies and it's taking time.' He digs his spoon into the soft, oozing brownie placed before him.

'Where is it on the map?' Robbie takes out his phone and they lean over the Maps app, finding the place the team have pinpointed.

'It's a long way from the centre of town, though,' Cal says, still troubled by the distance. Most of the students he's known shuffle from lectures to pubs and halls. 'Do students go and party in random places?'

'Anything's possible. Maybe one of them had a car,' Robbie says. 'Some students do. The well-off ones.'

'I guess so.'

'Or...' Robbie studies the map. 'There's always the Leith Walkway.'

'Oh, yes, I heard about that. I keep meaning to check it out.'

Robbie's fingers hover above the twisting waterway that meanders through Edinburgh to the sea. 'There's a path all the way along the river – for walkers and cyclists. I run down there sometimes.' His eyes cloud. 'I haven't for a while, but I should get back to that. It's really peaceful along there.'

Cal stares at the map. Is this pathway the right track or a bizarre tangent?

'When are you going to go and look at the building?' Robbie presses. His face is more animated than it's been all evening. Cal recognises the need to bury yourself in something new.

'I've got a couple of weeks before the trial reconvenes. If I don't hear back from the owners, I might go take a look anyway.'

'I could come with you. Show you the way.'

Cal looks into his hopeful face and doesn't have the heart to say no. Besides, he could do with the company and the clock is ticking – he wants to see the place before he heads back to the Midlands. 'You're on. I'll send you a message when I have decided on a day.'

It's only later, when he's walking back to the hotel, with the collar of his coat turned up against the cold, that Cal wonders if Shona would think this was a good idea. But it's too late now.

CHAPTER THIRTY

Cal meets Robbie at the end of Princes Street, carrying two large coffees and pastries in a bag. While this is bad news for his own waistline, he's decided to make the sacrifice and feed Robbie up as much as possible. Fresh air, food and exercise can't do any harm when it comes to the long and torturous process of mending a broken heart. He's trying to separate the knowledge that Chrissie is the cause of the sadness.

He finally remembered to call his mother. It's telling that she didn't seem to realise how much time had passed since they last spoke. She sounded distracted, her voice drifting away from the receiver and back again. There's a clench in his gut when he thinks about how distant he is from her, how soon it's going to be too late to change that. Maybe it's always been too late. Since he was nine years old, they've been at cross purposes. Even the trial hasn't brought them together.

They walk down to Dean Village, as Robbie is insistent that they start their walk along the river from there. Cal can see why, as they dip down into a quaint collection of streets. The view from the bridge is picture-postcard, the river curving away from them to the west, hugged by charming centuries-old buildings.

'This is incredible,' he says when they've traversed a little cobbled street to reach the spot.

'I know – it's usually swarming with tourists. We must be too early for them. This way.'

Robbie takes him away from the bridge, to where the path passes beneath a massive viaduct. The arches make Cal dizzy as he tilts his head to look up at them. It's like they've passed into a forgotten forest now, a green belt that follows the rushing Water of Leith, its body weedy and brown. It's dark and damp here, with trees crowding over their heads and traffic noise receding. Cal feels the urge to plunge his hand into the tannin-shaded liquid of the river, foaming and mysterious. It feels like he can't look at it long enough.

He falls into step with Robbie, marvelling at the river beside them as it cascades over small weirs. A runner emerges from twin columns that flank the pathway, sweating his way past them. A little further along, and what looks like a Greek temple – complete with columns, statue and a rounded roof – comes into view.

'St Bernard's Well,' Robbie tells him, and they stop and take a moment to breathe in the tranquillity.

'Pretty cool, eh?' Robbie sounds boyish, lighter again. 'I love it here. We've got a bit of a way to go if we're going to make it to Leith, though – we should get moving.'

His words jolt Cal from his reverie, reminding him of why they're here. 'I can see why you like it.' He turns to face east. 'This way, then?'

As they walk, the landscape changes over and over, winding through graffitied tunnels, wooded park sections, and close to old industrial buildings and new apartments. At one point, he startles, seeing a body standing in the river's flow. His instinct is to dash towards them to help, but then he realises it's a statue.

Robbie laughs at his shock. 'Antony Gormley,' he explains, naming the sculptor famous for the *Angel of the North*. 'There's lots of them.'

Cal laughs too – but all the same, he feels like the statue is watching them as they continue, so lifelike is the form. He cranes his head to check on it as it slips from view, balking at the uncanny likeness. He tries to imagine a group of students using this route after dark. It would be so difficult to see where you were going, passing close to homes and warehouses, under bridges, clinging to the river. He shivers, seeing how disorienting it could be.

'Would they really be able to come this way at night?' he muses, as the trail twists through a dark tunnel in a quiet stretch.

'Nae bother,' Robbie scoffs. 'You could use the torch on your phone, when you needed, and it would be quick to zip along here with the river beside you.'

They pause beside a massive weir, in the middle of which is a beached tree, no doubt torn up in a storm and washed downstream.

'We don't know that Arran came this way, anyway. It's all guesswork right now.'

Robbie is quiet for a moment. 'You're good at that, though,' he says. 'Working away until you get to the truth.'

They continue in silence and Cal knows Robbie is thinking about his mother, Bryony, and the way that she died when he was only five years old. It took almost fifteen years to get answers, and the ones they found blew Robbie's life apart.

As they get closer to Leith, they see a heron fishing and ducks surfing. Gradually, the river winds through old buildings until it opens into a dock area lined with pubs and restaurants, signs for coffee, and pontoons that lead to eateries festooned with fairy lights. It's a clear regeneration of the area – when they pass through and emerge onto the road next to a chic boat hotel, the old Leith Docks spread out before them: rusting machinery and cranes decorate the skyline, mounds of rubble and industry still in operation. The tranquillity they found next to the Water of Leith feels a million miles away.

'That's it,' Robbie says. 'You can't really see the sea past all this, but it's right there.'

They check the map on Cal's phone, following the road along until they find the behemoth they have been looking for.

The grain warehouse rises before them: the larger lower section is windowless and foreboding, separated from the dock water by more modern warehouses. The concrete edifice is fifteen stories high. It looks like an office block has been stuck on top at one end as an afterthought. Cal cranes his neck to look up at the roof. Is that really where Arran was on the night that photograph was taken? Dressed for a sophisticated evening but on his knees, drinking neat vodka? It makes him dizzy even from here.

'Look.' Robbie points at a notice attached to the wall. 'The building is up for demolition. It's supposed to have happened months ago.' Someone has pasted protest posters along the wall. *Save historic buildings! Remember industrial Edinburgh! Beauty in architecture!* 'Maybe that's why they haven't got back to me,' Cal says. He takes a note of the campaign hashtag to check it out online.

'Beauty? That's a bit of a stretch, isn't it?'

They both tilt their heads to examine the grain warehouse.

'It's an impressive building, that's for sure,' Cal says. 'I wish we could get in there for a look. If they're going to knock it down, then we don't have long.' He feels conflicted: he will soon be rushing away to Margot's trial, when he could be focusing on Arran. He knows his presence in court won't alter the outcome, but he has waited most of this life to see justice done. Cal wants to look into Barr's eyes when he realises he's finished. He wants him to remember his sister.

'They'll help, surely? The owners?'

'I wouldn't be so sure. You'd be amazed how unhelpful people can be. I wish I could be absolutely certain this is the right place. I want to tell Arran's mother something concrete. Not that that will reassure her, but...'

'Well, let's sneak in now...' Robbie gestures to a gap in the chain-link fence. 'Easy.'

Cal looks around and laughs, sure the boy is joking. 'It's broad daylight. We can't possibly—'

'Sure we can. Let's go up to the roof and check. Then you'll know.'

'Robbie, wait!' Before he can stop him, the young man slips through the gap and runs towards the building on his long legs, meeting the edge and skirting it, out of sight in moments.

Cal stands alone, the breeze pulling at his sleeves. 'Robbie!' he hisses, then curses when he realises it makes no difference, as Robbie can't hear him.

He waits for long moments for him to come back, gradually realising he can't stand here much longer – he is going to have to retreat or go in after him. The looming concrete structure is so bleak and soulless, it's making him nervous just standing beneath it. The thought of it at night is horrible.

'Fuck it.' Taking a deep breath, Cal runs to the building and follows the way Robbie went, round towards a set of doors that seem closed. He dithers for a moment, then jumps when one of them creaks open.

'Shit! You scared me, Robbie.'

He just laughs. 'You took your time. I climbed round that way, but this opens from the inside. Quick, before we're seen.'

He reaches out and pulls Cal into the building. The door shuts with a thud that echoes in the emptiness and he is sucked into darkness, his eyes taking some time to adjust to the gloom.

'The power is still on,' Robbie says, flicking a switch. A long luminescent tube flickers into life above them, humming and thick with dirt. 'Weird, huh?'

'Let's keep that off,' Cal says, reaching out to the switch. 'The wiring could be dodgy. We'll just head up to the roof and then get out of here. Don't touch anything.'

But Robbie can't conceal his glee as they walk the floors still filled with old machinery – huge grain hoppers and massive pipework that he trails his hands along, wiping the dirt on his jeans.

'Oh my God, look at this...' Robbie runs ahead to a spiral staircase in the corner of the building that reaches up through the stories, a twisted metal beauty. 'I can see why people want to save it. You don't get this in a modern factory.'

When they get to the top, the long floor plate is dark and echoing, crammed with machinery. The ceilings are low, making Cal feel claustrophobic. There are so many places someone could hide. The glass in most of the windows is smashed and their feet crunch in the shards. A musty smell crawls into his nostrils and sits there unpleasantly.

Robbie sneezes – the air is thick with dust, and bird droppings lie everywhere. The engineer in him is fascinated. 'All of these pipes seem to lead down. The grain must have been fed in at the top, and stored and moved to the bottom for export,' he tells Cal, gesturing to the machinery.

Cal has a horrible feeling now that they're in the building. He hates it. Just wants to get up to the roof and then get out of there. But it is nice to see Robbie distracted from his pain. He just hopes they aren't going to be arrested for their troubles. He'd have a lot of explaining to do to Sarah if she had to bail him and Robbie out for trespassing.

They progress through the building. In one room, they can barely hear each other over the sound of the pigeons, flurrying and panicking as their peaceful roosts are disturbed. Small windows offer only glimpses of grey sky.

Eventually, they make it out onto the roof. The sea stretches out ahead of them, flat and grey. Around them, cars move and the docks hum with life, but everything looks smaller from up here, like a toy town. Cal watches a boat being loaded with goods. Is that what happened to Arran? Did he jump onto a boat for a different life somewhere else? Anything is possible, but it seems so unlikely. Even if he was involved in transporting drugs, it's far more likely he fell foul of a dealer than ran off with the help of one. Cal's eyes drift to the water, still and deep, wondering what lies at the bottom. He shudders. Should they be bringing in divers to search? Maybe. But not yet.

'Have you got the picture?' Robbie's voice brings him back.

He pulls the image up on his phone and the two of them hunch over it. Cal whistles. It's immediately obvious that they're in the right place. He pivots so they're facing the same direction – the edge of the higher section of building on the left of the frame – and the landmarks that are just visible in the picture are laid out before them.

Robbie exclaims in wonder, his tone filled with an excitement Cal doesn't yet feel. 'This is it.'

'It really is.'

It's so lost and lonely up here. At night, how could you find your way? He snaps a few pictures as proof for Arran's family. It's frightening to think how close to demolition this building is and how in a few months maybe it won't be here at all. There are so many places where a body could be hidden or forgotten.

Cal starts recording, detailing their location, the views and the bleak dereliction of the factory they've passed through. Looking up, he sees that Robbie has crossed to the edge of the building and is peering over.

'For God's sake, be careful,' he calls.

'Look, down here… There are massive hoppers and other machinery – I wonder what that was all for. Looks like it's been cleared and dumped in a huge pile. It's all rusted. But there's one still hanging on the wall.'

Cal approaches carefully, dropping to his knees to look over. Robbie's right. There's a huge metal structure clinging by a thread to the side of the warehouse. 'Please move back,' he says. 'You're making me nervous.'

'Look…' Robbie is further back, staring at a shoe that lies on the floor.

'Don't touch that.'

Cal crosses to him. The black shoe might once have been smart, it's hard to tell – it must have been rotting here for some time. He peers into it but can't see what size it is.

'We could take it?' Robbie looks at Cal expectantly. 'It could be his.' He wants to tell the kid that they're hardly Cagney and Lacey, but maybe the boy's right. This could be evidence that Arran was here – the basis for a search, perhaps. If it's evidence, it should stay in place. His eyes dart to the edge and back, but not quickly enough that Robbie misses it.

'There's a fire escape ladder. I could climb down and look into that hopper thing.'

'Absolutely not.'

'But—'

'No. No way, Robbie. This place is a death trap. We'll take some more pictures and go.'

They head back to the stairs, both quieter now.

'Do you think he's in here somewhere?' Robbie asks, looking around as if expecting Arran to materialise from thin air.

'I hope not.'

'But no one has seen him since that night?'

'That's right.'

'And we know he was on the roof.'

As they make their way back down through the dereliction, Cal scans the gaps and passages around them, imagining how terrifying this place would be after dark. He's going to need to chase up the police again, pass on this new information. If this is the last known place where Arran was seen, then Robbie's right – it should be searched.

Something out of the corner of his eye catches his attention, making him recoil. Cal stops and peers into the darkness, his heart juddering at the sight of a black shape. Slowly, he steps towards it, shuddering at the feel of trailing strands of spider webs. He stretches out a foot and nudges the fabric. It flops, useless. Just an old sleeping bag, covered in bird droppings. He wipes the sweat from his face and laughs at his overreaction. This place is freaking him out, that's all.

CHAPTER THIRTY-ONE

ARRAN, 2009

Arran finds the corridor deserted when he gets in at eleven. He's been making pizzas for six hours, helping out front as well as in the kitchen, as several of the waiting staff are off sick. He stinks of garlic butter and basil, has an inch-long burn on his wrist and never wants to see another pizza again. In the communal kitchen, he fills a glass at the tap and drains a pint of water, dehydrated, tired but too wired too sleep.

Taking another pint of water with him, he knocks at Jonno's door, then Colleen's and Olivia's, but no one is there. He remembers now that Jonno is out with a set of his school friends, so many of whom seem to have decamped to Edinburgh, despite it being hundreds of miles from home, and Olivia was meeting up with some of the people from her course.

He feels bad to be a little relieved that Colleen isn't here. She's been shriller and pickier recently – has become obsessed with 'secret' drinking societies, deriding them with a vehemence that reveals her desire to be included. Olivia has been invited to some drinks events run by these exclusive male clubs – purely on the basis of her matriculation photograph. She turned them down. Colleen hasn't been approached and he can tell it's added fuel to the blaze. The result is that she spends a good portion of any conversation railing against the injustice of these closed groups. He finds it an exhausting reminder of ways he doesn't fit in either. What's the point in dwelling on it?

His head is spinning with the traces of conversation and the overall noise of the pizza bar – he isn't going to sleep until he unwinds, so he may as well work until someone else comes back, and he can make them a cup of tea and some toast to soak up the booze, as he listens to the stories of their night. He props his door open and puts on his desk light, getting out a textbook to make notes on the chapters.

He quite likes the peaceful scrawl of his pen on the page, the way the words seem to grip his brain better when he writes them down in his own bullet points. Colleen and her highlighter pen would say it's a waste of time, but it's how he learns. His handwriting is childish, not like Jonno's elaborate penmanship or Olivia's meticulously neat legal notes. At this time of night, it's almost easier to focus. The world is quiet and his brain is too tired to leap from one thing to another. It's meditative, like when he rises early at home and does his chores automatically.

He's so absorbed that he doesn't notice the swing of the door at the end of the corridor, or her quiet footsteps on the linoleum, until she's right there.

'Working late?'

'Olivia! I didn't hear you come in. How was your night?'

She sways in the doorway, strands of her normally neat hair floating around her face. 'I think maybe I had too much to drink,' she says. Her eyes are glazed and full, not like her daytime self. It's bewitching seeing her there; she looks vulnerable and so beautiful. But then a tear trails down her cheek.

'Woah, what's wrong?' She sways again. He jumps up and takes her arm, drawing her into his room. 'Do you want my chair? Sit down. What's happened?'

The tears are flowing freely now. Olivia lurches towards the bed and sinks down onto it, sliding off her heels. 'I could just sit here. If that's okay?'

'Of course it is.' He puts an arm around her and she leans into him. He rests his chin on her head. 'What's wrong?'

'I'm sorry to cry on you. It's silly, really. I told David I don't want to see him again and he didn't take it very well.'

The vibration in his blood is impossible to ignore, the thrill of being near her. She's ended it with David.

'I'm sorry,' he says, carefully. 'I thought you two were getting on well.'

'He called me a frigid bitch… when I told him.'

'What the hell? Dickhead.'

She sniffs and then laughs in surprise. 'Yeah, he is a dickhead.'

Arran gives her a squeeze. 'You're way better off without him.'

'I know.' She wipes at her eyes. 'I just didn't expect him to lose it when I told him.'

'Here…' He gets up to reach the box of tissues on his desk, passes it to her. She takes one and blows her nose. He can see now how much she's drunk, how tired she is. As if in confirmation, she flops onto her side on the bed, drawing her feet up, the tissue balled in her hand.

'Thanks, Arran.' She looks up at him, from half-closed eyelids. 'You're always so nice.'

Nice. She's right. He is nice. Maybe that's the problem.

He sits down next to her, and she moves so she's snuggled against him, their bodies touching. 'You can forget about him now,' he says. 'It's all done.' Olivia yawns. The inside of her mouth is pink. She wipes her eyes with her fist.

'Why are things always so complicated? Why are boys always so complicated?'

'Most of us are pretty simple,' he jokes. 'Sorry you got stuck with a wanker for a minute there.' He watches the smile that bursts across her face.

'I *like* you, Arran,' she slurs.

'I like you too.' He takes a breath. 'I like you a lot.'

He reaches out and strokes her cheek. Her skin is so soft. There's a moment when she's still, silent, and he thinks maybe this is it. The moment everything comes together. His breath catches with longing. Then she presses against him a bit more.

'I think it would be a mistake, though, wouldn't it?' Her voice is small and tremulous. 'It would ruin everything.'

And he doesn't need her to tell him what *everything* is, because he feels it too. Their bonded foursome. He, Olivia, Jonno and Colleen. They're the light and sparkle in his world. He's never had fun with people like he has when the four of them are together, has never laughed so hard or cared so much. When he had a head cold the other week, they all stayed in and watched films with him, feeding him chicken soup, crusty bread and then a hot toddy to send him to sleep. He woke, flushed and refreshed. No one has ever done that for him, not even his own family. They have so much to lose if they try this and it goes wrong. It's hard to explain, but he feels that he and Olivia are in some way fated. Just not yet. Not now.

So he whispers: 'Yeah, I know.' Her eyes stay closed, but she sighs, and he feels sadness flood through him.

Arran strokes her forehead until she falls asleep, then retreats to his desk and his work, watching over her, the way her breath rises and falls. He likes his room with her in it, drunk or sober, but it all feels too much tonight, like he really should be alone. Staring at the page, he understands he's not been imagining things. She's all but told him she feels this too.

Looking up, he sees her lashes lie thick and still on her cheeks, her hand tucked under her like a pillow. If only he could join her on the bed, lie next to her, even just to watch her sleep. Shaking his head at himself, he swivels on his chair, going back to the book and the essay notes. He keeps stopping, though, raising his head to check on her far more often than is necessary.

After a while, the door on the corridor goes again and he hears the thump of Jonno's footsteps. He knows Jonno will launch himself into the room when he sees the door ajar, so he leaps to his feet to intercept him, sticking his head round the door and putting his finger to his lips. Jonno's eyes are round with mischief. As he comes closer, Arran can smell beer and cigarette smoke, the remnants of Jonno's night clinging to him and following him home.

'Have you got a woman in there, Farmer Boy?'

'It's Olivia and she's asleep. She was a bit upset. She split up with David.'

'Really? Thank God. He was a dickhead.'

'That's what I said.'

Jonno forces his head round the door to look. Arran fights the desire to push him away. Tamps down the protectiveness that springs inside him.

'Leave her, she's sleeping.'

'Awww, sleeping beauty,' Jonno stage-whispers. 'Just another night, another drunk person for Farmer Boy to save.'

'Not my fault none of you can hold your drink.'

Jonno yawns. 'Where are you going to sleep?'

'I'm doing some work. She can sleep there for a bit and then I'll go to bed later when she moves. Do you want a tea?'

He edges out of the room, pushing towards Jonno's side of the corridor. What previously felt protective feels voyeuristic now that there's two of them. Arran pushes away the thought that he doesn't want to share her with Jonno, the more charismatic, undeniably the better looking of the two.

'Do we have any toast?'

'I'll see what I can rustle up.'

'Good man.'

Trundling down the corridor, he is relieved to hear Jonno banging into his own room. He fills the kettle and waits for it to boil, wondering if he should make Olivia a cup too, but deciding against it. Let her sleep. Then he rifles in the cupboard for bread, scanning the slices for mould as he slots them into the toaster, digging around for cleanish plates and knives.

'Boo!' The tea slops over his hand and he curses.

'Oh God, sorry,' Colleen squeaks.

'Nae bother.' His skin stings as he lets himself be guided to the cold tap. 'Just an accident.'

'No, no, no! I burned you. Look, it's all red. Hold it under a bit longer.'

She is so stricken, he has to laugh, even though his skin is stinging. 'I'm fine, lassie. Chill.' He pats her shoulder then passes her the teas he's already made. 'We're in Jonno's room. Olivia's fallen asleep on my bed – she came back pished.'

'Did she split up with David?'

'Yes. You knew about that?'

'She's been planning to do it for ages. He was a dickhead.' Arran laughs. 'What's so funny?'

He shakes his head. 'Nothing.'

When Arran joins them, Colleen is curled on the bed and Jonno is sitting next to her, face pale and eyes red. He hands them the plates of toast and takes the slightly deflated inflatable chair. Then he reconsiders. 'I'll just check she's okay.'

'She's fine, now she's got rid of that knob-end,' Jonno drawls and Colleen bites into her toast.

Arran goes anyway, slipping into the room quietly. Olivia's rolled onto her back and her top has ridden up a little. He feels his cheeks getting hot. It feels wrong standing here, gawking at her, so he grabs a blanket from the end of the bed and pops it over the top of her, feeling better when her flesh is covered. He wishes he could crawl into bed and wrap his arms around her. Stay that way until morning. But he thinks of Natalie, and of the acknowledgement that a relationship with Olivia would change everything, could tear their friendship group apart. It's just not possible. He has to live with that.

CHAPTER THIRTY-TWO

CAL

The police take two days to get back to him. Frustration builds inside Cal as time ticks on, closer to the trial restarting and him having to leave Edinburgh with Arran's story unresolved.

'I could take some leave, come with you.' Shona says this every time they speak. It makes Cal want to put more distance between them but he can't explain why, even to himself. It's like being trapped in a room with no door, the walls slowly gliding closer, destined to crush him.

'It's too unpredictable,' he says. 'The delays and the changes. You've got cases and people depending on you. You can't just take time off indefinitely.'

'I don't mind.'

'I'll be fine.' He repeats this over and over. *I'll be fine.* If he keeps saying it maybe it will become true. He *will* be fine. Just as soon as Jason Barr is rotting in a cell, facing years before the possibility of parole. It's that thought alone that sustains him. He busies himself with Arran's case – research on ships, bodies washed ashore – details that fend off real life. He calls Shona a bit less and tells himself it's only until after the trial.

When Detective Austin calls, he has all but given up, but she sounds so exhausted that he bites down the anger he feels over having to push so hard for answers. The lack of time and funding means the cold case is far from top of the heap. As much as that rubs like sandpaper on his skin, he does understand the apparent lack of urgency. She has no end of horrible cases on her plate.

'Sorry, it's been a week.' He can hear the yawn. 'I meant to come back to you sooner. What is it we can help with?'

'We confirmed the building in the picture I shared with you is the grain warehouse in the Leith Docks.'

'Right. Good…' Cautious, giving nothing away.

'It's the last place Arran was seen, and it's full of nooks and crannies – I really think it's worth doing a proper search. With a canine unit.' Austin lets out a strangled laugh but he ploughs on. 'Honestly, if you could see it, you'd understand what I mean. The whole place is a state – full of old machinery. A death trap.'

'How did you get into this death trap?' Cal falls silent. Caught. Her tiredness hasn't dulled her sharpness, clearly. 'Okay, never mind, I don't want to know.' Austin sighs. 'I can ask the question…'

'That sounds like you think it's going to be a no.'

'The whole department is squeezed right now, budgets being slashed. We're not even allowed to leave lights on. Cost of living crisis.' Her voice softens. 'I don't want to give the family false hope. I can put in a request and let you know.'

It's not much but it's better than nothing and he really wants to keep her on side.

'Thank you, I really appreciate it. How long will it take, do you think?'

'As long as it takes.' A note of humour back and then she's gone.

–

He travels down the night before the trial, relying on coffee to keep himself alert as the roads peel away before him. He feels like he's going to the gallows. The thought of having to listen to the shit that the defence team will be coming up with leaves him nauseous. He wants it to be over, wants to still this jittery restless feeling in his limbs. The constant sense that there's something he's forgotten.

Instead of going straight to his flat to inspect the piles of post and dead houseplants, he goes reflexively home. Only, he's not supposed to call it that. It's not his home any more, even if it's where he brought his daughter up and where his heart tells him he's safe. Today, as he turns down the bumpy track, Cal realises something is different. Allie has had the clapboard painted. It's no longer white, but a greyish tone. It just underlines the fact that this isn't his house any more.

The dog is lying on the porch and lifts his head, tail wagging when he sees the car approaching. He's a labrador, after all, ready to welcome anyone. But when Cal gets out of the car and calls his name, Rocket lives up to it for once, leaping down the steps and barrelling towards him. Cal crouches down and is hit by almost forty kilograms of wriggling, wagging dog, hot tongue covering his face. For once, he doesn't mind, just wraps his arms around his mutt and fruitlessly tries to contain the perpetual movement and excitement.

Rocket manages to push him so much that he's kneeling in the dust, rubbing his dog's fur and velvet ears. Something inside clicks in a way that tells Cal he has not been okay, not by a long way. This is what he needs right now.

'You missed him, then?' He looks up to see Allie on the porch, her arms crossed and a look of dry amusement on her face.

Cal grins and pushes himself to standing, though the dog doesn't make it easy, alternating between leaning on him and bumping his snout against Cal's legs in joy. 'Just a bit.'

'Silly boy,' Allie says affectionately, and Cal wonders if she just means the dog.

'You painted the house.'

Allie pauses, before she answers with a lightness that weighs heavily on him. 'Dave did it. It was starting to peel.' She watches for his reaction. He leans over the dog to conceal the blow to his solar plexus.

That's why she isn't inviting Cal in. Dave is here.

He looks up and makes himself smile. Allie holds out Rocket's lead.

'You can keep him overnight, if you like. I can pick him up from yours while you're in court tomorrow.'

'Really?' It's embarrassing but he feels his eyes fill. He hopes Allie doesn't notice.

'Yes, it's fine. He's missed you too.'

Cal pops the boot and Rocket jumps up. He has less spring than he used to, and the knowledge that he's getting old squeezes Cal's chest so that for a moment he can't breathe. He rubs the dog's head and closes him in. As he turns the car around and waves to Allie, he sees the door behind her open, sees Dave wrap his arms around her. There's a moment of utter dislocation – he feels he's back there, still in his old house and his old life – and then Rocket barks once and he's thrown back into his body, into the here and now.

'Come on, boy,' he says. 'Let's go have a really long walk and buy you a bone.'

CHAPTER THIRTY-THREE

WEST MIDLANDS

CAL

Cal parks outside his mother's house and waits, reluctant to go in, but drawn back by memory and duty. Listening to the closing arguments in the courtroom has left him feeling dirty, made his skin crawl. The prosecution laid out what they think happened to Margot that night almost forty years ago. Hearing their account of her argument at home with his father, and then the subsequent fight with her boyfriend, Andy, has brought home just how conflict-filled her last hours were. Even before she met Barr on a deserted country road.

But it is the defence barrister's words that have most inveigled their way into his mind. *Someone else was there that night when Margot died. Someone else is responsible for her death.* He means Andy, and Cal hates the way this line of thought plays on the seed of doubt inside him. He was friends with his sister's boyfriend for thirty-five years, until Andy revealed that he'd lied about that night and the argument he had with Margot. That he'd forced her to get out of his car on a deserted country road and left her to walk home alone.

Cal had, largely successfully, tried to ignore the presence of Barr in the room, but these words have put him in a spiral. He's exhausted, eyes drooping with tiredness, and yet he comes here like a glutton for punishment. The place where it began.

His phone is full of messages from Chrissie, Shona and Allie. He wants nothing more than to go home and call them, then open a beer and forget about today but instead, he sighs and unclips his seat belt, opens the door. Looking up at the house, he can see that some of the white paint is peeling – not the pristine perfection that his father insisted on. But his father has been dead for years, and his mother is old and suddenly far less capable. He'll need to do something about it, he realises. It's his responsibility. Maybe Dave will help.

As he steps towards the little gate leading to a short path to the doorway, he folds back in time, remembering how big this tiny slope once seemed to him, how he played here with action figures and the grown-ups walked above him as he went to and fro. His sister's kiss planted on his head, Andy calling from his car on the street where Cal's is parked now, his hair gelled and short-sleeved shirt immaculate. Waving shyly back at him. Andy whistling appreciatively at Margot in her bright green dress, the tut from his mother behind and her pinched face of disapproval. The stream of images flows through him like they were made yesterday. They feel warm, like summer.

But then he's back in the here and now, with his hand on the gate.

Cal shakes his head a little and steps forward, letting it shut behind him with a clang and feeling in his pocket for the spare key. He rings the bell to warn her and then slots the key in the lock, opening the door and knocking on the painted wood for good measure.

'Mum… it's me.'

A moment, and then a thin trace of voice that allows him to step over the threshold and follow it through to the living room. It isn't cold, but she is in her armchair with a blanket over her knees, silver hair sparser, skin greyer and cheeks seemingly more sunken than the last time he saw her.

Cal leans forward and kisses her cheek. She doesn't resist and there is no acerbic comment – does he imagine the slight whiff of stale decay? It is these details, even more than her physical appearance, that tell him how much she is ageing.

She peers at him as he perches on the couch opposite. The television is on, and she reaches out a gnarled hand to mute the sound.

'Well?'

Cal sighs. 'It's what we expected. Closing arguments, just rehashing over the same things. The judge will speak tomorrow and then the jury will go out to consider.'

It could take days. Cal wonders what he'll do with his time, tethered to the courthouse and its environs, waiting for justice.

'Was Diane there?'

There is no love lost between his mother and Margot's 'bad influence' school friend.

'She's been there every day.'

His mother tuts. 'She would be.'

Normally, this sort of comment would make his hackles rise, but he's too tired and her caustic remarks no longer pack the punch they used to. She's old – old and broken, with no more power over him. Every time she does this, he changes the subject. A small and petty way of taking control.

'Want me to put some tea on for you?'

She shakes her head. 'I had something earlier.'

He frowns. She's eating less and less. He's been stocking the fridge with high-fat foods and tempting snacks, but she just picks at them and so much goes to waste.

'Mind if I make a hot drink?' If he brings through a packet of biscuits, ostensibly for himself, maybe he can persuade her into eating some of them.

'Go ahead.'

He waits for the kettle to boil, with nothing to do but look around the once-immaculate kitchen. It's still fairly tidy, but when you look closely, everything is grubby round the edges. He reaches for a cloth and rinses it under the hot tap, finds a cleaning spray and gives the surfaces a good wipe. There are traces of food and crumbs she never would have left in the past. He can't decide if she isn't able to see them properly or if she's no longer able to keep on top of it – or if she just doesn't care.

There's a pile of papers on the side. Unopened letters among them, some of which look like bills. The kettle has rocked itself to a boil and clicked off, but he reaches for the pile and starts sifting, heaviness settling in his bones as he does. Her carefully maintained life is coming apart at the seams and, as her only living child, he needs to step up. Shona's face flashes into his mind, her hope that he can move to Aberdeenshire. He'd like nothing more than to walk away from this responsibility, but how can he?

His mother doesn't have many friends. People fall away when you lose a child and those that she does have are just as frail as her. He shoves a load of envelopes into the recycling and takes the tea down the small hallway, passing the place at the foot of the stairs where his father once struck his sister across the face. There's a question he needs to ask.

'Are you coming to the court for the verdict, Mum?'

Her head twists on her scrawny neck and he sees fear flicker, before obstinance takes its place. When he speaks again, he can hear the tight bowstring running through his voice, ratcheted so tight that it's going to snap.

'Mum? I can come and get you. The judge will hold proceedings to allow me to.'

She won't look at him. Just sniffs and stares at the muted television. It's been this way for the whole of the trial. His mother has checked out, chosen not to engage.

Cal's whole body seizes and he has to press his arms to his sides to stop himself grabbing something, anything, and hurling it through the window. The violence turns inwards, pinballing inside him until he thinks he will scream just to release the pressure.

'It's like you stopped caring.'

'Don't tell me what to think or do. Maybe they have the wrong man.'

Not this again.

He can't be here any more. He has to get out now. Setting down the cup of tea and a plate of biscuits beside her, he takes a deep breath.

'I have to go now, Mum. I'll see you soon.'

She doesn't look at him. As he walks into the hallway, he hears the sound of the television going back on.

—

Back at the flat, he can't settle. He dumps washing in the machine, does some cleaning, starts playing a podcast to drown out the voices in his head, then turns it off so he can think. He calls Shona but her phone goes to voicemail and his mind is too scrambled to remember what she said she was doing this evening, and he doesn't want to text and reveal his utter lack of information retention when it comes to anything but himself. He just needs the hours to move more quickly. He needs to get to the finish line. How can his mother decide not to be there? Pacing the hallway, he wishes he still had the dog with him, something to talk at, a way to fill the silence. This is torture.

It's going to be fine, he tells himself. Just one more night.

The doorbell goes just as he's thinking he should sort something to eat.

He can't see who it is on the monitor, so he presses the buzzer to let them in, craning his head to see down the stairs.

'Hello?'

Then a face he knows so well, so unexpected that it stuns him. She's coming towards him, dropping her bag, arms around him, grounding him, holding tight. Shona. 'You didn't think I'd miss this, did you?' she whispers as he drops his head to her shoulder and allows himself to be folded into the hug, all the air rushing from him, the vacuum filled by sheer relief.

CHAPTER THIRTY-FOUR

Cal looks up at the imposing red-brick edifice. His palms are sweaty and his shirt feels too tight. It's warm for November. He's regretting the third coffee – his hands are shaky and his body feels jittery. At least he can blame the caffeine. Shona squeezes his hand, but it's like she isn't there beside him. He feels so disconnected.

As he stands, poised to enter what feels like a final stage in a lifelong process, he tries to hold the image of the sister he knew in his head. He has sat and listened every day to the slurs on her character, skewed interpretations, defence lawyers twisting and distorting. He's seen so much of this online already.

Somewhere along the way, Barr has become a symbol to a certain kind of disillusioned young man, and it unnerves Cal to see the bile spewed in chat forums, to realise there are still sizeable groups of people who think of women as possessions – and these people walk past his daughter in the street, they could be at university with her...

'Cal?' A hand on his arm jerks him back to the present, the reassuring face and authoritative tones of Detective Inspector Foulds saving him from that particular thought spiral. Her brown hair is tied back in a loose bun at the nape of her neck and she's wearing a navy suit with a white shirt. Her brown eyes are curious, kind. Her stance is, as always, *don't fuck with me*. It's good to see her.

He tunes out as Shona and Foulds chat for a few moments. They've met before and get on well – both similar in their logical, methodical approach to life.

'Well,' Foulds says, 'are you going in?' Both women look at him. Cal forces himself back to the present.

'I can't believe we've reached this point.'

'It's been a long haul,' Foulds says.

He nods, relieved that she's here. 'I can't thank you enough.'

'Don't thank me yet.' But she's smiling. 'It's a strong case and they argued it well. I'm…' Her words are broken off by a commotion behind them.

Both swing round to look. Cal's stomach lurches when he sees it's Jason Barr and his wife, Naomi. There's a back entrance that Barr could have used today, but he's chosen to arrive publicly, driven up in a gleaming Jag. He is immaculately dressed, as he has been every day of the trial: a pinstriped navy suit elegantly fitted across broad shoulders, a white silk handkerchief in his pocket and sunglasses protecting him from full scrutiny. He walks hand in hand with his wife, who is every bit as well turned out – blonde bob blow-dried, skirt and low heels. A simple gold chain flashes at her neck.

Shona tuts and reaches for his arm, her hand warm through his jacket.

Cal knew they would be well advised, and they've played it perfectly from start to finish – the couple a picture of respect-ability, the ankle tracker invisible beneath his suit. Waiting reporters and camerapeople, who didn't stir when Cal and Shona arrived, leap into action. Lights strobe and loud voices call for attention, each desperate for the best picture, the one that will grace the evening editions. Barr stops to talk to them. Cal can see he's muted but affable, annoyingly well-briefed on how to play to his audience.

'You should go inside,' Foulds says, her mouth a tight line. 'You don't need to see this.'

'Aye. We'll see you in there.' Shona steers a mute Cal up the steps and into the court building. But when they reach the door, he turns back to look, compelled.

Foulds stands impassive and unmoving, acting as a human wall between them and the accused, who is approaching the wide set of steps that taper to the doorway. It takes Barr a moment to notice she's there, but Cal is flooded with satisfaction when he sees the millisecond hesitation in his movements as he spots her. Foulds is half his size, and it looks like Barr could snap her in two, but the fact the officer scares the ex-bouncer makes Cal very happy indeed.

–

After the judge sums up and sends the jury to deliberate, he and Shona wait in a different part of the building to Barr's team. The hours drag by. He goes to the toilet twice, unable to sit still for long, pacing while Shona takes a phone call about bones found in a ditch outside Portlethen.

He's grateful she's here, as their recent calls have been more strained than usual. But at the same time, he doesn't really want anyone that close to him right now, doesn't want anything to pierce the bubble of concentration. Their strength has always been their openness with each other and the fun they have together. A small nagging voice in his mind tells him he's brought far more darkness than light into her life for a while now. Ever since their accident in Inverness, when he almost lost her, he's felt an underlying layer of guilt and responsibility. Like he makes everyone else's lives worse just by being around. Once the trial is done, he really needs to sit down and work some things out. The thought of losing Shona makes him feel hollow, but is he going to be able to give her what she needs?

Time is moving on. He steps out into the corridor again, his mind convincing him that his bladder is full when it isn't, too preoccupied to see that Barr's wife is standing down the hall. He comes to a halt when he realises and dithers about whether to press on or go back. Then she looks up and their eyes meet. Hers seem to glint. She opens her mouth, as if she's going to say something. Cal takes a breath and keeps walking.

The hardest thing is resisting the temptation to ask her what the hell she sees in Jason Barr. Naomi Middleton is rich from her first marriage to a Birmingham property developer, has a huge house on the edge of Tamworth, spa membership, two cars and enough money to do whatever the hell she wants. Why she would harness herself to someone like Barr, he cannot fathom. Chrissie tells him it's the lure of the supposedly reformed bad boy. Naomi wrote to Barr and other men in prison. Do people really look that deep into the toxic sludge to 'save' someone? The thought makes him shudder.

As he draws nearer, he is enveloped in the mist of the strong perfume that surrounds her. His head feels light and it's hard to breathe. A few feet away now. Up close, she doesn't look as glamorous as she usually does. The nails gripping the coffee cup are short and painted pale pink, the silk blouse a muted colour, the heels of her shoes blocky and low. But then his eye catches the simple gold chain she is wearing, and his body feels like it's been doused in ice.

This is impossible. Cal draws level, swivelling towards her and, before he can save himself, trips over his own feet, so is forced to throw a hand out and steady himself against the wall. The icy feeling passes and his skin flushes hot. He looks up and she smiles at him. She knows. Stumbling on, he makes it to the toilets and bolts inside, ignoring the man at the urinals and locking himself in a cubicle.

He's burning up, feeling faint. Cal takes off his jacket and hangs it on the peg on the back of the door, undoes the top few buttons of his shirt and forces himself to breathe deeply. Then he sits down on the closed seat, gasping for air, slowly feeling the waves of nausea and panic dissipating.

'You okay in there?' A tentative voice. 'Want me to get some help?'

'No, I'm fine.' Cal deepens his voice to compensate for the tears springing to his eyes. He doesn't want this other man to realise that he's crying. 'Thanks.'

He hears the outer door open then close, and the stillness in the air tells him he is alone. His mind is chasing itself around and around. He must be mistaken. It cannot be. Cal looks down and pulls back his sleeve, pressing the small tattoo on his wrist. The little swallow he drew from memory of Margot's chain, the one she always wore, which was found tangled in her remains beneath a rusting car in a forgotten scrapyard. That symbol is precious to him. It's the essence of her memory.

It can't be the same one. The original swallow chain is locked in police custody, bagged and tagged, poked and prodded as they extracted evidence.

So the one he has just seen is new. It's a replica. A message from a man with no remorse. Barr's wife is wearing Margot's swallow.

—

Anger chases shock. When he can breathe, Cal bangs open the door. He needs to find Foulds, he thinks, tell her. She'll know what to do. Surely, this is evidence? He ignores the voice that tells him the swallow necklace is now public property, discussed in court. No longer something only the killer would know.

The hallway is empty so he doesn't go back to Shona, and instead strides down the corridors, looking for Foulds, praying that she's still here. She's in the lobby, with her phone pressed to her ear, so he waits for her to finish.

'What is it? Are you okay?'

'She's wearing the same necklace.'

'Who? What?'

'Cal?' Shona is behind him now, her hand on his back, but he can't stop babbling, can't make himself slow down.

'Barr's wife. She's wearing a swooping swallow.'

The DI's face clouds. 'Unbelievable.'

'I don't understand.' Does Shona think he's overreacting? He turns to stare at her, flabbergasted that she can't immediately see.

'They're taunting us,' he says. 'Isn't it obvious?'

Shona looks at Foulds. He has the feeling more is passing between them than he can see, and it makes the pressure in his head build even further. 'Can we speak to the judge?'

Foulds shakes her head. 'It's circumstantial. You know that, Cal. Look, I know it's tough but you need to ignore him. He wants a rise. He's getting off on this. Don't let him see it hurts.'

Shona takes both his arms in her hands and he can feel the steel in her running through to him. It helps but it isn't enough. She doesn't see this the same way he does.

'I don't know if I can do this,' he mutters.

'You don't have to wait here, Cal,' Foulds tells him. 'The jury could be days. Go home. They'll call you.'

'I need to be here,' he says. 'For Margot.'

Isn't that obvious?

'You need to do what's right for you.' Shona's voice is soft. 'She looked out for you. Margot would want you to take care of yourself above everything. You're still her little brother. Even now.'

'Cal?'

They all turn to see an older woman clutching a neat handbag. Grey hair elegantly pinned on her head, a grey silk scarf around her neck and a slash of red lipstick.

'Diane!' His voice is a hoarse croak.

She steps forward and hugs him so tightly that, just for a moment, it feels like someone else is holding him up. Diane, his sister's best friend, testified about the graphic pictures Barr took with unwilling women before they were allowed into the club where he worked. She withstood vicious questioning as she tried to persuade the jury that the image that appears to show Margot cuddling up to Barr is not what it seems.

'We're almost there,' she says. 'Last push.'

Her presence in the lobby fortifies him. Just enough. Diane grips his hand while Shona goes for sandwiches and coffee. For a short time, the darkness and fear recede enough that he can keep going. Diane knew her. The real Margot.

But the reprieve doesn't last long.

Just as they're considering leaving for the day – the light is dimming around them, the windows darkening – an usher sticks his head around the door.

Even he seems surprised.

After only six hours of deliberation, the verdict is in.

CHAPTER THIRTY-FIVE

EDINBURGH

ARRAN, 2009

Arran finds it strange that he doesn't see any of the others for days, but he is busy with uni work, a night out with the other students on his course, time with Nat and his shifts at the pizza bar, so he puts it down to everyone being as busy as he is. Until he bumps into Colleen in the kitchen one morning.

'Hello, stranger.' He flicks the switch on the kettle.

Colleen jumps as if he's burned her. She opens her mouth to speak but closes it again and Arran freezes, as it's so unusual to see her lost for words. 'Are you okay?'

Colleen doesn't answer him. Instead, she edges past, as if Arran is dangerous. He laughs, once, thinking she's playing a joke, but the look of disgust on her face silences him.

'Colleen? What's up?'

Arran steps towards her, but she speeds away from him. Her door slams, leaving him stunned, stranded in the doorway of the kitchen, his stomach churning with uncertainty. There was something like hatred in her look and he isn't sure what he's done. Should he go and knock on her door? Find out and apologise? He's not sure she's in the frame of mind to listen, her behaviour so extreme that he's afraid.

He makes his tea, unsettled by the encounter. Maybe he'll go and ask Olivia what's going on. Colleen can be funny; she has weird moods, and so it could be nothing. All the same, he'd rather be sure. He has sisters and knows full well the signs that the problem is him.

Leaving his cup in the kitchen, he walks along the corridor to Olivia's room. He knocks softly and waits, but there is no answer. He tries again after a moment or two. The waiting is excruciating. She isn't there. Arran stares at Colleen's door for a moment, trying to build up courage, but it doesn't come. When the door at the end of the corridor opens and another student appears, he turns tail and returns to his own room.

There's an essay to write that he should be focusing on, but all morning Arran feels on edge. He goes to his door whenever he hears a noise in the corridor but there is no sign of Colleen or Olivia. Jonno will be sleeping off whatever he drank last night, but at ten thirty he decides he can knock.

There's a groan from within.

'It's just me. Can I come in?'

The next groan doesn't sound affirmative, but Arran opens the door. Jonno is sprawled on the bed, with his head under the pillow.

'It's the crack of dawn.'

'It's not,' Arran says, perching on the inflatable chair. 'It's the middle of the morning.'

'You're a savage. What should I expect from a field-dweller?'

He isn't in the mood for banter. Arran chews at a piece of skin on the corner of his thumbnail.

'Look, I wanted to ask you… I bumped into Colleen earlier and she was acting really strange. She wouldn't talk to me – like she was upset with me or something. Do you know what I've done? It was really odd.'

Is it his imagination, or does Jonno go still at his words?

'Colleen *is* odd.'

'Odder than normal.'

'No idea,' Jonno says. 'I'm sure it will be fine later.'

Arran feels that Jonno wants him to change the subject, but he can't let it lie. He doesn't like being the bad guy. Colleen is his friend, isn't she?

'Could you ask her for me?'

After a second of silence, Jonno emerges from the pillow, pale and puffy, not the put-together version that will meet the world after a shower and shave. 'Sure,' he says. 'When I see her, I'll ask.'

He wants Jonno to go now – the waiting feels intolerable – but he knows his impatience is unreasonable, so he presses down the urge.

'Thanks. I'll ask Olivia too, but she's not there right now.'

'Oh, yeah. She's gone home for a bit. Didn't she tell you?'

'What? Why?'

Jonno's eyes shift away from him. 'Something about being tired and it not being long until the Christmas break anyway.'

'It's two weeks until the break. She had that law student party she was really excited about. Was she more upset about David than it seemed?' It's all he can think of.

Jonno throws back the covers and stands, stretching. He's only wearing boxers, and his skin is still brown from the summer, as if being Jonno means you're bathed in permanent sunshine.

'I guess so. Women, mate. Women.'

CHAPTER THIRTY-SIX

WEST MIDLANDS

CAL

The roar of noise that accompanies the verdict soars and surges. Cal's world flashes in and out of focus; his body is numb, stuck in position. Diane clutches his arm on one side while Shona turns and leans into him, as if she could protect him from the body blow of reality. *Not guilty.* The judge slams his gavel over and over, calling for order, threatening contempt of court.

Cal's ears aren't working and he can't turn his head. There's just a rushing sound inside his brain. Nausea sweeps through him as he stares at Jason Barr in the dock. He watches the man he hates, grinning from ear to ear, looking towards the public gallery, searching the rows for his wife. Barr's eyes rest briefly on Cal as they rake the seats, and he can't help but flinch at the joy he sees in them.

The defence team are shaking hands and clapping each other on the back, already mentally in the pub celebrating, while the judge is forced to wait for the furore to subside. *No. No. No.* Failure and despair sweep through Cal like a tsunami, knocking everything over. He's being tossed in the waves, tumbled over and over until he can't tell where the surface is. He can't think of his sister, he won't picture Margot.

The judge is still calling for order, the court settling to a rustling impatience. Cal grasps Diane's hand like a drowning man, not sure if he can listen to the judge declaring Barr free to go. But he has to. He's stuck in the front row – what was the best position to see justice done and is now the most exposed vantage point. His eyes prick with tears and he squeezes Diane's hand more tightly. He can feel her shaking with sobs beside him, but he can't cry here, has to hold it together. He won't give Barr the satisfaction.

The verdict is unanimous. The world is a fucking joke.

People are rising around him and Shona is saying something, but Cal can't tear his eyes from Jason Barr. The man's posture is light and carefree. He's going home. He should be in a cell for the rest of his life. All of the reassurance he was given about the other cases being excluded seems so fanciful now – of course it would have made a difference, why didn't he think it would? Why did he let them tell him that nonsense? He watches as the man nods to the jury. Bile rises as Barr shakes hands with the suits in the row behind him and then strolls out of the court.

This is not possible. It's not real.

He turns to look for Foulds. There she is, away at the side. Her face is grey. He can see her fighting back tears. She wanted this almost as much as he did.

'Cal! Cal!' Diane's voice is bringing him back to the present. 'Quickly.'

He turns to look behind him, where she is pointing. Shona exclaims and her hand drops from his shoulder. More shock floods in. His mother is sitting three rows back, alone, as the people around file away. She looks so small. Her handbag is on her lap and her hands are clenching it to her chest as she shrinks onto the chair. His chest contracts at the sight. Why didn't she sit with them?

But then he takes in the way the blood is draining from her face. Alarm runs through him, filling his body with adrenaline. She's looking around her, eyes darting, a glisten of sweat on her forehead, and then she finds him and they fix on each other. Just for a second they connect and he knows she needs his help. He can almost taste the anguish in the air. Then her eyes roll back and she slumps to the side.

Shona is already scrambling across the rows, pushing past people. Cal follows, crying out for someone to help them. He can see Foulds running as well, a strand of her hair flying free. None of them are in time to catch his mother before her head hits the chair arm and she slides to the ground. Court staff are running too, people shouting, clearing space, crowding over her. Cal can't get close. He stands helplessly as a man with a lanyard round his neck administers CPR.

Shona's arm is around him and it is the only thing keeping him grounded. 'I'm here,' she says. 'Hold on, Cal.'

In his pocket, his phone vibrates, and then stops and begins again. People have seen the verdict. Do they know what is happening in the public gallery? He stares at the melee in front of them, and all he can see of his mother are the sensible brown shoes and stockings. Her ankles are thin, her skirt rucked up above her knees. He wants to cover her, protect her. She would hate this fuss, the scene.

Other people are being ushered away, the crowds are clearing and a tense silence falls, not unlike the silence before the verdict. Every muscle in Cal's body is tensed, as he prays and begs silently. *Not like this, not today.*

Paramedics appear at the doorway, kit in hand. They speed to his mother and take over the CPR, bringing out an oxygen mask, calling to her. The younger paramedic, a woman with lilac-blonde hair tied back in a plait, stops what she is doing and leans in and presses her fingers against his mother's scrawny neck. It looks like chicken skin, not a living, breathing being. But then she moves. 'I've got a pulse. It's weak but it's there.'

The other paramedic passes her a mask. 'Let's get her in the ambulance.'

'Please.' The word croaks from Cal as he presses forward, able to move now he knows she's alive. 'I'm her son. Is she okay?'

The grey-haired man has a calm efficiency about him that reduces Cal's panic. He puts a gloved hand on Cal's arm, grounding him.

'We're doing everything we can.'

'She was just sitting there. She had a shock. The verdict...'

Here, he falters. He cannot say it. *My sister's murderer walked free today.*

'Right. Well, she's breathing now but we need to take her into hospital. Do you want to come in the ambulance with her?' The paramedic glances at Shona. 'I'm afraid we only have room for one.'

'Go,' Shona says, rubbing his arm as if trying to bring life back into a frozen body. 'Diane and I will follow you there.'

They watch as a stretcher is brought and his mother is lifted onto it like she is lighter than air, covered in a blanket, strapped in place. She hasn't regained consciousness and there is a lump on her head where she hit the chair arm as she fell. They follow as the paramedics wheel her out of the court fast, shouting at people to move out of the way. Eyes staring, curious shock.

'Talk to her,' the paramedic urges when they've bundled him into the back of the ambulance, Shona's anxious eyes the last thing he sees before the doors shut. 'Tell her you're here.'

So he takes his mother's hand, appalled that her skin feels like crinkled paper, and he tries to sound jolly and calm, unlike the last conversation they had, when he spoke the words in anger. If this is it, if she's going to die, then he can never take them back.

CHAPTER THIRTY-SEVEN

At the hospital, they wheel her away from him. Is this the last time he'll see her? Cal stares after the diminished shape, transferred now to a hospital trolley, not knowing whether to feel heartbreak or relief that she may not have to live through the media maelstrom that is about to descend.

He doesn't think he believes in an afterlife, but if there is one, then at least they'd be there together: his father, mother, Margot. He'd be the only one left on this side. His mother's deterioration has been stark in the last few years. It strikes him anew – the utter unfairness. She could never be whole again, never find peace after Margot. She lived the life sentence Barr should have been given.

She's not the only one. He thinks of Angela and Bill, their stoicism despite the obvious toll.

'Can you come with me? We just need to get some details down.'

He startles out of his reverie, finding the concerned eyes of a nurse before him. 'I'm Brian,' the man says kindly. 'This way.'

It's all a blur. Cal fills out the paperwork, then slumps into a chair with his head in his hands to wait for news. He tries to breathe deeply, shut out the noise of a man complaining at the desk about the time it is taking. Waiting, waiting, waiting, while life hangs in the balance yet again.

When Cal raises his head, he sees that the television screen in the corner is running a news channel. Footage of Barr trotting down the courthouse steps, waving at the camera and getting into a car with a smile on his face comes onto the screen, and his gut clenches. His face heats as he watches, eyes gritty and painful. He stares back at the floor.

He won't call Chrissie yet, he decides. There's nothing she can do. He'll wait until there is news. Shona said that she and Diane would follow the ambulance to the hospital in a taxi, so when he feels a hand on his back, he looks up, surprised they've made it through the traffic so quickly at this time, without a blue light.

But it isn't Shona he sees. It's Detective Foulds, her face chalk-white, apart from her eyes, which are red-rimmed. The thought of the no-nonsense detective crying is shocking.

'How is she?'

'No news yet.'

She perches next to him. Barr walks onto the television screen again, waving at the camera in a repeat news-cycle Groundhog Day horror.

'Do you want that on?'

'Fuck, no.'

She gets up and strides to the corner, pulling over a chair and standing on it to press the buttons, until cartoons fill the screen.

'Hey! I was watching that.' A man with a jagged cut on his forehead and bloody knuckles wrapped in a tea towel starts up.

Foulds steps down from the chair slowly. She's not as tall as the knuckle-dragger, but she flashes the man a death look and slowly pulls her badge from her pocket. The man sinks back in his seat, muttering. She plonks herself back down next to Cal, legs wide, posture tough.

'I don't know what to say,' she starts. 'About…'

Cal shakes his head. 'I can't think about it. Not yet. It's too much.'

'Yeah.'

They sit in silence.

'I just can't believe it's true,' Cal bursts out, the words coming without him meaning them to. 'How could that jury find him innocent?'

'They didn't have all the information we have. About his past.'

'But how could they not know? It's been everywhere.'

'Well...' she says. 'If they knew, then they weren't allowed to use it. You know that.' She rubs her face with her hands, as if trying to wake up. He's always thought she looks forbidding, with her strong, angular features, but from this angle she looks vulnerable, human. 'We had to prove the case on its own merits. I thought we had enough.'

'We weren't going to talk about this.'

'No,' she says. 'I'm sorry.' She isn't referring to the stilted conversation. It's a far bigger apology.

'It's not your fault.' He forces himself to say it, though in truth he wants to scream and shout and blame everyone. 'You wanted him put away as much as I did.'

She doesn't reply.

Cal's phone vibrates in his pocket and he takes it out. Allie is calling. He rejects the call. He can't talk to her, not right now.

Foulds watches. 'She'll have seen the news.' The phone vibrates again. 'They all will.'

'I just don't know what to say to them.'

'It's going to get out soon that someone collapsed in the courtroom,' she tells him. 'You need to at least text them.' He nods but does nothing. 'Do it now. I'm going to get you some tea.'

'I'm fine...'

'No arguments,' Foulds tells him. He's glad she's here, that he's not alone, going mad in the hot, claustrophobic waiting room.

'Cal!' They both swivel to see Shona and Diane approaching. The older woman has mascara trailed down her face and it looks like they've been running. 'I'm sorry it took so long,' Shona says, pulling Cal into a hug. 'It was mayhem outside the court, and we couldn't get a cab for ages. Is there any news?'

Cal shakes his head. Foulds stands to free her seat. 'Here,' she says to Diane. 'Take this. I'm going to see if I can find out what's happening.'

Diane falls into the seat in relief. 'I don't know what to say, Cal. I thought it would be enough. I'm sorry, I'm so sorry.'

Another person feeling guilty for something that isn't their fault. The fallout ripples are bewildering.

'You did everything you could,' Shona tells the other woman. 'The system doesn't always get it right.'

The system, he wants to shout. *How can she talk so calmly about the system?* Because she's part of it, he remembers. Shona testifies in court all the time. Sometimes they get a conviction, sometimes not. He tries not to think of her and Foulds as part of the process that's just failed him, but it's hard. He feels the adrenaline subsiding and exhaustion sweeping in.

–

He finally gets in to see his mother a couple of hours later. She is out of danger for now, but will need to have a heart operation in the morning, have a stent put in. The shock, along with an underlying condition, was too much for her. It caused a cardiac arrest.

She's sleeping when he sees her – sunken into the big pillows like a child, her hair wispy and her skin pallid, looking ten years older than she did only days ago. Her breathing is ragged, her muscles are wasted – he looks at her scrawny arms resting on top of the hospital blanket and feels the desire to tuck them under, just so he doesn't have to look at the reality.

'Two minutes,' the nurse says, closing the curtain around the bed. 'She needs rest.'

Cal nods. It's not like his mother will derive comfort from him being here.

She won't be able to live alone after this, he realises. She's too frail and there have been signs for a while now that she isn't coping. The thought of the task and the battle to get her to agree is overwhelming. But it's more than that. It's the sense that they are coming to an end. Dealing with his mother's mortality is like spinning out into space: new territory, adrift from life as it used to be. It feels as though everything is shifting around him – Chrissie going to university, his mother failing, Margot's trial over.

He doesn't know what life looks like beyond this. He doesn't know who he is without these things to anchor him. Cal stands another moment in the dim light of the ward, which is quieter after visiting hours, with only the machines beeping and low moans from a nearby cubicle rending the air. There's a heaviness pushing down on him. Despite the people waiting for him outside, he feels alone, so very alone.

CHAPTER THIRTY-EIGHT

Cal borrows Rocket from Allie and takes long walks while Shona works. The dog trots by his side, not going far enough to smell the revolting corners of the wetlands that he usually so enjoys. Maybe it's his age, slowing him down, but more likely he knows that Cal needs him to walk beside him. He goes to Margot's memorial bench and sits, gazing out across the water for hours, losing track of time. Sometimes he talks to her and he almost forgets what has happened.

He cannot watch television or read the papers. Apart from brief calls with Chrissie, he keeps his head down, refusing all media requests to discuss the trial. It is too hard to talk about Margot, even with the people he loves. It's just too much to come to terms with. The idea of Barr, out roaming the world, is not something he is able to fathom.

When he returns to the flat after these long rambles, he is worn out and good for nothing except curling on the sofa with the warm body of Rocket beside him, the dog's head on his lap. Shona wants him to talk to her, open up. But it's as if a wall has come down inside him, holding in the depth of hurt. If he lets even a chink of that through his defences, they will break and it will flood his soul.

Shona watches him. Every time he feels an absence of air, an intake of breath, Cal looks up and finds her worried gaze fixed on him. Like he's a problem that needs to be solved.

'Stop,' he tells her again and again.

'I can't.'

She sits at his kitchen table, logging into video calls, juggling her work from afar. He has the intense need to be alone, but he doesn't know how to tell her that. He can't. So, they edge around each other instead. She cooks and he tries to eat, all the while battling a grief that runs on a twin track in his head, accompanying his regular life. It's like he has a second brain now, which is always ruminating, grappling, failing.

At night, he lies awake and moves to his own side of the bed, needing space around his body, because it is too much to cope with someone else's needs, their breath, their aliveness. It is all he can do to keep his own body moving.

'I think I should go home,' she says after another long day, the challenge and apology equal in her voice. Neither of them is sure. There is no manual.

'You've been amazing,' he tells her, neither in confirmation nor denial.

When she goes, he buries himself in Arran's case, poring over documents and listening to recordings in between visits to his mother. He's convinced the grain warehouse is significant – all trails and traces of the student end there. He can't live with the idea of it being demolished without being searched. It feels so long since he and Robbie stood there together.

Austin calls from Police Scotland. She doesn't mention his sister, but he thinks he can hear pity in her voice, and he despises it.

'I'm sorry,' she says. 'Search denied. We just don't have the funds for this. The dog teams are backed up with current cases.'

Cal experiences a tightness in his chest, a wobble in his legs. He wants to scream at the injustice but if he loses it with her, he may not stop.

'What about a private search?' he asks instead.

'If you had permission from the building owner there would be no problem with that. All I'd ask is that you keep us informed.'

He resists the urge to scoff. Of course. All the glory, none of the effort. Maybe that's not fair, but none of this is.

Gradually, his mother stablises. She is too weak to live independently for now, so he arranges a temporary care home, pushing the decision of what to do long-term down the road. He moves like he's drugged – exhausted and washed out by the trial and its aftermath, driven forward only by the podcast and the need to find answers for Arran's family. If it wasn't for the case, he isn't sure he could function. It's tempting to crawl under the covers and stay there.

He applies himself to the issue of permission with dogged determination, making call after call until it is easier for them to respond to him than fend him off. The grain warehouse is owned by a corporation that has bought up land for development. With no emotion involved in the interactions, he is faced only with bureaucracy and a desire to avoid delay in demolition – a combination that proves possible to work around.

After jumping through hoops and making promises, he secures permission to search the site with dogs. The notification comes in on the same day his mother is settled into her care placement. Three hours later, he deposits Rocket with Allie and takes a train to Edinburgh, wishing it was fast enough to leave all his demons behind him forever.

CHAPTER THIRTY-NINE

EDINBURGH

CAL

It is Robbie who understands the most. When Cal gets back to Edinburgh, he finally answers the boy's calls, apologising for not being in touch. Robbie brushes off the apology, makes no mention of Margot, no loaded question of how *are* you? Cal exhales with relief. Every human interaction has become this minefield. Even Shona, every time they speak, can't help but ask him. He feels her worry as a weight and a guilt.

But when Robbie meets him for a drink, he grips Cal tight in a hug and then sits quietly. The boy doesn't probe or ask questions; he lets it be, adapts when he realises that it's the case that Cal wants to discuss right now, not his sister or injustice. After the first pint, Robbie goes to the bar for coffees. 'One is probably enough,' is all he says. Cal feels like there is a net beneath him.

'Can I come with you? When you search the warehouse?'

Cal sets down his coffee. His instinct is to say no. The police wouldn't like it; Sarah probably wouldn't either. But what harm can it do? And he likes having the boy around, derives solace from his quietness, his steady understanding. Everyone else is driving him mad. 'Fine,' he says. The combination of Robbie and no-nonsense dog handler Mel will be good for him right now.

Mel drives north with her canine team just days later – the clock is ticking on the demolition. Her well-trained labradors are relatives of Cal's own lazier Rocket, a reject sniffer pup. He's worked with Mel many times before and she is always a comfort to him – far more concerned with animals than humans, she is straightforward and straight-talking.

'I saw the verdict on the news,' she says by way of introduction when she's parked her van in the shadow of the warehouse. 'What a shitter.'

Despite himself, Cal smiles. He gestures Robbie forward. 'This is Robbie – he's here to help.'

Mel only nods and busies herself giving the dogs water. Her straw-coloured hair is scraped off her face and tied back with an elastic band, and she's wearing odd socks. By contrast, everything for the dogs is immaculate. Cal makes a reassuring face at Robbie, nudging him forward. The tough search expert softens when the boy ruffles the ears of one of the two black Labs she's brought with her. The way to Mel's heart is always through her dogs.

'That's Domino,' she says as the dog licks Robbie's face. 'And the other one's Cody.'

The air is so sharp that it bites the skin, and the dogs' breath makes clouds around him. Mel lights a cigarette and sucks on the end like she's taking in oxygen, while staring up at the warehouse.

'Well, this is a bit easier than that moorland you had me do last time.'

'Wait till you see the inside,' he tells her. 'Lots of nooks and crannies.'

'What's the ground like?'

'Plenty of smashed glass.'

'Right. You, boy,' she barks at Robbie. 'Make yourself useful and grab that bag there.'

With Domino's feet neatly encased in protective boots, Mel settles Cody in the van and follows Cal to where a representative of the development company is standing. The man, wrapped in a too-large luminous jacket, is stepping from foot to foot, holding a set of keys.

188

Mel whistles when they enter the ground floor of the building and she is confronted by the vast machinery housed inside.

'Told you,' Cal says, though his emotions don't match the cheer in his voice. He hates the warehouse just as much as he did last time. It feels watchful and knowing.

Domino doesn't seem to like the atmosphere either. Mel releases the dog, and they follow his lead as he trots round the machinery, nose to the ground. Although he's as methodical as Mel's dogs always are, Cal is surprised by how jumpy and agitated Domino seems. He keeps stopping and sniffing the air, then criss-crossing the parts of the building he's already visited, like he's confused.

'Huh,' Mel says, and he waits for more explanation, but it isn't forthcoming. 'It's okay, boy,' is all she says.

Gradually, they work their way up the building, until they reach the floor with the door that leads to the machinery attached to the wall. When Domino gets close to it, he whines and scratches at its base. Mel calls him back, while she looks out through the small window in the door.

'Can't go out there, boy,' she says, frowning.

Robbie looks at Cal, wide-eyed. He shrugs, and they follow Mel and Domino as they sweep the rest of the building. On the roof, Domino whines again, his nose in the air. The dog looks at Mel and turns in a circle.

'He sure doesn't like it here,' she says.

'What does it mean?'

'I don't know. He's got something but his alert is a bark, so...' Mel's voice tails off as she clips Domino's lead on, and they head back into the building. 'Maybe we try Cody.'

Getting the dog down the spiral staircase is harder than coming up. 'Can you leave us to this circuit?' Mel asks. 'Might be better if it's just him and me.'

'Sure,' Cal says, turning to tell Robbie they should wait outside.

But, when he turns, Robbie isn't there.

'Rob? Robbie?'

Cal retraces their steps, alert to any sound or movement in the dust. The hairs on his neck are vertical and he wants nothing more than to leave this building. There are footprints leading away to the outside wall, and the door that Domino scratched before is swinging in the breeze. Cal knows, suddenly, where Robbie has gone, what he's doing.

He reaches the threshold and halts, teetering on the edge of a metal platform leading to some steps. The structure sways violently, just from one moment of contact, lurching with a screech of angry metal. He pulls his foot back inside, clinging to the door and peering out.

Robbie is halfway down some metal steps, craning his neck to see into the old machinery they spotted from the roof. It's as if he is oblivious to the danger. Cal feels the cold seize his body.

'Robbie! Get back here, it's not safe.' But even as he calls the warning, the steps wrench from the wall. Cal watches in frozen disbelief as they swing out into open space. With a tearing screaming sound, the hopper falls away from the external wall, twisting and groaning in the air. Robbie's face jerks to Cal's and he can see the moment of realisation and regret.

Everything seems to happen in slow motion. The steps break away and slide downwards, as the machinery tumbles to the ground. The sound slices through the docks. Cal watches, terrified, as the steps peel away, metal wrenching. Robbie holds tight, dangling from extended arms as the stairway arcs slowly over him. When it grinds to a halt, he is suspended one or two storeys above clear ground.

'Hold on!' Cal calls, his hands clenching the door frame, splinters pushing into his skin. He can't look away until he's sure Robbie is still. But he needs to run down to him.

In the next moment, Robbie looks up and their eyes meet again. The boy's hands slide from the metal and he drops to the ground below, legs crumpling beneath him.

The movement breaks the spell that has paralysed Cal, and he turns and runs through the factory, shouting for Mel to call 999, pounding through the dirt and the cobwebs, scattering pigeons. His brain can't compute what is happening. He just needs to get to Robbie.

Down to the ground floor and out the door, he sprints to the corner of the building and comes face to face with the fallen hopper, its twisted metal carcass blocking his path. A shout goes up and he sees two men running from the other end of the building to the fallen shape. Mel is behind him, Domino straining on his leash, barking wildly.

As he nears the spot, Cal desperately looks for signs that Robbie is moving, sitting up, talking to his rescuers, but there's nothing. His heart constricts in his throat.

'Help him!' His words come out a pathetic squeak. Like a dream where you can't move properly, can't call for help. 'Robbie!'

He reaches the boy, dropping to his knees beside him. They're on a rotting mound of old grain, he realises. A crusted barrier between them and the concrete.

'What happened?' One of the men sinks down next to Cal, his face chalky. 'Did he fall from the roof?'

'From the steps up there.' Cal gestures behind him. 'Robbie!' He leans over Robbie, calling his name, afraid to touch him or move him. He can see the boy's leg is lying at an unnatural angle. Everything around him seems unreal, dreamlike.

'We were on our break and we saw him hit the ground,' the man says, leaning closer to Robbie. 'All right, son?'

Robbie is out cold, his face grey. Cal thinks he sees him twitch but then go still. He presses his fingers to the boy's neck, letting out a cry of relief when he feels the flutter of a pulse, life moving beneath his touch.

'He's breathing,' the dock worker says. 'I saw his chest move. He's just knocked hisself out, like.'

'I feel sick,' Cal whispers, touching Robbie's hand, not sure what to do to help him. Behind him, Cal can hear Mel speaking to the 999 operator. Domino is going wild, his barks sounding out across the dock.

'Gave me the fright of my life,' the dock worker says. 'I might just have a wee chunder me'sel. Fuck' sake.'

Robbie groans and takes a big shuddering breath. 'Robbie, can you hear me? We're here with you. Hang on, help's coming.'

Robbie's eyes open, clouded with confusion for a moment, until he sees Cal.

'I'm sorry,' is the first thing he says.

'God, you gave me a scare.'

'I don't think the stairs are safe,' Robbie says, and Cal's chest loosens at the sound of the boy making a joke, though he pushes him back gently when he tries to move.

'Just stay still, okay?'

'My ankle hurts like hell.'

'I think you might have broken it. The ambulance is on its way.' Cal pulls off his coat and drapes it over Robbie, realising how cold the boy's fingers are. The air is brutal and he must be in danger of going into shock.

'Can someone shut that dog up,' one of the men says.

Tuning back into the world, Cal turns to look for Mel. The warehouse looms above them, the metal staircase hanging limply from its flank. On the ground, the hopper lies broken. That's what the dog is straining towards, its barking frantic as Mel ignores his signal, speaking into her phone to the 999 operator.

Her eyes meet Cal's and he knows.

'What's that?' The other man, Danny, has approached – he speaks at the same moment Cal catches sight of it... a tangle of fabric and remains that could be anything: factory debris, gull or pigeon carcasses, ancient rubbish. Except for one thing. The unmistakable bleached-white ball of a skull has rolled free of the wreckage and come to rest on the grain, so it is staring up at the roof – sockets hollow and accusing.

Mel quiets the dog. Robbie gasps from his prone position. The dock worker vomits behind them, and in the distance a siren sounds.

CHAPTER FORTY

The police arrive before the ambulance. It's a shame it's not the other way round, because Cal's request to go with Robbie is immediately squashed.

'But he's had an accident.' Cal has one eye on the red-faced fury of the officer in front of him and one on Robbie, who is being strapped to a board and then lifted onto a stretcher with the help of the dock workers. Lurking behind the first officer is a junior PC who looks like he's barely out of school and is clearly just here to do what he's told. Cal can tell there is zero point appealing to him. He wishes he'd had the presence of mind to call the detective he spoke to originally, but his fear for Robbie overtook reason.

Behind a hastily erected cordon lies the skull – and the rest of what Cal is sure must be a body. Other sirens in the distance tell him more police officers are imminent. The luminous-clad keyholder from the development company is on the phone, his face beetroot, waving his free arm. This is not what they agreed to.

'Are you a family member?'

'No, I'm not…'

'Then I need you to stay here, sir, and we can contact the next of kin.'

Robbie's face falls and Cal pictures the call that will be made to his father on the west coast. How the man's already-reduced ability to cope would crumble to dust if he had to worry about his oldest son as well as everything else. The fact that Cal is involved will only make things a million times worse.

'You can't,' Robbie says, wincing as the paramedic cuts his jeans open from ankle to knee, exposing swollen skin and weeping grazes. 'He's not well.' He looks at Cal. His face is streaked with dirt. 'Don't worry, I'll be fine.'

'I really think I should go with him.'

'You've some questions to answer.' The officer steps closer to Cal, eyeballing him, chest stuck out, though he is a good few inches shorter.

'You need to speak to my boss too,' the luminous beetroot man squeaks at Cal. 'She's going mental. You said you'd be in and out, and no damage done.'

All three of them turn as one to look at the elephantine hopper.

'Well, that worked out, then,' the officer says, his words oozing sarcasm like honey. Cal likes him a bit better for it.

'Robbie, I'll call someone to come and I'll follow as soon as I can, just hang in there.'

He squeezes the boy's hand as the paramedics slide him into the ambulance, his heart rate still at panic level. Mel and the dog are over by the side wall, and Cal needs to talk to her; the building owner is on the phone, waiting to speak to him, and he is also going to have to explain his presence here to police detectives, as well as breaking the news to Arran's parents. Everything looms up in front of him like an impenetrable wall.

He holds one hand up to the officer to tell him to wait, then pulls his phone from his pocket and dials. For a moment, he thinks she isn't going to answer, but then he hears the out-of-breath tone.

'Dad, I'm just out, I can't—'

'Chrissie,' he cuts her off. 'I'm really sorry to interrupt you, but something's happened. Robbie's hurt.'

'Robbie?'

'They're saying he's okay, but he's broken his ankle and they need to scan him to check for other injuries, to be sure. He was helping me with a case and he had a fall...'

'What?!'

'I'm with the police and—'

'The police? What the hell? Are *you* okay?'

He feels like the child, not the parent. 'Yes, I'm fine. I promise I'll explain everything. Just… Can you get to the hospital and wait with Robbie? He's being taken to the Royal Infirmary. If you jump in a cab, I'll pay for it. I'm sorry to ask you, I just—'

'It's fine,' she says, though it sounds anything but. 'I'll go now.'

She hangs up before he can say goodbye. When Cal turns around, the officer is right behind him. He's not sure what's the easier to face: this man's officiousness or his daughter's shock and disappointment.

'Now, would you like to tell me what's going on here?'

'Can we call Detective Austin? She knows I'm here. I'm a podcaster and I've been investigating the cold case of a missing student, Arran McDonald. We had permission to do a private dog search of the building. Robbie fell from the walkway up there…' He tilts his head and is hit by the lurch of vertigo, making his legs sway a little, almost losing his balance.

Then he looks back at the discarded skull and the mess of the hopper. He's been too frightened for Robbie to really take it in. Now the shock is subsiding, and reality is rushing back. There are so many people he needs to tell. Already, one or two onlookers are gathering at the edge of the site, phones raised, and who knows how long it will be before the press are here.

'The machinery came down when the walkway did. I can show you some ID, and you can speak to my producer and the building owner's representative to verify this, but please…' He gestures to the onlookers. 'I think those could be Arran's remains. His mum doesn't know. I don't want her to see this on the news. He's been missing for thirteen years… He was nineteen.'

His words have an effect on his antagonist.

'You!' The officer's shout is so unexpected that it makes Cal – and the fresh-faced PC he's addressing – jump. 'Get those numpties back, will you?' He glares as the kid walks over to the gathering, his scowl deepening as he watches his attempts at crowd control. 'Wait here!' The older officer stalks over and starts shouting directions, chest puffed out and clearly in his element.

Cal exhales at the temporary reprieve and quickly digs in his pocket for his phone. He types out a quick text to Sarah, letting her know what he's found.

> Can you keep an eye on the news and call
> Angela if anything breaks? And I might need you
> to speak to the building owner… sorry.

–

Mercifully, Cal is rescued from the grumpy police officer when two plain clothes officers turn up. The first, a woman with close-cropped dark brown hair, stretches out a hand.

'Cal Lovett? DS Austin.' She steps up to the cordon and puts her hands on her hips. 'I was under the impression you might do this a little less… dramatically?'

He grimaces. 'It didn't exactly go to plan.'

She raises an eyebrow. 'I don't know about that. You seem to have a result.'

The detectives invite him to sit in their car.

'Pinker, give him a Murray Mint,' Austin instructs. The second officer flips open the glovebox and passes Cal a sweetie.

'Er… thanks.'

'Give that a sook. Good for the shock,' Austin says by way of explanation.

Outside the car, the clouds have darkened and he can see the first drops of rain hanging there, waiting to fall. He glances over at Arran's exposed resting place – if indeed it is Arran. Two men are pulling on forensics suits, and others are bringing screens and a tent to shield the work from prying eyes. Crime scene tape has sealed off the area and officers are swarming.

The detectives questioning him in the car remind Cal of Foulds, and he feels a sudden pang at the memory: the hope she gave him for the court case, the risks she took to follow the leads. He hopes, for Arran's sake, that these officers are also the sort of people guided by practicality and sense, rather than a myopic interpretation of a strict set of rules. He relaxes a little in their presence.

'So, let me get this right,' Austin begins when he's finished explaining. 'Your, shall we say...' She widens her eyes '...*assistant* took it upon himself to do a little exploring and just happened to dislodge a giant piece of machinery with a body in it?'

'I know it sounds unlikely, but the dog was acting strangely and we saw the machinery from the roof where the picture was taken. Robbie decided to have a little look. That's why he went out onto the walkway.' He swallows, feeling sick at how close they came to Robbie being much more seriously injured. 'Do you mind if I open this door? I need some air...'

The wind is rising and the structure towers over them like a malevolent giant. Cal just wants to escape it.

'And have you touched anything since then?'

'Nothing, I promise. I was more worried about Robbie. We didn't go near the hopper, didn't even see what was in there at first, until we noticed the skull. You can ask the others. They'll say the same.'

Cal's cold, shivering without his jacket. 'I really need to go to the hospital to see Robbie. And Arran's parents are expecting me to call. I need to let them know...'

'We can break the news, if you prefer? Obviously, we'll be speaking to them more once we ID the remains, if it is Arran.'

He shakes his head. 'I'll tell them.'

They leave the car, and the detectives cross to the cordon and start putting on protective suits. He scans the area for Mel and her van, finding where they've been moved to. She's just finishing giving her statement.

'Thank you,' he says when she's done. He feels like hugging her, but Mel is not a hugger and she'd probably set the dogs on him, so he settles for fussing over Domino and Cody instead.

'No problem. It was only half us – and half your clumsy friend. But the fee's the same. Think that's your guy in there?' Her face sobers as she jerks a thumb in the direction of the hopper.

'That's my guess. But we'll have to wait for forensics. Poor kid.'

'Helluva place to end up.'

'Are you staying in Edinburgh tonight?'

'Nah, best be off. I'll find somewhere to take them for a walk on the way back down and they'll sleep fine.'

Once Mel has driven away, it feels wrong walking away from the site, from Arran, but he has to go. After calling a cab, he stands on the side of the road, hunched against the chill, and dials Sarah.

'Cal, what the hell?!'

'I know, I know.'

'You *found* him?'

'We found remains – bones. It could be him. Have you told Angela?'

'No, I was watching to see if anything broke. Figured it was better coming from you. I've already had a call from a lawyer from the development company, though.'

'Yeah, their representative seems a little pissed. Not sure what they thought we were looking for.'

'Lucky for us that they didn't think it through. I'll deal with them.'

'Thanks.'

'What were you thinking? Letting Robbie search, though?'

'I know, I know, it was stupid.' He remembers the creaking squeal of metal and the unstoppable aftermath. Robbie's pale face and swollen leg. If he closes his eyes, the hopper falls again and again.

'Is he going to be okay?'

'I think he's had a lucky escape. Broken his ankle or leg, though.'

'Could have been so much worse.' Then Sarah's voice changes from admonishment to excitement, quivering as she speaks. 'But, Cal… Arran. You actually found him.'

'I hope we did. This might be the end of the road. Maybe he just jumped, Sarah.'

She's silent for a moment. 'I know. How likely do you think that is?'

Cal looks back at the doomed grain warehouse, its dark, shattered windows giving nothing away. He tries to imagine Arran making his way through those abandoned corridors in the dead of night, the forgotten lighting buzzing overhead, the wide expanse of roof with its view of an inky sea.

'Even if he did, something happened to him up there first,' Cal says. He thinks of the picture, the figures surrounding Arran, who was stripped to the waist in the brutal ice of an Edinburgh January. The wind coming off the sea must have cut through him. 'I'm going to try and find out what.'

CHAPTER FORTY-ONE

The taxi drops him at the hospital and he jogs towards the doors. He's been texting Chrissie and she's seen his messages, but there is no response. He almost cries out when she steps out from the doorway.

'There you are. I'm sorry it took me so long, how's—'

But he stops speaking at the forbidding look on his daughter's face. Her eyes are red, she's been crying. His hands fly to his mouth, his stomach falls away like he's skydiving. 'Oh God, is Robbie…'

'He's fine.' Chrissie wipes her eyes with the back of her hand. 'Broken bones and a bruised ego.'

He frowns. 'I'm sorry, love, that I had to call you. I really didn't want to.'

'Why were you with him, Dad?' Chrissie breaks in, her voice cracking.

Cal steps forward, reaching for her, but she pushes him away. It's not a hard shove, but it hurts more than any punch he's ever taken. Cold dread flows through him, making the side of the factory seem warm and inviting in comparison.

'I called to see if he was okay, when I came to Edinburgh. We went for a walk – and then, after the trial, he was just helping me.'

It sounds pathetic, even to his ears.

'You're my father, not Robbie's.'

'I know that. I… I'm sorry, Chris, I didn't think you'd mind if I saw him when you weren't around.'

'I do mind.' Her words fly out, shrill and aching. 'You wouldn't even speak to me about the verdict, Dad. You've shut it all away. And now I find out that you'll happily talk to Robbie.'

'It's not like that, Chrissie, it's really not. It's just that Robbie's been there, he—'

'Understands?' Her face is pinched with the effort of not crying. 'Thanks, Dad. Thanks a lot.'

It's hard to get his bearings, while he feels cold and riven with exhaustion, the clang of metal echoing in his skull. He's messed everything up today.

'No, please. It isn't like that. I'd like to talk to you. I would...'

But Chrissie's face has hardened with hurt.

'This isn't okay. You're here, Dad. In Edinburgh, in my first term of uni. This is my chance to be away from home, to work out who I am without you breathing down my neck. You've brought all this...' She looks around, as if searching for the right word. '...*chaos* with you.'

Cal feels tears prick his eyes. They've always been close. She's always wanted to help him, travel with him. He'd just assumed his being here would be welcome.

'And now, to make things worse, you've gone off gallivanting with Robbie, and I've got to deal with it all, explain to him again why I don't want to be in a relationship. You're the parent, Dad, not me. I don't want to be tangled up in this. It's too much, with Auntie Margot and everything. He isn't your son. As much as you wish he could be.'

Her words are bitter, so unlike her. She presses her fingers to her lips as if she could push them back in, eyes wide, her face drained of colour.

Cal feels the hit in his core. The shock of pillars he'd taken for granted crumbling. It had never occurred to him that she felt this way. It's like something inside him is tearing. His eyes are hot. How can he take it all back? Make it better? Shona warned him and he didn't listen.

'I'm sorry,' she whispers. 'I have to go. I need some space.'

She brushes past him, and he breaks from his paralysis to put his hand on her shoulder. 'Chrissie, wait...' But she shrugs him off and wraps her arms tight around her waist as she picks up speed. His hand drops to his side and he watches, lost and unsure, as she crosses the car park – scooped into the gathering darkness, so he can no longer see the flame of her hair.

He doesn't know what to do. Everything is broken. It takes every ounce of his willpower not to follow. She's his daughter, he should be there for her. But if Chrissie needs space, he needs to respect that. He's fucked up. Royally. Shaken, Cal slumps against the wall for a moment, pinching the bridge of his nose, stopping the tears, shaking them off.

He still needs to check on Robbie. After all, the boy is lying in there with a broken ankle and that's his fault – it was on his watch. As he walks into the hospital, needing to confront the disaster he has started, there's an oily feeling inside him. He's been a fool, blundering around where he isn't wanted. His loyalty should have been with his daughter. She's wrong – he doesn't want Robbie as a son. It's just that he's come to need him as a friend, and he shouldn't have let that happen.

Looking at Robbie has always been like looking in a mirror. He's intimately attached to the boy's progress, his prospects and happiness. Because, if there is hope for one lost child, maybe there's still hope that the one lost inside himself can find peace too.

–

Robbie looks subdued when Cal pulls himself together and makes it to the cubicle in A & E. His leg is strapped up and his face is still streaked with dirt. There's a cut on his forehead that Cal doesn't remember seeing when they were at the warehouse. They both start apologising at the same time.

'You told me not to...' Robbie says once they stop gabbling their culpability.

Cal's mouth quirks. 'Yes, but if you hadn't plummeted off the side of a building, then we wouldn't have found what we did.'

For a second, he sees the idea of a smile on Robbie's face, fast vanishing in the artificial light when a patient further down the line of cubicles cries out.

'Do you think it's him?'

Cal shrugs. The answer is yes, of course, but he's wary of rushing to conclusions. 'I hope it is and I don't, if that makes sense?'

Outside the cubicle, there's the sudden commotion of people and a trolley rushing past, voices injected with urgency and seriousness. The curtain billows in the wake of their movement. Robbie lies back and closes his eyes.

'It sounds like it could be a little while until they get to you.'

'Aye, they said as much. It's busy. Should have picked a quieter day.' Robbie opens his eyes and this time the pain is of a different flavour. 'Chrissie was here. Did you see her?'

'Yes.' The urge to elaborate is almost as overwhelming as the desire to ask what passed between the two of them inside the hospital, but he bites down on the words that come to his lips. Robbie watches him for a moment. His mouth opens and closes, but he stays silent. There's a wall between them.

'You should get some rest,' Cal says, finally. 'Have you spoken to your dad?'

Robbie's eyes meet his. 'He would either care too much or not at all.'

It's impossible to disagree with him. Angus is broken up, like tarmac where weeds have pushed their way through. He has lost shape and coherence, is impossible to predict and incapable of being someone his son can rely on. Cal set Robbie free and he orphaned him.

'Can I get you anything?'

Robbie shakes his head slowly against the pillow.

'I'll be back in a minute,' he says. 'I have to go and call Arran's mum.' Robbie doesn't answer.

On his way out into the cold, Cal checks the news. There is a small bulletin about police attending a scene in the Leith Docks, but nothing concrete – as yet, no mention of the remains. It will be coming and so he needs to act now, before the police make the call.

He pictures the farmhouse as the phone rings: dogs barking, family clustered around in boiler suits and overalls, perhaps showering after a hard day, sitting down to eat at the kitchen table that overflows with the debris of life. The place left for the missing son. He groans. He is about to extinguish the flame of hope that exists inside everyone who's missing someone – the chance that they will walk through the door again one day. He had it himself about his sister, though deep down he knew it was a fantasy. At night, before he fell asleep, he nourished the hope and luxuriated in it. He misses those pre-dreams and the escape from cold reality that they offered.

'Angela,' he says, when she answers. 'It's Cal. How are you?'

'Aye, well enough.' Her words are cautious. Like his, they are an entry into the conversation, feeling the way.

'Are the others there with you? Can you sit down a minute?'

'You've found something. In the search.'

The background noise dulls, and he pictures her holding out a hand to the room, alerting them to be silent.

'We found some remains at the grain warehouse, yes.'

'What? What do you mean, remains?' Her voice shakes.

'We found some bones. A body that has been there for a long time. We don't know if it is Arran, Angela, but you need to prepare yourself.'

The suck of air being drawn into lungs, slowly. He has to imagine the tears, for she betrays nothing. Is she feeling like he did when the news came to him? Like punching the air but sinking to the floor?

'When will we know?'

'The police are examining the scene now. They'll take away the remains and look after them, they'll see if they match. You'll have to wait a little longer, Angela, I'm sorry. They'll be calling you this afternoon to explain the process.'

'Were they…? Was he…?'

'The bones were in some machinery,' he says, softly, as if that could make things better. 'It looks as if maybe they came from the roof above – perhaps someone falling. They were hidden from view, that's why no one knew until now. We dislodged some machinery, and it fell and broke open.'

He rushes to speak, to give her the information.

'Oh.'

'Do you have any questions for me? Anything at all? I would have come in person, but I didn't want you to find out from the news. It's possible it might be covered in the papers or on television.'

'No, no. Thank you for calling,' she says, formally. An ambulance siren starts up close, piercingly painful. Cal plugs his other ear and strains to read into the void between them.

'I need to…' Her voice trails away. 'I should speak to Bill.'

He can tell she wants to be off the call, and he has to let her go.

'Call me back,' he says. 'Any time, day or night.'

—

He's not sure why he forgets to call Shona – probably just the overwhelm, the emotion, the preoccupation with his argument with Chrissie. His eyes are scratchy and dry, his throat hurts, and he wants nothing more than to sleep so he picks up a sandwich and some snacks from a grocery shop on his way back to the hotel, his legs like lead as he forces himself up the hill.

He's just dumped his bag of food on the bed in the hotel room, when his phone goes.

'Cal… I heard from Angela a while ago. I've been waiting for you to call. She's got all these questions, and I don't know what to say.'

How could he forget to call her when she's as invested in this case as he is? Cal slumps onto the bed. 'I've just got back to the hotel. I'm sorry, there's been so much going on. I haven't had time to…'

'Is it him, though? Have you found Arran?'

'We think so. There was a skeletonised body in some machinery. The police are testing the remains and they'll let us know as soon as there's an answer.'

This is Shona's area of expertise. She knows well what it means, and the processes and steps needed to identify bones of this age. 'I'll put in a call,' she says. 'Find out who's doing the analysis. Maybe they can hurry things along.'

'That would be amazing, thank you.'

Her voice is colder than usual. 'I just want Angela to have some peace.'

Cal could kick himself. 'I should have called you earlier, I'm sorry. I got caught up in going to the hospital, and Chrissie is furious with me and…'

'What? Why did you go to the hospital?'

He recounts the accident Robbie had, which led to the bones being uncovered.

Shona sounds confused. 'But I don't understand… What was he doing there in the first place?'

'I've… We've been meeting up a bit since I got back. He wanted to help.'

'I can't believe you thought that was a good idea.'

'He's not a child.'

'He could have died, Cal. That's pretty reckless, if you ask me.'

'He's going to be fine.'

'That's not the point. No wonder Chrissie is mad with you. You shouldn't be hanging out with him – he's her ex-boyfriend.'

'That's what she said. But before that, he was my responsibility.'

'You did a podcast on him, Cal. It doesn't mean you're tied for life.' Why is she shouting at him? He can't take this. Not today.

'Yes, it does! That's exactly what it means. I take them with me, all of them. And I ruined Robbie's life, Shona. I destroyed his family.'

He hates the note of hysteria in his own voice.

'You didn't do that. It was all done before you even came on the scene. You have to put some of these things down or you'll go mad.'

'I can't! Don't you get it? When you ask me to take on a case, that's what you're asking me. It's there for life. What happened to them, their families. It never leaves.' His chest heaves with the effort of trying to explain. He thought Shona, of all people, got this.

'I'm sorry if you took this on for me, when you didn't want to.' There are splinters of ice in her tone now.

'No, Shona… that's not what I mean. I'm tired. I need to eat something. I'm not explaining myself properly.'

'Yeah,' she says. 'I should go.'

Before he can say another word, the line goes dead. Cal drops the phone down on the bed and puts his head in his hands. His vision is blurred, his muscles aching. All he wants to do is sleep. Why does it feel that everything is whirling out of control?

CHAPTER FORTY-TWO

Cal is waiting to meet Angela and Bill off the train at Edinburgh Waverley. The wind is whipping through the station under the shadow of the castle, the day as bleak as his mind. He has been down to visit his mother in the intervening days, relieved to see she is being well looked after in the temporary care home, though the family home needed attention: a slow leak in the bathroom soaking the carpet only added to the sense that things are coming apart at the seams.

Though he and Shona have been speaking, there are cracks in their conversations, places where it is better not to step. Chrissie hasn't replied to the apologetic text he sent her. The more days that pass, the harder it seems and the less he knows what to do to make amends. Every time he checks on Robbie, he feels guilty. He woke early this morning and lay staring at the ceiling, unmotivated and too sluggish to get out of bed. His limbs feel heavy as he walks.

When the train wheezes to a stop, Cal scans the platform, searching the waves of people walking towards him: some of them are dragging luggage and chatting, while others appear stony-faced and move at speed, impatient at the slow crowds around them. He sees Angela first, stepping down from the train, one of the last to disembark. It's shocking to think she is the same age as Shona – she looks at least ten years older, her make-up-free skin clear but weathered and ruddy. Angela is fit from the physical work she does on the farm, but there is something wretched in her movements – it is as if she's aching from the inside.

Bill follows, taller than Cal remembers, looking different away from the farm. He's wearing jeans and a jumper, carrying a coat and a rucksack, as well as wheeling a small suitcase. He looks like he could be here as a tourist, to walk Edinburgh's Old Town and drift in and out of the pubs and cafes. Instead, he and Angela are here to meet detectives. They've asked Cal to accompany them.

Angela's face relaxes a little when she sees him. He leans in to give her a hug and she clings for a moment, tight. When she releases him, he shakes Bill's hand. The man avoids his gaze – choosing to look anywhere but into Cal's eyes. His fragility is so stark that he might shatter into a million pieces on this grey platform.

'I thought we could take a taxi,' Cal says, guiding them to the rank of black cabs as if this is his city and not a stranger to him.

Angela grips Bill's hand tightly as the cab lurches up the steep cobbled streets. She tries to smile but it's no more than a brief twist of her lips. Cal holds the grab handle as they round the corner at speed, trying not to fall from his perch.

'Why was he up there?' Angela says, looking at Cal, her face pleading. 'I don't understand.'

'I'm not sure,' he answers. 'It did look like the kind of place where kids might go for parties. Maybe the police will know more.'

'You are coming in with us, aren't you?' Her voice is shrill.

He studies their faces. 'If you want me to, then yes. But I do understand if you'd rather have some privacy. You can tell me about it after, if you prefer.'

Sarah would kill him if she could hear this.

Angela shakes her head. 'We need you there.'

Bill is silent, his gaze fixed on the streets outside.

'Bill?' Cal feels compelled to ask. 'Are *you* sure?'

Arran's father turns as if only just tuning into the conversation, his eyes slightly glazed. In the movement, Cal sees echoes of the son – a similar face structure, perhaps. He is reminded of Chrissie's similarities to Margot, of how it is a comfort to see his sister reflected in the next generation, but for Angela and Bill, it is the reverse – the loss of their son, some of their future.

'Aye,' Bill says, toneless. 'It's fine.'

Cal's tongue feels dry in his mouth. He wonders if he should push further, but Angela's teeth are gritted, her face fixed in an expression of determination, and her hand grips Bill's so tightly that he stays quiet.

The cab arrives at the police station too quickly. It's hard to gather his thoughts before he's paying the fare and helping Bill extract the bag from the back. A dart of bright sunshine sears them for a second. Then they are in and through reception, and walking towards a meeting room where Austin and Pinker are already waiting with a strict-looking woman he doesn't know. It's not a room where they interview suspects, he notes, but a more comfortable suite with softer chairs, carpet and a box of children's toys in the corner.

Austin takes Angela's hand, then Bill's, introducing herself. 'I'm DS Ellie Austin. This is my colleague, DS Ben Pinker.' She smiles a tight smile at Cal and he wonders what's going on, when the strict-looking woman steps forward. She must be a similar age to Cal, heavily made-up and with shiny blonde waves of hair that fall perfectly into place when she moves, like they're made of water.

'Hazel Patrick,' she says, her voice Miss Jean Brodie–posh and clipped. 'I'm from the media team here.'

Cal thinks maybe he catches Austin rolling her eyes but when he looks over to her, she is a picture of innocence.

'Nice to meet you,' he says. But Patrick ignores him.

'It might be better if it was just the two of you,' she tells Angela and Bill, as if it is a foregone conclusion. She holds out an arm to guide Cal to the door. 'I'm happy to take you to reception, where you can wait until we're done.'

The smile is false and brittle, and Cal thinks that, actually, she would prefer to shove him out of the door. Before he can look to Angela for support, Bill's voice sounds out, so loudly that the words bounce off the walls of the room, making them all freeze in position.

'No. He stays.'

'Mr McDonald…'

'It's because of him that we're here. Our son has been missing for thirteen years and you folk have done nothing. Five minutes, this man has been looking into this, and he's found out more than you have in more than a decade.' He looks at Austin and Pinker. 'No offence.'

'None taken,' Austin says, and Cal gets the distinct impression she's as happy to have the press officer put in her place as he is. 'That's fine with us.'

He didn't know until this moment that Bill appreciates the work he is doing.

Patrick huffs.

'I'll just stay over here,' Cal offers quickly, sliding into the space and moving down to a corner, his back against the wall, a safe distance from the carefully arranged chairs. 'You won't know I'm here.'

'I highly doubt that,' Patrick says. 'This is a very sensitive—'

'He needs to stay,' Angela interrupts, her voice trembling, and that settles it.

'No recording,' Patrick snaps at Cal. He takes his hands from his pockets and holds them up as evidence.

They settle onto the chairs and he watches – the fly on the wall. The room is hot. His chest feels tight and it is an effort to take enough air in. High in the corner of the room, a camera watches too, its red light indicating that it's running.

'I'm very sorry about Arran,' Austin says, leaning forward, her forearms resting on her thighs, her voice calm and quiet. 'As you've been told, we have confirmed that the bones found at the grain warehouse definitely belong to your son. We believe, from initial reports we've had from the autopsy, that the remains have been in the hopper somewhere around ten to fifteen years.

We are working on the assumption that Arran did fall or jump from the roof and that he has been there since 2010. Obviously, we will keep an open mind during our investigation.'

Angela draws in a shuddering breath; Bill's face is shuttered and pale. Neither speaks. Pinker passes the box of tissues across the coffee table, and Angela takes one and blows her nose, crumpling it into her fist.

'Our aim is to conclude our investigations quickly and release his remains to you for a funeral.'

'So… why was he up there?' Angela pauses, her eyes red-rimmed, her cheeks streaked with tears that she hasn't wiped away. This is the question everyone wants the answer to. Surely, the police will know more than they do? Cal leans in to hear properly.

Austin opens and closes her mouth, considering her words. When she speaks, her voice sounds less certain than it did before, her sentences slower, feeling their way into the room. 'We know, from talking to his friends and yourselves, that Arran was depressed at the time.' Bill makes a noise of protest. 'But in the absence of evidence that Arran intended to take his own life, we expect the procurator fiscal will find death by misadventure.' She leans in again. 'There really isn't anything for us to investigate, I'm afraid.'

'What about the photograph?' Cal can't stay silent. 'It shows there were other people there.'

Austin glances at the press officer. Patrick's mouth is a tight bud of displeasure. She's watching hawk-like from her seat. 'In truth, we don't know for sure *when* that image was taken. The building has been a target for student parties in the past.' Cal resists the urge to point out that, as the picture was sent the same night that Arran vanished, they could take a wild guess. He doesn't want to be kicked out and there's a tight line of tension between Austin and the PR – he can't quite read what's going on.

'Arran was pictured alone on CCTV, so the theory is that maybe he'd been there with friends on another occasion and

213

returned to the location separately.' *The theory*. Whose is that, he wonders? Austin doesn't look like she's buying it.

The officer glances at Patrick and continues, 'The photograph does suggest that there was a party of some description, but we haven't been able to identify the other people there. We do know from the initial investigation that there were friendship issues and a split from his girlfriend. We will, of course, consider any new evidence that comes to light. However, the manner of his death does fit with the impression that alcohol had been consumed and I'm afraid it may be impossible for us to ever know if it was intentional or not. I'm very sorry for your loss.' At least the last bit sounds sincere.

Cal's head throbs with the closeness of the room, the devastation of the details. He knows Angela and Bill are desperate to know why Arran was in the Leith Docks area at that time of night. Other people were there the night the picture was taken – who were they and where did they go? Did they know he'd fallen? Did they panic and run? Did they leave him to die?

'I'm afraid we have some more details. I'm sorry, but this isn't going to be easy to hear.'

Cal jerks his head to watch Austin. Her skin seems bleached in this light. What could possibly make any of this worse?

CHAPTER FORTY-THREE

EPISODE FIVE: LEFT FOR DEAD

Police tape still runs from the corner of a derelict grain warehouse to a metal hopper that lies rotting into the ground next to the Leith Docks. Destruction of the grain warehouse was scheduled to take place last year but has been delayed by the efforts of campaigners who are keen to preserve the building's history. Sadly for them, those efforts have failed and, next month, diggers are scheduled to raze it to the ground. Shops and a bowling alley are planned in its place.

For now, however, all work has paused under order of Police Scotland. That's because the remains of Arran McDonald were found inside the machinery when Finding Justice *conducted a private search of the building. The hopper was attached to the wall of the building, until it was dislodged during the search, exposing Arran's bones to the light.*

'I can't believe he's been in there and we didn't know.'

Natalie was Arran's girlfriend – they'd broken up right before he vanished. 'All this time and he was right there. How is that possible?'

It seems that the only way Arran could have ended up in the hopper was if he jumped or fell from the roof above. The same roof where he was photographed drinking vodka, surrounded by other people.

'I just don't know why he would have been there.' Natalie is adamant that Arran wasn't the type to participate in dangerous drinking games or initiations.

The thought of Arran dying alone in the remote location is upsetting enough. However, police have revealed further disturbing information. Listeners are advised to exercise caution, as they may find the following details distressing.

The stage of decomposition means it is difficult to be sure about some things — cause of death is unclear, for example, but we know from the autopsy that Arran broke his leg and some ribs. There was a fracture to his skull. This is all consistent with a fall.

Although partly clothed in the picture we have seen, by the time he fell, Arran appears to have been only wearing underwear. No traces of other items of clothing have been found. The night he went missing, it was typical Edinburgh January weather, cold and wild. Temperatures dropped as low as -2 degrees centigrade that night. The only item found with him was a striped scarf — it is not something his parents recognise.

But by far the most harrowing news from the report is that it seems Arran may have been alive for a while after he fell into the machinery. On examination, his fingernails appeared broken and torn, and there were deep scratches in the hopper that could have come from someone trying desperately to pull themselves free.

Who else was there that night? Did he cry out? Did they hear him? Why didn't they help him?

CHAPTER FORTY-FOUR

ARRAN, 2009

Hogmanay arrives, the weather clear and the cold tight as a bowstring, fields glittering with the hardness of frost on top of snow.

They've always organised a ceilidh for friends and neighbours, and this year is no exception. Kirsty is to be allowed to play the fiddle for the first time, joining the cribbed-together band for the songs she knows, and the house echoes with the sound of her practising, her feet stamping in time to the beat.

'She'll come through the ceiling,' their father complains, though he isn't actually angry. Kirsty is the one who unites them all – so different from the rest of the family that they all instinctively want to protect her from each other. She's their mother's baby, but no one minds.

Now, his father and Gillian are lining the walls with fresh bales to be used as seating, stringing lines of lights above. But his mother wanted him to stay with her. His father didn't put up the usual resistance. He and Arran have been arguing ever since he returned, constantly butting heads over the smallest thing, so maybe his dad doesn't want to be near him. He seems to prefer Gillian these days.

'How many of your pals are coming out, then?' Angela asks Arran, as she prepares great sides of beef to cook for sandwiches, piles mounds of floury baps and cuts trays of the sweet tablet that she's known for. Everyone will bring a dish and some drink. The trestle tables will be heaving, the air hot with voices and thick with alcohol.

Has she noticed that he's not been out to meet any of his school or farming pals since he returned? Does she know he's ignored the group chats and the pub meets? It's a small community. Someone will have been talking.

'I'm nay sure,' he says, shrugging. 'Haven't really caught up with them yet.'

His mother says nothing, and the silence between them is heavy.

He carries the meat to the oven for her, slides the trays in. Tiredness seeps through his bones and he wishes he could bury himself beneath the covers until it's all over. He keeps wishing Jonno, Colleen and Olivia were going to be here, drunk and different, shocking his family, no doubt, but something of his own. Only, he's fucked that all up and he doesn't know if he can fix it. Nat dropped hints about visiting, but he's told her it's too far, that he'll see her in the New Year.

His mother puts her hand on his arm.

'You'd say, wouldn't you, if something were wrong?'

His eyes slide from hers. 'Aye.'

–

It all explodes in the hour before everyone arrives. His father is shaving; his mother is wearing a fitted dress and gold earrings, her make-up done, looking pretty and pink with the heat and the anxiety and anticipation of guests. She loves this time of year.

He doesn't want to ruin it for her. Arran has showered and is forcing his unwilling limbs into smarter clothes, buttoning a shirt for the first time since he came home. His mother has only just ironed it for him and it's still warm. He straightens the sporran on his kilt. Kirsty is tuning up her violin for the tenth time.

He casts a glance around. Something is different.

Someone has been in here. In his stuff. His books have slipped from the shelves, some clearly shoved back in with no care, some of the pages creased. Someone has been rummaging in his space, in the one place he can get away from them all. His body tenses as he looks around for the red jumper that Jonno gave him as an early Christmas present. He relaxes as he sees it stuffed down the back of the bed, but when he pulls it out, Arran's breath catches. There is a long slash in the soft material, a hole too big to be accidental. He stands for a moment, disbelieving. And then he remembers Gilly's disdain for his 'posh ways', the petty jealousy in her eyes. She saw how important this was to him.

Arran is filled with a heat that won't be doused, a burning mist that moves through him, obliterating thought. He slams back his door and heads for the girls' room, where Gillian is scowling at herself in the mirror, forced into a skirt for the night, ungainly as a fresh calf.

'What the hell did you do this for?' He brandishes the jumper and his voice sounds different.

He sees the flicker in her eyes before denial. 'I don't know what you're talking about. I haven't done anything to your precious cashmere.'

'Don't lie, Gillian!' He's bellowing now, and Kirsty's tuning stops abruptly.

'I'm not lying. I'm sick of you. When are you going back? It's so much better when you're not here. We all hate having you here!'

Her eyes blaze and he advances towards her, fury running through him, incomprehensible and uncontrollable.

'Why are you always such a bitch?' he shouts, spit flying from his mouth.

Nothing makes sense. He loathes himself, is afraid of what he is doing and yet he can't stop. His hand flies out and he slaps her. Gilly's hand jumps to her cheek, hiding the pink flare of finger marks, the echo of horror.

'Arran!' His mother's voice from the doorway shocks him back into himself. His father appears behind her.

'Whit's going on?' The voice of authority.

Silence and stillness.

Arran feels his face on fire. He looks at them, quaking inside, and then back at Gillian, whose eyes are wide, though her hand has dropped now and the marks are fading. Then he steps back with his hands held up in surrender, the red jumper still dangling, and bursts into tears. As he pushes past his parents, slamming into his bedroom like a hormonal fourteen-year-old, he feels the shock in the air and sees Kirsty's pale face watching from the doorway of their parents' room, fiddle dangling by her side, bow in her hand.

He dumps the jumper into the bin and throws himself onto his bed, punching the pillow hard three times. Then he buries his head in it and screams and screams.

He can hear his sister's raised voice protesting over his mother's tones – nothing from his father – and a cold, scared kernel shakes inside his chest. He's pushed it too far, he's going to be for it now. But no one comes. He wishes they would. It's so much worse just waiting.

He lies there in the dark listening to the first cars pulling into the yard, and the laughter and greetings called. Doors slam, voices shimmer, the dogs bark and no one shuts them up. More people come, and more and more, and with the sound of their happiness comes the dark underlay of shame. He is not like them. He is not good. In the barn the music strikes up and as he lies there, he fancies he can hear the thread of Kirsty's music among it all. Something to cling to as he unravels.

He must have fallen asleep, because he's woken by a soft knock on the door to his room and then Kirsty pushes in, a silhouette with the light behind her.

'Arran?'

He wipes his face with the back of his hand. It's still wet – has he been crying in his sleep? How long has it been? He sits up to see her, making his voice soft because he doesn't want to scare her and he knows he did, earlier. He doesn't want to scare anyone. This isn't him, it's a monster who's taken root inside him.

'Yes?'

'Are you coming?'

He shakes his head. 'Maybe in a bit, I'm no feeling too good right now.'

She waits a moment, shifting from one foot to the other. She's wearing a dress of red sequins and she sparkles like Dorothy on the yellow brick road. His chest hurts.

'I want you to hear me play.'

'Me too. I'll be over in a wee moment, then.' He forces the tremor in his voice down, gentles it, for her.

'Okay.' And she closes the door softly, skipping away down the hall to the stairs, believing him.

CHAPTER FORTY-FIVE

ARRAN, 2010

He sloshes through ankle-deep slush, his feet and jeans soaking and frozen, but the heat of self-hatred keeps him going long enough to reach the road. It's dark and the snow is starting up again, but he doesn't care, just wraps his scarf tighter around his face and trudges in the direction of the village. The strap of his bag cuts into his shoulder, burning, making his body twist and ache, but he doesn't care. He just needs to be away from here.

He's been walking for maybe an hour, face tight in the cold, body wet with sweat, slush and falling flakes. It's starting to occur to him that there will be no buses or trains at any hour, not on New Year's Day. He's totally alone, walking the twisting country roads he knows like the back of his hand, the way only lighted by the lacklustre reflection of the moon on the snow-covered fields. Where is he going? What is he going to do?

He reaches the turn with the main road out of Inverness and stops, his breath heaving, sending clouds of condensation into the air. Now that he's still, he starts to shiver, the cold like a knife cutting him, reaching the innermost parts.

He starts to walk again, heading south, wondering if he can find somewhere to shelter until the trains start running and he can go back to Edinburgh. It seems unfathomable that he could turn around and face his family. He's so ashamed. Lost in self-recrimination, Arran doesn't realise there are headlights behind him until he hears a car making that wet-tyre-through-the-slush sloshing sound and realises he is about to be caught in an arc of ice water that is spattering onto the banks of snow on the side of the road. At the last moment, he cowers away, raising his arm to protect his face, bracing for the impact.

But instead, there's the slide of brakes on wet road and the vehicle turning away from him, drifting into the empty carriageway. He thinks that maybe the car is going to swerve off the road, but it corrects at the last minute. The slowing reduces the size of the arc so the spatter only reaches his waist, drenching his already-soaked clothes. Everything comes to a shuddering halt.

Arran lets out a held breath just as the door of the car clicks open, causing heavy music to fall into the cold outdoors. A hand must reach to turn it down, because it dulls.

'Shit, pal. Sorry, I didnae see you there.'

'It's okay,' he splutters. Though it isn't okay, nothing is.

'Wait… Arran? Is that you?'

He swivels to look properly at the driver.

'Donny?'

'Aye! Whit you daeing oot here in the early hours? Do you need a lift?'

He steps closer to the car, hope flaring beneath the ice of his skin.

'How far are you going?'

'All the way, min! All the way…' Donny throws back his head and laughs, and Arran sees it's a miracle the other boy didn't hit him: he's high as a kite.

'Woah, you sure you should be driving, like?'

Donny looks at him with red-rimmed eyes, suddenly sober.

'Maybe no, but I have a delivery to make and it's late. Wisnae ma fault. It come in late aff the boat. Was supposed to be in Edinburgh long afore the bells, so they're going mad.'

Feeling as though he'd been drowning, Arran looks up to the surface and catches the glowing serendipity above him, reaches for it.

'I can drive you,' he says, pointing at the undulating tyre tracks. 'You'll be stopped by the police if you can't go in a straight line.'

Donny pales. 'Dinnae say that.'

Arran holds his hand out for the car keys. 'We'll be fine,' he says. 'Just tell me where you need to go.'

–

Mercifully, Donny sleeps most of the way, waking up starving at about the time they're going to need to stop for petrol anyway. They pull into a remote service station and Arran loads up on snacks while Donny fills the car. The wind is howling now, but under the shelter of the forecourt, he stretches the kinks out of his spine. His eyes are dry and tired; he's been leaning forward, concentrating on the dark road and the difficult conditions. The ploughs were out yesterday but new snow is falling on the gritted roads, making it skitey.

He's shutting his mind off to it all, he decides. He has to be away from his family, back to Edinburgh to wait for the others, and he'll make it all right. He just needs to talk to them, that's all – Olivia, Jonno and Colleen – make them understand, make them see. It will all be just fine.

Donny awake is much more hassle than Donny asleep. He's jittery and twitchy now, jerking his arm across the steering wheel to point out imagined hazards to Arran, blethering about everything and nothing. Boats and fishermen, money and cargo.

'Just this one mair time,' he says, looking out the window in a calm moment. 'And that's it.'

'Sounds like a good idea to stop,' Arran tells him.

'Aye, but the money. It's hard to turn down the money.'

'How much do you make, like?'

'I'm getting a good cut. And a flat. It's a chance, for the future. I know what you think of me.'

The moment of clarity shames Arran – Donny's right. He's been judging the hell out of him, but who is he to judge? After everything he's done.

'No,' he tells him. 'You're all right.'

CHAPTER FORTY-SIX

CAL

Angela is swaying, moaning a little. Bill has her shoulder gripped in his hand and there's a wildness in his eyes. There's little more to say and the state Arran's parents are in suggests they won't hear it anyway. The horror floats between them all. Arran was alive.

Cal follows them to the doorway and down the corridor. 'I can take them to the door,' the PR woman tells Austin.

'No, no,' the DS says firmly. 'I'll walk you down.'

Hazel Patrick frowns, and then keeps up a pointless and chipper commentary about it being *this way* and *almost there* as they walk, as though she's filling the space so no one can say anything meaningful. Cal wishes she would read the room and shut the fuck up.

At reception, they guide Angela and Bill to plastic chairs that are bolted to the floor.

'Thank you, Hazel,' Austin says brightly. 'I can take it from here.' The dismissal leaves no option for the press officer but to clip off into the bowels of the place on her vertiginous heels. The jovial sound sets his teeth on edge. Cal follows Austin to the desk to get the number of a taxi, still reeling from the details they've just been told.

When they've put in the call, she pulls him away from the desk, to the side. He can see that telling Arran's parents the gory details has left her drained. 'Off the record...' She speaks in a low voice. 'It wasn't my idea to have her there, I'm sorry.

They're worried about legal action.' She glances over at Arran's parents.

'They just want answers. It doesn't feel right, given what we know: the photograph, the chance someone else was there,' he tries. 'Is there nothing you can do to check that out?'

Austin frowns. 'My hands are tied,' she says. 'Off the record, the official view is that it was thirteen years ago, all of those students are long gone and there are *competing priorities*. The feeling from on high is that they need to be grateful we've got any kind of resolution.'

'Resolution?'

She winces. 'I know. Their words, not mine.'

'How do I tell them that those are all the answers they can expect to get? The horror of knowing he was alive, conscious.' He feels his stomach hollow out at the thought of it.

Austin looks up at him. Her eyes are clear and piercing, a fierceness in them that reminds him again of Foulds. 'Well…' she says. 'They have you on their side and if I were you, I'd keep going. Between us?'

Cal nods.

'There's been unusual recalcitrance from the bosses on this one.'

'What does that mean?'

Austin shakes her head. 'I don't know.'

Without another word, she raises a hand to Angela and Bill. He doesn't have time to process her words before she is gone.

–

Cal drops Arran's parents at their simple bed and breakfast, watching the two of them supporting each other as they walk, bent under the regret and pain. He knows Gillian is holding down the fort at the farm, that she's capable of taking that strain, but they seem so out of place here, away from their comfort zone and purpose, doing the right thing for their son at such cost to themselves.

'I just don't understand,' Angela says as he turns to go. He pivots back, her voice barely a whisper. 'I wish I knew what he was doing up there.' Her eyes are glassy with tiredness.

'We'll try and find out,' Cal says. 'Someone must know. I'll talk to his friends again. Maybe now he's been found, someone will come forward.'

She squeezes his arm then follows her husband into the bed and breakfast, her shoulders stooped.

He backs away, suddenly desperate to walk, to be free for a moment, of all of it. And yet, he finds himself striding, of all places, back down to the Leith Walkway, cutting his way inland this time, through parts of the city, over bridges and across roads, following the brown churn of the river like a guiding star. The statues in the water never fail to startle him: faces turned downstream, some clothed like real people, catching the corner of his eye. He reaches the massive viaduct at Dean Village and emerges into the tourist trap, the tranquil view held before him.

He wishes Chrissie were here, or Shona. Not for the first time, he wonders if he can keep doing this, taking on the burden of other people's pain and adding it to his own. He wants to go back in time and shake Arran, hug him, get him help. It feels like so much of him is still hidden. What happened to him in Edinburgh to change him so much? Maybe drug-taking is the answer, though none of the friends he has interviewed have said they saw him using. It would perhaps explain the personality change, depression, moods?

His phone rings. It's almost dark now and the streetlights guide his way back up to the West End of the city, to the cafes and bars, to the relentless march of Princes Street under the shadow of the castle. He answers and it's Bill. He sounds uncomfortable, no good at small talk.

'Angela's asleep. She's very upset. We've been talking.'

'It must be so difficult for you. I'm sorry that I can't make this any easier.'

Bill pauses. 'These bobbies, they just want us to go away, to agree it was suicide. Angela is adamant it wasn't. I don't know… Maybe it was, but where were his friends when it happened? That's what makes me so mad. Why did they leave him? It doesn't make sense that he'd be up there alone. If they were just messing about and he fell, then we'd understand. It would just help… to know.'

Bill lapses into silence. Cal wants to tell him that there's always something else that will help, always something else to know, that it never ends, ever. But it isn't his place to say that. And maybe it isn't true for their family. His experience isn't everyone's.

'How do we make them listen? Can you make them listen?'

'We can try,' Cal says. 'I'll speak to them all again and the podcast might bring other people out of the woodwork. It has a good reach but that could be slow. Another option would be doing a public appeal for other people who were on the roof to come forward. But that's a lot to ask of you both – talking to journalists.'

'Like on television?'

'Yes. And newspapers. Though we could limit it to an interview with you both that we share more widely.'

'Could we do that?'

'I can look into it for you. Let me have a think and talk to Sarah. You should sleep on it, too, see if you feel the same in the morning. Talk to Angela.'

'Aye, I will. But I have to dae something. Angela's had to take a pill to go off. She's just not right. I don't think she's going to be able to rest without knowing. He was her boy…'

His voice breaks.

'He was your boy too.'

'I was too hard on him. I thought I had to be, that there'd be plenty of time to make it up.'

'None of this is your fault.' He sounds like a broken record with this phrase.

229

But when he rings off, he can tell there is nothing that can comfort Bill when it comes to the fractured relationship he had with his son. Realisation has come too late. Cal thinks of his own daughter. Of how lives can be broken off with no notice and with no time to say goodbye or make amends. He takes his phone from his pocket.

> I'm sorry. I should have thought more carefully about how all this would affect you. I want to give you all the space you need but I also want you to know that I'm sorry and I love you. There's only one child I want and that's you. Here whenever you need me. Dad xx

It's not perfect, but better than nothing. He presses send and his breath catches when he sees the tick turn blue. He waits a moment. She doesn't reply, but then a heart emoji reaction pops up on the message and his body floods with the warmth of relief. It will have to do for now.

Next, he calls and speaks to Sarah, as he walks.

'A TV interview? You're sure they're up for that?'

'I'll need to talk to them again tomorrow, but he sounded quite determined. Someone must know something, and it might put pressure on them to come forward. Is it an option, do you think?'

'Definitely, and it can only be good for numbers.'

Cal rolls his eyes.

'I can see that eye-roll from here.'

'You're a witch.'

'No. *You're* predictable. And your silences are loaded.'

He laughs.

'I've got just the thing, in fact.' Mischief has entered her voice.

'Really?'

'An old friend of yours has been in touch about doing a follow-up and this would be perfect.'

Confused, he waits a beat and then it hits him.

'Oh. No, no way. Absolutely not.'

CHAPTER FORTY-SEVEN

Shona is completely against the idea. She calls him, furious, as soon as she hears.

'I can't believe you're asking them to do this, Cal! They don't know how any of this works – they're going to be chewed up and spat out by the media. Remember what Jacinta did with you? And this is literally your job. I don't think they're psychologically prepared. This isn't fair on them. It's too much—'

'Hey,' he finally interrupts when it seems she isn't going to stop of her own accord. 'They asked *me*.'

'What?'

'They asked *me*, not the other way round. I've posed the same questions you have. I have reservations. They're adamant they want to do it. He was their son, Shona. It's their call, not mine.'

She's silent a moment. He can taste her unhappiness in it. Part of this is his fault, not keeping her in the loop, leaving her to react rather than be included, but ever since the trial, it's been a struggle to engage with the world. He finds himself doing the minimum needed, and still exhausted at the end of it.

'I'm sorry,' she says at last. 'I should have given you the benefit of the doubt.'

Her words linger long after their conversation. Neither of them really gives the other much leeway at the moment.

It's not Jacinta herself doing the interview, in the end. Cal insists and won't be budged, telling the station that someone needs to be with Angela and Bill in person, refusing a remote connection with the main studio as is originally mooted. He is determined that Arran's parents won't have the kind of experience he had on the show. No audience is worth that, and he wouldn't put it past Jacinta to use them to score points by hauling them over the coals.

At one point he threatens to walk away and go to a rival news programme, hanging up on the morning show's producer. When Sarah calls him ten minutes later, they have acquiesced to his demands. He still has to listen to Sarah berating him about the opportunity he's almost cost the podcast.

They settle on a Scottish interviewer, Hayley Laing, who is based in Edinburgh and a regular correspondent on the morning TV show that Jacinta fronts. Everyone is sort of happy, and that will have to do.

'Someone with a heart instead of a rock, I hope,' he growls to Sarah, and she laughs, thinking that he's joking. He really isn't.

They also agree to a pre-recorded piece, along with footage of the couple laying flowers at the grain warehouse where Arran's body was found. This, Cal raises with the couple over coffee the next day. Though they continue to be resolute when it comes to doing the appeal, he thinks they are still in shock, so he doesn't want to put pressure on them or engineer a situation they can't cope with.

'It might trigger memories for people, seeing the building,' he tells Angela and Bill. 'But if it's too much for you, just say and we can ask them to shoot that separately. It's fine.'

'I think I want to see it,' Angela says, looking at Bill for agreement.

He grips her hand briefly, the smallest indication of the deep affection that Cal has grown to appreciate lies between them.

Bill turns to him. Nods. 'Set it up,' he says. 'We'll do it.'

-

The warehouse looks bigger than he remembers it. They step from the taxi into thin drizzle and a low grey sky, the perfect accompaniment to the mood. Their heads automatically tilt upwards, looking for the place where he fell.

'I can smell the sea,' Angela says, faintly, though her eyes don't move from the warehouse.

She is clutching an armful of white roses, purchased from an eye-wateringly expensive florist off the Royal Mile. Cal was about to offer to pay for them, but this is their memory, their tribute to their son, and Bill waved away his wallet. A police officer manning the cordon lifts it to let them through. Hayley Laing is standing off to the side with a cameraman and Cal signals to her to give them a moment. Wrapped in a thick coat, holding a red umbrella, she offers out-of-place glamour – like a slick of lipstick on a hangover – but she makes no move to approach, giving them time to come to her.

Now that they are here, Cal feels overwhelmed with negativity and dread, almost shuddery and cold at the memory of Robbie lying on the ground, so close to Arran's remains. He'd be happy if he never saw this site again. What happened that night? Was Arran drinking on the roof with friends? Taking drugs? And why did they leave him?

Bill asks him to show him what happened when he and Robbie were here, so he points to where the walkway parted company from the wall and talks him through it – the support falling free, dislodging the hopper leading to the silo. The older man frowns and says little, just fixes his eyes on the rooftop above. The cameraman takes footage while Angela lays the flowers against the stained metal, and then he and Cal retreat to the cordon, leaving Arran's parents to their thoughts and memories.

'Quite a place,' Hayley says to him, offering a hand for him to shake. 'You found Arran's body?' Her voice is softer than he expected, but then he was bristling for Jacinta mark II.

'It was a fluke, really. One of the people I was with tried the steps and it all just fell away. He was in that hopper.'

Hayley shivers and Cal warms to her empathy. She speaks to the cameraman, who swivels to record the rusting hopper again, an intimidating giant of crushed metal.

'This won't take long,' she tells him. 'We'll just ask them a few questions and then come to you. If you could talk through the appeal you're making, that would be great.'

'No problem.'

Before them, Angela crumples. Bill reaches out and holds her steady against his side. Cal looks away, out to the almost-visible sea, and thinks of Shona, feeling the distance between them in the bleakness. They don't have those years of history to fall back on. That's what he had in his marriage with Allie. You can't recreate that in a short space of time; it takes knocks and damage, resealing the cracks over and again. It's painful and beautiful to watch.

Around them, industrial Leith continues its final death throes, encroached upon by the bars and restaurants, the apartment conversions. Soon, the warehouse will be razed to the ground too, making way for new living, plastering over old ways.

Finally, Angela and Bill are ready, and Cal stands beside them as Hayley sets everything up. Calm and unfussy, she reassures them by telling them what she's going to ask.

'We can do it again if we need to, but I don't want to keep you out here longer than we have to,' she says. 'Just relax, if you can.'

She starts by asking them about Arran and what he was like as a child. Cal feels Angela soften beside him as she talks. It passes in only a few moments: simple questions about him coming to university and going missing. Before he knows it, she's turning to him.

'Cal Lovett is the podcaster behind the *Finding Justice* series, which investigates cold cases of missing and murdered people. Cal, you helped find Arran's remains, using just a photograph of him taken that evening. He'd been missing for thirteen years. Do you think the police are doing enough to find him?'

Cal's mouth twitches and a moment of journalistic amusement passes between them. *I have to try*, she seems to be saying. He gets it, raising an eyebrow in acknowledgement and then dodging the invitation to criticise the police, remembering Austin and her frustration with the diktat from her bosses.

'When your child is missing, there can never be *enough*,' he says. 'The important thing now for Angela and Bill is to get answers about what happened to Arran that night. We believe another student or students may have been on the roof with him, perhaps having a party, and we'd like to appeal to anyone who knows what might have happened to come forward and speak to us in confidence.'

Hayley pivots to Angela.

'Angela, what would it mean to you to get some answers? What if the conclusion is that Arran took his own life? What would you say to people who think that?'

There's a second when Angela's face blanches and Cal thinks he will have to step in. A tear rolls down her cheek and her grief is palpable, a tortured creature beside them. Then she takes a deep, heaving breath and looks right into the camera.

'Please,' she says, letting the tears run freely, making no move to wipe them away. 'Arran was my son. I need to know how he died. I need to know what happened to him. No matter what that was.'

Then she buries her head in Bill's jacket and Cal steps in front of them.

'We've got enough,' Hayley says before he can protest.

The cameraman is already backing away towards the vehicle they arrived in – job done, deadline to meet. But Hayley, at least, has the decency to wait while Angela composes herself.

'You did brilliantly,' she says. 'It will be on the local news tonight and the breakfast show in the morning.'

–

Exhausted, Cal deposits Angela and Bill at their bed and break-fast. Pale as bleached linen, they don't speak in the cab. They don't even look around them at the vast city and its flotsam, just gaze fixedly ahead, each lost in their own thoughts and horrors. Occasionally, Angela gasps back tears, like she's coming up for air, and then Bill strokes her hand with calloused fingers, soothing her like he would an injured animal.

At six o'clock, he watches the news bulletin on TV, seeing again how isolated and forbidding the grain warehouse is. Somehow, Hayley and the cameraman managed to secure access to the rooftop. The camera pans across the debris up there, and he is plunged back to the first day they went to the roof. The shoe that he and Robbie found can't have been Arran's – it was way too small. But the memory of it lying there empty still gives him chills. Only seconds later, the report is over.

Tomorrow he will start again with Arran's friends, hoping that someone will know why he might have been up there and will be prepared to speak now that his remains have been found.

A couple of hours later, Cal opens his laptop and checks his email. Most of it is the usual jumble of spam and press releases, though there is an invitation to speak at an event in Birmingham next month, so he forwards it to Sarah to confirm.

Still preoccupied by the cloud of dark thoughts, he almost deletes the message. Has already clicked 'archive' when the subject line penetrates his mind and rebounds on the inside of his skull. *For Angela.* He recalls it to his inbox, his senses firing. The message comes from an email address that is a jumble of numbers and letters. Classic spam. And yet…

There is no text in the body of the email, only a video file. He sits up straight, glancing around the drab room as if the sender might be here, watching him. Knowing his luck, it's a virus that's going to destroy everything on his machine. He should leave it.

He stares at the file. Fuck it. Before he can talk himself out of it, Cal hits play. At least his audio is backed up to the cloud, so he won't lose any of the podcast.

A rooftop at night-time. A cold dagger through him.

Whatever sound there was has barely been captured. Only the fuzz of static and the echo of what might be shouts. It's easy to forget how far video technology has come in only a decade or so. Cal is forced to reduce the volume, as the loudness of the nothing hurts his ears. What he sees on screen turns his stomach.

Arran, in the distance. On his knees. He only knows it is the boy because of the location – clearly, the rooftop of the warehouse. Stripped to the waist in the glittering frost, his mouth making dragon puffs of condensation in the freezing Edinburgh night. But, they were right. He isn't alone, and there isn't just one person with him either. He's surrounded. There must be ten other students on the roof, all male, dressed in dinner jackets, bow ties hanging. Cal leans in.

The cold tick of the radiator and the hum of traffic on the road below his room recede. He exclaims as Arran doubles over, vomiting, and the crowd of young men jump back to avoid the splatter. The prone boy is shaking, the nubs of his spine visible. A burst of tenderness explodes inside Cal. He wants to take the youth in his arms. Wrap him in a blanket and remove him from the taunting, the prying eyes. Angela's child.

The video is seven minutes long. Seven minutes too long. At one point, Cal has to pause and take deep breaths, sickness rising inside him, jostling with despair. Moments like this demonstrate the bloodlust and absence of humanity that groups can display when they fire themselves up.

It feels so voyeuristic, watching this footage. Is he going to witness a murder? Maybe he should turn it in to the police without watching any more. But then he thinks of the instruction from the top for Austin and Pinker not to investigate Arran's case any further. There are some who see the media as no more than prying jackals, but he takes his role as a check and balance seriously. He needs to bear witness, owes that to Angela and Bill, even if seeing it changes him forever.

He sits up straight against the headboard, pulling the covers close around him for a semblance of protection or comfort. Then he presses play.

–

When it is over, Cal lies awake, unable to find the peace to sleep. He wants to speak to Shona, but he can't do that to her. Doesn't want her to have to fall asleep with the same thoughts in her head that are circling his. The covers feel scratchy against his skin, and the noises of the pipes and footsteps in the hotel seem louder and more intrusive than usual. How can he ever be free of this horror? Unsee what he's seen? Only when he feels his pillow is wet does he realise he's been crying. Dawn is peering round the edge of the heavy curtains by the time he finally manages to sleep.

CHAPTER FORTY-EIGHT

EPISODE SIX: ON THE ROOF

It's agony to watch. So, it's hard to imagine how painful it was to experience.

As a result of the appeal Arran's parents made for people to come forward with information, footage of the Edinburgh student on the roof of the Leith Docks grain warehouse has been sent to Finding Justice *anonymously. This sets the photograph we already had access to into a wider context. What the recording appears to show is some kind of hazing or initiation ceremony.*

Around ten other people were on the roof that night, dressed in black tie. Whatever their original intention, those ten people tortured Arran. Stripped to his pants in sub-zero temperatures, he is made to drink very large amounts of alcohol, despite begging them to stop.

The other men on the roof ignore his distress. They force his head back and tip vodka into his mouth straight from the bottle. He is also made to drink what appears to be some kind of oil, and a dead eel is shoved into his underwear. Arran is made to kiss the eel while the crowd jeer at him and some of them kick him in the ribs. As they turn to go, one of the figures unbuckles his trousers and urinates on the vulnerable student, while he lies curled into a ball. The footage ends shortly after, but Arran does not appear to move, remaining a foetal shape covered in urine, vomit and alcohol. They treated him worse than you would an animal.

Shortly after this was filmed, Arran would be dead. Whether he fell, jumped or was pushed from the rooftop, we don't yet know, because the footage stops before that point. But someone was filming that night, someone knows something. We think you want to talk.

Arran's parents have been told what the footage contains but have decided not to watch it. Angela says that's not how she wants to remember her son.

'I can't believe they would do that to another human being. He was my child, my boy. My only comfort is that if Arran took his own life that night, he won't have been in his right mind after what happened to him. He won't have meant to... will he?'

'No, I don't think so.'

[Sound of sobbing]

'It's okay. Take your time.'

'It's just... that's the best I can hope for, now. What kind of comfort is that for a mother to take?'

CHAPTER FORTY-NINE

While it's now becoming clearer what happened to Arran – some sort of hazing or initiation on the rooftop that ended in disaster – Cal feels he's at an impasse. What was the club or group he was part of? What bound them together? He has no record of Arran being a member of any societies, for example. Who was there? What happened after the camera stopped rolling? Did Arran, broken and out of his senses, simply walk off the edge? Did he jump as a result of the torture? Why did the little fucks just leave him there to die?

He can't rest, can't just leave it to the police, so he listens back to the recordings and previous episodes to refocus. The thing that strikes him most is that the friends Arran shared a corridor with in his only term have been so one-dimensional in their responses. He remembers the wistful jealousy he glimpsed on Natalie's face when she talked about the closeness of those relationships – surely, there should have been more depth and richness to their stories, their memories. Are they hiding something? Protecting someone?

He'll have to push them again, he decides. Hard. And maybe in the meantime the open-source experts can help him identify some of the figures in the video. If they can finger one or two, the others will fall like dominoes. It's human nature. No one wants to take the rap alone.

Right now, it's time to get to work. To analyse the footage, despite the horror of it. To do his job. Steeling himself, he returns to the video. He notices that none of the members of the group tormenting Arran on the rooftop look at the camera

– either they don't want to incriminate themselves or they don't know they are being filmed. Curious. He grabs his phone and scrolls to his photographs of the scene. There are the remains of a rusting tank in the corner, close to the stairs down. Could the camera have been positioned there? Why?

Did one of the group film without the others' knowledge? For insurance or blackmail, perhaps? Surely, the person who sent him the video… They must be the weak link, must feel bad enough to have sent it. It can be no coincidence that he's received this after the footage of Arran's stricken parents has been aired. Angela's tears are enough to melt the hardest of hearts. Professional satisfaction stirs inside him. It's working.

But the momentary lightness dissipates as he watches the screen. It terrifies Cal: the lack of feeling in the mob, the bloodlust and the cold cruelty. This time, he notices one of the figures holding out a phone at one point – the brief flash of light before someone beside him jostles him, perhaps in censure, and the device is tucked away.

Cal drums his fingers on the table – the photograph that led them to this point. He pulls it up on screen and checks. The original image looks even more sinister now. It has mutated, transmogrifying into something bigger in the wide-angle context. He compares the video and the still. The angle works. The picture was taken by one of the participants, then.

He goes back to the Facebook message again but all there is is that laughing emoji. The sender is simply Anony4321 – a defunct profile that leads to nothing. And yet, the profile image itself is distinctive. A silhouette on a rooftop, the Edinburgh skyline behind, lights gleaming. He peers at it, his mind idling, his eyes wired open. What if the profile is fake but the picture is real?

Cal clicks on a web page that allows him to search for the image elsewhere online. He expects a million options or none, but instead there are only four. His mind jerks awake. He makes an instant coffee and settles back at the desk to follow the breadcrumbs. They lead him to an old Flickr account – a series of pictures of Edinburgh: arty, moody shots – the kind of thing Chrissie takes to capture the atmosphere she needs for her drawings.

And then he looks at the profile name. A Runner. Someone into running? Or a name? Something pings inside him, jostling with the coffee-induced jitters. But the connection won't come. Cal types the identity into a search engine and adds 'Edinburgh student', his mind twisting around to remember, but before he can, bang, up comes the answer. A man, the right age now, gazing into the camera confidently, assured of his place in the world. The newest member of the Scottish Parliament. Andrew Runner. Son of a judge.

His fingers fumble the keys, and he swears and deletes, types slowly. When he finds it, he scans the MSP's biography page, scrolling until he finds the details he's looking for. Bingo. Runner studied economics at Edinburgh University. More googling, mistyping and frustration, before he traces the dates back, calculating the time the man spent in industry, working back from his selection as Conservative candidate and the campaigning years.

He grabs a piece of paper and jots down all the details, circling the gaps until he can fill them. Then, there it is: undeniably, the dates match. Andrew Runner was a student when Arran was a student. His mind quakes with the possibility. Cal stands and shakes his head, unsure if he's making something out of nothing.

He runs his fingers through his hair, feeling groggy still – he's had no sleep since he watched this atrocity. He makes another coffee and takes it into the minuscule en-suite, running the shower ultra-hot and standing under the stream, forcing himself awake. Making himself think.

Wrapped in a towel, he returns to the computer and googles again, scanning, reading, saving links. He's about to give up, when he finds it. An obscure reference to the 'Saltire Circle'. Cal frowns. He hasn't heard of it, but Runner was apparently its president for a year.

He searches for the society and surprisingly few results appear. Those that do aren't hugely informative. It appears in the list of university clubs and had filed accounts, had charitable status. There isn't anything recent, so he wonders if it disbanded.

He is about to give up and move on, when he finds an article in a student newspaper. It's a diatribe against the proliferation of old boys' clubs in the university, spaces that female students are excluded from – in fact, most seem to be excluded from. The author protests against the behaviour of the elite in these clubs, alleging wild parties, sexual assault and destruction of property. Above all, the article rails against the sort of closed shop where wealth opens doors to future leadership, and privilege is passed between a select few.

Past members are apparently now judges, politicians and business leaders. Cal clicks back to the image of Andrew Runner. Could he be the one who took the photograph on the roof all those years ago? If so, he could know what happened to Arran, who the other people were. But if that's the case, he's been keeping that secret for thirteen years. He's not going to thank Cal for bringing it out into the open now.

It's only when he looks back at the article that he notices the name of the writer. Another flare. He's getting closer.

CHAPTER FIFTY

He hangs around outside Colleen's office, determined to push for some more answers. Security is hardly top-notch – the man juggling three cups of coffee thanks him for rushing to hold the door open rather than realising he doesn't have a pass. Cal's heart rate rises as he walks past reception, hoping he looks confident enough that no one will question him. He retraces his steps through the corridors to her poky office.

The door is open and she's on the phone, her feet on the desk. Her face drains of life and then hardens when she sees him. She holds the phone against her chest.

'What are you doing here? How did you get in?'

'They said I could come up,' he lies.

She lifts her feet off her desk.

'I'll have to call you back,' she tells the person on the phone, clicking the receiver back into its cradle, the tangled spiral of cord pinging into place.

'I didn't think anyone used fixed lines any more,' he says, sitting opposite her without being asked.

Colleen scowls. 'What do you want?'

'I want to talk about Arran.'

She swallows. 'He's been found now. They can bury him.'

'They want to know what happened.'

'Isn't that obvious?'

'Is it?'

'Yes. He must have jumped off the roof.'

'You think he jumped?'

'If he was depressed, it makes sense.'

'How do you know he was depressed? You didn't mention that when we spoke.'

She shrugs. 'That's what was in the papers. And he kept phoning Olivia, begging her to give him a chance. She wouldn't. So he must have taken the coward's way out.'

Her eyes slide from him.

'There were other people on the roof that night,' he persists, gently. 'There's a video.'

Colleen stills.

'I heard that.'

'Going by the footage, there was a lot of alcohol in his system. Enough that he couldn't walk. He was a big guy. Did he often drink a lot?'

'No. He usually drank less than the rest of us.' Colleen's voice is quieter now.

Cal takes the original photograph of Arran on the roof from his bag and slides it across the desk towards her. She stares at the image of the half-naked student, surrounded by figures Cal now knows were torturing him and crowing. He notes that Colleen doesn't seem that surprised or horrified. But then, she must see so much worse in her job, maybe she has become inured to it.

'What do you think is going on in this picture?'

She shrugs again, her eyes hard. 'There were initiations. Stupid machismo... Ridiculous.'

'Like the Saltire Circle?'

Colleen's fingers flex. She nods. 'Aye. Like them.' Her lip curls.

'I read the article you wrote in the student paper.'

A long pause before she replies. 'You found that.'

'It's something you felt pretty strongly about.'

'Yes. Still do. Societies like that are abhorrent. They're everything that's wrong with our culture. Building these impenetrable structures of privilege that no one else can breach. The Saltire Circle should have been banned long before it was. It was one of the last bastions of old boys' clubs in Edinburgh

– closed door, women excluded, posh rich boys, misogynistic shit.' There's a venom to her voice that he hasn't heard before.

'It was a drinking society?'

'It was Edinburgh's Bullingdon Club. All privilege, arrogance and sleaze. They were notorious for getting drunk, really drunk, and doing stupid stuff – trashing hotels and playing pranks. They got girls pissed and rated them on how they looked, or kissed, or shagged. Then they got away with it because Daddy wrote a cheque or hushed things up.'

'That doesn't sound like Arran's background.'

'It wasn't.'

'So, how did he get involved with them? What was he doing there?'

Colleen shrugs. 'I wasn't his keeper.'

'Jonno came from that kind of background, though, didn't he?'

There's a heavy silence between them. She looks up at Cal.

Cal's mind races to find an avenue, a way to break through the walls that Colleen keeps around herself.

'I've read your article, Colleen, you hated those people.'

'Not all of them.' She falters, seeming to regret the words.

'Do you mean Jonno? You liked him, didn't you?' She shakes her head. 'Even though he was one of them. The elite.'

'He wasn't like them. Not really.'

'Was he in the society?'

'I have no idea.'

'Andrew Runner?'

A flicker of uncertainty. 'He's a powerful man. You want to be careful what you go about saying.'

'You don't strike me as the sort of person who worries about ruffling feathers.'

'Well, maybe once I wasn't. But look…' She gestures around at the tiny office, the suffocating piles of sadness around her. 'It hasn't exactly got me very far. Just been knocked back for promotion yet again. I've risen as far as I'm allowed. Best not get above my station, now.'

'You think people have blocked you?'

'I don't know what I think.'

She lapses into silence, and he realises he's losing her. Colleen doesn't see them as on the same side. It's time to get to the point.

'Arran didn't die right away, Colleen. He was alive in the machinery for some time after. He tried to get out.'

Colleen pales. Her fingers tighten their hold on her desk, and she sways a little, her cheeks circles of flame.

'Please. I don't like to think about that.'

He watches her push the horror away, her face calcifying, the mask back in place.

'They tortured him on the roof. They fed him alcohol and oil. They stripped him and left him there.'

The silence grows heavy. Colleen's earlier certainty has soaked into the grimy walls and drained away.

The woman purses her lips again and shakes her head. He remembers the softness on her face when she described their pseudo-family unit, the memories of that term before things soured. A group knit so tightly that it was like family. And then it all unravelled.

'I need to go for a fag.'

Colleen waits until he stands and then follows him to the door. He inhales the scent of stale smoke, but more than that, the air thrums with a loaded quality, like there is something he's missing. He casts a last look back at the cheerful faces on the wall, the touching talisman of her worth, searching for the thing that's out of place and not finding it.

She follows his gaze.

'It just seems odd…' Cal ventures. 'From everything I've heard about Arran, he really wasn't the sort of person who'd want to be in a society like that.'

'That's just the thing,' Colleen says, her voice tart. 'You never really know what's inside someone, what they're capable of. You think you do, but you don't.'

They walk along the corridor together and he wishes he had longer to question her, to mine the depths of her anger.

'Do you still see him?' He turns to say goodbye on the street and she is already pushing a fag from the packet, cupping her hand around the lighter flame. 'Jonno, I mean?' She exhales a long line of smoke.

'No,' she says. 'Never.'

CHAPTER FIFTY-ONE

Cal goes to see Robbie. Up steep stairs to a top-floor flat, the smell dank and musty. His skin prickles and he is dismayed that the boy is living somewhere unsuitable. One of Robbie's flatmates answers the door and lets him through, shouting that he's on his way out. Cal catches his breath, relieved at what he sees. The flat itself is a pleasant surprise: high ceilings with elaborate cornices, light bursting in through streaky windows. He finds Robbie sitting on his single bed, leg propped up on some cushions, textbooks scattered across the covers.

Robbie grins. 'I'm logging in for lectures online for now... No need to move at all.'

Cal unloads a bag of food from his rucksack – ready meals, fruit and treats.

'I wasn't sure how well you're being looked after.'

'I've got friends dropping in,' Robbie says. 'But this is great, thank you. Do you want a tea? I should probably try and move anyway. I'm not actually supposed to sit still all day.'

Cal helps him up and follows him to a kitchen filled with unwashed dishes, the sickly stench of a fruit-flavoured vape and a wall of photographs of the flatmates. He spots Chrissie in some of the pictures – her smiling face pressed close to Robbie's, the two of them out with his friends, arms wrapped around each other. A side of her unfamiliar to him. It's both uncomfortable and warming to see how happy she looks.

'It's weird, isn't it? I thought maybe I should take them down, but I don't want to airbrush her out... I know she's not speaking to me now, but maybe we can be friends one day.' He sniffs. 'You might want to open the window. It's pure minging in here.'

Relieved, both to let in the air and to see Robbie in a good mood, Cal pulls up the sash window over the full sink. Sounds of the city drift in on a rush of cool air and the atmosphere in the kitchen improves.

'You might not want to look in the bathroom,' Robbie jokes.

'How are you managing?'

'Not too bad – the nurse at the hospital told me about a cover that goes over the plaster so you can shower. It's working a treat. The guys are shopping for anything I need, and I'm getting visitors and going out once a day, even if it's just to the pub on the corner. The stairs take a long time to get back up. I can slide down on my arse.'

'I had visions of you starving in the attic.'

Robbie laughs. Then his face drops a little. 'I keep having dreams of falling. They're worse than the actual fall.'

Cal shudders. 'Me too – dreams of you falling and not being able to do anything. It gives me cold sweats just thinking about what could have happened.'

'Well, it didn't.' Robbie squidges the teabags against stained mugs, hopping the few steps to the fridge and back, adding milk. Cal accepts the drink and tries not to think about the state of the mug.

'What's happening with Arran? Have you found out any more?'

Cal fills Robbie in on the developments since that day – the confirmation of Arran's identity, the visit to the site and the video sent after the appeal.

'Can I see the video?'

'It's not pretty.'

'I know. I just keep thinking about him. How he was close to my age. Doing the things we're doing. It wasn't that long ago, but he's been there all that time and no one even knew.'

Cal digs his laptop out of his bag and shows Robbie the footage, sliding mugs out of the way to make space on the crowded kitchen table. It gets worse with time, not better. It's tempting to try to shout across the ages at the crowd of laughing tormentors – to reach through the screen and grab them by their collars, dash their heads together. He finds that he's gritting his teeth.

'I've sent the video to my open-source experts,' Cal tells him. 'The police have the footage, too, and I'm hoping they'll make progress, but maybe we can boost the investigation. They should be held responsible for what they did.'

'Some of their profiles are visible when they turn,' Robbie says. 'It's just pretty zoomed in and really bad quality. Can I watch again?'

'Sure. I'm going to do some washing-up.'

'No, no, you mustn't do that.'

'I can't bear to look at it,' Cal jokes. He clears out the sink and stacks all the dishes to the side, then fills the bowl with hot water, tipping a load of washing-up liquid in from what appears to be an unused bottle.

As he makes his way through the plates and cups, Robbie plays and replays the video. He is quiet for the next ten minutes, the tapping of laptop keys and the density of concentration a backdrop to Cal's housekeeping endeavours. He's moved on to drying and stacking dishes into cupboards, when Robbie calls him over.

'Look.' He points at the paused video. 'That MSP you mentioned. Could this be him?' Robbie clicks a few keys and Runner's mugshot appears alongside the paused footage. 'See? The hair colour is sort of right, and there's a mole on the side of his cheek. That could be it there...'

Cal squints at the screen.

'You *could* be right.'

A thought occurs to Cal, and he leans over to click through the history on his computer until he finds the images of Jonno on the investment firm's website.

'Could this man be one of them? I'm pretty sure he was in the society.' He's been trying Jonno, but his secretary says he's out of the country. Whether that's true or not, he isn't sure.

Robbie stares at the photo and then clicks back on the video, watching, slowing the frames, then forwarding to the end.

'There.'

'Where?'

'Right at the end. After that one... pisses on him. Someone crouches down and talks to Arran. Just for a second. All the others have moved away. Could it be him?'

'Maybe.'

'I wonder what he was saying.'

Cal meets Robbie's tired eyes. He straightens. 'You look exhausted. I should go – you need to rest.'

Robbie lets Cal help him to his room and eases down onto the bed. He passes the boy painkillers and fills a glass of water for him.

'What will you do now?' Robbie's head turns on the pillow, his face taut with interest.

'More research into these men,' says Cal. 'If they think we have footage and we can get some names, maybe one of them will talk. Especially if some weren't physically involved, more bystanders. It's worth a try.'

'I'd like to help.' Robbie yawns.

'I'll come back and see you,' Cal promises. 'Right now, you need to rest.'

He lets himself out of the flat and emerges, blinking, onto a busy street, sucked back into the light and life of the city at dusk. Traversing the road, he weaves his way through returning commuters with tired faces and dishevelled shirts. Patience. Maybe that's all he needs. Patience and faith that things will work out. A slow chipping away at the facts until the truth emerges. Someone knows something. They always do.

CHAPTER FIFTY-TWO

Cal drags his suitcase to Waverley station in a downpour and pulls his hood up tight around his face, feet sodden and the rain crawling into his collar by the time he gets under cover. He buys a coffee and sits on the train with his face held close to the cup, blowing onto the liquid to send the warm steam onto his cheeks. He needs better boots and a warmer coat.

Shona picks him up at Aberdeen and suggests they go for a coffee in the shopping centre next door.

'How are you?' Cal watches her face carefully when they're seated, his senses telling him that something is wrong, that something has been wrong for a while. Was it his imagination, or was their hug shorter than usual? Did she pull away from his kiss? He doesn't think he's being paranoid.

She smiles but it doesn't break her face into its usual sunshine.

'Work's a bit tough. And Angela has been on the phone most nights...'

'I'm sorry we don't have more answers for her yet.'

'That can't be forced.'

Even so, he feels the guilt and responsibility soaking through everything, just like the rain, crawling into all available spaces. 'We're trying, I promise.'

'Who's we?' Shona's voice is sharp.

'I've sent the footage to the open-source experts, and... well, Robbie has been doing some research from his sickbed.'

Shona pauses, setting down her coffee cup. 'I thought Chrissie was upset that you'd been in touch with him? What does she think about this?'

Cal squirms a little in his seat. He's been trying not to think about Robbie's ongoing help as a further betrayal of his daughter.

'She doesn't know. She's not been in touch since the day we found Arran and I saw her at the hospital. I've spoken to Allie, so I know she's all right. I'm just giving her space. She'll come round. Eventually.'

He tries to imbue the words with more confidence than he feels, which is hard because Shona's eyes don't have their usual reassuring sparkle. Her cheeks have no colour and she looks tired – he suddenly worries that his being here this weekend is a burden rather than an enjoyment.

Before he can say more, she drains her coffee.

'Shall we go for a walk on the beach before we go home? I haven't been out to Balmedie since we last went together.'

Going for a walk is the last thing Cal wants – his feet are still wet and cold, and he's tired after a long and frustrating week in Edinburgh, but he feels on edge and desperately wants to see the Shona he knows and loves. If this is what she wants to do, then he isn't going to argue. 'Sounds great.'

'It'll be dark in an hour, so we ought to go, if we're going.' She's already up and yanking on her coat, fast, businesslike.

He leaves the last quarter of his drink cooling in its mug and follows her to the door. As they exit the shopping centre, he tries to catch her hand but her arm swings away as if she hasn't seen the attempt. Cal's stomach clenches. He knows he's not imagining things now, and feels trapped here with her, barrelling towards a confrontation he doesn't understand or want to have, not today.

They drive to Balmedie in almost silence, Shona briefly agreeing with the inane comments he makes about the scenery. As they pull into the car park, a faint drizzle mists the air around them like a haar coming in off the sea.

'We're going to get pretty wet,' Cal says dubiously, thinking longingly of the pub they passed a few miles back and about to suggest they retire there instead, but he doesn't get the chance.

'Oh well, we're here now...' She locks the car but doesn't meet his gaze, just turns and trudges over towards the path to the beach. There is only one other car in the car park. It's bleak out, though the sand makes things glow, seem warmer than they are.

Cal zips his jacket to the neck and follows Shona up and over the dunes. Any protection they had from the elements vanishes – it's just them and the furious churn of the ocean. She plunges down the other side, regardless, and he jogs onto the sand next to her. Her hair is wild, Medusa-like: torn from her hands, strands thrash up in the wind and across her face.

'I just needed to be out here.' Her voice is high, and her eyes are bright and watery as she looks towards the might of the North Sea – he can't tell if she is crying or if it's the wind making her eyes stream. In front of them, the waves are crashing onto the beach, foaming and angry, and he just can't take it any more.

He moves so he is standing in front of her and she has to look at him.

'Shona, what's wrong? What's going on?'

She pauses for an excruciating moment, waves of emotion riding across her face. He sees flashes of pain and anger, braces for the impact. If he's honest with himself, he has known it was coming.

'I don't know where to start, Cal.'

'Pick something, anything.' He throws his arms out to the side and feels the wind get up into his jacket, swelling it as if he could fly.

'Okay, well... You spoke to Allie.'

'What do you mean?' His mind feels slow and stupid. Of course he spoke to Allie. This has never been an issue before.

'Chrissie hasn't talked to you for weeks and you talked to Allie about it. I had no idea, Cal. How do you think that makes me feel?'

Even though her voice is raised, the wind takes her words and whips them up into the sky, dashing them on the waves,

257

making it hard to hear. Gulls are swooping low over the water, buffeted by the stormy conditions, hardy and unconcerned. Their beaks are a startling yellow against the grey water and white spume.

'It doesn't mean anything,' he shouts back. 'I only spoke to Allie to check Chrissie was all right. I'm not going to stop speaking to Allie. Is that what you want?'

She makes a noise of frustration. 'Of course not! It's not about that. I'm supposed to *know* things about you, Cal – how you're doing, what you're thinking and feeling – and you give me nothing. I'm the last to know about everything in your life. It never used to be like that. Why are you shutting me out?'

Shona's face is red and her eyes are streaming. Cal notices that the trickles of rain are running down his neck again, but he can't feel the cold, not right now. That's what Chrissie said, too.

'I tell you everything,' he shouts across the weather, trying to make himself heard.

He does, doesn't he?

'No! You don't. I get nothing, Cal. I thought you'd open up, I thought you'd be different after the trial. I thought that's what it was. Sometimes I see glimpses of it, the real you, but the rest of the time you're shut down. I can't take this. It isn't what I want my life to be like, my relationship.' Her voice is strangled. 'You're not the person I thought you were.'

Cal feels the sand shift beneath his feet. Now he really feels the cold, the pain of it slicing into his bones.

'I am!' He reaches out for her arm, but she pulls away from him. 'Shona, I love you. Please. Let's talk about this.'

'No, Cal. It's not enough. I'm always getting the scraps. I need more. I *needed* more. I needed someone who loves me. I know you're grieving, and I'm sorry, I've tried to be patient, understanding. I just can't do it any longer.'

Her words hollow him. He notes the slide into the past tense. A gust of wind hits them, and she takes two steps back from him and it could just be the weather, but he can feel her slipping away like the tide – an unstoppable movement. Tears are running down her cheeks. This is hurting her, but she wraps her arms tightly around herself, turning away from him.

He rushes forward. 'No, wait. Shona, *please*, listen.'

'There's never anything to listen to, Cal. We should go.'

'We can't leave it like this.'

'I think we have to.'

And then she's gone, wrenching away from him, cutting their connection, her feet sinking into the wet sand as she leaves.

CHAPTER FIFTY-THREE

When Donny drops him in town, Arran trudges up the hill to Pollock, barely able to put one foot in front of the other. Most of the windows are dark in halls, which is good. He doesn't want to see anyone. He opens the door to his room and it looks even smaller, even more drab than it did when he left. There's a smell that suggests he left some food in here, so he throws open the window and sinks onto the bed.

His limbs are so heavy, and he only realises when the pillow beneath his head grows wet that he's crying. He just wants his friendships back. Surely, whatever he's done, it can be fixed? It's all been a mistake, and they will come back after Christmas and things can go back to the way they were. He, Olivia, Colleen and Jonno.

He can't bring himself to move – to turn the lights on or close the window. Instead, he just pulls the musty-smelling covers over his head and drifts into unconsciousness. When he wakes, it's dark. His mouth is dry and he's desperate for the toilet, so he has to force himself out of bed.

When he makes his way out of the bathroom, he hears movement down the corridor. Someone else is back. He peers along, seeing the light falling from another doorway, a slice of life projected into the darkness.

He follows the light like an entranced insect, realising now whose it is, who is here with him. Olivia. He creeps down the corridor to her room, footsteps quiet, his heart fluttering with anticipation, his cheeks warm. He needs to clear the air, to get their friendship back. This is his chance. Fate has intervened to help him.

But when he knocks and the door falls back, it isn't Olivia that he finds. Colleen looks up, startled. He sees the flash of fear in her eyes, the way she recoils just a little, and it wrong-foots him, but he ploughs on, so relieved to see someone.

'Colleen! You're back! What are you doing? Is Olivia here too? I need to…'

Arran steps forward but she backs away from him, her eyes darting to the door. 'I thought no one else would be back yet.'

'I thought so too,' he says, smiling. 'How was your Christmas? Is Olivia here? Why are you in her room?'

'I'm packing for her,' she tells him in a tone that makes it clear it's an instruction for him to leave.

'What? Why?'

'Like you don't know. Even Jonno is moving out of halls. You're toxic.'

'What?' Through nausea and confusion, he feels the unfairness travelling from his gut to his throat, words ripping out into the quiet.

'What's going on? Why are you being like this? What am I supposed to have done?'

'Are you really telling me you don't know?'

'I have no idea.' His voice raises and Colleen flinches as he throws his arms wide.

She stops stuffing clothing into a duffle bag and steps closer to him, planting her feet wide, her face purple with rage.

'The picture.'

'What picture?'

Colleen rolls her eyes and scoffs. He feels like he's going mad, that he's going to explode if someone doesn't put him out of his misery. 'Colleen! What bloody picture?'

'The one you took of Olivia. And shared around. That one. Remember now? That's why she's moving out of halls. It's all your fault.'

His belly swoops and drops.

'What? I have no idea what you're on about.'

'Oh my God, Arran, stop pretending. It's fucking out of order. I've told her she needs to report you. Get you moved off this corridor. You act like you're so calm and steady and quiet, but you're a bloody psychopath.'

'Colleen, what are you talking about?'

Furious, she stabs at her phone, bringing up a screenshot and waving it in front of his face. 'It's evidence. I'm keeping it as evidence and I'll tell them myself if I have to, no matter what she says.'

He tries to keep track of the moving image but she's waving it so fast that he can't see. Without thinking it through, he grabs her wrist to hold it steady but Colleen gasps and drops the handset.

'Get off me, Arran!'

But he's too busy scrabbling on the floor to listen to her.

'What the…?'

He's got the phone now and what he sees shocks him. Colleen is breathing heavily, words flying at him, but he can't listen to her.

'Give it back, Arran, I swear. It doesn't matter if you delete it, I've got a copy safe. I can't believe you'd do this just to get into some stupid society.'

It's a picture of Olivia. She's asleep or unconscious, her eyes closed, her hair in disarray. Her top is pulled up and one breast is spilling from her bra. It takes him a moment to realise where this was taken and when he does, his stomach plunges over another drop. It was taken on his bed.

Colleen snatches the phone, and he looks up at her and experiences a second of vertigo. How does she have this? How is it possible? His mind falls over itself in a bid to understand. His mouth drops open. There is only one night when that could have been taken – he remembers the outfit she was wearing, how he covered her with a blanket and worked by the light of his bedside lamp, occasionally checking on her, just happy to be nearby.

Colleen stares at him, her face a strange mixture of triumph and loathing that reminds him of Gilly. It makes her eyes glitter, her lips redder than usual. No wonder she hates him, no wonder they've blocked him, if that's what they think he would do. How can he explain to her, when he can't explain this to himself? His mind won't compute what he's seen. That was his bed, his room, but he would never – could never – do that to Olivia. He flushes hot and then cold as the thought intrudes: *even when he was really drunk?* But immediately he banishes it. No way. Never.

'I didn't...'

His words can't form, his mind won't catch up. The floor feels like it's falling away from him. What does this mean?

'Get out,' she spits at him. 'And stay away from Olivia. You make me sick.'

CHAPTER FIFTY-FOUR

CAL

He can see it so clearly – the journey back to the station, her driving away from him, shivering on the train back to Edinburgh, having fucked everything up once again. The thought of his life without Shona is an unbearable bleakness. He needs to get her to stop; he needs to assemble the turbulent thoughts in his head; he needs to do something now, because she is walking away from him, striding up the beach and out of his life, and this cannot happen.

Everything builds up inside him and it's like the worst thunderstorm ever going off in his brain. All the feelings he's been holding back for weeks now – the pain of Chrissie's anger, the horror of what happened to Arran, Margot's injustice, his mother's frailty, the sense that half his life has gone and it's too late to make things right – are crashing and breaking open inside him. The hurt and the panic engulf him. Cal's ears are ringing with it. But he has to fight. As he hurries after Shona's bent figure, he knows he's watching the woman he loves leave him, detach and move on alone. This is it. This is the moment when it ends.

His brain flashes with memories of her: waiting on the footpath for him when they first met, her blonde hair tucked behind her ears, the warm shiver of her laughter. The two of them, walking together, climbing hills on the west coast, eating in cosy pubs. Then he remembers her pale face in her hospital bed, those moments in the darkness on the hillside with her blood on his hands, her long recovery. He's bad for her, he brings disaster, he's always known he's cursed.

It's all too much: too many thoughts cascading, not enough time to form words. His legs won't work properly and she's getting further away from him. Cal's knees buckle and he sinks down into the wet sand, letting out a wail that sounds like the howling wind. 'Shona!'

The desolate, animal sound makes her turn and he stretches out his hands to her, crying now. The hairs on his arms feel like they're in an electric storm, alert to what he's about to lose. She thinks he doesn't care. 'Please, please, wait.'

Shona staggers back towards him. The wind is stronger now. It wants to push her away from Cal. He can taste salt, doesn't know if it is from the ocean spray or his tears.

She's crouching beside him. 'Cal, get up, we have to go.'

'Please,' he says into the lee created by their bodies, the tiniest shelter of calm. 'I just need to tell you. I know you're going to walk away, Shona, and I've known deep down this would happen, that I'm terrible for you. But please, do not walk away not knowing how much I love you.'

'What are you talking about? Why are you "terrible" for me?'

'Are you kidding? Do you remember the sabotage last year? The accident? You ended up in hospital and it was all my fault. You saved Chrissie, Shona, you fought off that madman and that's how you get repaid. You've been put in danger so many times because of me. Robbie just fell off a fucking building, for Christ's sake. I'm a liability to be around. There's a common denominator here.'

'Cal.' She puts her hands on his shoulders and shakes him. 'Those things were not your fault. That's not why things aren't working between us.'

'I didn't know you felt I was shutting you out, I swear.' The tears won't stop running down his cheeks. He doesn't bother to wipe them away, and they mix with the rain. He's soaked to the skin, talking fast while she's listening. 'I just don't want to be on the phone whingeing to you about things all the time. I don't want you to have to listen to that. You're so strong and capable, Shona, and I admire you so much. Honestly, I feel like a total fuck-up and I don't know what you see... what you *saw* in me.'

She's shaking her head, looking furious. 'That's just such bollocks. We're supposed to be partners, tell each other everything. How can I cry on your shoulder, when you won't cry on mine?'

'But you never cry on my shoulder!'

'What about all the times I bend your ear about the cases I see at the lab, the nightmares over the kiddies' bones? Doesn't that count?'

'But that's completely understandable – you do a really tough job and see things most people couldn't comprehend.'

'And how does that differ from your job?'

'I'm just a journalist.'

'Oh my God, Cal Lovett!' Shona screeches at him. 'You can be so fucking annoying.'

'Sorry.' He is sorry, but he's also glad she hasn't walked away yet – the two of them are still kneeling on sodden sand in a miserable gale, stuck between breaking up and staying together. He seizes the moment she's granted him, puts his cold hands on her cheeks, wiping away the tears, so relieved that she doesn't flinch. 'Shona, I'm sorry. I never ever meant to shut you out. I love you. I miss you so much when I'm away. I want to be with you all the time.'

'But you won't even commit to moving in with me. You freaked out when I asked you.'

'That's because I'm an idiot who struggles with change. It's not because I don't want to be with you.'

The side of her mouth quirks, like it remembers how to smile. She immediately covers it back up with annoyance.

'You are an idiot,' she agrees.

266

'But I'm an idiot who does want to move in with you one day, if you can wait for me a bit longer?'

'Really?' Her forehead wrinkles. 'I just don't know what's right, Cal. I can't cope with being shut out.'

'Well...' He takes a deep breath of salty, rain-swept air into his lungs. 'Shall we talk it through? See what we both think when we're warm and dry – maybe not make the decision on a really fucking cold beach in November?'

'I can't feel my fingers.' She leans forward until they are forehead to forehead. 'Your teeth are chattering.'

Before he knows what's happening, her lips are on his and he's kissing her back, hungrily, both of them clumsy with cold. Shona topples against him and he wraps his arms around her, his heart still beating fast with the fear of her walking away. He's been pulled back from the edge of a terrible precipice, but the drop is still there, right beside him.

CHAPTER FIFTY-FIVE

When they pull up to the house, he looks at the tall glass windows, the thick stone walls and wooden cladding, and feels a sense of rightness. A single light is burning, the one she keeps on a timer, and it looks inviting, like a life you could step into if you only had the courage.

He wants to be here, with Shona. No one else is going to be at the centre of his life; it is wrong to keep that space clear for other people, when it should belong to the woman he loves. He needs to open up to her, to give her more. He can see that now. Chrissie is moving on. She'll always have a home with him, but he can't put her at the centre of his universe.

His imperfect mother is going to die, and he's going to have been an imperfect son, and there's nothing either of them can do about it. He'll visit her, call her, keep her safe, but he won't feel guilty that their lives and their relationship have not been the ones they might have liked. Those runes were cast a long time back, even before Margot vanished. He's holding out for something that never existed.

Shona is asleep, he realises, still against the window, her breath steady. He touches her arm gently and she stirs.

'We're home,' he says, testing the taste of the word in his mouth.

–

Cal persuades Shona to go and have a hot shower while he unloads the car and locks up. The rain has slowed to hardly anything now, but his soul is chilled. He can see the clouds in the distance are splitting and dispersing, letting the stars peek through and sending icy daggers down towards the land. He retreats into the warm of the house, lighting the fire – success- fully, for once – closing the curtains and opening a bottle of wine.

While he is alone in the open-plan room, he looks around, seeing it through new eyes, mentally moving into the space. It could feel like home; he just has to make the leap. The real truth is that part of his heart is still back in that clapboard house in the Midlands, with its wrap-around porch – the place where Allie was pregnant with Chrissie, where they brought up their daughter, where his beloved dog still lives. Rocket would love it here, he thinks, looking at the warm hearth, the crackling fire.

'Your turn.'

He looks up from his musings to see Shona, pink and warm, her hair in a turban and her body wrapped in a huge furry dressing gown.

He smiles, searching her face for reassurance, then hands her a glass of wine and makes for the bathroom, realising that his clothes are still damp, the material sticking to his skin.

'You lit the fire?'

He turns at the doorway, smiling at the surprise in her tone. 'I know – I must be learning,' he says.

It takes a while for the feeling to come back into his limbs, the numbness to leave. He stands under the shower jets, gradu- ally creeping the temperature hotter as his body adapts. By the time he's dry and dressed, Shona has heated up a casserole and garlic bread, made a salad, and set out plates on the kitchen island – the smell makes him realise how ravenous he is.

They sit opposite each other at the table as they eat, socked feet entwined beneath, both too tired to say much, though he can feel how conscious they are of each other. He can barely take his eyes from Shona, woken from what feels like taking her for granted and seeing her anew. She looks gorgeous in the soft light, her hair wet and her cheeks pink with warmth and wine.

They leave the dishes and move to the bedroom, crawling beneath the covers and lying facing each other, their knees, hands, foreheads touching. He breathes her in.

'What you said on the beach, about thinking things would be different after the trial?'

Shona grimaces. 'I was angry.'

'No, you were right. I thought the same. I've been waiting and waiting for a day that isn't going to happen, and I've been putting the most important things on hold.'

She kisses him, softly. 'I wanted it for you.'

Cal thinks back to the trial and the shock, his mother's collapse. 'I know. Me too. But it's okay. We tried. And now I need to think about the future.'

'What is it that you want, Cal?'

'You. To be here with you.'

'Are you sure? You haven't seemed sure. We're a long way from the Midlands, it's a big decision.'

Cal pictures Jason Barr free and living so close to his home and everything slides into relief. The thought of bumping into his sister's killer on the street is intolerable. There are so many reasons to move on now. To leave who he was behind.

'It's not,' he says, squeezing her hand. 'It's just taking me time to get where you are. I'll need to go back down regularly to see my mother, and that's fine. But my work means I'll always be away a lot. I don't want to lie to you about that.'

'I understand that,' she says. 'I'm independent, busy, I don't need you here every second. Don't want you getting under my feet.' She smiles. 'I just need it to be your home. Whether you're here or not.'

'That's what I want too.' And he realises it's true.

'We can make a bedroom for Chrissie as well – it's important to me that she feels at home here. I know things are hard between you now, but they'll be back to normal before you know it.'

'Thank you. I hope so.'

He loses himself in kissing Shona for a moment. When he pulls back, he nestles into the pillow, still and looking into her eyes, which are glazed with tiredness. One tear slides free, making his heart constrict.

'What is it?'

'I just… I'd prepared myself for that being it. I'd hardened myself to it and now… I'm relieved, that's all. Almost more frightened than I was before. It's silly.'

He pulls her close. 'I know what you mean.'

'I don't want to lose you.'

Cal keeps his arms tight around her, listening as her breath deepens and she slides from exhaustion to sleep. He's dodged a bullet. Shona is one in a million, yet he came so close to losing something he could never get back. As tired as he is, he lies awake, watching the light of the moon hit the wet field outside, staring into the quiet silver of the Aberdeenshire countryside where the peace is broken only by the rare movement of headlights on the single-track road in the distance. He lies there and thinks of ways he could change, of things he has to say goodbye to, determination seeping into his veins.

–

They spend the weekend quietly, going for walks hand in hand, and breakfast at a local garden centre, followed by coffee and watching the rain drip over the awning outside. Mainly, they talk. They talk about Cal's plan to give up his flat, how and when they will move his belongings, what he will say to his mother, daughter, Allie.

Then they talk about Arran and the case, about Angela and Bill, and the toll the truth is taking on them. Shona catches him up on work at her office and lab, a series of lectures she's been invited to give at Glasgow University. The more they talk, the closer he feels to her, the bond reinforced.

They cook and curl up on the sofa, and read and have sex and sleep, and do it all over again. Cal feels like he's holding a fragile thing between his hands. He needs to take care not to break it.

'What are you going to do this week?' Shona asks on Sunday afternoon, her feet up on his lap and an intimidating book about decomposition in her hand.

He sighs. 'I don't know. It feels like we're finding things out and they're just raising more questions. How am I going to work out who those men on the roof are, when no one will talk to me? It's so frustrating. Someone was filming up there, someone must know what happened to him. The police don't have the resources to keep chasing, and I understand that, but it must be possible to find out more. Sarah and I are going to reconvene. We may have to wrap things up for now and return to the podcast later if more evidence emerges.'

'Will Sarah be okay with that?'

He shrugs. 'From a podcast point of view, it's not the worst outcome – we found the body, so we have a resolution of some kind. From a personal point of view, it's awful. For Angela and Bill...' Silence falls as they contemplate Arran's family. 'I just have the feeling that some of the people we've spoken to know more than they're saying. And who sent that video? Surely, they care about getting the truth? It came just after Angela and Bill's appeal. Why wouldn't they come forward?'

'Because they're scared? Or involved?'

'Yeah. If Andrew Runner is any indication, then they've got links to power, that's for sure.'

'Keep going. You can do this.'

He smiles at her. But inside, his stomach is churning – why can't he see how the pieces fit?

CHAPTER FIFTY-SIX

Cal plans to take the train south from Aberdeen on Monday morning. His phone rings just as Shona drops him off, so he answers it as he's waving goodbye. It takes him a moment to tune into the conversation but when he does, he's completely alert. It's Jonathan Keble.

'I can't believe it. I just can't. I don't… It doesn't make sense.'

Cal listens to the thickness in the man's voice, thinking that maybe he is crying or close to it. Turns out, his secretary wasn't lying about him being away, after all. He's been in Argentina on a trek and missed the news that Arran's remains had been found. His upset is unexpected, as is his seemingly genuine surprise that Arran's remains were at the warehouse.

Playing for time, Cal strolls down the platform to his train.

'Tell me about that night. Tell me why you were up there.'

A long pause. A couple of sniffs.

'What do you mean? I wasn't.'

The hope that this call would be the key to unlocking the events of that night fades and Cal can barely keep the exasperation from his voice.

'Arran's parents just want answers, Jonathan. I think you know more than you're telling me.'

'You're wrong.'

Cal tries another tack. A brutal one.

'If you haven't listened to the podcast, you might not know: Arran didn't die right away. He fell into some machinery and couldn't get out again. He was alive for a while.'

'What?'

273

'I'm sorry to be the one to tell you this.' Cal repeats the horrible truth: 'It does look like Arran lived for a short while after he fell. There was evidence that he tried to get out. But he was very badly injured and it was a cold night.' He thinks of the scratches and the student's damaged fingernails. This detail always makes him feel sick.

'I don't... I don't understand.'

'I think you do.'

'I need to go.'

'Please...'

But he's talking to thin air.

Frustrated, Cal settles into using the intermittent internet connection to catch up on some research as the train glides south. He googles the grain warehouse again, looking at articles about its imminent demolition. It's hard to believe that such a behemoth will be razed to the ground. He loses himself in irrelevancies, such as the demolition company explaining how they'll use a mixture of deconstruction and explosives to reduce it to a pile of rubble.

He wonders, if the building had been demolished without their snooping, would Arran have been found? The chances are his bones would have been lost in the destruction, the hellish mess and the dust. But then, he discovers from the interviews that all the machinery was due to be taken off the side of the building, and from inside first, and the metal recycled. He doesn't know why, but that makes him feel better, knowing that Arran's discovery was coming, not just down to chance and Robbie's adventurousness.

He's so focused on the screen that he almost doesn't notice when they arrive in Edinburgh, and it's a scramble to shove his things in his backpack and get off the train before it continues the long journey south. His mind is churning over and over like

274

the muddy brown waters of the Leith. He stands in a daze on the platform and his phone alerts him to a message. Jonathan.

> I need to talk in person. I'll be in Edinburgh tomorrow. Can we meet?

It's rapidly followed by another message. At last, Chrissie is ready to talk to him.

—

She's at the bar before him. He buys her a glass of wine – it still feels wrong to do that, but he's trying to remember she's a grown young woman, not a child. He's trying to do better. As she sips it, he studies her over the rim of his own glass. She is thinner, more angular, less smiling. The urge to ask what is wrong is almost overwhelming.

'I'm sorry,' he says, instead. 'It never occurred to me that by taking a case linked to Edinburgh I was very much stepping on your toes. I can see that now. It wasn't fair of me.'

She sets down the glass, playing with the condensation on the side of it with a finger.

'It's not that I don't want to see you…'

'I know,' he says. 'You need to form your own life here and be your own person. I understand, I do. I should have talked to you about it before accepting the case. By the time I realised, it was too late to back out.'

'What I said… about Robbie, and you talking to him and not me – I'm sorry.'

'No, you shouldn't be. I can see why it felt like that.' He thinks about how he's shut out Shona; he has been doing the same to Chrissie. 'I should have talked to you about it.'

'I feel awful for thinking this way. With everything that's happened – the trial, Barr… I know it's selfish of me.' Her eyes fill with tears, and he reaches across and rubs her arm. It's thin through the wool.

'Those are not things you should be worrying about or trying to fix, love.'

'I know. It's just that…' She looks up at him and he can see she is exhausted. There it is again, that parental urge to wrap her in cotton wool and take care of her. 'I thought he was going to be found guilty. I thought it was all going to be over. And now… It never is, is it?'

Cal feels the shadow of Margot beside them. Sees the full burden of being your dead aunt's doppelganger. How the weight of it has been pressing down on his daughter, and so much of that is his fault.

'It isn't ever going to be over,' he says. 'I thought the trial was the answer. But I can see now that even if he had been found guilty, it wouldn't have been over. It's not something that can ever be made right, but I have to move on from it. Margot would have hated me wallowing. We gave it the best shot we could.'

'It's just so utterly shit.' Chrissie's face morphs into a recognisable set of creases – those lines on the forehead that come from anger and injustice. He sees them on himself and doesn't want this for her.

'It really is. But it's part of what makes us who we are. You're sensitive, Chrissie, and wise in ways that others your age haven't had to be. Maybe you can see that now, as you make new friends… I don't know.'

She frowns in a way that makes him see the words have hit a nerve.

'Maybe we need to embrace it.' He sits back and looks around the pub. 'As hard as it is, I love my job, Chrissie.' As he speaks, he realises the words are true. 'And I don't think I'd be doing this if Margot hadn't vanished. And you know, sometimes, it makes a difference. And maybe, that's worth something.'

His daughter's face clears as he speaks.

'It does make a difference,' she says so quietly that he can hardly hear her in the noisy pub. 'I just...' She pauses.

'Go on,' he says, overriding the instinct to hide from whatever she is going to say. 'Get it out on the table.'

She cups her wine glass in her hands. 'I just get so worried about you.'

'Oh, love. That isn't your job. I'm fine, I promise you. More than fine. Coming through my midlife crisis.'

'How's Shona?'

'She's getting impatient. She doesn't want us to live apart forever.'

'That's fair enough, Dad.'

'Yes, but if anyone is going to move, it should be me. She's tied by work in a way I'm not. It's just that I've got responsibilities at home, it's hard to up and leave...'

'You mean Gran?'

'Yes.' He chances a look up from his glass. 'And you.'

She smiles a wobbly smile.

'I understand if you need to move.'

'You do?'

'Yes, I mean, I'm in Edinburgh for four years and then I don't know where I'll be, but I don't think it will be the Midlands, not for a while.'

'So, if I was in Aberdeenshire, you would be okay with that?'

'Do I get to come and visit?' His mouth quirks. He loves that she's teasing him again.

'Whenever you want. You'd have your own room, ready for you. You'll always have a home with me, Chrissie, whenever you need it. That's the most important thing. Shona loves you. She doesn't want to come between us.'

'So that just leaves Gran.'

Cal sighs, feeling the lightness leave him.

'Dad,' Chrissie says. 'You just need to make sure you go and visit. That's all you can do. She's in a good place, now.'

'I worry that I'll regret not spending time with her. That when she's gone, there will be no way to fix everything.'

'I'm not sure there's a way to fix things, even if you're right there, though, is there?'

He shakes his head slowly. 'Maybe not.'

And when he pictures his home, that's not what he misses. In leaving, it feels that he's abandoning someone else.

'It's her, isn't it?' Chrissie's watching his face, her voice soft and knowing. 'Margot.'

'How did you know that?'

'That's the look you get when you think about her.'

'It's silly that I'm scared of saying goodbye to someone who's been gone a long time. She doesn't need my goodbyes.'

'But getting a guilty verdict would have been enough to release you?'

'Are you sure you aren't training in clairvoyance?' He laughs. 'But yes, maybe. I would have done my duty. Got justice for her. But then, maybe I'm just a bit scared.'

'What of?'

'Change! Mourning the life we used to have, your mum and I, the dreams we had.'

Her smile turns wistful.

'I think Mum's moving on, though. With Dave.' She rolls her eyes.

Cal chokes on his pint. 'Don't say his name like that! What's wrong with *Dave*?'

Chrissie laughs. 'Nothing. It's just… they get all soppy.' She makes sick noises.

'Okay, well nobody needs to see that.' He makes a mental note to talk to Shona about them not making the same mistake. 'Are you hungry?'

'Are you changing the subject?'

'Yes,' he says.

'I'm starving.'

'Right, come on, then, let's go and find some food.'

He waits for her to bundle herself into her coat, and pull on her gloves and hat, then they link arms as they take the winding cobbles of Fleshmarket Close down towards the New Town, the castle looming above them.

CHAPTER FIFTY-SEVEN

Cal meets Jonathan in a discreet snug in a private members' club off the Royal Mile. Whisky bottles line the walls and a waiter serves them silently before gliding away and vanishing into a door set into a bookshelf. It swings back to reveal a secret passage, like something out of a children's adventure story.

He's shocked to see the tanned, good-looking Jonathan Keble in real life. His skin seems grey and his chin is stubbled. He looks like he hasn't slept at all – or if he has, it was in the clothes he's wearing.

Cal takes a sip of single malt and feels it burn the back of his throat. He waits, poised for the other man to begin, but Keble spends some time shifting in his seat and swilling the liquid in his glass.

'I need to tell you… the full story.'

He looks up at Cal and back at the glass.

'It was that stupid society I was in.'

'The Saltire Circle?' Keble nods. 'What was it?'

'A drinking club, supposed to be full of the leaders of the future.' The laugh is bitter. 'Rich kids hanging on to privilege. My father was a Circle member in his day, and he was determined I would be too. I had no choice.'

'No choice?'

Shame crosses his face. 'I was young and stupid, and dependent on family money.'

'But Arran doesn't really seem like the usual Circle candidate? No family money or political influence. The son of a Moray farmer.'

'He wasn't.' There's a hollow to Jonathan's tone now. 'He wasn't up for consideration.'

'But the initiation on the roof? The hazing. Why would he have been there if he wasn't in the running?'

'It wasn't his initiation,' Jonathan says. 'It was mine.'

Cal's mind folds in on itself.

'I don't understand.'

'It was stupid and cruel. I'm so ashamed of myself for it. But part of my initiation was to convince someone to make this crazy journey across Edinburgh to the factory, thinking they were going to be let into the society.'

'But they were never going to be allowed in?'

Jonathan shakes his head. 'No. It wasn't just me, though. There were three of us up for admission that night, but... Arran was the only one who made it there.'

Cal lets the weight of the thought rest over them.

'He didn't even want to be in the society. I persuaded him to do it for me. Colleen and Olivia weren't talking to him, and he was lonely, I think...' Jonathan trails off into thought.

'Why weren't they speaking to him?'

Jonathan can't meet his gaze. He sets down the glass and drops his head into his hands. 'I'm not that person any more. I promise.'

'It was your fault?'

'It was the other part of my initiation.' He looks up and Cal sees the torment. 'I had to get a photograph of a woman – a compromising one.'

'Okay?'

'Olivia came back drunk from a night out. She fell asleep in Arran's room. He was taking care of her, and he went to the kitchen and I... took my opportunity.'

'What did you do?'

Tears come to the man's eyes. He looks haunted. 'She was out cold. I pulled her top up and took a photograph. It was just for the society. It was never supposed to be shared outside the group. But somehow...'

'It was.'

'Colleen was dead against the society and someone sent it to her. She and Olivia thought it was Arran who took it.'

'And you let them?'

'No! I was going to tell them. After the initiation, I promised Arran I would.'

'So, it was an exchange. Arran didn't want to be in the society, but he did want you to clear his name.'

The look on Keble's face tells Cal it was.

Curiosity overcomes him. 'And did you ever tell them?' Jonathan shakes his head slowly. 'He was gone. Things were bad with his family, so I thought he'd run away. He wasn't there. I didn't think there was any point.'

'Colleen still hates him.'

'I can see that now. I should have said something.'

Cal feels a deep sadness for the damage to Arran's reputation. But he needs to keep Keble on side and get to the truth.

'So, tell me what happened when Arran came to the roof that night.'

'I didn't know,' Jonathan gabbles, clasping his hands tightly together to stop them shaking. 'I didn't know what they were going to do. I thought they were just going to laugh at him, make him drink some more, not...'

'Humiliate him.'

Keble puts his face in his hands again and Cal listens to the sniffs as the man composes himself. He thinks of the horror of that night on the roof, of Arran's drunkenness and confusion, the mob mentality.

'But you watched it happen. You could have stepped in and protected him, but you did nothing.'

'I...' But there is no excuse.

'And then you just left him.'

'I had to.'

'Had to?'

'I was weak, okay? I should never have done any of it. I didn't think he would vanish. I went back and he was gone.'

'You went back?'

'Yes. When we left, I whispered to him that I'd come back as soon as I could get away. We piled into cabs and I went on to the bar for my official initiation, but then I slipped away and went back to get him. I took a taxi.'

'And what did you find on the roof?'

'Nothing! There was no one there. I called his name, I looked everywhere. I thought he'd gone home.'

'In that state?'

'He was big and strong, and he could hold his alcohol. I thought he'd be sleeping it off and I'd see him the next day. That's why, when you said he was alive for a bit...' He sobs into his hands. 'How was I to know he'd fallen off? What if I could have helped him?'

'Or jumped.' Cal lets the thought hang there.

'Oh, Christ.'

'Why haven't you come forward before now?' he asks.

Keble takes a moment to pull himself together. When he speaks again, he sounds wary, like he knows how poor the excuse sounds.

'The people in the Circle are powerful. It was made very clear that there would be repercussions if anyone spoke out. And not just for me – for my father, my family, the work he'd put in his whole life to build the estate. I just... I let it go. I hoped he'd run away, was starting a new life somewhere. I tried to forget about him.'

Cal finds he can't summon any sympathy – all that he has is reserved for the family working the land without their eldest child, with no answers or knowledge about what befell him for all of these years.

'And anyway...' Jonathan continues. 'Some of them were friends, good friends. This was a stupid night where people got carried away. They'd have lost their places if the university had found out. We all would have. No one should have their life ruined by one stupid drunken night that got out of hand.'

'Except Arran.'

Silence.

Eventually, Cal moves on. 'Who was filming that night, Jonathan?'

'What? Filming? No one.' He frowns, confusion etched on his brow.

'Someone was. I've seen the footage.'

'That's not possible. It would never have been allowed.'

'Maybe if I show you…'

'No!' His voice rings with panic. 'I don't want to see it. I swear, none of us were filming that night. Someone took one photo and Andrew – the president – made them put their phone away. Said there was to be no record.'

'Well, someone made one.'

Jonathan is silent a long moment. 'All I can think is that maybe Andrew knew he might need some leverage one day. No one else in the Circle would dare.'

CHAPTER FIFTY-EIGHT

ARRAN, 2010

The door to Jonno's flat is painted a shocking scarlet, like a soldier's uniform, complete with brass fittings. Arran is almost afraid to touch it, but he presses the button on the intercom and announces himself, daring to touch the shining handle to push open the door when the buzzer sounds to release it. His phone vibrates with a call but he sees it's Donny so he rejects it. As he climbs the stairs, the phone rings again and again in his pocket but he wants nothing to do with the other boy's chaos. He has enough of his own.

Up to the top floor, because of course that's where the best light is, the best views. So obviously that's the one that Jonno will have. Nothing but the best. As he climbs, his anger builds. Every step ratchets the fury higher and higher. He's going to punch Jonathan Keble in the face as soon as he sees him – all this stress and darkness building up, running down his arm into a fist. Arran is far from full strength right now, but he can still land a punch. He's a strong farmer's son; the muscles may be dormant but they're there.

But when he gets to the inner door, and Jonno throws it wide and beams at him, Arran's intention to hit him, hurt him, withers. He takes one look at the warm, tanned face and bursts into tears.

'Oh my God! I mean, I know it needs work, but it's not that bad.' Jonno's exclamation makes Arran smile through his tears – the flat is immaculate – and then hate himself for succumbing to this yet again. 'Seriously, come through.' Jonno steers him into a bright living room with velvet sofas and the slight pleasant smell of a just-lit cigarette curling through the air. 'What's wrong? You look like shit.'

Arran drops onto the nearest sofa and presses his hands to his face. He takes deep steadying breaths before looking up at Jonno. It's a face he knows so well and clearly not at all.

'The picture. The one you took of Olivia sleeping in my room.'

Jonno's face spasms. 'Ah…'

'That's why Olivia and Colleen aren't talking to me. They think I took it.'

He waits for Jonno to say something. Anything but stare at him with that sheepish look on his face.

'What the hell did you do that for?'

Jonathan's hands shake a little.

'I know. I know it was shitty, okay? You wouldn't understand.'

'No, I don't think I will, but you need to explain anyway.'

'I didn't want to do it.'

'So, what, you just accidentally pulled up her top and took a picture?' Arran's voice is stronger now, echoing from those beautiful high ceilings with their elegant cornicing. 'I thought you were my friend!'

'I am.' Jonathan jumps to his feet. 'I'm sorry, I really am. I'll make it right.'

'Why did you do it in the first place?'

'It was part of my initiation for the Circle.' Jonathan mumbles the words, looking at his feet, his whole posture changed as he confesses.

'What? That stupid drinking society?'

When Jonno looks up at him, his eyes are wet and pleading. It makes Arran recoil a little. 'I had to. My dad insisted. He was in it, and it matters to him. I wasn't going to do it, but then he

286

went mental. No one was supposed to share the image – it was just for the Circle committee to see.'

'Well, that's okay, then.'

'I know, I know. It was shitty.'

'You have to tell them.'

'The girls?'

'Yes. You have to tell them today. Now.'

Jonno turns away from him and looks out of the window. It's getting dark, starting to snow.

When he turns back, his eyes are blank, fish-like. He looks defeated. 'I will. Tomorrow, I promise. I'll tell them I fucked up. I'll tell them it wasn't you. I just need you to do something for me first.'

Arran feels his eyes widen. This can't be real. 'You want *me* to do something for *you*.'

'Yes, in return.'

He doesn't know whether to laugh or cry. Instead, he stands and launches forward, shoving Jonno to the ground. They roll over and over, and something smashes – and all Arran can hear is the roaring in his head, and Jonno groaning and then yelping like he's scalded. About to launch a fist, he pulls back, shocked at the kicked-puppy sound.

Jonno scoots backwards from him, cowering in a corner. He covers his face with one hand and cringes, his body shaking.

'Please, please, stop,' he cries, holding his other hand up.

Arran sinks back to the ground, too stunned at the transformation to pursue him.

'All right,' he shouts. 'I've stopped. What the hell?'

Jonno is still crying and shaking. Arran crawls towards him and peels back the hand covering his face.

'What's going on?'

'He does that.' Jonno sobs. Arran can't get over the shock of seeing his confident friend reduced to a snivelling heap.

'Who does what?'

'My father.' Jonno lifts the hem of his shirt and Arran is shocked to see a pattern of bruises in different shades of purple, some edged with yellow or green, a demented rainbow of pain.

'Jesus.'

Jonno's laugh is bitter. 'You'd never guess it, would you?'

Arran shakes his head slowly.

'I told him over the holidays that I didn't want to be in the Circle. He wasn't happy.'

Sinking back on the floor, Arran stares around him at the trappings, the luxury, no longer seeing the privilege he imagined moments earlier. His friend is a prisoner. All this time, he thought he was the one who was caged, and it isn't true. He's free.

'What is it you want me to do?' he asks, softly.

–

Arran listens to what Jonathan needs from him. He doesn't want to do it. But he does want his friend back. The two of them sit facing each other on the window seat, legs stretched out, watching the swirling flakes of snow outside. Is it weird that he's never felt closer to anyone?

All their secrets are out there, all their doubts and fears.

So very different. And yet, not that different after all.

'It's too much to ask, isn't it?' Jonno says eventually, like he knows the answer already. He's going to give in. 'I'll tell the girls anyway. You don't have to do it.' His voice is shaky. He looks around at the unpacked boxes and chaos. 'I really screwed things up.'

'What will you do? Will your father understand?'

Jonathan shakes his head sadly, slowly. 'I don't think so, but this has been coming. Maybe it's better to get the disinherited bit over with.' He starts to laugh but the sound is too sad to join in.

Arran, thinking of his own family pressures, wants to ask if it would really be that bad to be cut free, but he knows that to

Jonno it would be. Jonno's family are rich enough to ensure he never has to worry about a bill or take a job he doesn't love, but that kind of wealth comes with ties.

Maybe it's not that different to his own situation – he's tied to the land, to a way of life that's uncompromising in its demands of you. You can't be half-hearted: farming takes body and soul, no mornings off or spontaneous trips abroad. Funny how he's started to crave it these last few days. Since their corridor family crumbled, the lustre has faded. He misses the physicality of life at home.

He shrugs. 'It's just one night of drinking till I puke, right? And then you're in. Home and dry.'

Jonathan's face widens in hope and surprise. 'Oh my God? You'll do it?'

'As long as you put it right with Olivia.'

'I promise.'

'Only one problem,' Arran says. 'I don't have a dinner jacket.'

'I'll find one for you.'

Jonno punches his shoulder, sending Arran off balance but not hurting him. Jonno could never hurt him.

'Just as a warning – they take your phone and cash, give you a location and you've got to get there on your own, using your wit and charm.'

'My what now?'

'I know. You're fucked, really.' Arran swipes at him. 'When you get there, there's another clue and another, and so on until the end. They'll do the initiation when you make it to the final location, which is usually somewhere we're not allowed to be.'

'Can't you just tell me where it is now and save me the bother?'

'Only the president knows. And his closest advisers.'

Advisers. What a bunch of dickheads. Arran's tempted to back out, but looking at his friend's face, he can't. There's colour in his cheeks again.

It's only while they've been sitting here that he's seen how hollow Jonno's face is. He waves his cigarette in an anxious way, more riled than Arran has ever seen him, thin and uptight.

'Are you eating?'

'Yes. Why? Do I look slim?' Jonno sucks in his stomach.

Arran rolls his eyes. He's never had a friend like this before. All charm and neediness. Sometimes it's intoxicating, other times exhausting. He misses last term. Misses their old corridor camaraderie, misses Olivia, even Colleen. Nothing is ever going to be the same between them again.

Suddenly emotional, he turns his face to the dark glass and the swirling flakes of pure ice. Arran pictures the farm and the fields coated in a white blanket, the surface a frozen crust, the cattle brought into the byre to be fed hay, because they can't scrape to the solid ground. Iced-over drinking troughs, numb fingers and air so cold that frost clings to your eyelashes and hair, melting when you go inside and dripping on the kitchen table.

He hates how he left things with his family. Until he goes back home and apologises, it is going to fester. After tonight, he needs to do it. He has to make amends before carrying on here, if that's even the right thing to do. He can't believe he stepped into Donny's car with God knows what he was transporting, rather than face his family and apologise. It's like he's been blinded. Deep down, he knows that after tonight he can't stay friends with Jonno. Not after what he did to Olivia.

Jonno has the window open and is catching snowflakes with his tongue.

'Try this.'

Arran rolls his eyes but kneels up to the window and leans out. The street lurches below him, cars rolling slowly through settling snow, the flakes illuminated in headlight beams. He wobbles, high above the street, suddenly dizzy with the height.

'Careful,' Jonno says, grabbing him and steadying him.

Arran sticks his tongue out, and fat, lazy snowflakes drift onto his hair and face. In moments, his mouth is numb but it's strangely intoxicating. When he looks up, the world seems to slow down and the sky's heavy purple-grey presses onto him, filling him with contentment.

He pulls his head back in and sees that Jonno is watching him, quieter, more serious than his usual irreverent self. His eyes seem deeper and the quality of the light makes the room eerie.

'Thank you,' he says.

Arran shivers. He reaches out and closes the window. 'It's nae bother.'

'Nae bother,' Jonno echoes, mouthing the words like they taste of fine wine. The phrase sounds funny in his cut-glass accent, the cold air twisting around the room and the feeling of snowflakes instead of tears on his cheeks.

CHAPTER FIFTY-NINE

ARRAN, 2010

He meets three shadowy figures in dinner dress under a bridge down by the muddy waters of the Leith. They're masked, so he can't tell who they are, and it doesn't matter – they make him drink neat vodka and laugh like braying animals when it burns his throat and he coughs and sputters.

'Phone and wallet,' one barks, hand outstretched.

'I left them in my room.' There's an icy pause of displeasure. The message on his phone from Donny, that he'd been arrested, still echoes in Arran's head. He wants nothing to do with it, but after tonight he's going to call the other boy's parents to tell them the mess their son is in, so they can help him and get him clean. After tonight, a lot of things are going to change.

'Fine, shoes instead.'

'What?'

'Give us your shoes.' The boy repeats the words like he's an idiot. 'You have to pay a tax.'

Arran could argue, but he knows there's no point. If he wants to make everything right in his life, he has to jump through their ridiculous hoops. Once this is done, Jonno will tell Olivia and Colleen the truth. Maybe, slowly, he can get back what they had.

'That way.' One of the boys shoves him downstream and Arran sets off, his socks immediately wet from the damp ground. It is cold, so cold. The stars are out, the air is clean after the snow, and it could be beautiful if you were in the right frame of mind. He tiptoes along, trying to choose smooth patches of ground in the dark. There is no point to this.

The boys meet him twice more, and each time they expect him to drink more neat spirits and foul concoctions. The second time, they take his watch; the third, his jacket. At this, Arran protests. The world is lurching in front of his eyes. He feels sick and blurry. The alcohol has hit his system so fast that it feels like it's dancing in his veins.

'Naw... come on... it's freezing.'

'Fine. You won't make it either. Here...'

They hold out his shoes and jacket, and for a moment Arran sways and is tempted to take them – to leave and go back to his warm room in halls and forget all about it, but then he pictures the mess he is in and the determination rises once more.

'All right,' he says, though the words come out twisted and slurred even to his own ears. 'Where now?'

'Go to the docks,' they say. 'Find the grain warehouse. We'll meet you at the top.'

Arran groans. He wishes he had his phone, but he's going to have to do the best he can. He follows the path by the Water of Leith, conscious that he's not walking in a straight line as he veers into the undergrowth a couple of times, unsettling the occasional roosting waterfowl.

As he goes on, the paranoia builds and he feels sure he's being followed. Footsteps that stop when he swivels. He knows for sure there is someone in the bushes at one point, because he hears the clink of cans and smells the sweet weed smoke, but he blunders through, quiet in his socks, the river a burbling companion. At one point he stops and folds in two, heaving into the mud, bringing up the alcohol he's been forced to drink. His vomit spatters the ground and his ankles. It's vile, reeking of booze, and makes him heave again, but when he is done, he feels a little better, enough to keep going.

Tilting his watch, he sees it is almost midnight. A fox darts across the path ahead of him and he staggers on. When he emerges at a bridge at the end of the Walkway, Arran feels self-conscious stepping into the glow of the streetlights, so he slinks in the shadows like the fox.

He just has to get through this. He's so drunk that he has to focus on walking, and finding the grain warehouse seems impossible. He presses on, crossing a road and moving into an area of docklands, lost and panicking. If he can't get to the right place, it will all have been in vain. Is he supposed to ask someone? Who? There's no one to ask. But then he catches sight of a car ahead of him, a taxi pulled over. Three men in dinner jackets, carrying clinking bags, get out, laughing.

He presses himself against the wall, and watches as the car draws away and the boys slip down the side of a building. His chest fluttering, Arran lurches after them, scuffing his soles painfully on the ground. His feet are blistered and sore, his fingers frozen, his body numb with cold. They slip through a gap in a fence and cross to the door of an immense building, its windows dark and forbidding. Arran follows, triumph rising now that he's almost completed the task. Jonno is going to owe him for this.

The door to the warehouse has been levered open. He steps through. In the distance he can hear echoes of footsteps on metal stairs, snatches of laughter. It's no warmer in here, but somehow being indoors is a relief.

He crawls up, bit by bit, using the stair rail, the walls, anything he can to inch himself higher up the building. *Must keep going.* Finally, he does it, emerging on the roof into a raucous wall of sound that, when they notice him, turns into a mocking cheering. He tries to focus on the faces before him but they're so blurry, they slip from view. Hands slap him on the back, too hard. He jolts forward, footsore, ready to be done, ready for his prize.

CHAPTER SIXTY

CAL

Cal waits over the road from the office building. Jonathan's words have been circling his mind. He left the man staring into another thick finger of whisky, already slurring his words. There's no way to undo the sins of his student days, the stain they've left on the person he is. Cal has the impression that Jonathan has kept all of that guilt and truth locked in a box.

But his words have hastened a realisation that's been coming. He needs to take a chance, trust his instincts.

Just when he thinks his wait is pointless and he'll have to come back another day, Colleen emerges from the office, one hand in the pocket of her leather jacket and the other clutching a raft of folders, scarf round her neck, collar turned up. He can't miss the lilac flash of hair and her distinctive rolling walk. Cal hurries across the road. She moves quickly and he has to jog to keep up.

'Colleen. Colleen?'

At last she hears him and turns, pulling an earbud out, frown in place. He swears that when she sees it's him, there's a flicker of fear, hastily concealed.

'What do you want?'

'I'd like to talk.'

'I've said everything I need to.' Colleen turns away from him, lifting the bud to her ear. It's now or never with this hunch.

'It was you. Who sent the footage. You were there that night.'

She falters in her movement. And he's sure. He's got her.

A beat too late, Colleen spins around to face him. 'What are you on about?'

He waits. 'You wanted the world to see the Circle was to blame. But they're powerful men. I get why you didn't come forward back then. I do.'

It's like trying to calm a wild creature. The woman's face relaxes a fraction, but her eyes are still tight with distrust, her shoulders turned away from him as if she wants to run and never look back.

'You don't have any proof.'

'You knew, Colleen. You knew Jonno was in the Circle. You hated it.'

She hesitates, looking up and down the street. Her hands are tight around the folders she carries.

'Why did you come forward now, after all this time?' he pushes.

'His mother on the news... I just couldn't bear it. No matter what sort of person he was. She doesn't deserve that. She needed to know.'

'Shall we go for a drink? Talk about this? You could help now, Colleen. We can protect you and make sure those men pay for what they did.'

Colleen's face contorts with calculation. 'I could lose my job.'

'If everything is out in the open, they'll be the ones who are scared.'

There's something hungry in her eyes – a long-held desire to see some justice. To right the balance between the world she battles in and the way they skate above it all.

She jerks her head and he follows her along the street to a rough-looking drinking hole that looks like it's barely changed in a hundred years. He goes to the bar and gets her a pint of Guinness, as well as a bottle of beer for himself. Then he sets the recording going.

'So, tell me why you were at the warehouse that night. Why you took the footage.'

Her face seems to fizz with heat – too much anger to conceal, tamped down over the years but building inside her, nevertheless.

'I wanted to take them down. I bumped into Arran going into halls and he let it slip that he was going to a Circle initiation, so I decided to follow him and get some proof to show the university, so maybe they would finally grow a spine and ban those drinking societies.'

Cal sips his beer and nods along, not wanting Colleen to clam up.

'You followed him all that way?'

'It wasn't hard. It was dark and he was so drunk by the time he got there. I just hung back and watched him. When they went into the building, I followed them in.'

When she stops talking, he nudges her along, gently.

'What they did to Arran was pretty shocking.'

'Aye.' She looks away and then back at Cal. 'They'd already started by the time I made it up to the roof. They were like animals. I realised I'd been stupid – going out there, following them into that building at night. I was just so worked up, so angry. I hid behind a metal tank at the top of the stairs. I took the footage and then left.'

'You didn't think to check on Arran? To help him?'

Colleen's eyes blaze.

'There were so many of them, drunk. And he was one of them! There was no way I was going near him – you don't know what he was capable of.'

This is the moment that Cal has known has been coming. It's going to puncture the story she's told herself about that night. The way she's justified her silence.

'You mean the picture? Of Olivia?'

'She told you?' Her voice is barely more than a tremble. 'Olivia told you what he did to her?'

Cal shakes his head.

'Jonno did.'

Colleen swallows.

'He came to Edinburgh to meet me,' he adds. 'He's been abroad and only just learned about Arran's death.'

'He knew about the picture?' Her initial softening at the mention of Jonathan has given her away – even all these years later, Cal can tell how much she liked him. This student who seemed to have such charismatic power over them all.

'He took it, Colleen.'

'What?' She sets her pint down too fast and it jars loudly against the wood. 'No. That's not…' She sits back, hands to her mouth. He can see her thoughts spinning, the emotions rippling across her face. 'You're lying.'

'It was him. Part of his initiation. He slipped into Arran's room while he was in the kitchen. Arran knew nothing about it until you told him. Jonathan promised that if Arran went to the rooftop, then he'd tell you and Olivia the truth.'

'I don't believe you.'

'It's true.'

Two men have come into the deserted snug. Their voices are loud, their office talk cutting across the space. Colleen doesn't appear to notice.

'But if that's true, then…' She stares at Cal, tears in her eyes. 'Arran was innocent.'

'I don't believe this. I don't trust you.'

'I'm not lying to you, Colleen. I have Jonathan on the record.'

'I need to go to the toilet.' Colleen pushes her way out and hurries through the bar. Cal lets out a long breath.

So many things led to that moment, to the lack of mercy shown to Arran. Even now, they still don't know exactly what happened at the end. Did he decide to jump after being unable to bear those betrayals? Or did he fall, unable to walk after the alcohol and abuse?

Maybe they'll never know. He died alone.

What they can do is seek justice for him. Those men on that roof are culpable. Maybe a court won't give them much time, but the court of public opinion can do just as much damage. You only need to look at Margot's case to know that. Those powerful men. They're going to find they can't run away from the past.

—

When Colleen comes back from the toilet, her skin is pale and her eyes dark and deep.

'I need to go,' she says. 'I need to get my head around this.'

Cal nods. 'Arran's parents deserve justice. His little sisters deserve justice. You know who those men were, Colleen. I know you do.'

Her eyes widen for a moment and she slumps into the chair.

'You don't understand,' she says. 'They could make my life hell.'

'We'll help you. Protect you. You can be anonymous.'

Colleen chews at her fingernails for a moment and Cal is struck by the transformation in her. In just a short time, her hard shell has cracked.

'Turn off the recording,' she says.

Cal reaches out and presses the button on his phone.

'I have one name,' he says. 'Andrew Runner.'

She nods. 'He was one of them. I can give you more names, but they didn't come from me.'

Colleen looks around and Cal feels a chill run through him, despite the warm bar and the comfort of music and conversation. Colleen's brand is bolshie and abrasive to the extreme – he admires that, although finds her hard to like. But as she reaches for a pen and scribbles the names onto a page ripped out of one of her files, she is clearly afraid.

'There.' She slides the sheet of paper over to him. Five names. Pressed hard into the paper. She points a bitten nail at the top name and runs it down the rest as she details them. 'Son of a sheriff, police officer, magistrate's kid, lackey to the First Minister, television presenter.'

Colleen looks at him, a fearful satisfaction entering her eyes when she sees she has his attention. The instructions the police have had to leave this alone make a lot more sense now.

'They were on the roof that night? All of them?'

She leans back and slides a packet of cigarettes out of her pocket, along with a lighter, holding them with shaking fingers.

'They were there. I have to go. Please.'

Cal nods. 'Thank you, Colleen.'

She stands, gathering her things in a chaotic, haphazard way. She drops the files and he helps her collect them, holding them while she slides her arms into her jacket. When she takes them, she looks up at him, her voice shaking as she speaks.

'If that's what they do to their mates for fun, imagine what they do behind closed doors, to their wives, their kids. And we let them run the country. We hang on their every fucking word.' A tear runs down her cheek and he knows it's not the group she's thinking of, but one in particular.

'Jonathan would like to see you,' he tells her. 'He asked me to pass that on.'

She doesn't wait to be told more. Seconds later, Cal is alone in the pub, the list of names held as carefully in his hand as a stick of dynamite.

CHAPTER SIXTY-ONE

ARRAN, 2010

Breathing hurts his lungs, and his skin stings and throbs where it is drenched in sick, oil and piss. There's a graze on his chest that is burning a hole in him. He wants to go home, but home is a distant concept, no longer real. Nothing is real, except the darkness and the jeering voices, laughter that comes in and out of focus as he sways and shivers, his breath making brief clouds of warmth that dissolve in front of him.

Arran closes his eyes, too afraid and ashamed to look. They took his trousers after he climbed up here, the world blurry and lilting. At that stage, maybe he was laughing along, but it's been a long time since any of this was funny. What time is it? The world is just endless night. How is he going to get back to halls? The thought makes him whimper but he pulls the little scraps of sound back down his throat or else they'll hear him and all of this will start over.

Initially, he felt so exposed in his cheap boxers and socks, but he has long stopped caring what they think of him. His tongue is coated with the taste of fish oil and vomit. It lies like a thick, furred creature in his mouth, something that doesn't belong to him. Arran's thoughts flit in and out. He wants water but that is not allowed. Only more vodka – the cheap paint-stripper brand from the corner shop, though they could afford anything.

He can't hear Jonno and he wonders if he's gone, left him, or if he knew this was the plan all along. It has been another lie. That's a hurt that can't be blotted out. It chases him. Then thoughts of his mother, the farm and the fields – a longing almost as intense as the physical pain – flood him and pull out like the tide again, leaving him washed up, fifty metres above ground.

There is no point in begging.

'One more!'

Hands grab his chin and he groans involuntarily, his eyes flying open to see a kaleidoscope of faces whirling. He gags again, and they shout and jump back – he can feel the recoil and disgust like a slap, as vomit spatters on the concrete. He keels over to the side, crumpled on the cold surface.

'Wait. Is he still breathing?'

One note of sense in a feral frenzy.

Another bends over to check. 'Yeah. He's fine. God, he stinks.'

'Come on, up we get.'

Strong arms, wrenched up, tilted chin and hot breath on his face that rotates in his mind until it is the steaming breath of cattle. He can hear them stamping their feet in the byre, smells the farmyard effluent – the mixture of cow piss and hay, warm and intoxicating. But then one of them kicks him and he is back in the present, the burn of more vodka in his throat. He gulps it, diabolically grateful it's not fish oil.

A moment of quiet now, like the intake of breath, and he thinks he hears his mother's voice calling him in. He opens his eyes to check but the world spins on its axis, vertigo sailing around him, so he clamps them shut again but it doesn't help. He has been so sick that he should be sobering up, but he can feel himself slipping further into drunkenness, his body protesting at all the substances he has been made to drink, the foul liquids poured over him, burning his skin.

'Enough,' he tries to say, but his face is wrenched around and the world turns into a gargle of choking-thick fish oil and stinging vodka. Hands cup his chin, lifting so that the concoction pours down his throat and he thinks he will die, but has no choice but to swallow. They cheer and slap him on the back, but they aren't congratulating him – only themselves.

He tries to focus on them but the alcohol inside him has distorted everything: they are blurred and shaking devils, dancing hazily before him in the cold. He feels his gorge rising. His belly spasms again and they leap away like imps, cheering and cursing as he brings it all back up, infused by bile. It spatters on the roof, splashing over his legs. He wipes his mouth, wishes for water.

'Careful,' a voice rings out, jovial as Christmas. 'We don't want to kill him.'

Don't they? Because it feels to Arran that they do, and he is a plaything, like the mouse toyed with by a bored cat. Surely it must be over soon.

But there is worse to come. Before he can fall, he is gripped again. His boxers are ripped down, and he moans in horror and fear as he feels something cold and slimy slither between his legs. *Not this.* Inside, he is screaming but the sound is caught in his throat and all that comes out is an awful moan that sounds almost sexual and makes him want to rip his own skin off.

'Fuck,' he screams. Whatever it is feels like death, like a nightmare.

His instinct is to call for his mother, but the thought of his family just drives more shame into him, like he's sullying them by bringing them into this situation, even in his mind. Panicked, he fights the arms that hold him.

Grey and hideous, with sunken eyes, the dead eel slides to the floor, flopping between his feet. Its stare is glassy and cold in the moonlight. He screams again, and propels himself backwards, completely unprepared for this part of the initiation. An eel. It's only an eel. Yet his skin crawls with panic and uncertainty. Laughter around him.

'Careful,' someone shouts, and a hand reaches out and pulls him away from the edge, where he has been teetering without realising, the glittering lights of the city spread into the distance.

Time passes, and he slides in and out of it.

'I'm cold,' a voice above him says. 'Let's split.'

Please, he begs silently, *please leave*.

They're moving around him now, like he doesn't exist. Gathering things, bagging the evidence. They're taking his clothes. Then he hears the clang of metal, and he spasms and shudders at the notion of how high they are, so far above the ground, though he honestly feels there can be no further to fall.

Their laughter rings out across the rooftop, the confidence that they can operate with impunity, a privilege of their birth, not his. He is not stupid enough, even in his slurring, disintegrating state, to have missed the camera flash and click, taking and storing evidence of his shame. Because that is what they do. They pass it around between them, share it for edification and delight. It's what they did to Olivia.

Some of the voices are fading now. His body is wracked with shivers, his fingers and toes are numb with cold. Is it over?

And then he hears the voice he knows so well. *He's still here.*

'I'll be right there.'

And into the pause he feels the shift of air and the rattle. Hands touching him. He is too tired and broken to flinch away.

'Arran, it's me.'

Jonno.

'I'm sorry. I had no idea it would be like that.'

The hot whisper in his ear is so comforting that he wants to cry. It is too late to say sorry, when you have taken a person to pieces. You can't pretend, after that, that it was all a game. A tear runs down his cheek. He should just leave him to die.

'Go away.' The words are croaks into the night.

'I have to go. But I'll come back for you as soon as I can, with a taxi.'

Arran is so far beyond resistance that he stays limp and neutral. He can never face anyone after this, he can't ever look his family in the eye.

'Or I could stay…'

'Just go!' Arran uses the last iota of strength he has to roar and he feels Jonno fall back at the force of it, scramble to his feet.

There is no doubt that a dark, private bar draped in gold is waiting for him. Champagne on ice and admiring girls in elegant dresses, clean and glittering. Nothing like this sordid rooftop. So, Arran knows he will go, but all the same he hopes he won't. Because that is the one and only thing that might get him through it all.

He closes his eyes and waits. There's the longest pause, and hope starts to flicker into his freezing limbs. And then the clink of the steps, the sound of weight being transferred to them and the metallic clangs that fade into the night the further he goes.

Arran rolls onto his back and opens his eyes. They sting with the fresh onslaught of tears. The night is perfect, and still it feels like the stars are laughing.

CHAPTER SIXTY-TWO

CAL

Cal walks slowly back to his hotel, unable to shake the sense of melancholy that's fallen over him. Arran's short time in Edinburgh ended in a lonely, horrible place, his body rotting far from home and the people who loved him. Yes, he's managed to solve a mystery, but increasingly it feels like this isn't enough. It isn't justice. And that was what his podcast was supposed to be about. It was what his life was supposed to be about.

He'll sit down again this evening and comb through everything, trying to put a case together against these powerful men – but what hope is there of ever getting any kind of conviction? And for what? The open-source experts are comparing the footage to the names Colleen provided, they're matching faces and bodies, lining up the evidence. Lawyers are going over the letter he's written to send to each of them. All hell is about to break loose, so really he should enjoy the calm before the storm.

Instead, he rings his mother.

She has her own number now, in the care home, her own mini-apartment, with a bathroom and kitchenette. It takes a few moments for her to answer. When she does, her voice is frail. A fraying line to the past.

'Mum? It's me, Cal. How are you doing?'

A shaky breath. 'I'm fine. Where are you? Are you coming to see me?'

'I'm in Edinburgh, Mum, but I'll come and visit next week. See your new pad.'

'That will be nice. I can see the birds from my window. I was wondering if you could bring me some bird food.'

'That's a good idea. We could get one of those feeders that stick on the glass.'

From her exclamation, she sounds genuinely excited by the idea. It's both reassuring and sad that it's becoming about the small and simple things, though maybe there are lessons in that too.

'I have to go in a minute,' she says.

'No problem.' It's a relief that she's the one bringing the conversation to a close.

'I'd like to talk but we're playing Cluedo at five.'

Cal smiles, taken aback, repressing the urge to laugh. 'Who's playing?'

'Oh, me and a couple of the other ladies. And a man called Wilf. But he can be a bit interfering, truth be told.'

'That sounds great, Mum. Well, except the interfering bit.'

'I told them about your pod thing…' she continues before an awkward silence can intrude. 'We're going to listen to the next episode together, me and Eliza.'

'That's brilliant, Mum.'

'That poor boy. Eliza was quite shocked when they found his body.' She pauses. 'I haven't told them about your sister.'

Her voice is so matter-of-fact. Cal feels a strange sense of a door tilting shut, blowing in the breeze. It's going to close soon.

'Maybe that's best,' is all he can manage.

When they finish speaking, he can't quite believe it. He spent the whole call waiting for the usual sting in the tail, but there wasn't one. As he strolls along the road to his hotel, he finds there's a lump in his chest.

–

With nothing much to do until the lawyers come back to him, Cal ends up down an internet rabbit hole. There are still some things that bother him about Arran's case, but he can't quite put his finger on what they are. Maybe it's simply that, aside from Natalie, his friends haven't really offered much insight into him, the person he was to them. Like scratching an itch, he finds himself googling the grain warehouse again – the beast of a building that disgorged its secrets so dramatically.

All the pleas to save it have failed, he discovers. As soon as the police give the word, it can be demolished to make way for the future. He clicks through old images taken by urban explorers who broke into the site like he and Robbie did. The staircase looks ethereal and ancient, like something on the Titanic. There are pictures of empty offices and files, clipboards and hulking pieces of industrial machinery. All these things Arran must have walked past that night.

Maybe it's good that the building won't be there any more. It's seen too much. It's now an empty, ghoulish attraction.

As he clicks through media images of protesters keen to see the site preserved, he searches his mind. What is it about this case that still niggles at him? He's tired, that's all. Shona is out at a lecture this evening, so he tries Chrissie, surprised when she answers.

'Hi, love, is this a good time? I thought you might be out on the town.'

'I'm revising,' she says. 'I have an assessment tomorrow.'

'Oh, I should leave you to it.'

'No, wait, I'd like to talk for a minute.'

He chats with her, though she sounds deflated, tired perhaps. In the end, he breaks the golden rule. 'Chrissie, are you okay?'

There's a long pause and then a tearful sniff. 'Yes. I just… You're going to think I'm so stupid after everything I said, but I kind of miss Robbie.'

'Oh, love, I'm sorry. That must be hard.'

'What if I made the wrong decision?' Her words are a gentle wail.

Cal stills. What is the right advice to give her? What is the right or wrong decision?

'There's no such thing,' he says, finally. 'We just do our best with the information and the feelings we have at the time.'

'It felt like the right thing,' she says, her voice small. 'But now I'm not so sure. He just *got* me. Here, I've met all these new people and I like them but… sometimes I feel so alone.'

'It'll take time to find the true friends. The first term of university is exhausting, Chrissie. You're not doing anything wrong.'

'I'm not? Because it feels like I'm pretending all the time.'

'Not at all. Just keep watch for the people who make you feel good.'

'Thanks, Dad.'

'Now get on and study.' He makes his voice strict and schoolmarmish, and is rewarded with a chuckle.

They say their goodbyes, and then Cal sets down his phone and moves the mouse to bring his computer back to life. The screen opens on a picture of protesters holding placards. *Our story, not history! Grain down the drain!* He realises there is something about the image that has his attention, a pinging inside his mind. But what?

Tired, he leans back and closes his eyes, massages the crick in his neck. Then he goes back to the computer. What is it? He peers closer. Enlarges the image. He's about to give up, when it hits him.

'No way!' Without meaning to, he has jumped to his feet.

There's a figure, standing at the back, looking up at the building instead of at the camera. He knows who it is. The electric purple hair is now a more muted lilac, but he'd recognise her anywhere.

–

He manages to get the resident of one of the other flats in her building to buzz him in by claiming to be a confused pizza delivery man, then takes a single flight of stairs to her doorway. He knocks and waits, a moment later hearing footsteps within

309

– his mind is humming with the connections he's making. A flicker of doubt tells him his thoughts can't be true, but his gut disagrees.

Colleen must be looking at him through the spyhole, because when she opens the door, there is no surprise on her face. They look at each other. Something passes between them.

She steps to one side.

'Come in.'

Cal follows her down a hallway covered with framed photographs. There are more in the tiny lounge, so many images of Colleen with her university friends, treasured moments papering the walls in which she lives. He finds it sad that there aren't more recent examples of fun and friendship, like she's stuck in the past. She seems softer here, in her own space. It's immaculate, apart from a tray on the sofa, a ready meal eaten from its container, scraped clean.

'Have a seat. Do you want a drink?'

Cal sinks into an armchair, relieved not to be towering over her.

'I'm fine, thanks.'

She watches him, waiting, so he takes out his phone and unlocks it, holding it out to her.

'I found this picture when I was researching the grain warehouse. That's you. There, at the back.'

Colleen nods. Her eyes are wide and fearful.

'You didn't want it demolished.' Colleen doesn't move. 'Because then they'd find him.' She seems to deflate, punctured, no trace of the fight and defiance he is used to from her. 'You knew he was there, all along.'

Colleen puts her hands between her knees, shrinking in on herself. She nods. Her skin is pasty and her eyes well up.

'I need you to tell me,' Cal says, softly. 'Everything that happened that night.'

There is a long moment of silence.

'You saw the video,' she says eventually. 'He was so drunk, and they kept making him drink more and more, disgusting things that made him sick. It was awful. I stopped the filming and I was going to go, but I couldn't get to the stairs without them seeing me. So I waited until they left.'

'Then it was just the two of you on the roof.'

'He fell.' Colleen swallows her tears. 'It was awful. He was so drunk, and one minute he was standing there and the next... he'd gone.'

'Why didn't you call for help?'

'I thought he was dead. I panicked and ran. I was going to call for help but I thought for sure he'd be found, and then days passed and... he wasn't. And I started to think that maybe it wasn't real or the Circle people had hushed it up, and I was scared and...'

Cal nods. Her distress is clear.

'There are going to be questions now. You know that, don't you?'

Colleen wipes her nose with the back of her hand. When she speaks, she sounds like a child. 'Will I lose my job?'

'I hope not.' But the truth is, he isn't sure.

'So,' he pushes on. 'Can we tell Arran's mother it was an accident, not suicide? That he didn't mean to do it?'

'He didn't mean to do it,' Colleen says, her eyes fixed on Cal, her gaze unwavering despite the tear stains on her cheeks. 'It never should have happened.'

CHAPTER SIXTY-THREE

Jonathan is only in Edinburgh for one more evening. Cal wants to talk to him, to tell him who was filming, get his reaction and some of his thoughts on record for the podcast. When he calls him, the man sounds drunk.

'I've been looking through pictures,' he says. 'Of that first term.'

When Cal is admitted to the same snug where he met Jonathan before, he sees regret swilled together with whisky. Even the expensive surroundings can't dampen the acrid taste of shame in the air. The man looks up with red-rimmed eyes.

'Any progress?'

'Yes.' Cal takes the wingback chair opposite. 'I spoke to Colleen,' he says.

'She won't return my calls.' At Jonathan's signal, the waiter sets down two glasses of whisky in front of them. He holds a gleaming silver tray, moves with ease – like a dancer.

'She was the one filming that night.'

Jonathan pauses, glass suspended between table and mouth. 'Colleen?'

'Yes. She wanted to expose the Saltire Circle. She followed Arran and filmed the initiation.'

Jonathan takes a mouthful of the amber liquid. He looks stunned.

'I thought it was Andrew.'

Cal shakes his head. 'She saw him fall.'

Jonathan closes his eyes for a second, as if in pain. 'Then why didn't she tell anyone? All this time…'

'She was scared.' But Cal finds this odd as well; Colleen seemed such a moral person, to the point of self-righteousness.

'Christ. What a mess.'

'We're trying to identify the men in the footage, Jonathan. I think the people who fed Arran the alcohol that night should be held accountable. If he hadn't been that drunk, he wouldn't have fallen. You could help us…'

Jonathan doesn't say anything, just stares into the crackling flames of the small fire beside them. The smell of smoke is oddly comforting, mixed with the peat of the whisky. 'Maybe,' he says, eventually. 'It's all coming out in the wash anyway.'

'It's the right thing for Arran's family. They need to know.'

Mention of them galvanises the man. 'I've been thinking,' he says. 'Arran's family might want some of these.' He swivels his laptop to show him a kaleidoscope of snapshots – the four of them, so young and hopeful, arms thrown around each other, walking down a street, posing in front of the Scott Monument, drinking together. Some of the shots were taken at night, and the movement of the camera has created a blurriness that fits the impression Cal has of Arran and this case.

'I think they would,' Cal says. 'They don't have any of these kinds of pictures.'

Jonathan gazes at them through misty vision. 'We had a lot of fun those few months. Before it all went wrong.'

'Do you mind if I have a look?'

'Not at all…'

Cal picks up the laptop and clicks through the pictures, seeing an Edinburgh of the past, the kids pulling faces, their fresh skins testament to their youth. He looks and he sees his own daughter, and it strikes at the soft parts of him, the fear and the protectiveness.

He lands on one photograph in particular. An image of the four of them standing in front of a building, holding glasses of steaming mulled wine in gloved hands.

'Where was this taken?'

Jonathan leans across to look. 'Oh, that was Bonfire Night – before we went to see the fireworks.'

Cal puts his finger on the screen. Time bends as he looks at the past, clicking a final piece of the puzzle into place. One that could change everything.

'That scarf. It's distinctive.'

Jonathan laughs. 'Oh, yeah – it's colourful, that's for sure. Very much of its time, I guess.'

He doesn't seem to catch the relevance. But then, he wouldn't. Certain details have never been released, after all.

'Would Colleen ever borrow that?'

'Colleen? Definitely not. She used to go on and on about how much she hated it.'

Cal's jaw drops open. Because now, he sees.

CHAPTER SIXTY-FOUR

ARRAN, 2010

It's time to move. He has to move. Arran rolls onto his side, the cold making his movements slow and sluggish – or is that the alcohol? He can no longer tell, only dimly aware that this level of chill is dangerous, this prolonged exposure to the elements. A memory of hearing about the drunk his father once found in a ditch – a local man who'd walked back from the pub and sat down for a rest, never woke up. Arran was six at the time.

It's only when he's on his knees, groaning, that he hears another sound that cuts him silent, bracing for a strike, for another wave of torment.

But these footsteps are different. They are the soft shuffle of trainers rather than the arrogant clip of dress shoes.

'I guess you have to be careful what you wish for.'

Her voice is like an electric shock. Worse than the torture he expected. He'd swap back to those boys in a heartbeat. The only thing that could ever make tonight bearable is if no one else bore witness. A wave of dizziness strikes and he leans forward, sick again on the frozen rooftop, little left to bring up, just retching into nothingness. It feels like he's been poisoned, and there's no way to get it out of his system.

This is not what he wanted. Not like this.

But now could be his only chance. He needs to tell her the truth. He has to pull himself together.

He stumbles to his feet and tries to focus on her face, but her image lurches from side to side and all he can take in is an imprint of anger, hands on hips.

'What are you doing here?' Another voice. Arran staggers, turns, sees Colleen striding across the rooftop to them.

He opens his mouth to explain, but she isn't talking to him. 'I followed you.'

Olivia's voice, instead of its usual melody, is a needle in his brain. She turns on him again, her face filled with hatred. 'Was it worth it? What you did to me? For this? I thought we were friends!'

'We are,' he slurs.

'No. You treated me like an object.'

'It wasn't me, please...' He's trying to form the words, but they keep coming out wrong. He's drenched and nearly naked, stinking, sick. It's every horror you could ever imagine.

'Please, Olivia, let me explain.'

'You deserve to be treated like this.'

He doesn't mean to, but he lurches forward towards her; he becomes aware too late of her recoiling and tries to step backwards but fails to execute the move properly, his legs refusing to obey his addled mind. He's so close, he can smell her perfume for a brief, beautiful second. Only then, her hands fly out and strike him, hard. He's forced back, winded, teetering. His arms windmill in space. He reaches, finds cloth, softness sliding through his fingertips, and grasps tight, like he won't ever let go. He hears a scream and wants to tell Colleen not to worry, that he's got this.

But he can't. Because he's falling.

CHAPTER SIXTY-FIVE

EPISODE SEVEN: ARRESTED

Last night, Jonathan Keble was taken into custody by police in Edinburgh. The arrest was made after Jonathan, once known to his Edinburgh friends as Jonno, turned himself in for the manslaughter of Arran McDonald.

We've been investigating Arran's disappearance on behalf of his parents, Angela and Bill. For years they've been desperate to know what happened to their vanished son. The gentle boy they depended on. Now they finally know the details of his last moments.

Jonathan Keble has revealed to police that Arran fell from the roof into machinery on the side of the building after a drunken altercation between the friends. It was, he says, a terrible accident. His lawyers have provided a statement for us to read out on his behalf.

'Arran was my friend. He took part in an initiation that evening on my request – he had no desire to be part of the society himself. After the initiation, I tried to help him up. If we hadn't been drunk, he never would have fallen. The reason I haven't come forward before now is that I was afraid of the consequences, and deeply ashamed that I failed to step in and protect my friend. I was also threatened by the other members of the Saltire Circle. I was young and stupid, and I sincerely regret my decision not to speak out sooner. I know there is nothing I can do to ease the pain this has caused for Arran's loved ones.'

While Keble has taken responsibility for Arran's death, that's not the full story. After all, this is an accident that would never have happened had Arran not been plied with alcohol by older students in the Saltire Circle. It was a terrible initiation that went too far when there were so many opportunities to stop it. If only one person had spoken out.

The footage that we revealed in the last episode was taken by a student keen to expose the practices of the society. It shows the events of that evening in detail. Before his arrest, Jonathan helped with the identification of the other students in that film – including those who assaulted Arran by forcing him to drink neat vodka and fish oil. Many of them are people you would recognise in public life, men you might look up to. We plan to continue our coverage and reveal their identities, to ensure they take responsibility for their part in Arran's death and the silence afterwards.

Next week, Arran will be buried in the family plot at the churchyard near their farmhouse in Moray. Jonathan will be remanded in custody until his trial.

CHAPTER SIXTY-SIX

CAL

He isn't sure why he goes. It's only a building, after all.

The protesters have stayed away for the main event. Battle fought and lost, individuals have faded back into the community to mow the lawn and cook tea for the kids. On the appointed day, there's just a smattering of locals, a sole reporter and a cameraman standing in the drizzle, watching as workers in luminous vests walk back and forth, shining yellow diggers primed and ready. There's much pointing and waiting.

Cal gazes across the dock, which is rippling in the wind. It's a dreary place. The sky will look different without the old grain warehouse. The past obliterated. In front of him, a spaniel scurries around the building, nose to the ground, breathing in the smells of the brownfield site as it sweeps the area one last time. Just to be sure no one sleeping rough is left inside before Armageddon begins above them.

It must be close now. The council officials with clipboards are here, standing off to one side, hard hats in place and biros quivering. He records a short piece – observations, bearing witness. He thinks of Arran, high on the roof above, under-neath a brutal sky of stars. Then he thinks of the men now being questioned by police – their privilege in the end less of a barrier to justice than they had hoped, and that gives him some satisfaction.

Who knows what the court process will bring. It cannot be relied upon. But what you can do, he's realising, is disrupt. Take their perfect lives, and their attempts to move on and forget – and break them in two. Less justice, more revenge? Possibly, but he doesn't like to think that way. Surely, there will be a chance to disrupt Jason Barr in future.

The weather is keeping most people away, but Cal scans the perimeter and notices another watcher in the distance, down the side of a vacant-eyed building, her hair whipped forward by the wind funnelling down the street. He stares at the woman a moment or two, unsure if he's really seeing her, but she's there: gaze directed up to the roof, arms folded as if in self-protection.

Expecting her to bolt when she sees him, Cal creeps along the cordon towards her. Olivia is wearing a pale grey suit, though she looks less pristine than he remembers her. She doesn't notice him until he's a few metres away, but when she does, she makes no attempt to avoid him.

He can see it, he thinks, the luminous fragility that captured Arran all those years ago. But it's deceptive, because underneath the surface is a core of steel and a legacy of hurt. She went on, anyway. She got her degree, achieved in her career – all the while knowing that the body of a man she thought assaulted and humiliated her lay in this factory. A push from her sent him there – that's what Cal is fairly sure happened. Arran's fingers closed on her scarf as he fell, pulling it from her, taking a piece of her with him.

He doesn't know what to say to Olivia. He only knows what he suspects. He isn't sure why he's colluded in their silence.

'Maybe I shouldn't be here,' she says, head tilted to the sky. 'I just wanted to say goodbye.' She looks at Cal. 'I never really did before. I didn't think well of him.'

'Colleen told you, then?'

'That it wasn't him who took the picture? Yes. Jonno was always so plausible, so charming, you know.'

He waits, the silence between them stretching into all the things that cannot be said.

Cal pictures Jonathan, due in court this morning to be charged with manslaughter. His lawyers have tried to persuade him to contest the charges, but he will not. He admits them fully, says he wishes to atone. Only a few people know exactly what he wishes to atone for. It isn't pushing Arran from the top of a building. Just everything that led up to that moment. Maybe if he pays the price, then he can be free.

The luminous ant-people retreat behind the cordon in front of them, a sense of nervous excitement sending bolts through the air. A shout goes up, there is a pause and then the explosion inside the top half of the building causes it to crumple as if in disbelief. Dust billows as the structure folds. The noise sends birds into the air from the rooftops; there is a ringing in Cal's ears and then the perfect absence of sound.

When the clouds of dust subside, he looks up to see light and sky. A smattering of self-congratulatory applause emits from the cluster of hard hats, then beeping sounds as the diggers clank into motion.

He turns to say something to Olivia. But, like a ghost, she has gone.

EPILOGUE

He visits Jonathan in the jail where the investment banker is awaiting what will be a brief trial, given his admission of manslaughter and the lack of appetite to push for a murder charge.

He always forgets how noisy it is in prison. The artificial light, the poor diet and the lack of exercise have already had their effect on Keble. He seems diminished and exhausted, but strangely accepting of his circumstances. But then, he's chosen them, after all. In the visiting room, they sit opposite each other while families meet around them, fathers greeting children and partners, the atmosphere muted yet loaded. Snippets of conversation drift to him. He hasn't been given permission to record, so this is just between the two of them. Cal lowers his voice.

'It wasn't you, Jonathan.'

'What wasn't me?' The side of Keble's mouth draws down slightly, his eyes meet Cal's reluctantly.

'You didn't push Arran that night. I don't think you were even there when he went over the edge. The discovery of his body was a total shock to you. I know it was.'

'Maybe I'm just a really good actor.'

Cal shakes his head. 'Why are you doing this?'

'I bear responsibility. I'm taking it. I've spent my whole life running from the things I've done, the privilege I've abused. It stops.'

'This is for what you did to Olivia? The picture?'

Jonathan's face tightens. 'The first in a line of actions. But yes, if I hadn't taken that photograph and let everyone think it was him, Arran would never have needed forgiveness, would never have come to the warehouse at all. Colleen and Olivia wouldn't have been able to follow him. In a parallel universe, none of them were ever there. I wasn't in the Circle. I failed their initiation, my father was furious.' His eyes moisten. 'Arran is running a farm somewhere. We go and stay once a year and get mud on our wellies. He laughs at our easy lives. We send Christmas cards.'

Cal gives in to the fantasy. 'You think you'd still be in touch?'

Jonathan nods. 'There was something about him. He understood me. We were more similar than people knew. Arran was special.'

Cal watches a woman reach out to a man across the table. A guard steps in to stop their hands from meeting.

'I could tell the police they're wrong. That you're lying. The scarf – she's wearing it in pictures of the four of you.'

'I'd tell them it was mine, that I lent it to her. Would they believe you?'

'Yes, they might. There's a chance.'

Jonathan's voice takes on a different tone. 'Olivia went through things she shouldn't have had to. All because of me and the Circle. Yes, we could drag all that out in court, find the picture, humiliate her, but…' Keble closes his eyes and Cal sees the pain on his face.

'You loved her.'

The man sits back in his chair. 'I loved them all.'

Cal feels right and wrong weighing so heavily that it makes his mind stupid. He doesn't know what he thinks about anything any more.

'So, you'll do time to protect her?'

'Too little, too late, but yes.'

When the visiting hour ends, Cal watches Keble walk away. Maybe he's a shadow of the man he was outside, but somehow he steps more lightly.

Outside, in the car park, he breathes deep lungfuls of air, relieved to be out of the building. He thinks of the podcast, of what Sarah would say if she knew, whether his duty to the truth outweighs his duty to justice. What should Arran's parents be told? What should make a difference? He isn't sure.

His phone rings in his pocket and he answers, expecting Shona. He's driving back up there tonight. Christmas is coming, and she's decorated the barn with sparkling lights and great swathes of pine. It smells like a forest.

'I need to talk to you. I've been trying to reach you, but…'

He doesn't recognise the voice, is still smiling in anticipation of Shona.

'Sorry, hang on. I missed that. Who is this? You've reached Cal Lovett.'

'I know. It's Naomi.'

Cal frowns. He doesn't know a Naomi.

'I'm sorry, I…' But then it strikes him. He almost drops the phone.

'We shouldn't be speaking.' He's taken aback by the anger that fires into him, making his voice shake. He grips the handset so hard it hurts.

'You shouldn't be calling me.'

'I know. It's just, Jason…' Even the name makes Cal want to strike something. He hates this woman. 'He's not what everyone thinks.' *No shit, Sherlock.* 'He's different.'

'I expect he's exactly who I think he is.'

'That's why I'm calling you.' Her voice drops to a whisper. 'I don't know where else to turn.'

He wants to tell her that serves her right, that she legitimised Barr, that she's a huge part of the reason his sister's killer walked free, but he's frozen in place. Thoughts of the man behind the prison walls are too close, skewing his ideas of right and wrong. Does Barr know she's calling? Is this his latest game?

Her words rush into the silence. 'He says things, in his sleep. You should know what he says. You need to know.' The fear has gone from her voice. Is it sick satisfaction he hears?

He can no longer be sure, but the thought of lying next to that monster makes Cal want to vomit. 'What things?' He asks despite himself.

Naomi takes a breath and holds him in suspense for long seconds.

'Allegra. He raves about Allegra.'

The name nags at him. Must be a woman Barr once dated. Is he really listening to a woman's jealousy. 'Is that it?'

'No,' Naomi whispers. 'He tells her to get away from the buggy or the baby dies too.'

Her words send a shot of electricity along Cal's spine.

'Allegra?'

'Yes.' Her voice muffles for a second and it sounds like she's talking to someone in the background. Is it him? 'I have to go. Don't call me back. He'll know.'

Cal leans against the car in shock, staring at his phone, not caring that the cold metal cuts through the layers he wears. Adrenaline and fear are coursing through his body. Is this a joke? Are they making this up as a prank to mess with him? What would there be to gain?

Allegra Carlo was killed thirty years ago in woodland, miles from Birmingham and Barr's usual haunts. There has never been any connection suggested between them. Another man sits in jail for the crime. No one has any sympathy for him. Allegra was walking with her three children and the family's dog when she and her girls were stabbed to death. The only one to survive was the baby.

He stands too long, staring out at nothing. Cars come and go around him. Several times, he lifts his phone to make a call and then shoves it back in his pocket. This is a box he has finally closed. A promise to Chrissie, to Shona, to himself. Tonight he drives to Aberdeenshire, to his new life and his new home. How can he possibly open it all up again? He can't. It's simple. Even if she's telling the truth, this is somebody else's fight. Finally, Cal opens the car door and slides into the seat, blowing on his fingers to warm them. He starts the engine and drives out onto the road, pushing down the voices inside him, turning the radio on loud. A fine rain starts to fall and he likes the way it covers the imperfections. If he concentrates, he can forget all about Naomi Barr. It's Allegra who will haunt him.

Acknowledgements

If you haven't already read the book, a warning that there are slight spoilers coming up...

Writing *Unsound* has been a wonderful excuse to immerse myself in my own memories of student life, and trips to visit my friend Genevieve at Edinburgh University. The city is a gift to writers, packed with drama and atmosphere. I hope readers will forgive me setting such a dark tale there. The starting point came from news reports of student initiations and hazings elsewhere in the world – with Cal committed to Scotland, I chose the university city with which I am most familiar. A huge thank you to Genevieve Loveland and Chris May for supplying me with student details I was missing. Any errors in the text are my own.

Diving into the changing landscape of the Leith Docks area was a delight. The fictional grain warehouse featured in *Unsound* is inspired by the old Imperial Dock Grain Warehouse – which I couldn't see in person as it was demolished in 2021. I am grateful to the urban explorers who have posted such extraordinary video and photographic evidence of the building, particularly the Urbandoned Team. If you're interested in seeing where I pictured Cal, Robbie and Mel on their dog search and where the main action takes place, check out youtube.com/@Urbandoned for their footage.

Eagle-eyed readers may spot that Cal relies on a Facebook Messenger post at one point in the story... I've knowingly stretched the truth here as Messenger wasn't around in 2010 – it didn't appear until the following year.

As ever, the wonderful team at Canelo have continued to champion the Cal Lovett books and have been a brilliant support in the writing and production of *Unsound*. Louise Cullen's insights are invaluable, while Alicia Pountney has managed the process so efficiently (and kindly when a struggling writer needed more time!). Thanks to structural editor Radhika Sonagra, copy editor Daniela Nava and proofreader Jan Adkins for working their magic on the manuscript. Thank you to Kate Shepherd, Thanhmai Bui-Van, Miles Poynton, Nicola Piggott and the rest of the team for the work that goes on behind the scenes getting my books into readers' hands. And a big thank you to Andrew Smith for Cal's first urban cover.

Charlotte Seymour is always a source of calm and reassurance, as well as being great fun to talk books and publishing with. I couldn't wish for a better agent. Thank you for championing my writing and keeping everything going so smoothly. Thanks also to Hélène Butler, Anna Dawson and the rest of the Johnson & Alcock team.

This book has tied me in knots at times and I'm so lucky to have writing friends who could help me untangle them. Thanks to Rachael Blok and Louisa Scarr for early reads and advice, and to Jo Furniss for abandoning the inflight film selection to read and edit the manuscript. Thanks, as always, for the monthly dose of sanity and feedback, Tammye Huf, Gillian Anton, Chris May and Eugenia Hall. Thank you to Dom Nolan for eloquent reassurance at the eleventh hour.

A big pincers up to the Criminal Minds group for the daily chat and to all of the authors who've kindly read and blurbed my books (and to those who let me read theirs).

Huge thanks to all of my friends and family for their support – it's hard to convey just how much it means to have you all rooting for me. Most especially, thanks to Will, Rachel and Adam, who spent many lunchtimes brainstorming the plot for *Unsound* while we were on holiday. I'm so very lucky to have you three behind me, willingly debating death and destruction over pizza.

So many people have helped me during the writing process and in bringing *Unsound* to publication that's it's impossible to name them all. If you're a reader, reviewer or blogger who has bought or borrowed this book, thank you. It's wonderful to hear from people who've enjoyed Cal's stories so please visit heathercritchlow.com and sign up for occasional updates if you'd like to stay in touch. You can also find me on Instagram: heather.critchlow and X: h_critchlow

CANELOCRIME

Do you love crime fiction and are always on the lookout for brilliant authors?

Canelo Crime is home to some of the most exciting novels around. Thousands of readers are already enjoying our compulsive stories. Are you ready to find your new favourite writer?

Find out more and sign up to our newsletter at canelocrime.com